LIZ NEWMAN

Evernight Teen ®

www.evernightteen.com

THE ANGEL OF SHADOWMIST

LIZ NEWMAN

DEDICATION

For my beautiful children, your dedication and commitment to excellence inspires me! For DB, for your never-ending love and support and energetic joie de vivre that encompasses amazing you. You make life so much fun! For Zeus and Lola, I appreciate your soothing presence, your warmth, and your lively vocals. You make our home truly an abode, a retreat, and a writer's haven. And for the benevolent spirit guides who make this world the magical, fantastical, and larger than life place that it truly is, thank you for always bringing my soul back to the light.

LIZ NEWMAN

Liz Newman

Copyright © 2023

Prologue

Halloween

In every person lives not one, but two different people. There is the person who is good and honest, who tries their best to be the person everyone knows them to be. The one made of sunshine and laughter and all the beautiful things. And therein exists another, the one that, if given a face, would harbor red eyes and pointy teeth and seethe with malicious thoughts. The one who might kill if they could get away with it. That's the tricky part about paying the blood price to the Demon of Shadowmist: one is certain they will get away with it. There will be no recourse, no repercussions. We flit back into normal life while the payment remains dead, incapacitated, or silenced. One thing is for sure: they never get a chance to talk about it.

I tried to scream as my fingernails grasped at the moist soil with confusion. My hair, tangled and matted, held my face to the earth as I struggled to raise myself by my fingertips and look around. I gave up and rolled over, staring at the night sky, the beautiful San Francisco sky.

For a second, I thought I had been buried under the ground.

The obscurity was a fitting backdrop to the ghostly fog that hovered above Lyon Street. I untangled my hair from my fingers and dug my heels into the dirt, soon standing in front of Ben Bach's home as I shuddered in an attempt to remove the demon's thoughts from my own. Or were my thoughts his? I wondered if I was dead or demon-possessed. Or like the way a zombie movie hero would define it on screen... just having a real bad night.

I longed to find Ben and soothe him, to surround him in an embrace and tell him everything would be okay.

How I yearned to be with Ben, to feel his touch upon mine just one last time, as he would raise my hand and press his lips to my skin with his eyes downcast. His gaze would meet mine. How I loved meeting his eyes as if the winter sky inhabited a vista of profound mystery. With his touch, we were bonded as one. Perhaps our presence in each other's lives was not truly happening and would never happen again.

"It can never happen again. You belong to me."

The demon's voice ran amok within me, or were these thoughts my own?

A ghost whispered with the voice of a child, as thin as the wind through reeds, though as high-pitched as a scream.

"AJ, can you see me? Now, can you see me?"

I shook my head, pulled myself to my feet, and walked toward the side door of Ben's home.

Lie down and sleep the eternal sleep, I told myself. *Sleep and dream from a sleep from which there is no awakening. Because when you sleep there is always the possibility that this could be a dream. That you will awaken back into a world of teenage angst, a crush, and the never-ending crusade for meaning in a big world that has little tolerance for girls your age.*

But there was no soft bed, no sleep. Only foggy, moist air surrounded my body, creeping into my sweater and up the legs of my jeans as I stood on soft mulch outside of Ben's home on Halloween night.

I grasped the handle of the side door and twisted the knob. I peered through the window on the door. Phoebe, Ben's gray-and-white cat, stared back at me as she perched on the linoleum.

I crouched down to the ground, dirty and hideous, I am sure, like a monster. Night-of-the-living-dead girl, perhaps, or the prom date who clawed her way out of the grave to return for sweet revenge. I chuckled to myself. *Ah, revenge on the awful Hyannis McWolfe, who may very well have killed me.* The very idea made my blood boil. Perhaps there were signs of life in me yet.

The cat cocked her head as she stared at me from the other side of the plastic window on the pet door. Her tail twitched and slapped on the kitchen floor in a splash of fur. I pushed the door with my shoulder, the feel of my slight force upon the wood making my heart race as I imagined Ben's mother appearing to discover a teenage girl trying to break into her home.

Or perhaps she would not see me.

Perhaps... I am only a ghost.

I knelt and groped about freshly tilled soil for a fake rock or some other silly contraption hiding a key.

Nothing.

Part of my being wanted to sob. Part wanted to flee back into the sky, the nothingness. Yet my entire soul willed me to stay, willed me on. Willed me to find a way inside, where Ben might be waiting.

A curious trill cut through the silence—the meow of a cat.

Phoebe's wide body squeezed through the pet door and stiffened upon contact with the cold. She meowed again as she sat on the mulch before me. Her pupils shone in big black circles upon spots of green. I reached out to pet her. Her body curled sideways like a spring as she hissed and snarled.

"Easy, attack cat," I murmured. "All I'm trying to do is break into your house. Shush."

Phoebe backed away, her eyes glowing and teeth bared as she softly wailed and then ducked into the bushes.

"You act like you've seen a ghost," I tittered. I rose to my feet and pushed the door with more force. It wouldn't budge.

"Ben!" I called as I pounded my fist on the glass.

Of course, he wouldn't answer. People don't answer doors when dead people knock. Or they shouldn't. In horror movies, they always do, but not in real life.

Or… dead people don't answer doors.

Unless *he* was alive. And I was not.

Accidents happen all the time. People survive. Hospitals keep them alive. Perhaps Ben's mother had forbidden him to see me again, presuming I might have been the cause of the accident. Please, God, let Ben be alive. Please. Please.

I turned away from the door and folded my arms.

A bit farther away, tiny lights shone from ships as they cruised about the bay. I sighed and stared out over the hills at the city lights downtown. In the distance loomed the Coit Tower, the tall cylindrical building set upon a base of misty black and gray sky.

The door creaked. I whirled around. The back

door to Ben's house gaped wide open.

I crept inside and locked the door behind me, taking one quick glance out the window to make sure I was not being followed.

The kitchen was dark, save for a light burning over the stove. I drifted up the stairs and up to Ben's room, passing by his shoes lined up against the hallway door, by his leather jacket hung on a hook with its faint scent of aftershave, and by shadowed photos of Ben smiling at various stages of life. Signs of life, signs of him, that his mother cannot bear to put away.

If he really is dead, too. Or perhaps he is like me, floating in this otherworld. I have to find him. I need to know.

Ben's bedroom was quiet, his bed made neatly and a few items of clothing strewn about the floor. A tiny light from a lamp burned on top of his dresser, illuminating the garish face of the lead singer of a band in a painting on the wall.

If he is dead, the fault lies with me.

Maybe, just maybe, everything is fine, and he's still alive. He'll call me tonight to tell me he's fine—he was out with Gideon and their friends. Tomorrow, we'll go to the café on the corner and have pastries and pumpkin spice lattes.

"Stop it," I murmured. "Just prepare for the worst."

The mechanism for the garage door downstairs churned. I jumped, startled by the sound.

I slid along the hallway wall, then ducked into the shadows of Ben's room.

The door to the kitchen opened with the familiar creak of a spring. Ben's mother sounded as if she had an armful of groceries. Cabinet doors opened and closed with soft pats and taps, and paper bags rustled. *That's a lot of groceries to feed just one.* I knew if I stayed quiet, she would never know I was there. I closed his bedroom door softly.

My fingers drifted over the mahogany furniture in Ben's bedroom. The scent of lemon polish tickled my nostrils.

Ben's image resounded in the reaches of my memory as I pictured him riding his Indian motorcycle through the mist on a day when the fog receded over the Pacific Ocean and hung over the streets of San Francisco into the early afternoon. I had the strangest feeling Ben would open his room door and find me waiting as I dug the toe of my shoe into the carpet in my usual gesture of confusion. Strangely enough, I longed to flee down the stairs and back into the past, to a life devoid of him. A time when my heart did not tug within my chest when we were apart.

A time when Ben's face was not forever emblazoned behind my eyes.

Maybe he would call me by my real name instead of AJ, for the dead know everything. He would know the real name I hid from, the name that would make me blush with embarrassment. I would hush him and pull him toward me, swearing him to secrecy that he would never speak the name aloud unless we were alone. He would flash that crooked smile of his. That smile...

I picked up his hairbrush and ran my fingertips over the dark, silky hairs embedded in its bristles. I could still feel him here, still smell his scent, a scent of fresh, clean skin and light cologne. Strange that someone as rough as he appeared on the outside, in his rugged jeans and leather jacket, could smell so beautiful. Strange that his eyes could hold such gentleness for one who had been through so much pain. I placed the brush down on his bureau and blinked back my tears. A lump welled up in my throat as my gaze rested on the picture he had taken of me just last week on the shores of Lake Stinson.

You don't have to die to know a thing or two about death. You shouldn't have to. For he may be dead. I know I could see him if he appeared.

I could see *them*. The ghosts.

I sighed as I lay down on his bed.

Sleep. Maybe this is all a dream. Maybe, when you wake up, he will be lying next to you, and you will be worried about whether your parents are going to come home from vacation a day early with baby Frances and find you dead.

I stretched my arm out, resting my head.

"It's all right, AJ," Ben whispered. "I'm here."

My chest bloomed a rose of fear as a shadow on the wall danced, but the shadow was only a branch from a tall oak tree swaying back and forth with the breeze. A gasp of hope escaped my lips.

Ben spoke again, louder this time.

"I'm here, AJ."

Could that really be him? Was he alive?

Or was the Demon of Shadowmist playing tricks again?

LIZ NEWMAN

Chapter One
Just Perfect

Eight Weeks Before Halloween Night

The doorbell rang three times in quick succession, true to my best friend Caslin Perez's penchant for flare. I glanced in my bedroom mirror as I arranged my dark hair to cascade over my shoulders and wondered if my lips and cheeks looked too plump. Sucking in the middle of my jowls gave me a scary face in the mirror, like a dying person wasting away.

I stuffed my cell phone and notebook into my backpack as I raced down the stairs. I could not even summon the strength to pull open my own front door. My fingers seemed too weak to grip the handle and too frail to pull the door open.

I had to talk to Caslin about my nightmare. I tried to think of what I could say, a way I could tell her about it without sounding childish.

A shadow stalked me, like a murderer, inside a building with high ceilings and laminate floors. I tried to hit, but my punches landed on empty air. I tried to run, but my feet were frozen to the ground. In my mouth, I tasted blood. The walls closed in. I was smothered, suffocating somehow. Then everything became red. Red walls, red lights. Red eyes and smoke.

I screamed, but I had no voice. I screamed again and again in silence.

The doorbell rang again. I twisted the knob and pulled the front door open.

Caslin Perez stood on the front step with her cell phone to her ear. She tossed a lock of freshly bleached blonde hair over her shoulder. She looked pretty as a blonde.

I opened my mouth to speak.

Caslin held up her index finger. "It's Hiya," she whispered. "On the phone. Shhh."

I nodded. "It's okay. I'll just get my stuff together."

Then everything exploded. The darkness, black smoke instead of walls, the people... doors and dust and metal were flying, and everything blew apart. All I could hear was screaming.

My hands were sweaty. I wiped them on my jeans, then reached for my backpack and took out a pack of gum. I took two sticks from the package and stuffed them in my pocket. Today, I wore my usual leggings, cropped top, and sweatshirt. The ensemble was comfortable and helped me feel ready to deal with Hyannis McWolfe, the rival who seemed intent on stealing my lifelong best friend.

"Oh, that's awful," Caslin said into the phone. "Johan is so smart. Tell him to stay focused. Of course, I'd be happy to. Are you kidding? He's a doll. You're lucky to have such a sweet twin brother. And he's lucky to have you, too. I wish I had a sister like you. Or a brother."

The saccharine in Caslin's gushing made me want to stick my finger down my throat and retch. I stifled the urge and rummaged through my backpack for my own cell phone to check my messages.

Need you to watch Frances tonight, my stepmother had texted from the master bedroom room upstairs. ***Group meeting***.

I groaned as I stuffed my phone back into my backpack.

Ever since Nancy had quit drinking and stayed for a three-month stint at a fancy rehab center in Wine

Country, of all places, she used me as a babysitter on the nights my father worked late. Which was every night except our family dinner night on Tuesdays.

"I was shopping for school supplies the other day and you'll never guess who I ran into," Caslin continued into the phone. "That's okay. I should go, too. See you later." Caslin pressed a button on her phone and smiled. "You ready?"

"I'm leaving," I called into the house. No one answered. I closed the door behind me as I slung my backpack over my shoulder and stepped down onto the pathway leading to the sidewalk. A white butterfly flitted around my head as the lawn sprinklers whirred on, tiny droplets of water sparkling in the sunshine and leaving spots on my jeans. I fell into stride beside Caslin as she tilted her face up to the late summer sun.

She flipped her hair over her shoulder. "Where did summer go? Or better yet, where did the money I made this summer go? Oh, right, to my college fund. Because my broke-ass parents can't pay."

"You'll win a scholarship. This is our last day of freedom. Then it's back to the weekly drudge. I don't miss being treated like a worm every day."

"They're not so bad," Caslin said.

"Not so bad? Hyannis McWolfe and her friends not only laughed at your clothes, your hair, my face, and our parents, they toilet-papered your house every weekend five years ago. I spent every Saturday morning with you cleaning up."

"It's just toilet paper, AJ."

"That's not what you were saying when you were scraping wet wads from the walls outside your room. And some of the stucco. You still have nicks in the paint."

"My mom fixed them. I hung out with Hyannis a little bit over the break. She's alright. We were both counselors at Lyell Elementary Science Camp. She knows you don't like her, but she doesn't know why."

"I never even gave her a thought until she set out to make my sophomore year a living hell. No one plans on spending their afternoons in the library, hiding from the quote, unquote in-crowd. Right? You were there, too."

"I wasn't hiding. I was catching up on some good books and keeping you company."

"Well, thanks for your support."

We took a seat on the bench at the bus stop and waited. "This is kind of exciting and scary at the same time," Caslin said. "Seeing a brand-new school, new theater, new everything. It's just weird to change up schools right at junior year."

I agreed as I rested my elbows on my knees and glanced across the street.

Mrs. Faria, my elderly neighbor, swept the dust off her porch across the street while dressed in a pink robe and floppy slippers. Her home was a humble one-story brownstone with bright pink and red rose bushes in front. She lifted a hand up in the air in a shaky wave.

"Good morning, Mrs. Faria," I called. Mrs. Faria held her hand up to the side of her ear with her palm open. "Good morning!" I shouted. "Do we have a few minutes?" I asked Caslin.

Caslin slipped on her headphones. "Five."

Mrs. Faria pointed to her ear as I jumped to my feet and ran across the street.

"Good morning, Mrs. Faria," I said as I stopped in front of her and reached for her broom.

Her gray hair stood on frizzy ends like a troll pencil topper. Her wrinkled face smiled sweetly, and her voice sounded like a tweeting bird.

"Good morning, sweetheart. Now, you remember

to look across the street when you cross. Always look left to right. Sometimes, I think you're a little careless."

"Let me help you. Caslin and I are a little early for the bus." Dust clouds floated up as I stroked the bristles over the concrete. Mrs. Faria started to bend down to move the doormat from the broom's path. I reached down quickly and picked it up for her, tossing it aside.

"Have a seat. I'll finish up."

Endearments lilted from Mrs. Faria's lips as she settled herself onto a porch bench.

"Would you like to stay for a glass of orange juice?" Mrs. Faria asked. "Fresh-squeezed with oranges from my tree. Dagan bought me a juicer. Best orange juice I've ever had." She shook ever so slightly as she spoke, the wisps in her hair feathery as if spun from a cotton candy machine.

"I'd love to, but I have to get to class. Another time." I propped the broom up against the wall.

"Door's always open to you." Mrs. Faria lightly fanned herself with a newspaper. "Nice sunny day. My son is coming to check on me. Maybe you can stop by later for some *arroz con pollo*. Extra green olives on top, just as you like it."

The memory of Mrs. Faria's *arroz con pollo* made my stomach rumble. My sense of scent suddenly attuned to the delicious smell of saffron and simmering juicy chicken from her kitchen. "I wish I could, but I have to watch Frances tonight. If I didn't have orientation, I would love a plate right now."

"Another time, then." Mrs. Faria did not extend an invitation for Frances, as her face grew pinched when Frances was in tantrum mode, which was often since Frances just turned two.

Bus number 21A rumbled down the street. Caslin waved frantically as she pointed at the municipal vehicle, her words drowned out by the churning noise. Mrs. Faria groaned as she rose to her feet, leaning on me for support as I walked her into the foyer of her home. She stood on the step, calling out, but I could not hear a word she said over the loud engine as I turned and headed for the bus stop across the street. I broke into a run. Not intending to be rude, I turned around then to wave at Mrs. Faria as my feet hopped from the sidewalk onto the street. The bus had already pulled in front of the stop. The doors creaked open, and a couple of passengers disembarked.

I turned toward the bus and quickened my pace.

Car brakes screeched as I whipped around to see a red sedan bearing down on me. It was too late to dodge out of the way. I held my hands out, and my heels flew in retreat of the chrome bumper.

I tipped backward and fell onto the ground.

Then the driver of the sedan was in my face, yelling, asking me if I was all right while sounding accusatory as well. I scrambled away and ran for the bus. "Fine, thank you!" I said over my shoulder.

"You're going to get yourself killed, girl!" the driver screamed after me.

"I'm sorry," I said when I found my voice. I waved half-heartedly into the air. My palms were covered with dirt. I tried to wipe it off on my jeans.

"Be careful when you cross, sweetie!" Mrs. Faria yelled from her doorway, shaking even more violently. Her hand fluttered about her throat, and she trembled. "Look left and right, then left again!"

"I will!" I booked it to the bus, my heart pounding. "I'm all right! I'm sorry if I scared you!"

Caslin was engrossed in typing into her cell phone as she rose from the bench and climbed the stairs into the belly of the bus. I hopped aboard and placed my transit card under the scanner. The scanner beeped loudly. I am not sure why I felt more flustered at the loud noise rather than the fact that I was almost run over by a bus. The portly driver gave me a once-over, then grunted and shifted gears as if to warn me to take a seat quickly. Caslin sauntered along, staring at her phone. She teetered as the bus lurched forward but casually gripped onto a pole as if she meant to, all the while intent on her messages. Another passenger stared at her with a combination of hysteria and admiration.

"Okay, freak-out!" Caslin said as we settled into seats. A rose with baby's breath wrapped in cellophane peeked out from Caslin's backpack.

My heart pounded from the near accident as adrenaline finally kicked in. "Right? I almost got killed!"

"When?"

"Just now! You didn't see?"

"I can't see through a bus! Are you all right?"

"I'm fine." I reached into my pocket and removed a stick of chewing gum. The driver's eyes met mine in the rearview mirror. He shook his head. I stuffed the pack of gum back into my pocket. I brushed the dirt from my hands and checked my reflection in the mirror.

"Good." Caslin patted my back. "Hyannis called back and said she can't find her flower barrette. She's tearing up the dressing room."

"Why doesn't she just put up her hair in a bun?"

"She wants to pin the barrette on the side of her head. You know how she is. Everything has to be 'just perfect.'"

I chuckled. Clasping my hand over my heart, I pursed my lips into a grin as I performed my best Hyannis McWolfe imitation. "Just perfect." I sighed as I batted my eyes. Caslin guffawed, her trademark laugh sounding apprehensive as she peered around the bus to make sure no one she knew was eavesdropping.

The bus chugged and churned down the city streets. Caslin's cell phone rang again.

"Hey, Hiya," she answered, bright and cheery. "You found it! I'm glad. I can't wait. You are going to be amazing. You own the choreography, so you'll do great. I wouldn't worry if I were you. Uh-huh. So excited to see you on stage." She smiled as she tucked her phone into her purse.

"I had the strangest dream last night, Cas. A nightmare."

"What was it about?"

My insides churned with the memory to match the ache of my skull. I worried Caslin would think I was silly if I brought it up, but the thought of the dream troubled me so much I needed to give voice to the vision.

The bus lurched to a stop. I took my first look at the brand-new Addison High School.

I inhaled sharply, for I knew this was the setting even before I could step inside.

"My nightmare happened here."

Chapter Two
The Red Room

"This is the first time we have ever been here," Caslin said. "We've never even seen this school before. They just took down the barrier walls. See?" Caslin pointed to trucks across the street with civil engineering logos, their trunks packed high with lined portable fence walls.

"In my dream, I walked up the front steps, down to the left corridor. An office is on the right, kitty-corner from the courtyard. To the left of that is the theater. Red. At least that was what was in my dream."

The school faced a corner where two streets intersected as if the building were the base of a triangle. The stucco of the new building gleamed immaculately from our vantage point on the bus. A wide expanse of grass in the shape of a half circle abutted the curve of the school's driveway and filled in the space near the sidewalk. The flat part of the half circle ended just below the wide expanse of steps that led up to the front entrance of Addison High, which was made up of floor-to-ceiling glass windows. The front windows were cathedral-like at two stories high. My breath spirited away as I marveled at how beautiful the school was. All thoughts of my nightmare vanished as the bus driver pulled a lever to open the doors.

Caslin and I stepped off the bus, trying not to stare in wonder at our brand-new school as we strode down the concrete walkway and climbed the steps. In the lobby, there were two sets of carpeted stairs that met in the middle and continued to the second floor, from which the vantage point afforded a view of the neighborhood through the floor-to-ceiling-height picture windows.

Caslin whispered as new members of our junior class surrounded us. "This building is just...gorgeous."

We wandered down the corridor, following the signs directing us to the theater for orientation. To the left of the office, which was kitty-corner to the courtyard. Just like in my dream.

The new principal, Miss Overton, lurked in the hall, her cheeks slapped pink with cream blush in contrast to her pale skin, her lips a slash of gooey red. She beckoned us forward. Across the hall, a tall, slim girl with a sheet of shiny onyx hair turned toward us. Her nose was pert, and her eyes a luminous black with thickly mascaraed lashes. Hyannis. She spotted Caslin and strode toward her.

"Hiya!" Caslin shrieked in smiling glee.

They enveloped each other in a huge hug. Hyannis looked at me, and her mouth twitched upward in what might be mistaken for a smile.

Miss Overton bustled about as we were led into the theater. It seemed as if everyone around me was chatting as we walked up onto the scaffolds, giggling about the giddiness of being in a new building, the smell of fresh carpet and paint, the darkness, and our name tags as we followed parent volunteers through a tour of the school's theater. The parents pointed out details that would mean little to those who did not plan to take drama classes (I did), such as the locations of the trapdoors and dressing rooms. Our tour parent droned on and on about the integrity of the performance programs and the generous contributions of the McWolfe family, oblivious to teenage smirks and titters.

"Then I say to Johan, could you get up the nerve and ask her out already?" Hyannis whispered as she and Caslin moved forward in their own world. I trailed behind.

Caslin squealed with delight. "Do you think he likes me?"

"Of course, he likes you," Hyannis said. "I told him I hang out with you. It's not like you're some dum-dum, like— " Hyannis glanced at me over her shoulder and looked away. "Tahoe was so much fun. You two should be shipped."

Hyannis's hair swung in a long, perfectly smooth black sheet down her back. Every minute or so, Caslin looked back and nodded as if to invite me into the conversation. Hyannis kept her back turned.

At the end of the tour, Hyannis embraced Caslin, then ducked backstage. Caslin marched right up to the third row and plopped down in the middle. I settled into the seat beside her.

The theater was drenched in red. Red seats, red curtains, red carpet. Blood red. I didn't know I was color-sensitive until this very moment when the sight of red made my pulse quicken.

I sensed danger. *Is this the place, the scene of my nightmare?*

I jumped up to leave.

Caslin placed a hand on my arm. "AJ, Hyannis will be on any minute. Are you okay?"

I swallowed the large lump in my throat. My hands shook. My head began to throb.

"Everyone *sit down!*" a student behind me snapped in the tone of Hitler, and a few other students giggled.

I sank back into my seat. "I... I'm not sure exactly what... I think I'm fine."

"On the bus." Caslin's eyes filled with concern. "You said something happened in your dream last night..."

"Yes. Oh, yes. In the dream I had last night," I

whispered in my best friend Caslin's ear as the lights dimmed, "I was fighting, trying to hit something. Trying to keep something off of me. I couldn't scream. I couldn't punch. I'm fighting whatever it is, a shadow or a stranger, maybe a person, fighting, fighting, I cannot land a punch. The ones I do land hit like they're hitting something soft and sticky, not real skin. I was powerless. But I know somehow, whatever it was or who it was, it wanted to kill me. And then—"

Caslin patted my hand. "I can't sleep anymore either. I'm too excited for school to begin tomorrow." Caslin ran her fingers along the red velvet seats of the theater. "I love the way everything feels at Addison. So soft and new. Like being in a new car. We'll be the first established seniors next year. We'll be immortalized. This is so awesome."

As I rolled my eyes, a shadow darted above. With the whole theater dripping in the color red, the shadow reminded me of a Lunar New Year parade dragon writhing across the domed ceiling. I looked up and stared. Something up there seemed ominous to me, or perhaps it was just the pervasive feeling of doom and gloom that plagued me at night. A feeling of helplessness welled up in my chest. A feeling that I could not talk myself out of, for what I was guilty of, I could not even imagine. I heard unintelligible words as if they echoed off the ceiling, words which I knew were only in my head.

Or were they?

The students around me chatted, oblivious.

"This place is going to give me nightmares. Like the phantom of the opera is lurking in here. I should have skipped the tour."

"What?" Caslin said as she typed a text into her phone. "Ooh, Hyannis is upset. Her leotard tag is itchy."

"I should have skipped orientation. This place

creeps me out."

"Why?"

"It's too red. Blood red."

Caslin grimaced. "We'll get used to it," she whispered.

Johan McWolfe, Hyannis's twin brother, arrived with his entourage of athletes, wannabe actors, and otherwise notable secondary friends. He sat next to Caslin and spoke in a low voice. His dark eyes were hooded and dreamy, and his chestnut hair parted to the side and flopped fashionably around his head. He wrapped his fingers around hers as she blushed and smiled down at the carpet, then met his eyes again as he continued to speak softly.

I shifted in my seat. The seat made a popping noise, and the cute guy sitting next to Johan turned, looked at me, and raised an eyebrow. Caslin tittered with embarrassment. *Touchy.*

A rift had grown between Caslin and me over the summer. The floor might as well have opened up, and the tectonic plates lurking under the city of San Francisco might as well have separated and created a hundred-foot chasm between us, for our inseparable friendship was fast descending into a casual shrug. We used to talk on the phone almost every night. Now, she took days to return my calls.

That rift grew even wider as her hair lightened several shades over the course of the summer. I glanced at her lip-glossed mouth and her expertly contoured cheekbones, wondering if she knew we were growing apart. Wondering if she knew how much I missed her, how I longed to spend time with her as the twosome we were instead of the threesome we had become now that Hyannis had entered the picture. Hyannis with her wallet stuffed full of cash and credit cards that she could always reach for to purchase Caslin a pack of gum, a tube of lip balm, or a new nail polish at the drugstore. She would begrudgingly tell me I could throw one on the checkout belt, too, but I always refused. Once, she offered to buy me a Dum-Dum lollipop. *A special treat for you, AJ, because you're a real sweet one.* She grinned, the first time she had ever smiled at me, then burst into laughter. I seethed in silence as my cheeks burned.

The students erupted in half-hearted applause as Miss Overton lumbered out onto the dimly lit stage wearing a wool-skirted suit and a shirt with a fluffy neckline that appeared to be choking the life out of her, although the redness in her face was likely rosacea. The front of her hair was pulled back in ponytails with springy streamer barrettes that grown women should never wear.

"Welcome to the new students of Addison High!" Miss Overton said. Her voice reverberated through the theater, clear and booming as the real and imaginary voices in my mind were eviscerated. "As you can *hear*, the acoustics on our new performance theater are top of the line. One particular benefit of this new theater is the area underneath the stage, a space of exactly twelve hundred square feet, which will enable our drama department to teach students the mastery of illusion and stunt performance. The size of the space below spans almost the same square footage of the stage and backstage area. That is the brilliance of Renfield Construction."

Miss Overton continued her speech with a warning that cell phones were banned at Addison High except during breaks for use in one designated area between the dumpsters and the restrooms. I tucked my cell phone back into my pocket as several students did the same.

"There will be parent volunteers stationed at every entrance and exit to the school," Miss Overton droned on. "They will assist you with everything we have gone over today. Maps of the school can be found online and will be handed out by our parent volunteers throughout the week. Please try and take only one, and place them in a recycling bin when no longer needed.

"And now, for the highlight to showcase our amazing brand-new theater, it's time to enjoy a performance by a member of our incoming junior class. The McWolfe family's generous support has made it possible for Addison High to provide supplies such as learning tablets and top-of-the-line noise-canceling headphones for our computer lab.

"Who better to warm up the stage than our own prima ballerina-in-training. I present to you Hyannis McWolfe!"

Hyannis's twin brother placed his hands around his mouth and *whooped!*

The lights onstage dimmed as the curtain pulled back. There posed Hyannis, frozen in a backdrop of flowers, her leg stretched forward prettily. The stage illuminated, and Hyannis danced to the tune of *Gymnopédie*. She rose to pointe and twirls. Caslin remained fixated on her every move, as every member of the audience was.

Hyannis danced with grace, unbelievably, charmingly, annoyingly perfect.

Just perfect.

The cords of her neck pronounced themselves beautifully as she moved one delicate foot after the other, prancing and pirouetting. The song drew to a close, and the students erupted in applause as she took her bows. Caslin reached under her seat and threw the rose tied into a bundle with sprigs of baby's breath. The flower landed on the stage at Hyannis's feet. Hyannis swept them up and blew Caslin a kiss.

"Bestie," Hyannis mouthed as she held the bloom to her heart.

A feeling of intense ire and disgust welled up in my chest. Caslin's shoulders drew up to give her own neck a hug as she grinned back. My heart dropped to the floor. Caslin and I had been best friends since kindergarten. We even donned those silly heart charms where she wore half a heart hung from a necklace, and I wore the other until the eighth grade. She was done with me. I was no longer the friend she cared for most.

How could I compete with Hyannis McWolfe and all her beauty and perfection?

Hyannis caught my eye, and her gaze glittered with the thrill of competition. I waved and congratulated her with a smile. The expression returned with a perfunctory nod and arrogant curl of one side of her mouth.

I sank down further into the red velvet seat. The seat popped again. Caslin shot me a look as if I had made the noise on purpose.

"I'm sorry." I shrugged. She patted me on the hand.

"Beautiful performance, Hyannis McWolfe!" Miss Overton boomed into the microphone as she maneuvered her way back to the center of the stage. "Here is where we will be holding our talent show in November, in less than twelve weeks. Sign up on the boards outside the office, and get that talent ready. I can tell by looking out at all of your faces that we have some great talent ready to be unleashed, so please do sign up. Singers, dancers, actors, yodelers, jugglers. Whatever you would like to do, we would like to see it. And did I mention that the McWolfe family will be donating their home in Kauai for a week-long vacation as the grand prize? Hyannis, can you tell us about your family's vacation home?"

Hyannis shimmied out on pointe like a marionette, her arms wrapped around the flower from Caslin and a bouquet of red roses someone had handed her backstage.

"Our vacation home is located in the beautiful complex of Wahili Beach Club," Hyannis said breathlessly, her eyes bright. "We have a three-bedroom, three-bath with a loft right on the beach, with maid service and all of the amenities of the Wahili resort: room service, three restaurants on-site, and three baths with soaking Jacuzzi tubs and marble rain showers."

A blond, shaggy-dog kid who I recognized as a member of my karate dojo raised his hand. Logan Worley. "Does it have a pool?"

Hyannis's pained smile read, *Of course it has a pool, you dum-dum.* "Three pools, including a teen pool with a swim-up smoothie bar. And a fitness center with yoga and Pilates classes."

Miss Overton applauded, and the entire theater joined in. Hyannis blew a kiss and exited stage left, ever the cartoon bunny on pointe with her eyes batting and one foot shuffling prettily ahead of the other. *Retch.*

Caslin gripped my hand. "Are you going to enter?"

"And do what?"

"A karate presentation. Wu Shu. You would be so amazing. You practically fly. We could go to Kauai together and bring Hyannis, of course. Whoever we want to bring. Sleeps twelve, so I hear. Will your parents let you go?"

"They'd let me go for as long as I'd like," I said with a lump in my throat. The thought of going anywhere with Hyannis made me want to toss up the wheat cereal I had for breakfast.

"Perfect. Because mine won't care at all. So you're going to win the talent show?"

"Caslin, I don't even want to enter."

Miss Overton shushed everyone as Addison High's new faculty lined up on stage. They sang the new school anthem, with Miss Overton wailing in full operetta soprano, while the students looked around at each other and giggled. When the song ended, the faculty took a bow. The students applauded half-heartedly as many began to gather their belongings.

"Thank you all for coming," Miss Overton called out. "We'll see you on Monday morning at eight-thirty. Please be on time to your classes."

Caslin squeezed my hand as everyone rose to leave. "Gotta go," she said. "I'm going to catch a ride home with Hiya and Johan. Hey, don't worry about that dream. My worst nightmare is that I will be naked on the toilet and leave the camera on my phone on, but it's never going to happen, see?" She showed me where she kept a piece of electric tape affixed over the camera on her phone. "*They* are watching. Always watching."

"Who?" I asked with a half-hearted smile.

"The Man." She laughed. "That's what my dad says." She pushed past students as she climbed the blood-red carpeted steps toward the exit. Everyone followed along, teenage cattle roving up a flight of stairs.

I sighed and sat back in the now empty row. The feeling of heaviness sank into my chest. I wished it were three days ago and I was giddy with the ignorant notion that once school began, Caslin and I would be best friends again.

As the crowd at the top of the steps thinned, I rose to my feet. The face of my watch read eleven twenty-nine.

My bus home came every hour on the half hour.

I silently prayed the bus was running late and sprinted up the red steps two at a time until I came to the top. I ran down the sparsely filled hallway.

"No running in the halls!" a faculty member called out as she spoke with another teacher. I slowed to a trot until I came to the glass door at the front of the school, then I bolted out the door toward the bus stop. The bus, which was running late, four minutes late to be exact, pulled away from the curb with a load of students.

The wind slapped my hair against my cheek as I pulled my sweater tighter around me. The day was blustery with cold winds, and somehow the sun shining through like a prop in community theater and just as cold and dead as yellow cardboard. I stood on the steps, watching the bus churn away up the hill. Out of nowhere, the drizzle began to fall, that San Francisco drizzle that could be a result of sprinkling from the skies above or the wetness of the fog. I shivered. The fingerlike tendrils of mist rolling downhill eclipsed the sun, stopping short of embracing the school.

A wall of fog formed. Curiously, the mist created a wall. On one side was the mist, which stopped at the street just before the school, on the flat end of the triangle. On the other side, me... shivering in a patch of faraway sun, standing on the steps of San Francisco's newest flagship high school.

A brand-new, sleek Mercedes convertible screeched to a stop in front of the sidewalk.

"AJ!" Caslin called. "Hop in!" She scooted over next to a girl with long blonde hair, who bleated in protest as I jumped down the steps, grateful for the rescue.

Hyannis sat in the passenger seat. She slapped her

brother lightly on the shoulder for stopping.

"No room," she said.

"Sorry, AJ." Johan shrugged. "Not enough seat belts. It's the law." He stepped on the gas, and the car sped away.

"You're popular, AJ!" Hyannis yelled over her shoulder, her eyes filled with glee. "You're so popular!"

Caslin's voice rose in protest.

Chapter Three
The Boy in the Theater

The convertible sped down the street with the laughing Hyannis and Johan inside. *Hyannis, the hyena. Hyannis, the wh-...* so many choice words sprung to mind as I weighed my options on how to make my way home, hopefully not with my head hanging down the middle of my chest in despair for the whole time. I supposed I could wait an hour at the bus stop, but I did not fancy sitting there blinking back tears lest the McWolfe crew decided to take one last spin and heckle the late bus riders just to round out the day's torment.

You're popular, AJ! You're so popular! Hyannis's gleaming white teeth flashed before my eyes.

The slight of being left behind while the in-crowd sped away left me cold, dead, and empty. I climbed back up the steps with a longing just to sit in the dark somewhere. I trudged through the school's wide, empty hall.

A janitor looked up from his task of sweeping the last of the construction dust off the linoleum floor. His eyes were sunken in, the blue of dashed hopes and broken crayons. His pale hands were huge like a costumed character's hands wrapped around a broom. The smell of clothes that once sat too long in a damp dryer hovered about him. His hair was disheveled and bald in patches. I glanced at his nametag. *Mr. Jim Sievely*. Perfect name for a creepy staff member, in my opinion.

"Hi," I said.

"Shhhhh." He brought his finger to the middle of his earthworm lips.

I startled a bit, wondering why he was shushing

me. He reached up to his ear and turned the volume up on his headphones, shaking his head as a song by Tom Petty floated into the air. Even he looked as if he felt sorry for me. I could not stand the pity anymore. I had enough self-pity welling up inside me to justify an act of *hari-kari*.

Craving solitude, I broke into a run before I remembered the "No Running in the Hall" rule. Last thing I needed was some nosy faculty member who didn't know or care about me telling me to go home. *I tried to go home. Thanks.*

I threw open the door of the theater and walked in.

The theater was empty, perhaps not a soul inside, but the eerie feeling I had walking in told me there might indeed be souls present, and perhaps I could not see them. The floodlights hanging down from the stage glowed softly. I trudged down to the fifth row in this sea of blood-red upholstery and plopped down in a heap on a chair.

"Welcome to Addison High School!" read the big banner festooned over the curtains.

The empty stage seemed to appraise me in a disapproving manner, the heavy curtains closed shut. I draped my arms over the seat back in front of me and rested my head. I imagined my new black Converse shoes with white laces side by side with Hyannis's small, pretty feet bound in pink satin.

Of course, Caslin would choose her over me. Hyannis McWolfe was smart, talented, and filthy rich. Her father had founded a startup in Silicon Valley, and her family was worth millions. Over the summer, she told Caslin she would invite her to her family's new cabin in Lake Tahoe, their vacation home on Kauai, and their 10,000-square-foot apartment in Manhattan.

At first, Caslin would turn to me and ask if I

wanted to go, but after the fifth, sixth, or seventh request, or after Johan, Hyannis's twin, had flashed Caslin that interested smile that made her eyes melt into stars, Caslin soon forgot to ask. All this could be forgotten. I could make new friends and move on to a different crowd, for droves of new kids would be transferring over from the redistricted Oceanside and Chula Vista high schools into the brand-new Addison High campus. Caslin and I could still hang out on the weekend when she wasn't drooling over Johan or on a luxury vacation with the McWolfes somewhere.

Tears should have welled up, but instead of grief, a bottomless pit opened up within me. I sighed. After several seconds, a sob welled up in my throat and came out like a croak. Then the sobs racked my chest and came up unbidden, one after the other, yet the tears refused to fall. I placed my hands on the velvet seat back in front of me. Its smooth texture brought comfort, like a favorite blanket. I lay my head down on my folded arms. My chest ached with sadness and self-pity.

Someone, something, whispered into my ear.

Can you see me?

The voice was near as if someone sat beside me. I lifted my head up and turned. The seat next to me was empty. The theater was empty. *See me*, the voice said again, drawling out into a hiss. *See meeeee.*

My heart jumped into my throat. My chair creaked as I slowly turned around. The row behind me was deserted. The back of the theater was dark.

Goose bumps appeared on my arms as the little hairs on them rose. I swallowed hard. Someone, or something, kept company with me in the theater. Someone had spoken. I stood. The chair creaked, and my heart jumped into my throat. As I turned around and around. All the red velvet seats were empty.

But the whispers…voices surrounded me like the whispered taunts of a child. First one, then another…whispers like the flutter of a broken bird's wings.

A smell of thick smoke hit my nostrils suddenly, so intense that I coughed. There was a fire inside the building somewhere. Underneath the curtains, a thin line of black smoke puffed out onto the front of the stage. I rose and walked down to the front of the aisle.

"I wouldn't go that way if I were you," a deep voice called out.

I whirled around.

A guy my age sat in one of the chairs in a row far back. He hid in the shadows where the dim light did not reach. I turned and stared at the curtains. The line of black smoke disappeared. In the air, only a trace of the burning smell remained.

I wondered if he had heard the ghostly voice and smelled the smoke. Perhaps I was simply going crazy. The memory of my sobbing croak was enough to make my cheeks flush hotly as I waited for a glimpse of scorn to cross the guy's face. I slowly walked up the stairs to get a look at him, stopping at the end of the aisle where he sat. His face was finely chiseled, with just a hint of boyish fullness to his cheeks. His chin jutted forward with a half smile. Even in the semi-darkness, I could tell he was very handsome, for his skin glowed. His shoulders were broad, and his belly lean and flat. He wore a leather jacket that looked well cared for, oiled even. His hair was freshly cut, shaved on the side and in the back, and a bit wild and spiky on top. I longed to rush out of the theater, for I didn't expect someone as good-looking as he was to be sitting alone in a theater, watching me at perhaps the lowest moment in my sixteen years of life.

"How long have you been there?" I said.

"Longer than you have." He shrugged, casually leaned back in his seat, and rested one elbow on the seat beside him. He gestured to the seat on the other side of him as if offering me the chair. "You okay?"

"Sure," I replied as I remained standing. "Why wouldn't I be?"

I shifted my weight to one side and dug my toe into the ground, a gesture I usually performed when I was nervous. Folding my arms, I stared at him. He raised his eyebrows and stuffed his hands in his jacket pockets. My pride swelled, for maybe he thought I was like him. Impossibly cool. Tough. Unfortunately, my insides felt as mushy as the cereal I had for breakfast, with lots of milk.

"Thought you were crying. Or looking for someone."

I gazed about. "Yeah... no." I was unsure what to do at this point, so a pantomime of myself seemed to be sufficient for the moment. "Does this theater feel strange to you?"

"Yes." He chuckled. "Like there is someone backstage. I had the same feeling the second before you walked in. Like someone was watching me, watching the stage."

"From where? Behind the curtains?"

"Definitely."

Maybe he was a stagecraft student about to play some lame joke on me. *Hey, by the way, check out Addison High's new smoke machine! Har har har.*

I had too much on my mind to play coy with him. "Are you here for the demonstration, too?"

"What demonstration?" He bent his leg and crossed a foot clad in a black leather boot over his knee.

"The new smoke machine."

"Don't know anything about it." He faced forward

again, staring at the empty curtains. We both remained silent.

"Well, nice meeting you." I turned to trudge up the stairs toward the exit.

"We never formally met."

"My name is AJ."

"Is AJ short for something?"

"Maybe."

"What's it short for?"

I shrugged. "I go by AJ. I don't like my full name."

"See you around, AJ."

"Be nice if you could tell me *your* name."

His eyes narrowed as if he were deep in thought. "The crowd you were sitting with earlier. Friends of yours?"

"You could say that."

"You're in with the popular crowd. Good for you." He rose and walked away from me.

"You didn't tell me your name," I called after him.

He turned and stared at me for a long moment. "I'm sure you'll find out soon enough." He raised two hands up in peace signs as he walked up the stairs. Pushing open the door, the daylight from the hallway illuminated his form, so he appeared almost ethereal. He stood in the doorway. "I heard the voice, too. You should probably leave."

"What voice?" I stood there defiantly, grinding my toe into the carpet. "There was no voice. I didn't hear anything."

"You didn't?"

"No." I stared at him as if he were crazy, even though I felt crazy in my denial.

"You didn't hear a voice in there?"

I shook my head. "It's all just a joke, you know. This whole thing. One big joke, I am sure. None of it scares me."

"You really want to play it that way?"

"What do you care?"

He raised his eyebrows. "Forget it," he said as he moved out of the doorway. He twirled his finger around his head. "Could be my imagination. Maybe *I'm* hearing things."

I stood there, stunned. A second before the door closed, I called back, "Like what?" I shouted at the door.

I rushed up the stairs. Pushing open the door, I scanned the hallway. The mysterious leather-clad stranger was already rushing through the tall glass doors to the school parking lot. He trotted down the steps as the doors shut behind him.

As if drawn by a magnetic force, I drifted back into the theater, the door closing behind me. I was intent on finding the source of the voice, the smoke. My bus home arrived in fifteen minutes. Fifteen minutes to linger in the cold drizzle or to shelter in the warmth of the theater and take a chance on the ghost, the Muumuu, or the jerk-faced drama students hiding under the theater testing out the smoke machine.

Chuckling, I recalled spending evenings at Caslin's while her mom used to flip her long, thick black hair over her face and chase us. Muumuu, she would moan as we giggled with fright and ran. *Muumuuu.*

I remained in the creepy theater, ready for the Muumuu to appear, but really just trying to find some kind of diversion to take the pain away from my aching heart.

I blew out a breath. There settled that empty feeling in my chest again. I took each step, watching my own shoes, one step, two steps, three steps, down, down to the stage, thinking of the Muumuu.

The curtains moved as if someone hid behind them. A high-pitched voice giggled. If I turned around and ran, perhaps the good-looking guy who spoke of voices would be waiting in the hallway with a group, all of them chuckling and snapping cell phone photos at their practical joke.

Drawing my breath in, I puffed out my chest. I would not run screaming and hear them laugh at my expense. Not me.

My feet reached the very bottom of the theater below the stage. Placing my elbows on the flat surface, I gazed up at the red curtains. A light breeze lifted the velvet. I didn't recall seeing a window backstage when we took the tour. I scanned my memory, recalling the walk on the scaffolding, the tour of the dressing rooms, and the trapdoor.

The trapdoor!

Perhaps some stagehand hid there with a little smoke machine, ready to pop out and say "boo" while another student snapped a picture. Ha! I'd show them who the scaredy-cat was. I slipped on the steps of the stage, quiet as a mouse as I climbed upward. I ducked behind the curtains. A light filtered into the backstage area from a window above the scaffolding. I sneaked over to the trapdoor and shoved it open.

"I know you're in there!" I shouted. The gaping interior of the trap was empty. I expected to see a couple of kids hiding under there with a smoke machine and microphone. I stuck my hand in and groped around for a fistful of hair or a limb. Nothing but empty air.

The daylight filtered in from the vents at the stage level, illuminating the area just under the trapdoor. The backstage area was so new only a thin layer of dust sat on the floor. The door was hinged in a way so that it opened outward to the stage or inward to the floor below. I lowered the door, then hesitated.

I had to peek inside.

Another tendril of smoke wafted into the air. "Who's down there?"

I thought of the caterpillar from the book *Alice's Adventures in Wonderland.*

"Whoooo are you?" I murmured, mimicking the creature's first words to Alice. Surely, someone hiding down there would giggle at the words. I listened. Nothing but silence. My fingers loosened on the lid of the door as I slowly brought it down.

A tendril of black smoke danced in the breeze. I changed my mind and slipped underneath the trapdoor.

My feet hit the cement surface of a shallow landing below. The landing inclined like a ledge, allowing me to stretch my body out to my full height and peer out from the trapdoor to the empty rows of chairs in the audience. *How clever. The actor can slip down to this level as if disappearing and not worry about falling so far.*

Lowering myself down so I could walk down the dark passage, I turned my cell phone flashlight on and crawled into the space, which grew progressively larger until I could stand without my head hitting the ceiling. The passage opened into a large room about the size of a parlor. The room was unfinished, essentially concrete floors and concrete walls open and empty.

My throat tickled as I coughed softly. There was a scent of acrid smoke in the air. Something else that reminded me of the smell of the grill my dad would attempt every summer before bringing the charred tri-tip sirloin back into the house and popping it into the microwave to fully cook on the inside, then chucking the whole thing in the trash and calling for the local barbecue takeout.

I walked into the parlor-sized room where the smoke smell was coming from. I crept slowly, contemplating calling out a greeting but still worried about being scared by a bunch of drama team members armed with the same photo chat apps as Hyannis, Johan, and the rest of the popular kids. The light from the flashlight hit the dark walls, scanning the surface one by one.

A sense of fear tickled the back of my neck as my breath began to quicken. I continued to scan the walls with my flashlight. As I passed over the dark, shiny surfaces, the dark shadow of a man appeared.

I gasped. Turning my flashlight back in its direction, I scanned the wall again. Nothing. Simply my imagination working overtime.

The trapdoor slammed shut. My cell phone slipped from my hand and clattered on the ground. The flashlight shut off.

Darkness. I was in complete darkness. I shrieked and crawled around on my hands and knees, searching for my phone.

Footsteps pounded above my head upon the stage, steps that ran in all directions, much like the steps of children running.

"Open it!" I shouted. "I'm serious. Hyannis? Caslin?"

No answer except the pounding of running feet.

My hands closed around my cell phone. I pressed the power button to no avail. The phone remained unlit. Shoving the device into my pocket, I maneuvered my way in the darkness, my hands reaching up as the passage to the trapdoor narrowed and the ceiling lowered. My fingertips grazed the smooth ceiling above as I felt for the trapdoor. I could not tell where it was. My heart fluttered with panic as I gripped at the concrete, desperately searching for the cracks that would reveal the trapdoor or any type of exit. Nothing. Just smooth walls. My breath came harder, faster. Someone, something… had shut me in there.

"It's dark. Please." The word escaped my lips as I realized I was trying to reason with myself not to lose my mind down here under a trapdoor in a dark, dank school theater. Talking out loud had always comforted me. I always felt like someone was listening. "Pitch dark. You'll find a way out. Don't worry."

A high-pitched giggle emitted from somewhere nearby. "Show me," the voice whispered.

"Sh-show you what?" The vibrato in my own words scared me even more.

"Whoooo…?" the voice sang. "Whoooo are you?"

I moaned as my fingertips danced over the surface, searching and trying not to imagine what being down here would be like when the day turned into night, and I was eclipsed in total darkness, with nothing but the smell of fire and the sound of ghostly laughter.

I wished I could scream. I knew I would begin screaming the moment I was convinced no one was hiding in there with their cell phone camera. *No one human.* Five minutes of this terror would be enough to break me. Perhaps less.

I heard it, too. The sentence the boy in the theater had called back resounded in my mind. A low, guttural moan rose from my throat. I had to get out of here. Before nightfall. Before the voice came back. Before the fire.

"Can you see me?" the voice said. I closed my eyes and crumbled to the ground, a mouse in a dark maze scrabbling about the floor, searching for an opening.

"Can you see me?" the voice repeated desperately. "See me. Tell me you can see me." The voice was above me, below me, and whirling around me all at the same time.

"No," I groaned, keeping my eyes closed. "It's dark, you moron. Help me. Whoever is there. Please help. Hello?" I slid on the floor, reaching one hand out and groping in the darkness.

A loud slamming noise sounded. I jumped up and hit my head on the low ceiling again. The trapdoor had opened. Hints of daylight filtered through and slightly illuminated the space where I stood.

I ran to the trapdoor as fast as I could, lifting myself out of the opening. I slammed the door behind me and rushed out of the theater.

Bursting out into the hallway, I struggled to catch my breath.

Mr. Sievely, the janitor, dipped a mop into a yellow bucket. The air smelled sharply of lemon cleanser. He settled the mop on the linoleum and pushed it back and forth, back and forth. I walked swiftly past him. His mouth opened and closed slowly as if he were mouthing a silent word or a dying fish taking its last breath.

And then there he was, the boy in the theater, walking back toward the theater doors I had just exited. He stopped, his eyes wide as if he were caught just by standing there. I strolled past him, cool and casual, even though my heart pounded hard enough to spring from my chest. He smiled softly, his eyes filled with concern.

That was all the bravery I could muster.

I sprinted toward the glass doors at the front of the school and threw them open. The area in front of the school was deserted. Out over the steps, a patch of circular lawn met the sidewalk. An American flag waved from atop a flagpole. The fog coming in from the ocean caressed the pole and caused the flag to wave in a manner that reminded me of the old Jolly Roger on a pirate ship. My body erupted into chills.

In my mind, the voice echoed.

Can you see me?

LIZ NEWMAN

Chapter Four
You've Got Talent

"Nancy?" I called for my stepmother as I walked into the downstairs hallway of my home. My voice shook. "Frances?"

I plugged my cell phone into a charging cable. The battery icon lit up. *Good. At least the spirits didn't break my cell phone.*

No answer except the patter of soft paws from our cat, Carlos, as he wound his way around my ankles, purring.

"Hurricane Nancy has left the building." I sighed.

I hung my jacket up on a coat hanger and placed my key on a side table laden with our family pictures. I shook my head and convinced myself that I would ignore the incident underneath the trapdoor altogether. My head sat on my shoulders like an anvil, and my body moaned with the day's injuries, both physical and emotional.

I turned to look into a mirror on the wall, hung over a side table. Upon examining myself, I realized I looked very little like my father. His nose was sculpted but slightly hooked, his chin was broad but pointy, and his forehead wide and long. The one thing we did have in common was our wide-set, almond-shaped eyes, although his were blue and mine were hazel green. My hair seemed too thick and bright compared to Hyannis's silk sheet of onyx. I had the Aleutian coloring of my late mother, with her warm and feminine earthiness and golden-toned marshmallow-soft skin.

I wondered what the boy in the theater thought when he looked at me. I wondered if he thought I was pretty. I headed for the kitchen and pressed a glass against the ice machine. The sound of the machine churning made me jump, and the sound of the ice clattering into the glass caused my heart to pound. I soaked a paper towel in cool water, sat on the couch and, pressed the compress to my forehead, then closed my eyes.

A loud knock sounded on the door. "Jesus!" I shouted. My heart somersaulted. I wondered if this is how my father's cardiac patients felt right before they died. Slowly, I tiptoed toward the front door.

A figure moved in the shadowy glass side panels of the doorframe, dark with an oval head like an alien, the top of its head an illuminated yellow reflection from the porch light.

"What the hell is this?" I muttered. "Creature Feature?" I deepened my voice even as my heart pounded with apprehension and intoned, "Beyond that door lies the Lake Stinson Monster." I laughed, though the sound lacked humor. The knock sounded again. I sighed, pretty much resigned that something slimy with webbed hands and feet was going to yank me out and drag me into the lake the moment I opened the door. The pounding resumed, more insistent this time.

"AJ," Caslin called. "I hear you in there. Open up."

I turned the knob and opened the door.

"Hi," I said glumly. "Thought you'd have plans this afternoon."

"We stopped for a fro-yo at Skyline Mall, and then Hyannis and Johan dropped me off. Do you want to hang out?"

"Sure."

Caslin strode in.

"Hi, Nancy!" she called.

"Nancy isn't home."

"Oh." Caslin looked surprised and pointed

upstairs. "I thought she was here. In your room."

"No one's here."

"Are you sure? Maybe she's straightening up your room."

"That means she's definitely not here." I snorted with laughter. "She never straightens up my room." Caslin gave me a wide-eyed look as if she were seeing me for the first time in a brand-new light. It appeared that this brand-new light was not favorable.

"Someone is here. I saw a shadow of someone in your room."

"Stop. There's no one else here." My eyes widened to the point where I thought they would pop out of my head. Perhaps *I* was turning into an alien.

"Fine. Maybe I didn't."

Denial kicked in. I decided not to wonder about the possibility that something that followed me home from Addison High and was lurking somewhere here in the house. Maybe *in my room*. I was certain that if I probed, Caslin would insist she saw someone upstairs, at which point I would come unhinged.

I shrugged and sank back onto the couch.

Caslin hunched down and cooed to Carlos, rubbing him on his white belly as he flipped over and playfully swatted at Caslin's hands with white-tipped paws. "Hey, cutie. How are you? Haven't seen you in forever. You too, AJ."

"I missed you over the summer," I said. "We spent almost every day together last year."

"Work is the curse of the lazy class, as my father says. I had to work with boogery little kids at science camp. Luckily, Hyannis got stuck having to do some hours for getting in trouble last year, so I had someone to talk to."

"What did she do?"

"It was so dumb. Do you remember the fourth period phys ed teacher, Mrs. Metcalf?"

"Kind of heavyset?"

"That's her. Hyannis typed her name down as Mrs. Fatcow in the yearbook, and Mrs. Fatcow decided to stick her with two weeks of detention. Hyannis swore she got the name wrong because they were so similar, which I thought was absolutely hilarious."

"She was pregnant."

"I know, but she kinda looks like a cow. Anyway, Hyannis didn't show up to detention, and the next thing you know, she's in the principal's office, and the principal called in her parents, who backed her up and told the principal she had simply made a mistake with the teacher's name. A typo. These things happen. But the principal kept scheduling Hyannis to come to detention, and Hyannis kept not showing up. And on the last day of school, Hyannis received a letter saying if she didn't do eighty hours of volunteering to assist staff in community summer camps, she would be expelled. So unfair."

"Sounds fair to me."

Caslin groaned. "Are you hungry? I'm hungry. Can we raid the fridge?"

Our shoes echoed on the hardwood floor as Caslin and I made our way to the kitchen. Although the kitchen had high and wide floor-to-ceiling picture windows looming above almost every counter surface, the room was filled with gray light due to the fog. The narrow gardens were bordered by a light-brown fence and gave the room the feel of being blanketed with green wallpaper, as the trees grew close to the house. In the distance, from Lake Stinson, I could hear rowers call out to each other in a cadence. *Heave ho, heave ho, one two three four*. Often, geese or larks would fly into our yard, and I would bring Frances out to feed them. She'd squeal with delight as they nibbled the bread from her fingers.

"Where is Frances?" I thought aloud. "Oh, she has gym tots class today."

I opened our Sub-Zero refrigerator, and a cloud of cold air floated out. The offerings on the shelves were plentiful but unappetizing since I had crawled through an underground dungeon under the stage merely an hour before and was pretty sure at the time that I would be trapped there for the night. I'd only had a small container of yogurt and nothing else to eat the entire day. My stomach chewed upon itself with anguish.

Caslin reached in for a box of frozen hot pretzels and busied herself at the microwave. The smell of hot bread filled the air, a yeasty smell I couldn't resist.

"Pop one in for me, please."

Caslin and I sat down with our snacks in the breakfast nook by the French doors leading out to the garden. I shook a packet of salt crystals over my pretzel. "Johan asked me out on a date," Caslin said. "We're going to dinner on Friday."

"Ooh, nice. I'll bet he'll take you somewhere fancy."

Caslin tore her pretzel in half and nibbled. "Maybe."

"Tell him to take you to Penatisimo. Best Mediterranean food ever. White tablecloths."

"He said he has a surprise place for me."

"I'm sure it will be a great restaurant. It certainly beats the days when a date was a cup of caff'. Now we can drive to places. I can't remember the last time someone asked me out on a date. Or when I met someone I wanted to go out on a date with. Actually…"

"Now that the Chula Vista students are going to Addison High, there is a whole new crop of possibilities."

"Hmmm." I thought of the boy in the theater, of

his glowing, tan skin and dark eyes. Refusing to speak of him to Caslin gave him all the more of a dreamy quality. I decided to keep the secret just a little longer.

"We should study."

"Right." Caslin polished off the last bite of hot pretzel. "Can't wait for AP tests tomorrow. Honors classes, here I come. Every time I look around at that rathole of a house I live in, I think about how I'm going to fix it up once I graduate college and get a decent job. First to go, my useless drunk dad and his La-Z-Boy chair."

"Your house has so much potential. I love old Victorians." I rose from the table to retrieve a bottle of Dijon mustard from the refrigerator. Squirting a dollop onto my plate, I dipped a piece of pretzel in and stirred it around. "Just needs a little remodel on the inside and it'll be gorgeous."

"The plumbing needs to be fixed. The whole house smells rank. That's why I haven't had you over in months. Hey, can I sleep over on Friday?"

"After your date? Of course. I want to hear all of the juicy details."

"Perfect. I'll come over at about ten, okay?"

We spent the afternoon pouring over AP and Pre-SAT workbooks on the floor of my bedroom. Nancy had papered the walls last year with cherry wallpaper in an effort to decorate. I complained to my father, but he hushed me, his eyes somewhat frantic as he mentioned how crushed Nancy would be if I said I didn't like it and then bender time for Nancy. Whiskey sours in midday, the smell of alcohol wafting about her, baby Frances pungent from not receiving the proper care. I bit my tongue and went shopping for a few posters, string lights, and throw pillows to make the room more my style.

Lying on beige carpet near dark oak furniture with

cherries everywhere made Caslin look like she was floating in a fudge sundae. I opened my mouth to crack the joke, then pressed my lips together quickly. After all, this was my bedroom. *Thank you, Stepmother.* I'll bet Nancy was just like Hyannis McWolfe when she was in high school.

Caslin glanced up. "What's wrong?"

"Nothing," I said defensively. "What's wrong with you?"

"You're quiet lately."

"I'm having trouble with Hyannis. She's kind of mean. I know you like her... I just get a bad feeling around her."

"She can be mean." Caslin's eyes met mine and softened a bit. "Just don't let her walk all over you. Sass her a little. They like that sort of thing. They won't like you if you're a pushover."

"How about if *I* don't like them?"

"Everyone likes them or hates them because they are not liked by them. Why wouldn't you like them? You're with me, and I'm with that crowd."

"Because they're mean."

Caslin made a dismissive gesture. "You have to be mean in high school, or you're going to get walked all over. Same as in real life. You're going to get along with them fine. You're just a little shy. We're juniors now. It's time for us to have a social life, go to parties, be popular."

"Do I have to work so hard to be popular and suffer people I don't like?"

"Some people. Look, most of the kids coming into Addison High are from Oceanside. Our high school. If we band together in a big group, all the hip kids, then the rest of them will have to kiss our butts to belong."

"All I want is to ace the SATs and do karate this

year. I don't want my butt kissed."

"You need to tighten up your ambitions." Caslin smiled. She raised two fingers to her lips and smacked them with a loud kissing noise, then slapped them down to the outside of her butt cheek. "How did you get home? You didn't walk, did you?"

"I took the bus."

"We swung back around after we drove a couple of blocks to come pick you up, but you weren't there anymore. We could've squeezed in together. See what I mean when I say Hyannis and Johan are good people. They came back. They were just giving you a hard time."

"Felt great. Thanks. I walked back into the school and hung out in the theater."

Caslin grew serious. "You didn't cry in there, did you?"

No, I just inhaled smoke and heard strange voices. Heh.

"I met a guy. Good-looking, nice. Leather biker jacket."

"Stop there. Biker jackets were cool back in the eighties. Whoever he is, he needs a makeover."

"I like it." I shrugged. "You have to meet him. He's handsome. Tall, amazing skin, deep-set eyes."

"I'll believe it when I see it." Caslin glanced at her red plastic watch and jumped up. "I've got to get going. My mom is making dinner."

I walked Caslin to the foyer as she gathered her backpack. Her lips tightened, and she frowned as if she were deep in thought. "What are you up to for lunch on minimum day? School's out at half day, so we're free as birds."

"No plans. Do you want to meet somewhere?"

"Sure."

"With others?"

"I don't know." I dug my toe into the floor, pivoting my foot in a circle as I leaned my weight on the opposite foot. "Who else?"

She shook her head. "I have plans. You could join us. Think about it." She spun around on her heel and threw open the door, trotting down the front steps as if I were chasing.

****

I looked up to the ceiling as I lay on my queen bed with my hands behind my head. The comforter underneath my body seemed too cheery, too flowery. Nancy had been so happy when she redecorated my room over the summer, replacing my chocolate-brown walls with cherry wallpaper and my window blinds with flowing curtains and fluffy valances. The room looked as if an enormous forest fairy came in and threw up cheesecake all over the vanilla-scented candles she placed on the bureau did smell nice, though. Probably there to camouflage the stench of fairy vomit.

The door of my room opened a crack. My eyes widened as I stared at the door. Here *It* comes. But what was *It*? Why did *It* follow me home? Suddenly, my cat, Carlos, jumped onto the bed, tearing me from my train of thought. I shrieked, then giggled as I reached over and stroked his silky black-and-white fur. "Carlos in charge, huh?" He blinked his sleepy eyes as he settled on the coverlet. "You tell me if something is coming to get me. Cats are supposed to do that, you know."

A toddler's voice called out, "Jay Jay!" The door to the garage slammed shut. I heard Nancy protest, along with what sounded like a heap of grocery bags crashing onto the garage floor.

Frances's little baby footfalls resounded on the steps, coupled with the sound of her hands slapping the carpet as she climbed on all fours to the top landing.

Frances burst into my room, her little head hovering only inches from the edge of the bed. "Jay Jay, why you sleep?"

"Hi, honey." I brought her little head to my face and inhaled deeply. "I'm just resting." The top of her head smelled like plumeria-scented shampoo. "How was music class?"

"Boooring," she droned. "Too many babies."

"You're a baby, too." I laughed. I planted a kiss on her head.

She shook her head. "*Noooo.* Frances a big girl." She pointed to herself and smiled, her gums pink with baby teeth poking out. Nancy appeared in the doorway.

"'Nooo,'" Nancy said mockingly. "I wonder where she picked that negativity up from?"

I raised my eyebrows. Gosh, Nancy could be so combative sometimes.

"I need you to watch Frances this evening. I have a meeting up in Potrero Hill. There's a famous actor who lives in San Francisco and is scheduled to speak."

"AP tests are tomorrow, and the PSATs are next week. I was planning on studying tonight."

"I'll be out pretty late, so you'll have plenty of time after Frances goes to bed." Nancy placed a hand on her hip. "Please, AJ. Your father and I really need you to pitch in and help out. Then there's the stress of Frances starting preschool, and now we need to get you on track to college. It's been too much for me, and I'm faltering. Please." Her voice shook.

The last thing I needed was for Nancy to relapse. "All right. What time are you going to be home?"

"Late." Nancy turned away and padded down the hall in slippers. The water in the pipes made a creaking noise as she switched the shower in the master bathroom on.

Frances climbed up next to me on the bed, and I read *The Count of Monte Cristo* aloud as she and Carlos the cat snuggled up next to me, both warm balls of comfort that eased the gnawing feeling in the pit of my stomach when my mind wandered to the guy who saw me crying in the theater. I sighed and ran my hand down Frances's curly blonde hair. Her lips puckered out softly like a little angel as her rib cage lifted up and down with the deep, heavy breath of sleep. Carlos stretched out onto his back with his eyes closed and his paws in the air. I tucked my body into a furry throw blanket, being careful not to awaken Frances.

"That book puts me to sleep, too," I murmured. "But the movie is great. Someday, when you're old enough, we'll watch it." Carlos meowed softly. "Not you, silly cat. Well, okay. You can watch it, too. Only if you warn me about ghosts and swamp creatures. Deal?" I rubbed his belly, and he fell back asleep.

Nancy's heels clattered down the hallway, and she appeared in my room doorway again, fastening a set of pearl earrings to her ears. "No complaints," she said in a low voice as she held up her hand. "Probably futile asking that of a teenager. I signed you up for the school talent show during the PTA meeting today."

"What?" I whispered as indignantly as possible. "You should have asked me first."

"Then you would have said no. You are great at martial arts. Do that jujitsu thing."

"You need to have a partner for jujitsu. Everyone is going to laugh their ass off watching me wrestle someone on the stage."

"Language, please. Remember Frances. Do jujitsu with Logan Worley."

"Frances is sleeping. I don't want to do jujitsu with Logan Worley. Do you know how embarrassing that would be wrestling on the stage like that?"

"Do something else then. For God's sake, AJ, you need to reach out to people. I was a hundred times more popular than you when I was in high school."

That worked out well for you and the drinking was on the tip of my tongue, but I knew her face would crumble and then...relapse. And more babysitting.

She flipped a curled lock of blonde hair out of her eye with a flick of her head. "You're doing the talent show, and that's final. Think up a routine with the Boukwajang."

"His name isn't the Boukwajang. That's not even part of his title. It's Kwan Jang Nim Luis."

Nancy rolled her eyes to show that she really didn't care about his title. "Tell your father to heat up the Paleek Paneer in the freezer for dinner when he comes home. I bought five so there's plenty for you and him. Frances should have one of the organic kids' meals. Any one. It doesn't matter." She closed my door, her heels clicking away down the stairs.

I groaned as I lay my head down beside Frances and planted a little kiss on her nose, then planted a kiss on my cat's head as he meowed softly.

****

The hospital texted me at seven in the evening with a notice saying my father was flown out to Lake Tahoe to perform an emergency open-heart surgery. Later, he called, asking me where Nancy was and talking to Frances as she babbled on and on in her cute little baby voice. After ten minutes or so, he grew exasperated with not being able to understand her and struggled to hide it with a smooth tone of voice as he said goodbye over the speakerphone. I placed Frances in her crib and read to her again, this time moving on to Fitzgerald's *The Great Gatsby*. Frances's eyes grew heavy, and she fell asleep.

I switched on the nighttime music and then the baby monitor. Tiptoeing out into the hall, I closed the door behind me. Frances snoozed on the viewing screen display on the unit in my hand, her sleeping form appearing a bit green due to the lighting of the room and the way the digital monitor worked. I tucked the belt clip unit into the pocket of my robe.

Padding downstairs to the kitchen, I poured a glass of water from the spring water dispenser and sipped as I stared out the window. Ground lighting illuminated the climbing ivy and eucalyptus trees near the fence border. The dark trees, outlined by the black of night, waved back and forth with the breeze coming in from the ocean. The stars were out, which was a rare occurrence in Fog City. I took another sip of water, letting the liquid cascade down my throat, feeling soreness. Maybe I was coming down with a cold. No, it was the smoke at school. Definitely the smoke from beneath the trapdoor.

There wasn't any smoke, my rational mind piped up. *The school would be burned down by now. The story would be all over the neighborhood and the news. There was no real cause for the smell of smoke, and so you are imagining your sore throat.* I took another sip of water and noted how my throat ached.

I saw the smoke in the theater, smelled smoke, breathed it…

And the guy in the theater saw it, too.

I bit my lower lip as I thought about the way he left the theater against a background of ethereal light that caught the natural highlights in his dark hair. His lower lip puffed out a bit fuller than his upper lip, and his eyes were almond-shaped, set perfectly above his high cheekbones.

"You'll find out soon enough," he had said when I asked him his name. I wondered if he was full of himself.

Since he was so good-looking, I would not be surprised. My mind pondered the various faces of my new female classmates, wondering whose heart he could have broken at Chula Vista High.

I checked the screen on the baby monitor. Frances lay sleeping, her valentine lips parted and her chest rising and falling. In the background, I could hear the last notes of *Clair de Lune* playing over a wireless speaker. As I took another sip of my water, I peered out at the garden. Thoughts of Addison High and the voice in the drama theater entered my mind.

Can you see me?

The shadow in the parlor room below the trapdoor came to mind.

I glanced to the hallway, half expecting the shadow to be standing there, watching me. Instead, Carlos crept around the wall and gave me a quizzical look.

"Cat," I muttered. "Just the cat." I shivered and took a seat at the breakfast table in the kitchen. Carlos jumped up on my lap and curled into a ball there as I placed the baby monitor on the table. He purred as we gazed outside at the garden, cloaked in the shimmering blanket of a windy night. The greenery outside quivered with the breeze. The plants stirred out of the corner of my eye. Even the bushes seemed to wait in anticipation as if something very bad was going to happen.

Near a popular destination called Pier 39, men would often hide behind bushes and pop out and scare the tourists with a friendly *boo!*

The bushes rustled. *The wind. Just the wind.*

I reached up and pulled down the window shade.

I thought of a line from The Great Gatsby. "The loneliest moment in someone's life is when they are watching their whole world fall apart, and all they can do is stare blankly." Propping my chin on my hand, I opened up the Pre-SAT test book to the geometry section. I solved each problem, one after the other, sketching my work on a piece of scratch paper. I peeked over the pages to the end of the book to check my work. Smiling at an entire page of my correct answers, I snapped my fingers. "Yes!"

The baby monitor buzzed loudly, and I shrieked. Carlos curled up his tail and fled down the hallway, scratching my legs as he made his escape. The noise burst into a loud, crackling static. From the baby monitor, an elderly woman's voice spoke in a gravelly tone. "Help me. Please."

I jumped with such surprise I knocked the unit over, which clattered to the floor as my heart pounded.

"Just Frances," I said to myself. "Just Frances and this piece of junk monitor."

Why does Nancy always buy these? They only last a month or two at the most. The voice came from a neighbor's cordless phone. Or a cell phone. Television interference. Anything but a person. Anything but a ghost.

The device lay face down on an area rug. Slowly, I bent down and reached for the parent unit. My fingers shook as they ran over the cover of the battery compartment and curled around, turning the unit over so I could see the screen again.

A pale face loomed over my view of Frances on the screen, all nostrils and quivering lips and eyes that rolled into the back of her head as she gasped.

"Help me," the woman begged, "I can't see!"

I screamed as I dropped the monitor and ran up to Frances's room, taking the steps two at a time. *I should call the police, but I have to make sure Frances is safe.* I ran down the hall and threw open the door of her room.

Frances was standing in her crib, giggling. As the light from the hallway flooded in, a white light flashed from beside Frances's crib and, in the blink of an eye, rushed to the window, where it hovered.

"Lady!" Frances shouted as she pointed to the window. "Lady! Lady! There." She clapped as if she were watching a show. The white flash glided over the walls of Frances's room to the high window opposite her crib. Then, the light disappeared.

I picked up Frances and clutched her, my body shuddering as I carried her to my room and lay down on the bed, keeping all the lights on. "Hush, sweetie. Just a dream." I tried to sound brave even though Frances did not seem frightened.

Frances rested her head on my chest. As the digital numbers on my clock switched to the midnight hour, my eyes grew heavy, and I allowed them to close.

"Lady," Frances whispered right before she fell asleep. "There." My eyes popped open.

Nothing but stark white furniture against cherry wallpapered walls and knickknacks. Just a teenage girl's abode minus ghosts. A picture of a fairy flying over a river and casting glittering dust over plants hung over my desk, the fairy gazing at the flora upon which she performed her task. I closed my eyes, afraid her gaze would shift, and I would find her staring at me.

I willed myself to sleep and fell into nightmares.

"Just perfect," the fairy growled like Hyannis but through a mouth full of drool and pointed teeth. "Perfect." Disembodied red eyes floated in the darkness somewhere in my dream. Or somewhere above my bed.

I hoped I was dreaming that voice. I hoped that the voice was not real.

Chapter Five
School Daze

"Love the wheels!"

Hyannis McWolfe's twin brother, Johan, heckled the students who clambered down from the steps of the bus, most of our heads hanging as we emerged onto the curb in front of the student parking lot. Hyannis stood near her brother, clutching her books to her narrow chest. A brand-new designer handbag hung from her shoulders. The goths, punks, loping gangsters, and poor kids who looked forty years old with their horrible hairdos, even though they were only eighteen at the most, hit the sidewalk, some smiling shyly at the beautiful Hyannis. She tossed her onyx hair over her shoulder and ignored them.

"Bunch of winners here," Johan went on. He stopped short when he saw me and Caslin. "Hey, Caslin."

"It's a bus, Johan," Caslin said. "Not a parade float." She enveloped me in a tight hug as we hopped down from the bus onto the curb. "You look gorgeous today, AJ."

Hyannis stared at me, her expression blank.

Johan breathed out a wolf whistle. Caslin elbowed him playfully in the gut. He reared back and pretended he never uttered a sound. "What's up with the bus, Cas?" He worded the question with disgust as if we had ridden to school on donkeys. As if we somehow embarrassed *him*.

Caslin smiled and shrugged. "It gets us where we need to go. On time."

I ignored Johan and patted the top of my head to make sure my loose curls were still in place. At home, I had rolled my hair with a flat iron, then arranged my tresses to give them a bit of fullness. I had applied a coat of mascara, blush, and a dab of lip gloss.

My heart fluttered with nervousness at the thought of seeing the boy in the theater again. The more I thought about him, the more I wanted him to see me looking nice. "I heard the voice, too," he had said before opening the door and stepping out into a flash of daylight. If I needed to camouflage myself to corner him and talk about the voices, I would. I just needed to know I was still sane. The fact that he was handsome motivated my newfound vanity.

Hyannis was surrounded by a group of guys and girls dressed in clothes I wasn't sure I'd ever have the patience to shop for. Her mouth widened to reveal perfectly even white teeth, but for a minute, I expected them to be pointy like the fairy in the painting in my room, a painting that I shoved into my closet this morning. Her brilliant smile gleamed white in stunning contrast to her cascade of onyx hair. Even her smell was intimidating. She exuded the scent of calla lilies in a concoction that screamed expensive.

Johan enveloped Caslin in a hug. "Unless you're going to drive me to school every day"—Caslin pouted—"don't make fun of my city wheels."

"You got it, gorgeous. Pick you up every day at eight." Johan kissed her on the top of the head, and Caslin grinned as she pulled away. Her mouth tightened in a thin line before the expression of discomfort fled her face. She smiled brightly once again. "How about AJ? Maybe you could give her a ride, too."

"Sorry," Hyannis said, "but after Caslin, the car's full. It was a stretch yesterday to even come back." Hyannis surveyed me with cold eyes. "I've never seen you fixed up, AJ." She spoke my name as if the mere feel of the sounds on her tongue put her out of her way.

"What are you all glamor glitzed for? Selfies on Social Butterfly?" Her group laughed at the mention of the archaic social network.

I inwardly cursed Hyannis as I ran a hand down my hair. "Just wanted to look nice, I guess."

"Yeah, well—" Hyannis began.

The sound of engines drowned out her voice and prompted all of us to turn our heads as a group of leather-clad motorcycle riders glided into the high school parking lot. The leader of the group had a physique of slim yet muscular legs that straddled relaxed on the sides of his vintage Indian motorcycle. He was flanked by two other guys on Harleys. The narrow motorcycle parking spots were situated next to the handicap section.

"They'll be moving over parking spots by December," Johan quipped as the group laughed.

The leader flipped up the shade of his helmet, and his eyes met mine. I recognized his deep-set eyes immediately. The boy from the theater.

I smiled as I watched him park his bike. He swung one leg over the seat as he dismounted. He removed his helmet, running fingers through his shock of dark hair, and held my gaze. My heart fluttered. He was even more handsome in the daylight, with piercing eyes and beige skin. He was beautiful, ethereal in the blue-tinged foggy light.

Hyannis, Johan, and their group stared in stunned silence as I shifted uncomfortably.

"Welcome to the black parade," Caslin murmured.

Hyannis giggled.

The boy turned to me and waved. I lifted up my hand and casually waved back. Kicking the stand on his bike, he propped the vehicle up. Hyannis's glittering eyes remained fixated upon me.

"That's Ben Bach," Hyannis muttered.

"Ben Beethoven?" I replied, seizing a moment to be witty.

"No," Hyannis said. "Ben Bach."

"What?"

"Ben Bach. You said Ben Beethoven."

"What?"

"Ben Bach!"

"Oh, sorry. Beethoven was deaf."

No one laughed. Caslin chose that moment to examine her manicure. Hyannis made a hissing noise and shook her head. My ears burned with embarrassment. Caslin found her voice again and tittered nervously at our exchange, leaning in closer to Johan as he chatted with his friends about surfing the waves of Ocean Beach during summer break.

As Ben removed his riding gear and conversed with his buddies, Hyannis leaned in and spoke quietly as we watched him. "Ben and his mom lived next door to us before we moved to a bigger house. A couple of years ago, freshman year for us, she called about something he did and how she had to take him to the hospital. She needed someone to watch their cat while she drove him to some juvenile center in Calistoga."

"What happened to him?" I said.

"To him?" Hyannis smirked. "Nothing happened to him. The authorities locked him up in a mental hospital and let him go after a few weeks. He picked a fight and nearly killed someone. His uncle or someone he knows is a criminal lawyer and got him off the hook. He's got a bad temper, so I hear. He's dangerous. Hurts people and then blames it on them, not himself. And no one suffers more for it than he does. As he should."

I stood there in shocked silence as I watched Ben walk up with his motorcycle gear casually hanging from his hands. He gave a polite nod to Hyannis, Johan, and their crowd. Johan ignored him and took Caslin's arm, offering to walk her to class. Caslin whirled off with him after a quick farewell and headed toward the school's entrance.

"I'll catch up," Hyannis said as she remained by my side.

Ben glanced in her direction and flicked his chin upward in acknowledgment. "Hyannis," he said pleasantly. "How are you?"

"Better than you," she replied.

"Everyone is entitled to their own opinion." His glorious gaze settled upon mine. "AJ. Good to see you again."

Her head turned to stare at me so her gaze could bore into the side of my skull.

I searched his face. His eyes were soft and lit, his gaze soulful. Despite his leather jacket and rugged look, I knew he was a gentle person. I could find no trace of a violent person, no trace of anyone resembling the picture Hyannis had painted. If I were to look only at the black leather, only at the motorcycle, perhaps my mind could formulate some idea of him as someone who would willfully beat someone else to the brink of death. Yet his eyes were gentle pools with vulnerability lying in the depths beneath. His face was boyish and good-natured, even crowned by his shock of dark hair.

"Good to see you, too. Ben. I'm glad to finally know your name."

"I'm sure Hyannis will provide all the details. Some true, some false."

She bristled and looked away, ignoring him.

He breathed in quickly, then exhaled, appraising me with a look that was glorious to bask in when coming from someone as handsome as he was. "You look nice today. Beautiful eyes. The minute I saw you, I was like, wow. If you don't mind me saying."

"Thank you," I said.

As his friends caught up with him, he gave me a tight-lipped smile and ambled toward the school building, resuming conversation with his fellow riders.

"Do you know him?" Hyannis asked. Her eyes were glittering stones. They reminded me of riverbed stones where salamanders and other slimy things lurked underneath.

"I met him yesterday in the theater. After I missed my bus, I went back in and sat for a little while."

"So now you're boyfriend and girlfriend?"

"Not at all." My voice sounded defensive, quivering as if spoken through the reeds surrounding Sleepy Hollow, even as my mind reeled with thoughts of the smoke and the voices. No way I could tell Hyannis the entire story of what happened yesterday. The only person who would understand was Ben, and I needed to talk to him as soon as I could about what we heard in the theater. "He said hello, and I said hi back. Why am I explaining this to you? Why are you still standing here?"

Hyannis huffed. "You and I share a friend. Caslin. You could really try and be nice, you know. I know it's difficult, but you could at least try. And get over yourself. Your eyes are weird. They're too brown to be green and too green to be brown. They're just creepy." Hyannis tucked her designer bag farther up her shoulder and sauntered away as the sound of the morning bell shrieked into the foggy air.

****

I breathed a disappointed sigh three classes later into my schedule after I found Ben was not enrolled in any of them. Even though I despised Hyannis, my common sense longed to override my instincts and stay as far from Ben as I could for as long as I could. At the beginning of my fourth class, I sat in one of the middle rows. I recognized the blond guy behind me as one of Ben's rider friends. He glanced at me curiously, then hunched back over his textbook as he opened it to the page the teacher instructed.

"Hey," the blond guy whispered. "You AJ?" He reflexively flipped a lock of bangs back as it fell over his eyes.

"Yes. Who are you?"

"Gideon. Ben was talking about you yesterday."

"What did he say?" *Please let it not be that this girl named AJ was acting schizophrenic in the drama theater. Please, please.*

"He said you're pretty. And smart. What a minute. I think he said you're pretty smart." Gideon's mouth widened into a grin.

"So?"

"You're going to have to prove it. Because the teacher's staring right at you."

"Ahem." The teacher cleared his voice loudly at the front of the room. I made a mocking sneer face at Gideon before I faced forward.

"Miss. Excuse me for interrupting our lesson, but what's your name?" my biology teacher inquired as he sat atop his desk. He folded his hands and let them rest upon his knee, raising his eyebrows.

"AJ Covington," I replied.

"Great. Now that I have everyone's attention, including Miss Covington's, let me begin by clarifying that the lessons will almost always take place in the front of the room. My name is Arnold Spinky." The class giggled. "Go ahead, get it out." He waved his hand as if he were a music conductor. "Most of you can call me Mr. Spinky but if you decide to call me Arnie, please expect you will most likely fail. If I'm purposely ignoring you, and this will only happen while either myself or someone who has been given permission is speaking, then you may not address me at all until I take notice of your request. Miss Covington, you'll learn more facing forward than you will looking back. That goes for everything in life." The class tittered as I opened my textbook. My cheeks flushed hot with embarrassment.

"We will begin this course talking about the cessation of life and study the causes, diagnosis, and social and cultural facts and theories of physiological death," Mr. Spinky continued. "Thus, you will have a test on these subjects shortly before Halloween. I am structuring the class this way, not so you can fall into the gloom of morbidity, but so you young people can further appreciate the life you've been given once we delve further into the study of the wonderful systems and organs you've been blessed with. This approach is akin to studying a machine from the inside out. How can you appreciate how it works until you've seen it defunct?"

"Dum da da rumm…" Gideon intoned in a low voice, mimicking the foreboding jingle of a scary television show. The class erupted in titters again.

Mr. Spinky waved his hand again and waited until the laughter died down. "Young man, to whom do I have the pleasure of speaking?"

"Gideon Glazier, sir." The rider extended his arm out over the top of his desk, resting his head on his leather-clad elbow. He looked up at the teacher with a churlish smile, then flipped his dangling lock of hair out of his eye. "I'm listening."

"Nice reply, Gideon. I couldn't have put it better myself." Mr. Spinky rose and walked down the middle aisle of the classroom, his hands tucked in the pockets of his slacks. He switched on an overhead projector.

"Gideon, the lights please." Gideon obediently stood, walked to the back of the room, and flicked the light switch down. Mr. Spinky slid a picture of a human skull onto the projector. "This is the most important piece of your shell."

I propped my head up on my hand as I stole a glance at the clock and thought about Ben Bach. I wondered if it would be wise to bring up the rumors Hyannis had no doubt already begun to spread all over school about Ben when I had the chance to speak to him again. Could he really be psycho?

A note slipped onto my desk from a hand that snaked around behind me. "What's up?" the note read in blue ballpoint pen. I looked over my shoulder. Johan, Hyannis's brother, sat two rows behind me and tilted his head to the side. "Are you cold? You can borrow my jacket."

I'm okay, I scribbled on a slip of paper. *Thanks*. I passed the memo back under my elbow.

I stiffened my shoulders, now aware that Johan watched my every move. The students in the classroom seemed fascinated by the pictures Mr. Spinky displayed on the screen: pictures of inanimate blood cells under a microscope, marine life both dead and alive, and a dead human hand outstretched with rigor mortis. If my stepmother, Nancy, were here, she'd lean over and retch. Then…relapse!

The rear door to the classroom creaked open, and a gust of wind blew in, sending another chill through my body. I clasped my upper arms as my teeth chattered. Mr. Spinky continued his lecture as he walked to the door and closed it shut, twisting the knob so that it latched and was immobile from further intruding breeze.

The students surrounding me were dressed in typical summer in San Francisco garb: light, textured, long-sleeved shirts with loose pants, jeans, or shorts. Some girls wore jean shorts or short skirts. Why was I so cold? I pressed my knees together and rubbed my calves, trying to generate warmth.

"AJ," a voice behind me said. "AJ."

Mr. Spinky talked on at the head of the class, oblivious to the disruptive member.

"AJ," the voice said again. Louder this time.

I turned around slowly. Johan doodled in his notebook. Gideon's eyes were closed, and his mouth slack as if he were sleeping. A burly guy staring at me raised his eyebrows. Eyebrow, actually. His face was so hairy there was a bridge of hair over his nose.

"What?" I said.

"What are you talking about?" he said.

"You keep saying my name."

"No, I don't, cuckoo. Turn around." He looked over my head.

"Excuse me, Miss Covington and friend. Are you aware class is still in session?"

The hairy bear pointed in my direction.

"She turned around and started talking to me," he said. I faced forward and sighed.

"Uh-oh," Gideon drawled in the croaky voice of someone who just woke up. "Maybe not so smart. But pretty."

The bell rang, and the students began to stuff their books into backpacks and heave sweaters over their shoulders. "Read chapter one tonight for homework. Have a great rest of your first day, class."

Mr. Spinky switched off the projector.

I gathered up my bag.

"Answer me, AJ," the voice behind me insisted. I whirled around. The hairy bear boy who sat behind me was several feet away, already opening the rear door of the classroom and engrossed in conversation with his friends.

Johan glanced over his shoulder at me with one eyebrow raised, shaking his head as he made his way through the door and out into the hallway, presumably to find his sister and tell her how weird I was.

Frozen to my chair, my focus wandered around the room as the last students grabbed their backpacks and purses. Mr. Spinky picked up a stack of files, and his eyes met mine. "Did you have a question?"

"I thought… I heard someone speaking. I'm sorry. That's crazy, isn't it? Uh, thanks for the lesson."

Mr. Spinky looked as if there were words on the tip of his tongue. *He probably thinks I'm a lunatic now, wondering if the school nurse has my size in a straitjacket.* Shaking my head, I rose from my desk, rushed out the door, and smack into Ben's leather jacket.

"I'm sorry!" I shrieked. My books tumbled to the linoleum floor.

"Whoa," Ben said. "Where's the fire?"

I stopped and stared at him, wondering if he was referring to the smoke in the theater. The smoke I thought I had imagined.

"Joking," he said. "There is no fire. Are you okay?"

"Fine."

He picked up my books and handed them over. I shot him a look over his choice of words, then shoved him out of my way. "Excuse me."

He murmured something to Gideon and walked after me down the hall as students flooded in. "AJ, wait. Bad joke," he called, "yesterday considered. I didn't introduce myself properly. I should have. Wait."

I whirled on him. I thought about running my Ben Beethoven joke by him, but let that one die flat in the cerebral water. There would never be a right moment for that joke, judging from my experience with Hyannis.

"Why did you say you heard the voice, too? What voice were you talking about?"

He ran a hand through his hair. "Cutting right to the chase, huh?" he said. "And inquiring about my medical history. All right."

A freshman wearing glasses with red plastic lenses rushed past and tripped over the tip of Ben's boot. He flew forward and crashed onto the ground. Ben placed a light hand under the kid's elbow and helped him up. "Sorry, man."

The freshman flinched as if he thought Ben was going to shove him, then relaxed. "'S okay," he mumbled before he walked away.

Ben lowered his voice, stuffing his hands in his pockets. "You really want to talk about that? Right here?"

I glanced around. "Not really."

"Will you join me for lunch?" He reached for my backpack. I handed it to him. He slung it over his shoulder. "Let's drop this off at your locker."

"My wallet is inside. I can pay for myself."

"I'm buying. I insist. Penatisimo?"

"I love that restaurant."

"Me too." He fell into stride beside me. I dialed the code into my locker, and Ben placed the bag inside. I gazed up at him. His demeanor was far too collected, for inside, my emotions raged. I was afraid if he leaned too close, his touch would burn me. The thought was so random I squelched it immediately.

"I'm going to put my books back, too. My locker is one row down."

He strode away, slapping hands with another guy in a jean jacket. The guy passed by me and gave me a small smile. From the looks of it, Ben had wasted no time telling his friends about the girl in the theater. That would have pleased me had it not been for my sobbing and subsequent freak-out session. I worried about how much Ben saw. And if he did smell the fire, if he did hear the voices, did that make him crazy, too?

I removed my wallet from my backpack and slipped the wristband up my arm, then closed my locker door. Hyannis, Johan, and their friends watched me from a few lockers down, leaning into each other and giggling.

Caslin came up behind me and tapped me on the shoulder. "Are we having lunch?"

"I'm... uh... I'm meeting Ben Bach." My gaze darted around the hallway as people started to leave in groups and head toward the cafeteria or outside the door to the parking lot. "We're going to the Mediterranean place up the hill that I mentioned yesterday. Would you like to come?"

"Hyannis knows all the dirt on Ben. You should stay away. He's trouble."

"She shared the news with me this morning. I think I owe it to him to at least get his side of the story."

"You don't owe him anything, AJ. Not your time. Not your reputation."

"I don't have a reputation."

"Yes, you do. The popular kids will eat you alive if they think you're going to try and keep that up without being friends with them. If you align yourself with someone like Ben, you'll find yourself alone the moment you decide he's not worth your time. Trust me. Let's make our junior and senior years the best years they can be. Hyannis is dialed into the seniors because of Johan and the football team. We'll be invited to all the in-crowd parties and get-togethers, and then next year, we'll rule the school. We might even be nominated to the homecoming court if we play our cards right and stick with Hyannis."

Caslin gently wrapped her hands around my long dark hair and spread the tresses out over my shoulders. "People have been waiting to get to know you, AJ. You're shrouded in mystery, and that drives people mad. They want to know what you like, who you are. It only helps us even more that you and I look nice." Caslin peered in Hyannis and Johan's direction. They were engrossed in conversation with their friends and seemed to have forgotten about us. "Shine the lunch with Ben. Tell him you're sick. Whatever you want. Or just ignore him, and he'll go away. Come on, let's go."

"We can have lunch together tomorrow."

"What is it about him that's so irresistible to you? Because whatever it is, just say it out loud, and you'll hear how dumb it is."

"You're being a little harsh on me, don't you think?"

"I'm your best friend. I'm trying to help you."

"It doesn't help that you're telling me who to pick as friends."

"Ben Bach is… Hyannis told me everything about him. He's—"

The crowds near the lockers thinned, and Ben emerged.

"I'll find out for myself," I whispered as I watched him. He walked toward us with that tight-lipped, crooked smile that made my heart do flip-flops. My lips stretched into a small smile.

"Oh god," Caslin groaned. "I'll catch you later." She spun on her heel and trotted toward Hyannis and her group. "Hiya, wait up!" Hyannis and Caslin murmured and waved at me over their shoulders as they walked away.

Ben gave a half-hearted nod. Hyannis grimaced.

She and Caslin flounced off to join their crew, which seemed made up of twice as many fit, well-dressed, and good-looking members as it was this morning. They had recruited swiftly.

"Ready for some amazing Mediterranean?" Ben said.

"For sure."

We walked down the hall and through the double doors leading out to the front steps of the school, making small talk about our teachers as we crossed and turned the corner onto Sutter-Hayes Street. There was a steep upturn on a hill where we passed by a decrepit, crooked house surrounded by a chain link fence and made famous by an article about San Francisco's ever-sinking streets. The house at the bottom of the hill resembled a worn-out, saggy brown boot as it leaned into itself. It had been long since abandoned, with a slight tuft of mossy grass growing on a patch that might have once been a small lawn. I could almost hear it sing a pitiful and plaintive tune of *You'll be sooorry* to whichever family had left it for dead as they loaded a moving van and drove away long ago.

"It's too much of a landmark to knock down," Ben said as if he could hear my thoughts.

We stopped in front of the house as the haze of fog drifted by, caressing us. "Yet another site for the tourists on the double-decker bus to take a photo of. There's a sinkhole inside with a scary story to it."

"And what is that?" I stopped and stared at the home. It seemed to stare back at me through dirty, cracked windows, its blankness making it all the more ominous.

"Supposedly, if one goes inside, the sinkhole will swallow them, and they never ever come out."

LIZ NEWMAN

Chapter Six
A Lunch Date

The windows fashioned of broken glass and mud ogled in my direction. The roof caved in on the lowest side where the house met the bottom of the hill, literally almost sliding onto the sidewalk, the only barrier to its spread of materials being a sturdy fence plastered with signs reading "Keep Out" and "Condemned."

Behind the window of the top floor, now depressed as if a giant had reached a finger down from the sky and pressed the roof of the house in like Play-Doh, a figure darted. I could make out the black shadow of a hunched-over woman staring at us.

"AJ, what is it?" Ben asked.

"Somebody is watching us." I heard my own voice like an echo upon an echo. I shook my head as Ben placed his hand on my lower arm. "Let's go."

We turned toward a side street to continue our walk to the restaurant.

A young woman with messy, raven-black hair stood on the sidewalk in the distance. Her figure was dark and imposing due to the clothing and the sidewalk's heightened incline. We walked toward her as she stood her ground in the middle of the path. She held her arms folded over her chest, her hands tucked under her armpits. The thin woman rocked on her heels from front to back, dressed in a black sweater coat and short black boots, her hands hidden away in ruffles. Her lips were a slash of red, and her dark hair was a tangled mass of mats and knots. Her face was broad, coming to a sharp point at the chin. Under her skin shone a blue undertone as drab and gray as her expression. Perhaps she may have been pretty once before. As we neared, I noticed she had a smell about her, a smell of old clothes and soil where worms would grow and dark things scurried to hide. Her worn-out knit booties were caked with dirt and mud in between folds of yarn.

I thought she would rush and hit me as her hands flailed. I shrank away. Ben placed his body in front of mine.

She bared her teeth and growled the snarl of a dog. Her teeth were those of a dog, pointed with layers and with lips curling back.

Ben held his arm out in front of me as she muttered under her breath, her black eyes fixated on me. Ben stared her down as we walked past until we left her behind us. I was mesmerized by her dark gaze. I couldn't stop staring. The woman and I both turned to follow each other's movements in some kind of primeval stare-down.

She clawed the top of her head, raking her fingers over her scalp, then her face, pulling the skin on her cheeks downward. "Hey. Do you know they can see you?"

Ben placed himself between us. "Get out of here," he commanded.

"They can see you. They can *hear* you."

"You heard me," Ben said. "You're freaking us out."

"They can see you in there," she whispered. "They can hear you." I shot Ben a nervous glance.

"The children," she repeated. She hunched closer, like a hobbit. "He hurt them. He burned them. He burned them all."

I stared back at her in silence. The fog blew in curling tendrils around us, eclipsing the sun.

"What are you talking about?" I said, feeling chills run up and down my spine. I advanced toward her slowly, holding my hand up in a gesture of surrender I hoped she would interpret as peaceful. She glared through narrowed, bloodshot eyes tinged with yellow. Her breath reeked of sour milk.

Staring, her mouth opened and closed like a fish. She lunged so quickly that I jumped.

"Their *home*, you stupid girl! Stay away, Dramadaaaaah!"

She raised her hands into fists and lunged to punch me in the face. I fell backward in retreat. Ben ran forward and caught me before I hit the ground. He cursed at her as she ran down the block. She huffed, shrieking once again as she turned a corner by the school. Her laughter, or screams, sounded like the cry of birds.

"Who is that?" I asked as I pulled my sweater tighter around my body to stop from shivering, although I knew I shivered not from the cold. "How did she... why?" My teeth chattered together. The name she had called me. How did she know?

"She looks like she's got feathers under that coat, or like a flock of magpies is just going to fly out of her hair. The Magpie. That's what we'll call her. The name Dramada. Does that mean anything to you?"

"Nothing," I lied. *Dramaaaada.* The Magpie may as well have cawed in my ear. I heard her so clearly in my mind. *How could she know if a name is what she screamed?* "Like magpies are hidden in her coat." A vision of magpies erupting from her chest, with tearing claws and snapping beaks rushing toward us, gave me a little shiver. "I hope I never see The Magpie again."

"Maybe there's a halfway house around here or something. She's probably loony." He looked away as he spoke, his brows furrowed with concern.

"Maybe."

"You know what's weird?"

"Tell me." I watched the condensation of my

breathing as it hit the cold, foggy air.

"Oh, nothing. I just realized what I was going to say will sound pretty dumb. I don't think I know you well enough."

I shook my head. "Like I care if it sounds dumb. Just say it."

Ben hedged a bit before shifting his weight from one leg to another. He turned in the direction of the hill. "Let's just get going. We're going to spend our whole lunch hour standing here talking about some crazy person. Another time. She's probably another displaced tech worker, on drugs and out of a job."

"You sure she's not out here to haunt Addison High's brand-new theater? Perhaps a starlet rehearsing for the next horror show?" We giggled softly and started up the sidewalk again. The incline grew so steep the top of the hill looked as if we would need our hands to climb up. I dug the toes of my new black Converse shoes into the ground as we puffed up the hill.

At the top stood the restaurant Penatisimo.

"Five times tasty," Ben declared as he ran his hand from right to left below the sign. "That's how you say *delicious* in Greek."

"How do you spell it in Greek?" I shot him a mischievous smile.

"Triangle, triangle. Five triangles, just like the sign," he joked.

I smiled. Slowly, the ice that had frozen inside my soul from the encounter with The Magpie melted under his warm presence. The leather of his jacket smelled fresh and new as the desire to be close to him overwhelmed my fear of the strange woman in the black sweater.

"If I brought my cell phone, I'd Google it. I leave it in my backpack as much as possible. It's another have-to."

Ben opened the door and walked in behind me. The bell jingled slightly as he pulled the door closed.

A squat, wrinkled man with big, round eyes and a thick Greek accent walked out of the kitchen and greeted us. Ben held up his hand in a peace sign. The Greek man responded with, "Table for two. A window seat for the young couple and a flower for the pretty lady." The man plucked a carnation from a vase behind the hostess stand and presented the bloom.

"Thank you," I said as I wrapped my fingers around the stem.

We sat at a table that faced out to the sloping sidewalk. The host unfolded a napkin with great aplomb and draped it on my lap, doing the same for Ben before he disappeared into the bar area to retrieve the drinks we ordered.

"The *spanakopita* here is unbelievable," Ben said as he surveyed the menu. "Like a dessert made out of spinach and cheese."

The air was scented with basil, garlic, and freshly baked pita bread. Much as our encounter with The Magpie had unsettled my stomach, I had only consumed a cup of green tea for breakfast, so my stomach rumbled with anticipation. "I'm going to order the Greek flatbread if that's all right with you."

"Anything." Ben peered at the menu. "Which one?"

"Feta cheese, tomatoes, basil, and artichokes."

"I've had that before."

"Me too. Have you been here often?"

"My mom and I have been coming here every year after Tax Day. April the sixteenth. It's our tradition. She's a tax attorney by trade. No expense spared if the year's client load has been heavy, and her private client load usually is. She's a wiz at crunching numbers."

"Planning to follow in her footsteps?"

He shook his head. "I'm still trying to figure myself out, let alone what I'm going to do for a job."

I giggled.

A tall, thin woman who stalked the sidewalk like Hyannis appeared in the corner of my eye. I glanced out the window. The model type dug her stiletto heels into the ground as she prepared to walk down the steep sidewalk.

"Ten to one," Ben said, "she'll plant on her way down."

I gave silent thanks that I was born with a cushioned bottom and the sense never to wear five-inch heels while walking in San Francisco.

Her feet gave way from under her, and her bottom hit the sidewalk. The hill was so steep it appeared she simply sat back rather than actually falling. "Down," Ben said. He turned back to his menu. The woman pulled off her heels and carried them as she resumed walking the hill in stocking-clad feet.

The waiter flounced out of the kitchen with a silver bucket, a plate of lime slices, and a big green bottle of sparkling water. The cap twisted off with a *chhhh,* and tiny droplets of carbonation shot up into the air, reminding me of the tiny droplets of water that danced in the fog outside of my home when the lighting was just right. As he poured the water into chilled glasses, he stole a look at me, then back at Ben. He glanced at Ben's leather motorcycle jacket, and he raised his eyebrows before placing the water on the table. Removing a notepad and pen from his breast pocket, he looked at Ben expectantly.

"The lady will have the feta cheese, artichoke, and tomato flatbread," Ben said.

The rest of his order was lost as my heart jumped

around in my chest. No one had ever ordered for me in a restaurant before, besides my parents, when I was a child. The way he did it was so unexpected and yet so smooth. The gesture reminded me of the flicks about British royalty that my stepmother loved to watch, with an open-mouthed gape as if her underside just imploded every time Lord Dobbins would speak.

"Excellent choice, Master Bach." Our waiter picked up our menus and hummed as he walked back to the kitchen.

"That always gives me a laugh," Ben said. "I think I've ordered everything on the menu here, and he always said I've made an excellent choice. And calls me master. That's why I like to come back." He smiled wryly. "Here, I'm always a master."

"What do you want him to say? 'The meatballs flambé taste like charcoal, dude? Pick something else.'"

Ben cocked his head to the side and surveyed me as my cheeks flushed at my own candor. His smile spread out over his face as he shot me a look of disbelief, and then he chuckled heartily.

"Sorry," I said.

"You know, you apologize way too much."

"What do you want me to say?" I joked. "Sorry?"

"I was spying on you in the theater, and you said you were sorry. I was blocking the doorway of your class, and you said you were sorry."

"Hey, if you would have fallen on the hallway floor, you would have been a lot sorrier than I was."

"True." Ben raised his glass in toast. "To being sorry. Or not."

"Not," I replied as our glasses clinked together. Our waiter's voice carried over from the back room as he sang a song in Greek.

Ben's profile was almost... godly, even with his

spiky hair that somehow still looked soft, with every spike in exactly the right place to make him look edgy, modern, and unbelievably attractive. Ben turned his head to the side, listening. "I've heard that song before. The one the waiter's singing."

"On a date?" I tapped my fingers on the white tablecloth as I parodied a look of extreme jealousy. Half parodied, half truthful.

"You're the only girl I've ever brought here. Besides my mother."

The waiter's voice raised in song and vibrated on a tremulous, deep note. "Do you know Greek?"

"Actually, I do. My grandfather on my mother's side was from Crete."

"Translate, please."

"That I can do." Ben cleared his throat dramatically and leaned forward. Reflexively, I leaned in his direction as he parted his lips to sing. "*Shoobeh-doobeh doobeh doo it's love. Babadoobeh-doobeh doo it's love.*"

My body shook with laughter as Ben kept a straight face. "Thank you." He placed a hand on his chest and half bowed mockingly to the right and left.

"Is he cooking back there, too?" I picked up a slice of lemon and squeezed the juice into my water.

"Might be. This is a family-owned joint."

The front door opened with a jangle, and a gaggle of office workers walked in, chatting in low voices as they sat at a table. Our waiter came out and greeted them exuberantly. Ben and I faded into the background, now in our own little world, as the door opened again and yet another group of patrons rustled in.

"I'm glad you came out to lunch with me," Ben said as he stole a glance at the table and then at my hands. His hands twitched ever so slightly. Oh, did he want to take my hand in his? My palms began to sweat as I knew if I placed my hands on the table, the moment might be gone, and they might twiddle there desperately. Or I would be behaving like one of those girls Nancy would always speak of with a tone of disapproval dripping from her voice. "I saw your last name on the talent show roster in the hall. Do your parents always enroll you as AJ?"

"That's what I ask them to do."

A man in a white apron placed a platter of olives, sliced grilled lamb, assorted dips, fresh vegetables, and warm pita triangles in front of us. I dipped a pita in red pepper hummus and relished the taste of bread fresh out of a brick oven.

"Are you ever going to tell me what AJ stands for?"

"My dad has this great trick he uses on my little sister Frances where he tells her if she keeps asking for something, he's going to tack on another minute before she gets it. Works like a charm because the minutes go by, and then she forgets she asked."

"I won't forget."

"It stands for something, I'll tell you that much."

"I'm here when you are ready to share. How old is your little sister Frances?"

Buzz off, Dramadaaaah! The Magpie echoed in my head. I reached for another pita triangle.

"Two and a half."

"I'm glad having a toddler at home has gotten you used to socializing with the mentally ill."

"Who's mentally ill? You?"

"No. You?"

"No."

"I was talking about our friend today. The Magpie."

I averted my eyes for a moment, thinking about

the drama theater and Hyannis. Was now the time to bring up the smoke? What if he didn't really hear what I heard? What if he was just placating me for some strange reason, telling his friends I was crazy and hanging out with me just for the joy of being able to bring back some gossip to his group of rebel punkspunkers. I wasn't exactly friends with Hyannis, but maybe his side was recruiting as well. I would be caught in the crossfire for not choosing a group to hang with. Somehow, I would become the odd girl out if I didn't hang out with the popular kids or become absorbed by Ben and his crowd. I decided not to bring up the incident in the theater. Not until we became better friends. Not until I could trust him. And if he had tried to murder someone, I needed to know the circumstances of that before I could even really count on him as a friend.

"I usually hear from people that it's the other way around," he said.

"Like who?"

"My friend Gideon, for example. His little brother is a toddler, and that drives Gideon bat crazy. He asked his parents about fifteen times for a motorcycle just to escape his house, then he bought a clunker and rode that around once. The footrest fell off, and he crashed into a parked car, so his parents finally let him use his savings for a new one. Me, I had to ask, take lessons, ask, buy the license, ask, work a summer job, ask, and then I bought one and quit asking. My mother moans and groans something fierce every time I take my helmet out of the closet. She's even offered to give me her Lexus, and she would take a cable car to work if I promised her I'd quit riding."

"Hmm." I swirled an olive around in the hummus and popped the bite into my mouth.

"You want to take a ride on my motorcycle after

school? I'm a good driver. You'd be safe with me."

"I'll never get on that thing. Never. I'll die before I get on a motorcycle with you."

Ben shrugged. "It's a lot of fun. We could just ride on the city streets or around the parking lot first to see if you're comfortable."

"No way."

"Never say never. Never let popular opinion sway you from living your life the way you want to live. That's what my dad always says."

"What does your dad do?"

"He's a senator. Lives out of state, in DC. What does yours do?"

"He's a doctor."

"That explains why you're so afraid of bikes. And here I thought it was just the looks Hyannis and her friends gave you when I rode up. Thought you were just giving in to popular opinion."

"I have a beach cruiser that is perfectly harmless. I'm not at all afraid of all bikes." On the tip of my tongue danced a multitude of stories my father used to share with me about when he did his residency at St. Luke's Hospital and the broken or worse-off patients who came in with injuries from riding their motorcycles.

Instead, I blurted out, "Hyannis said there's a rumor about when you were at Chula Vista High."

The heavenly taste of the lamb turned to dust in my mouth as Ben's eyes turned from warm pools to glittering stone.

"Did she? And what did you say?"

My mind turned and turned as I tried to remember what I said. All I could feel was the cold, blue stare upon my face and the sinking feeling in the pit of my stomach. Our waiter appeared out of nowhere and murmured something melodic with his accent, but the words were lost on me as Ben waited for my next sentence. The waiter set a plate of flatbread in front of me and a gyro with feta cheese and French fries sprinkled with herbs before Ben and spun on his heel, humming the *doobeh doobeh doo song* with far less enthusiasm.

Ben tapped his fingers on the tablecloth as I sat frozen, struck deaf-mute. "I might have told her to mind her own business," I choked out.

"That would have been very brave. Did you?"

"A little bit. I asked her why she was still standing next to me. Then she told me I was being terribly uncool. That Caslin was our friend, and I could be a lot better with her." I frowned and picked up a piece of the flatbread, taking a bite. The cheese oozed off the edge, and the tomato slices were plump and sweet. "Mmm." I hoped the presence of our entrees would change the subject. "My mom… my stepmom, actually, always said it's better to get along with people rather than make waves. Even if you don't really like them. Just the way of the world, I guess."

Ben folded up the gyro and took a bite, chewing thoughtfully. "It's better for you to get along with the popular people. Especially as a girl."

"I don't think so," I said as I shook my head. "That's how every stupid thing has happened in history. Hitler, wars, violence, you name it. Because of people just trying to get along, not make waves, and let something they know is wrong go on under their noses. Then again, you're talking to someone who spent most of her lunches hiding out in the library last year."

"You don't want to do that again."

"Not unless you like books."

Ben smiled, but there was not much joy in his expression. More of a sad, melancholy smile, which drew away from our former convivial energy. We finished our meals, and he flagged down the waiter for our check. As a black leather folder was placed on the table, I reached for my wallet. Ben waved my money away and inserted four twenties into the billfold. "Least I can do for yesterday. I shouldn't have left you in the theater. I should have stayed."

"Yesterday was my fault."

I reached for the check, but Ben whisked it away. "Today is mine."

On our way back to school, as we walked down the steep hill and past the sagging, decrepit house, the need to inquire about Ben's secret overwhelmed my better judgment. "Would you share with me what happened at Chula Vista? I'll keep it between us."

"You'll get a more entertaining version from your buddy Hyannis." Ben stuffed his hands in his pockets and inhaled the mist, his nostrils slightly flaring as he sucked in a deep breath. As we approached the stone steps leading up to the school entrance, the bell signaling the end of lunch sounded in a long drone. "I'll see you around." He flashed me a crooked smile devoid of all humor and rushed up the steps into the crowd.

****

After the last bell rang, the parking lot swarmed with students as I stood on the front steps of Addison High, searching the crowd for Ben. I owed him an apology for prying, and I wanted to let him know I would never bring up the subject of his past again. I spotted Ben pulling his helmet over his head and straddling his bike in the second row of parking spaces. I waved and trotted down the steps.

Hyannis and a gaggle of her friends brushed past me and then stopped. I glanced away to see Ben watching me. Hyannis met his eyes and shot him a disgusted look. "Do you want a ride home?" Caslin asked. "I'm going with Hyannis and Johan."

"It's fine," I said. "I'm going to head home and change and then go to karate."

Hyannis's face stretched out in a smirk. "AJ takes karate?"

"I like karate."

"I did, too, when I was twelve." Hyannis nudged Johan. "We'd love to see where you take karate. Let's go. We'll make room in the car."

"No thanks," I said as I moved in Ben's direction. The sound of motorcycle engines cut through the air as Ben, Gideon, and three of their friends revved their bikes, speeding away. My shoulders slumped. Today would not be the day for that apology. I sighed as Caslin called out a goodbye. She rushed to catch up with Hyannis and Johan, tossing her purse and backpack into their silver Mercedes convertible and hopping in the back with a Barbie type and a gorgeous girl with amber skin.

I trudged toward the bus stop before I realized my bus was pulling away from the curb. I broke into a sprint, waving and hoping to catch the driver's eye in the mirror, to no avail. The bus pulled away with a chug of black exhaust, and I threw my hands in the air in frustration.

Johan sped by in the packed convertible, and Hyannis shouted, "You're popular, AJ!"

"Getting old!" I yelled back. I turned away and shook my head.

With the roar of engines and the sounds of other students, I doubted Hyannis even heard me. She shot me a wicked smile as Caslin protested yet again. The convertible turned the corner. I waited a minute or two. They weren't coming back.

I turned toward the hilly street and began to climb. Footsteps sounded behind me, perhaps clad in heels or some kind of shoe with a hard sole. Perhaps the woman who fell on her bottom outside of Penatisimo. I turned around, hoping to make small talk with a friendly high schooler to ease my own mental discomfort. There was no one behind me. A slip of paper blew in the wind, coming to rest upon the chain link fence of the sagging brown-boot house, and the breeze blew cold and dank. I started walking again. The footsteps started up immediately. *Clonk clonk clonk clonk...*

Only your imagination, I told myself. *Just your imagination.* I squelched thoughts of The Magpie as I walked fifteen city blocks, counting my own footsteps and the footsteps of my invisible follower as they fell into the same pace as my own.

Relief flooded through me as I neared Mrs. Faria's house. The porch light shone softly. The curtains were drawn back in her wide living room window. Inside the home, Mrs. Faria reclined in an easy chair, her head thrown back and her eyes closed. Her thin body seemed so fragile in her pink flannel nightgown.

My brow furrowed. Her cheeks held no color in contrast to the pink. They were a sallow shade of gray blue.

A man stood in the kitchen. He turned, saw me looking through the window, and waved at me. Dagan, Mrs. Faria's son. He was dressed in a suit and tie and busied himself around the house as he washed dishes and placed them on a drying rack right next to the sink. I lifted my hand and waved back. I stopped at the front of the window, and the stepping noise that trailed behind me stopped as well.

Drying his hands on a towel, he disappeared from my vantage point and opened the front screen door a few seconds later.

"Hi, AJ," he called. "How are you?"

I strode up to Mrs. Faria's front door and greeted

him. "Fine, thanks. Is Mrs. Faria all right?"

Dagan bared his teeth in something not quite a snarl or a grin. "She needs to go to a residential care facility for a bit, as I'm headed to London on a business trip." He leaned closer and whispered, "Dementia. She's not doing so well. They'll take good care of her for the next couple of weeks. Could you keep an eye on the house for a few days? I'll pay you."

"You don't need to pay me. I'm happy to. I'll bring in the paper and check the mail. I'll sweep the porch, too. I know she prefers it nice and clean."

"Great." He smiled. "If you can just do the outside stuff, I'd really appreciate it. And I'm going to write you a check when I get back. Make sure to cash it. Or I'll just buy you a touchscreen tablet. Mom always said you like to read. Matter of fact, that's what I'm going to do as well as pay you so you won't turn the job down."

"No need, but you can if you want to, I guess. Is your mom going to be all right?"

He sighed heavily and wrung the dishtowel in his hands in such a way that he was probably unconscious of the motion. "She's getting along in years. I think... we should be prepared."

"Oh." My brow tightened with worry.

"Rest easy. The docs know how to keep someone alive for years nowadays. Far longer than they'd like to stay alive, I'm thinking. Mom is a strong woman. How are you doing in school?"

"Good." On the tip of my tongue was my impression of haunted Addison High, but Dagan clearly had his own problems. I didn't want to burden him more. "The subjects are interesting. Especially biology."

"Perhaps you are a doctor at heart, just like your dad. Silicon Valley would be the perfect place to set up shop as a cardiac surgeon. High stress. We tech guys are crazy with stress and late-night eating." He widened his eyes and made a face that reminded me of the facade of a smashed cartoon fly. "Hey, be careful when you cross the street. Mom said you were almost in an accident the other day."

I nodded, embarrassed. I spun on my heel to leave, then turned back to Dagan. "This might be an odd question, but do you know anything about this neighborhood? Have you heard about ghosts around here?"

"Nothing like that. Why do you ask?

"No reason. Just some strange lady following me all dressed in black, and then last night, I thought I saw a ghost on the baby monitor."

Dagan chuckled. He gazed at me thoughtfully before looking down at the doorsteps. "Sometimes I get a feeling. Could be Lake Stinson. There's something creepy about the mist, the way it hangs over. The Gloam is what we used to call it in high school. When the wind comes in from the ocean, over the dunes, when the air is just right. It almost sounds like something screaming in the fog." He gripped the edge of the screen door tighter, his knuckles whitening a bit. "Anyway, I don't want to scare you. Be careful out there."

I turned away from Dagan, a pang of worry shooting through my chest as he closed the front door.

The ghostly footsteps behind me resumed as I returned to the sidewalk. My breath came out cloudy from the cold as I stared at the Italian oak tree outside of my home. Fifty more paces, I counted to myself. Thirty, and I'll be home. I lifted my feet over the cracks.

"Step on a crack, break your stepmother's back," I murmured to myself as I jumped. "Where's the neighborhood hippie when you need him? Anything to make the footsteps stop. Anything." I stopped walking.

The footsteps stopped, too. Slowly, I turned around, and for a second, I thought I would see The Magpie looming yards away and rocking back and forth with her fists ready to pummel me like a charging zombie. I would have welcomed her presence then for at least a second before she killed me, for then I would have known for sure that I was not hearing things.

Nothing was behind me except for the empty sidewalk of an affluent street in a grand neighborhood. I turned and walked on. The footsteps accompanied me until I reached my double front doors, where they ceased. The craggy oak on my lawn with circles in its trunk that resembled eyes stared as I swung the door closed. Through the window, the mossy branches hanging beneath the oak swung forward from the breeze as if catapulting a specter into my home.

Chapter Seven
The Dragon Katana

At the Rising Sun karate dojo on Sutter Street, I padded softly in bare feet on the mats as I approached the mirror. I surveyed my reflection in the mirror, my long dark hair tied back in a ponytail, my white *gi* hanging from my body, with a black belt tied in a knot around my waist. The dojo was deserted except for Kwan Jang Nim Luis, my master teacher, who spoke pleasantly into the phone at the front desk even as he glanced up at me and held up a finger to signal that he would be with me in a minute.

My reflection stared back at me in the mirror: an oval face with what my stepmother had dubbed a bow-like mouth and wide, brownish-green almond-shaped eyes with curled dark lashes. Maybe I wasn't the best-looking girl in school, but I knew I wasn't weird, as Hyannis had said. Not in a bad way. For a minute, I wished I had the cool blond Nordic features of my father or the pleasant but plain girl-next-door features of my stepmother, but an image of my father's beak of a nose and Nancy's sun-damaged, freckled, pale skin flashed before my eyes, and I silently took the wish back. I had ethnic features, with golden skin, high cheekbones, and slightly hooded eyes, and for one of the rare times I was not shrouded in a haze of insecurity, I liked how I looked. My eyes blinked back at me in the mirror, and a smile crept over my lips. I looked all right.

Get over yourself, girl, Hyannis's voice echoed in my mind. *Your eyes are weird.*

My smile fell. I sighed and began warming up my arms and legs for training.

Luis opened his desk and retrieved a pen, jotting a few notes down before hurriedly ending the call and hanging up. I brought my hands to my sides, allowed my lids to fall shut as I focused inward and concentrated on my breathing, inhaling deeply through my nostrils and letting each breath out with a soft whoosh. With every breath, I saw the darkness behind my eyes grow more luminescent, the color of a cloudy midnight right before the full moon breaks through in a patch of clear sky.

Instead of a moon in my imagination, the white face I had seen on the screen last night on the remote unit for the baby monitor loomed. I gasped as my eyes flew open. I closed my eyes once again.

Ghosts can't hurt you. Focus. Focus.

"Sorry about that," Luis called as he rose from the desk. He was short and stocky, with dusky skin and a goatee. "Think I've spent all day on the phone. This place has been open five years, and we're finally taking a vacation. Marie is excited to go back to Russia and see her family tonight. I keep thinking I'm forgetting something."

"No problem," I said, happy to be lifted out of my thoughts. "Who's going to hold down the fort?"

"Couple newbies and Joseph. There's a huge turnover among karate instructors, it seems. They find new jobs, go pro, or decide that they're better suited for office work." Luis strode to the far wall of the dojo where supplies were kept. "You all right, AJ? You seem kind of sad." Luis glanced up his place near a set of tall cabinets as he removed a pair of foam swords for Wu Shu practice. His feet also made soft squishing sounds on the padded mats as he strode forward and handed me a sword. "Rough day at school?"

I nodded as he handed me a sword.

"Focus on combat." He placed his feet in battle

stance. "Begin."

Luis extended his right leg behind him and drew the fake sword upward, the blade slightly tilted in my direction. His fingers were curled around the hilt gracefully. He held the sword while slightly curving his wrist, in the true style of a master. I tilted my own wrist to match his. He advanced toward me, spinning around as he brought the blade of the sword close to my torso. The foam blade grazed my abdomen.

"You're disemboweled. Your focus is way off."

"You'll think I'm crazy if I tell you what's happening." I stood up straight and bowed, a signal that I was ready to begin again.

"Try me when we're done sparring."

He grunted as he jumped up and twirled in the air, slicing the blade over my head as I bent back. The blade just barely scraped the tip of my nose.

"Now you're missing a nose." He ceased his motion, bringing his hands to his side. "Do you want to trade in that black belt for white?" His laugh emerged as an infectious giggle, which countered my warrior image of him. I'd seen him kick through solid wooden boards and break a stack of fifteen bricks with one downward chop of his hand. He was death in a *gi*, yet he had the gentle aura of a teddy bear.

I sighed, bringing my hands to my side stiffly and bowing. "Yes, sir. Again." I crouched into battle stance, squeezing my brows together with the intent to focus.

Luis held the sword in front of him and curled his other hand up in the shape of a tiger's paw. With a war cry, he lunged, slicing the sword in my direction. I dropped to my feet and rolled under him as he jumped back, my sword slashing at his ankles as he jumped high in the air several times, evading each one. Agile as a cat, I hopped back on my feet and jumped in the air, twirling as I brought the foam sword down on his head once, twice, three times.

"Thank you for your scalp." I bowed mockingly, then readied myself for his counterattack.

He bowed, then stepped farther back, and he advanced once more. Now, he danced with the sword, gracefully swinging the blade through the air as he brought his hand out in front of my face. My blade shot out with the intent to slice off his wrist. If the blade had actually been real, it would have.

In a flash, he brought his hand up and threaded his own blade millimeters away from his midsection, pushing the tip into my abdomen. "You're dead"—he breathed—"because you're lost in your own mind. I lost some hair, but you lost your life. Not a good trade."

"Right," I panted as I brought my arms to my side and bowed. I threw the sword, and it hit the bottom edge of the mirror with a soft thud. "My focus is off today."

Luis perched on the mat and patted the space beside him.

I collapsed down and sat cross-legged, placing my elbows on my knees. "Strange things are happening. You're going to think I'm insane."

"Already do." He smiled.

"Thanks." I chuckled. "I'd have to be crazy to take eight years of karate lessons with the ultimate master, right? I start every day with a beginner's mind, and I truly feel like a beginner every single time. In everything." I decided I wouldn't bring up what happened last night while I was babysitting Frances. "Net-net is Nancy signed me up to participate in the school talent show, and that's the last thing I want to do. I'm freaked out over that and other things. Hyannis is almost a prima ballerina, and she considers herself the talent show headliner. And she is merciless when it comes to me because she wants to be Caslin's best friend, and I never thought about making other friends besides Caslin. I'm not exactly a social butterfly. I want to be nice to Hyannis, but something about her makes my hair stand on end. There's something about her that's creepy."

"Could be simple chemistry. Some people we like, some we don't jive with. Sometimes, we know it right off the bat that there are people we are meant to stay away from. Whatever the reason. I think you should listen to your instincts."

"Have you met her before?"

"Hyannis? Black hair, long. On the skinny side. Really pretty."

"That's her."

"She came in with Caslin to try out a lesson, but when she couldn't perform the kicks or punches the first times she tried, she gave up. Told me my teaching was *lame*. Her exact word."

"That's Hyannis. She recycles the same words over and over. Stupid, dumb, lame. Weird. My two-year-old sister is in that phase, too, but she's growing out of it."

Luis chuckled sympathetically.

I glanced at my reflection in the mirror, then frowned and looked down at the floor.

"The talent show performance gives Hyannis yet another reason to laugh at me. She'll probably get her friends to laugh at me while I'm on stage. Hyannis's crowd is at Addison. Caslin and I have drifted apart, and Hyannis... if she has her way, which she will because Caslin is soon to be dating her brother, then Caslin and I won't be friends anymore."

"A guy shouldn't change that. You might drift apart, but when they break up, she'll come back to you. We all make mistakes in high school."

"There's a new boy in school who caught me sobbing in the theater over all this, and he is beautiful and friendly, and I like him and I think he likes me, too. His name is Ben, and he has a bad reputation. Hyannis said he almost killed someone. But I also think... he knows there's something weird about Addison High. Like I do."

"Just be true to yourself, to your principles. You don't have to like everyone, but you can treat them with kindness and respect. Cheer up, *chica*. You're going to be all right."

I curled my hand into a fist and softly pounded my knee. "I have a brilliant idea. Caslin and I can do the talent show together. We don't need to do jujitsu. We can perform a sword-fighting dance. Wu Shu. Like you and I just did."

"This might be upsetting to you, but Caslin called and said she no longer wants to take lessons."

"I may as well sign up for homeschooling," I moaned as I buried my face in my hands.

The white face on the monitor loomed before me in my mind's eye. A headache, dull and throbbing, threatened to course up from the sides of my brow.

"Human beings are funny in that sense, AJ, but life goes on. It will go on anyway, whether we want it to or not."

"And Addison High... there's something very strange about it. It's not the students, or the administration, or even the way it looks. Something is wrong there."

"Every site in San Francisco has its past. I saw a story in the news about Addison. It was built on a site where a mansion hundreds of years old once stood. The old governor's estate when Benicia was the capital of California. The governor had his city home there." Luis's lips thinned as his brow furrowed.

"Forget about it. Let's train. I need to get my mind off this." I hopped to my feet, and Luis slowly rose to his.

"Sit down. I have something to show you." He gestured toward the edge of the mirror.

I obeyed and rested my back against the mirror as he strode to a locked cabinet by his desk. He opened the cabinet door and removed a long, sheathed black sword with a golden hilt. He walked toward me, holding the sword outstretched on the top of his hands as he gazed at the sword with wonder.

"The Dragon Katana. The sword of fire and vengeance. The dragon is the guardian of souls, who warms those who are cold. Brings fire to those who are dead inside. Ignites passion in those who have lost beyond hope. I bought it at an auction in Japan. What luck this had to arrive right before Marie and I head out for Russia because I can't carry it on the plane and admire it. Not thrilled about leaving it at home because someone could break in and steal it. This Katana was crafted for almost a year. Handcrafted by the finest steel maker in Tokyo."

He placed the sword in my hands. I unsheathed the blade, and the light pouring in from the floor-to-ceiling windows flashed on the silver. A golden dragon curled around the top of the hilt, partially onto the blade. Crouching into battle stance, I extended one leg behind me as I swung the sword from side to side.

"You handle the sword well."

"Let me hang on to this while you're gone." I made a decision I decided not to share with Luis.

"The Katana is a dangerous weapon, AJ."

"I won't even unsheathe it," I lied. "Please, Luis. There will be substitutes and all kinds of people in the dojo, too. You don't want to leave it here. Someone could steal the sword from you. I will keep it safe, I promise."

Luis shook his head, gently unwound my fingers from their grip, and repossessed the sword. "Today, you lack focus. Today is not the day for tackling new responsibilities. I will take the Dragon Katana home. You will keep it in your bag for now since mine is too small while we go grab a pumpkin spiced latte at the coffee shop around the corner. My treat." He sheathed the sword.

"Sure."

I shoved the weapon into my gym bag and we left for the cafe on Fillmore.

****

The cafe was decorated with artsy paintings of the California countryside and the rocky coastline of Half Moon Bay. An eclectic band played softly over the speakers, the music so vastly influenced by different eras that I couldn't decipher when the music had been made or where in the world the band may have been from. I swayed in my chair to the melodious beats of the melody, all heavy bass mixed with electronica, and an occasional soft buttery voice breaking through to sing a chorus.

The coffee shop was half full with patrons coming in for a late afternoon jag of caffeine and chatting all the while. The sound of the blender crushing ice for frappes broke through the music and conversation as Luis spoke animatedly about his new home in the Sunset District.

"Marie was getting out of the car with our dog, and she was about to set up a little blanket and gate area where the dog could play with toys while we unpacked the stuff from the van. Our new neighbor is out watering this little patch of a lawn, so I wave my hand and walk over and introduce myself. She seems nice enough. Bad teeth, though. Marie always said beautiful inside, beautiful outside, but I tend to disagree with that a little bit. I know a lot of people who are not that great looking who are some of the sweetest people I've ever met."

"Some beautiful people can be really ugly inside." I thought of Hyannis and her smooth, onyx hair and creamy skin.

"Agreed. The first thing our neighbor says to us is that the former owner committed suicide in our bathtub. And she has only gotten worse as time goes on. I know her every single health problem at this point."

The door to the cafe opened, and the sound of the voices of young men carried over to our table. I knew his voice before I even looked up to match the face with my auditory memory. Ben Bach.

"Oh." I ducked my head. "It's him."

"Might as well look up because he already saw you."

"Okay." I kept my eyes averted. "What's he doing?"

"Ordering."

"Pumpkin spiced latte for AJ!" the barista shouted.

"Do you want me to get it?" Luis said.

"Please."

Luis rose from our table, his back broad in a snugly fit t-shirt that showed off his muscles. Ben looked over his shoulder and gave Luis the once-over. A look of jealousy flashed, for he looked at Luis a bit too long. Then, with visible relief, he might have realized Luis was too old to be dating me. Luis picked up our coffees and glanced in Ben's direction as Ben made conversation with his friends. Luis turned, raising his eyebrow with an impressed expression that made me want to giggle.

I stirred the milk leaf that crowned the foam of my latte. An aromatic cloud of steam puffed up. My nostrils detected the enticing, light scents. *Ahhh, autumn heaven.*

Ben, Gideon, and a fellow rider milled about the counter, waiting for their drinks with motorcycle gear tucked under their arms. I could almost smell the scent of Ben's leather jacket. Ben laughed at something one of his friends had said, his face turned in profile where I could see the angle of his perfect nose and the soft pillow of his lips as they retracted over his teeth. I sighed as I slouched and hugged my elbows closer to my body.

"That's why you can't focus," Luis said softly.

"That's not why," I said. "Although I certainly botched any hope of being friends with Ben. This isn't a time to tell me how dangerous motorcycles are, by the way. I'm never going to ride, not that he would ever invite me again." Luis dropped another teaspoon of honey into his tea and took a sip as I relayed everything up to the lunch, where I stuck my foot in my mouth. "It's not like I care about his big secret. I have secrets of my own."

"Maybe he's so embarrassed he doesn't want to be reminded, and now, when he looks at you, he's reminded yet again. It's probably all about what's going on in his head and not so much about you."

"Hyannis said he almost killed someone. "But I don't think that's how it happened. Somehow, when I brought it up, he gave me this look. Like he was... being hunted. Persecuted." Right then, Ben turned around and met my eyes as I whispered the last word. My face flushed hotly. He had caught me talking about him, looking straight at him and speaking in hushed tones. His eyes narrowed as he glanced at Luis, then strode in our direction toward the leather couches and coffee tables set up in the back of the cafe.

"AJ." He nodded politely.

"Hi." I paused, embarrassed. "Ben, this is—" Ben

had already strode past and began settling down into a leather easy chair at the far end of the room. "Okay." I pressed my lips together as Luis gave me a sympathetic, tight-lipped smile.

Gideon stopped by with a short stack of napkins in his hand. "What's going on, AJ?" He lifted his chin upward in acknowledgment at Luis. "Black belt. I'm impressed. I took some karate lessons, too. I only made it to red, though."

Luis extended his hand and introduced himself. "You should come by the dojo sometime and take it up again. We're at The Rising Sun on Sutter Street. My wife and I own the place. I'll give you a free lesson."

"Nah, bruh. Most of my time's taken up by riding. Thanks, though, man." He slapped hands with Luis in some secret handshake only the male species was privy to. "See you in Spinky's class, AJ." His boots clomped on the stone tile floor as he walked over to the seating area where Ben was engrossed in the *San Francisco Daily*.

Luis and I rose after we finished our beverages. I pushed the door open, and we walked out onto the sidewalk near Columbus Avenue. Trucks and cars drove by on the busy city street. I shot one last glance at Ben, who appeared to have forgotten about me. But right before I walked out of the door, he raised his eyes and met mine. I coquettishly looked away and turned to Luis as we left the coffee shop. "He hates me, doesn't he? My chances with him are shot."

"I wouldn't say that. I sense a definite interest."

"I sense a definite disinterest. I feel like he wants me to not know anything about him. He has to tell me who he is, what he's like, what he did. How else will I know not to believe lies about him?"

"Maybe he wants you to trust him, but he has to

sense that trust before he can open up to you."

"Why does this have to be so difficult."

"It isn't always. Sometimes, things are perfectly clear."

"Yeah, for a guy."

Luis chuckled. "The day I met Marie, I thought, 'I'm going to marry her.' We met in a karate dojo on Taylor Street, both of us black belts and on our master journeys, and I told my sensei, 'That's the girl for me. The One.' I asked her out on a date, and flash forward five years later and we're married with a baby and building a life together. You're a long way from that. Zen mind and heart places your path on the place where you are destined to go. If you're not meant to go any further with Ben, you won't. If you are, you will. The universe will make it happen. Or not. You just have to be willing to accept and not chase."

"Well, I'm glad I didn't stand in front of him and scream, 'Why don't you like me?' It was tempting. Although I keep asking myself why he doesn't. Then I come right back to the moment in the Greek restaurant where I sounded like a nosy gossip monger and seeing his eyes turn to stone." A group of people crossed the crosswalk, filtering around us as Luis and I talked on the busy city sidewalk.

"Don't worry, AJ. The universe will lead you to the place you need to be. That may be by his side. Maybe not."

"Do I have to do anything in the meantime?"

"Yeah."

"What's that?"

"Work on yourself." Luis glanced at his watch. "I should get going. I've got to run home, finish packing, drop off the dog at the kennel, and catch a plane."

A bike messenger pedaled past us on a ten speed

with a rolled parcel under his arm and glided by with both hands stuffed in his fleece jacket's pocket. The parcel made a loud thumping noise as it whacked Luis in the funny bone. The bike messenger did not notice and pedaled away. Luis groaned and rubbed his elbow as he moved us farther away from the bike lane. "My advice is to find out the truth about what happened when Ben was fifteen. Find out direct from the source."

"He's going to tell me it's none of my business."

"He might. Maybe the first time you ask. Maybe the second time. Maybe the third. Or maybe he'd like to tell you what happened, and you merely need to ask with the intent to listen rather than with the intent to judge. People can sense these things. Those with a more acute connection with their emotions. I'd like to think that—" Bus number 21A rolled by and drowned out Luis's words.

"Oh no! Not again! I'm going to miss my bus!" I whirled in the direction of the bus stop and ran, watching the bus as the vehicle slowed down. My breath grew rapid as I sprinted into a run, flailing my hands in the air, trying to catch the attention of the driver. "I'll see you later, Luis! Have a good trip!" Luis raised up his hand in a wave and called out. My mind was set on catching that bus.

The bus was a good five yards ahead. My feet pounded on the pavement as I gave chase, with the lugging of my gym bag weighing me down. *I can make it, I know I can, just a little faster…* With no passengers waiting at the stop, the bus rumbled with a churning noise and continued down Columbus Avenue, turning right. I chased the bus for blocks before giving up.

"Ugh! My *life*!" I realized Luis had shouted out an offer for a ride home. I turned back in his direction into a crowd of people on the city sidewalk at the onset of evening. Peering over bald heads, sailors, and other chuckling people spouting out conversation, I could see Luis was long gone, probably headed home to pick up Marie and go to the airport. As the sun began its lofty descent behind the hills, the street felt chilly and foreboding, even while flooded with droves of people. Life in the real world seemed very lonely in the midst of countless strangers.

I clutched my coat closer around my body, heaved my bag over my shoulder, and trudged most of the fifteen blocks back to my neighborhood. My legs began to ache even as the sky grew darker. It was time for my parents to purchase me a car, although I could already imagine the conversation if I called would go something like this:

Hi, Nancy. I missed my bus. Could you come and pick me up?

AJ, your father and I are trying to teach you responsibility. Now, if I came to pick you up after you missed your bus, you would be missing out on a valuable lesson, and you'd probably expect me to pick you up every single time.

I wouldn't. I just lost track of time.

Next time you won't. (Click.)

One more call placed after that might send Nancy right back into The Echo Bar on Pacific Street and Bay Avenue. She was the perfect wife for a doctor who liked to be as useful as my dad. She always needed some kind of attention. My gear bag weighed down my shoulder, and I hoisted it over to the other side of my body.

The thought of what made my bag weigh so much brightened my step. *The Dragon Katana!*

Luis would probably slap himself on the forehead as soon as he realized his gaffe. Surely, Luis would trust that I would care for the sword. Little did he know I had decided in the dojo I would use the sword in the talent show performance.

No guts, no glory.

Of course, there was the possibility that I would cut off my own arm, or worse, during the performance. I shook off any feeling of dread or fear, as a true warrior would. I would show Hyannis I could be daring and strong. That I was a force beyond her comprehension. I had been training for combat for twelve years of my life. I would not make a mistake.

The chill of the fog rolling in from the coast sent a sudden shiver through my body. I looked up to find myself standing directly in front of Addison High. The two-story school building, eggshell white and new, stared back, disquieting like the face of a mentally ill person about to snap. The empty windows seemed to watch the street, blank and lifeless, yet with teeming menace. A wisp of fog ghosted over the wide landing over the cement stairs. I breathed as I watched a rush of dead leaves blow up into the air by the force of a light wind. The American flag waved over the school on a post near the newly laid lawn, giving the school the appearance of a ship. A ship inhabited by invisible spirits with secrets of very bad things that took place within.

I stubbed my toe against the cement and dragged it forward. *Shoop. Shoop.* I half expected the school to leap at me like a stalking tiger and swallow me whole.

The school's brand new. Just built. What could have possibly happened within its walls? It's your imagination running away with itself. Thinking about songs and rhymes always seemed to help ward thoughts of bad things away. "*London Bridges falling down, falling down, falling down. London Bridges falling down, my fair lady. Pins and needles bend and break, bend and break, bend and break, bones and fingers bend and break, my fair lady.*"

"Caw," someone whispered in my ear. I broke

into a run. My feet flew on the pavement until I reached my home and slammed the front door behind me.

Chapter Eight
Announcement

The pounding of Ben's motorcycle boots heralded his arrival into the hallway from a classroom, even as the hall was flooded with students who chatted and laughed. Ben looked right through me in the school hallway. He nodded as I walked by, his gaze fixated on the wall at the other end of the hall. I sighed and clutched my books closer to my chest. He could just forgive me for one prying question, really.

The halls were festooned with banners announcing the "Sign-up for The Thursday Night Talent Show! Thursday, November 17th at 6:30pm. Ballet, Bands, Bodybuilders, and More!" Bodybuilders was written in all caps, and someone had written the words "Beefcake!" underneath in pencil. A senior with her hair strung up in two buns shrieked as she read the addition. She reached into her backpack, retrieved a pencil, and scribbled out the words with an eraser. The banner ripped at a Scotch-taped corner. I jumped in and held the banner up while another student ran to find some tape.

Ben chatted with Gideon at the end of the hall, the two boys facing each other. *Look at me*, I willed. His gaze remained on Gideon. Perhaps it was only my imagination, but by the way Ben reached up and began massaging the back of his own neck, he knew I was watching him. I contemplated walking up to him. He couldn't just turn around and walk away from me, could he? Gideon and Ben turned in the opposite direction from my vantage point and turned the corner. My cheeks burned hotly as I struggled to suppress the weird gnawing feeling bubbling up from somewhere between my ribs.

After the banner was reattached to its former place, I picked up my books and placed them in my locker, then pulled out an advanced geometry textbook for my next course.

"He's an idiot," Caslin said as she wrinkled her nose in Ben's direction.

"He's not."

"I live in the aftermath of a woman starstruck by a bad boy on a bike. Flash forward seventeen years, and he'll be a useless alcoholic while you try to keep kids fed in a decrepit old house that your parents left to you. My mom used to ride behind him in a tube top dress and bare feet, holding on to a sissy bar. She thought she was so cool. One day, the motorcycle tipped over while he was driving drunk, and she burned the side of her leg on one of the chrome pipes. Left a big ugly scar. Then she found out she was pregnant with me and stuck with him because her family was Catholic, but mostly because of that scar. End of the fairy tale, if there was ever a beginning." Caslin leaned against her locker and placed her foot upon the lower half to steady herself. "Tonight cannot come fast enough."

"Where are you going?"

"Sharkey's Grill on Embarcadero."

"I hear they have a ten-dollar fajita special on Fridays. Johan's dad is a tech millionaire, Cas. You should at least ask for dinner at Epsilon. First dinner date and all. Let him know you will only settle for the best."

"He gets fifty dollars a week for allowance. He has to pay his own car insurance."

"He could sell a pair of his three-hundred-dollar sneakers on eBay. Or work like every other high school kid."

"Sharkey's is fine with me. I can't even remember the last time I had dinner at a restaurant."

Caslin surveyed the crowds coming down the hall, the goths with their heavy black eyeliner and gaze set just below eye level, the rockers with their ripped flannels and torn jeans, and the wannabe gangsters with their hats titled off to the side and one hand stuffed in a pocket of their jeans as they lurched along using the inertia of their swinging hand. Bright as a scene in a pretty pony cartoon came Hyannis wearing a bright violet-pink shirt and lipstick to match, with a yellow-blonde Barbie girl at her side.

"Who is that?" I asked Caslin.

"Gigi. Her name is Gigi Alvarez. She uses way too much bleach."

"You think?"

I decided I didn't like Gigi Alvarez. Judging from the approving stares she received as she glided down the hall, I was alone in that feeling. Even Caslin shot her an envious look. She flipped open her compact and examined her face in the mirror, raising a darkened eyebrow. Behind Gigi, speaking in low tones, walked Johan, Hyannis's brother. Caslin hurriedly applied lip gloss. She snapped her compact shut. He spied Caslin, and a smile crept across her face.

"You should be coy and play hard to get," I advised.

"Like you just did?"

"Ben doesn't give me the time of day, so it doesn't really matter. I could play hard to get and he would never notice."

"Oh, AJ. He's so not worth it. I hope you realize that someday soon."

"Maybe we both should. Hyannis hasn't proved herself to be a nice person in my book. Not quite yet. A few conversations while you're stuck together working doesn't make her a good friend."

"What does?"

"Time will tell." I closed my locker door and clutched my books to my chest. "One thing we know about Hyannis is she has to control everything and everyone. And she and Johan are twins. They're very close. The minute things end with him is the minute you lose her as a friend. I guarantee it."

"I like him. I'm going to like him for a while, and I'm fine with showing it. He said he never dates girls who play games. Hyannis is a good person and a great friend. I wish you would believe that."

Johan stopped and chatted with a group of boys, brushing his knuckles in a play punch against another boy's upper arm. Gigi held out her hand and announced something to the group, and the group responded with a loud *woo*! Gigi high-fived Johan and wrapped her arm around his waist, smiling up into his face. He wrapped his fingers gingerly around her wrist and removed himself from her grasp, whispering in her ear as he did so. She shrugged and turned away from him. A lazy grin crept across Johan's face as he tucked his books into his locker and headed in our direction.

"Johan is in high demand," I remarked.

"If you only knew." Caslin ambled toward him with her backpack slung over one shoulder, her expression dreamy. Johan wrapped his arms around Caslin. She tilted her head up toward his and planted a kiss on his lips.

Hyannis ignored me and continued chatting with Gigi, who ran her fingers through her hair and tugged on a curl. She worked her hair again, the curl springing back into place. Hyannis and her friend looked up to catch me watching them. I smiled cordially and turned away.

"I'll see you at lunch, AJ," Caslin said over her shoulder as she and Johan walked away, arm in arm.

"In the cafeteria or the library?"

"Out at the tables. Hey, the day after tomorrow, after the PSATs…" Hyannis nudged Caslin and shook her head. A look of guilt flashed in Caslin's eyes.

"The day after tomorrow, what?" I asked as I opened my locker. The entire contents came tumbling down around my feet. "Oh, gosh." I bent down to pick up my books, my binder, and pens, which had spilled everywhere. Hyannis smirked as she watched me. "What's going on after the PSATS?"

Caslin paused as Hyannis clutched her binder tightly to her chest and appeared to be silently laughing. Caslin's brows furrowed.

"Nothing," Caslin said. Caslin and Johan disappeared into a classroom down the hall. The rest of the lingering students filtered out into doorways and classrooms.

I finished placing my belongings back into the receptacle, closed my locker door, and dialed in the combination. From the look of the weather, the fog outside had won its battle with the sun. The empty hallway became darker, and the automatic, energy-saving lights switched on with a thumping noise. Just as I reached the door to my geometry class, the bell rang out in a shrill tone. I swore under my breath at myself for being late to class again.

Out of the corner of my eye, I saw someone walking down the middle of the hall. Great. The principal. I turned, ready to apologize for being late and using foul language. A child in tattered clothes stood in front of me and stared, his eyes round and his mouth half open. His hair sat upon his head in a bowl cut, and he was abnormally skinny. Holocaust skinny like in the history books where his clothes hung from his body, and you knew all that was under there were knobby bones and jutting ribs.

"Can you see me?" he whispered.

"No." I took a step to the side to walk around the child.

The boy nodded vigorously and reached out. "Please. Help us."

His fingers hovered inches away from my arms. I reached out to slap his hand away. My fingers gripped for purchase upon empty air. My hand recoiled as I shut my eyes tightly.

This was not a real child. This was a ghost. *Oh no, oh no, the woman on the monitor screen, the footsteps, the voice.*

Peeking through my lashes, I opened my eyes slowly. Nothing but the empty hallway and a buzz coming through the solar-powered lights. *The boy spoke to me. He knew I was there.*

"Can you see me?" echoed in my mind. Ash, where the child once stood, was strewn upon the floor.

I stooped to gingerly place my fingers upon the gray dust. I had to know if it was real, even though my mind screamed somewhere in the background of my thoughts to run. I touched the smooth surface of the linoleum, coated with a light layer of dust from the passing of students. Nothing more. The ash was now gone as if it had never been there in the first place. The hallway was empty, with only the windows shining with gray light and the lockers standing in staid rows.

The school office door opened and I looked up, my eyes so wide I felt the moisture of a tear fall from my cheek. Hyannis emerged, carrying a stack of attendance sheets in her hand. Her lips curled.

"You're late," she snapped as she strode toward me. "Why are you down there on the floor?"

I could do nothing but shake my head. I turned

and walked away, throwing open the door of the classroom as I heard her make a hiss of disgust.

****

The smell of freshly baked brioche wafted from the kitchen. Nancy hummed an indiscernible tune as my father's footsteps clambered down the wooden stairs. I folded my hands in my lap as Frances poked my cheeks with her soft little fingers.

"Chubby cheeks," she said as she backed away and squeezed her cheeks together so her lips squished into a tulip shape. "I have chubby cheeks."

I squeezed my cheeks together. "I have chubby cheeks, too. Want to see me smile?"

Frances squealed with delight. I gnashed my teeth and scrunched my face up to allow my front teeth to peek through like a chipmunk's. She wailed with laughter as she picked a grape from a fruit plate and stuffed it between my lips. I blew air through my lips with a *poof,* sending the grape flying across the hardwood floor and rolling underneath the toy bin.

"AJ," Nancy said. "That's disgusting."

Frances chased the rolling grape, crouching and leaning on her plump little arms to peer under the bin. She felt around under the bin until she pulled out the orb, holding it up like a prize and readying to pop it into her mouth.

"No, no. Dirty," I said. "Throw it in the trash, and I'll cut another one." Frances tossed the grape into the sink. "You're right, sweetie. Into the disposal it goes." I lifted up a knife and plucked a few grapes from the fruit bowl, cutting them in quarters. "Here you go."

"No." Frances shook her head and sat on the carpet.

"No, thank you," I corrected.

"No." She began to stack blocks.

My father, showered and out of the day's surgical scrubs, hiked up the waistband of his fleece sweatpants and sat at the head of the table.

"Good to be home." He sighed. "The procedure on the mayor of Redwood Shores went well. Standard ventricles clogged up with platelets and all sorts of evidence of a bad diet. I'd never be able to tell by looking at him. The guy's probably in as good a shape as an Olympian. You never can tell what hand you'll get dealt when it comes to health."

"You're a poet, and you know it." I smiled as I handed the busy Frances her cut grapes. This time, she took them and popped one into her mouth with a wide-opened, flat palm, as toddlers are apt to do.

"Cut them, or she'll choke," Nancy called from the kitchen.

"I did."

Nancy sashayed into the dining room and placed a salad on the table. She stood there and watched Frances chew. When she was satisfied the baby was not going to choke upon the grapes I gave her, she nodded at me, then fixed my dad with an exasperated look. My dad gestured for me to pass my salad plate, then filled it with spring greens studded with bleu cheese, pomegranate seeds, and tomatoes. He placed the plate in front of me and I thanked him, shifting uncomfortably under Nancy's critical eye.

"How've you been, AJ?" Dad said. "Sorry I've been so busy at the hospital. Shall we check out a museum soon? The De Young has a new exhibit. Monet, I think it is."

Nancy moved through the open door in the butler's pantry as she removed a platter from a cupboard. Her every move came with a clatter of dishes, silverware, or cookware banging together louder than necessary.

"There's something strange about Addison High," I whispered to my father as Nancy busied herself removing a roast leg of lamb with root vegetables from the oven. "It's haunted. I'm haunted. I'm seeing things at school and at home. Weird things."

Frances shrieked from the living room and ran over to us with a block in her hand stamped with the letter B and a picture of a baby. She laughed and pointed at Nancy's stomach as Nancy emerged from the kitchen. "For baby. Baby."

"Watch out," Nancy said. "Hot plate." She rolled her eyes as she maneuvered around Frances.

"Baby?" I raised my eyebrows.

"Yes," my father said. "AJ, your mother and I are having another baby. I wouldn't worry about the other thing. It'll resolve itself in time."

"What other thing?" Nancy said as she placed a serving platter on a trivet upon the tablecloth. She put an oven-gloved hand on her hip. "What other thing?"

"Nothing," I said. "Mmm, that smells good. Thanks, Nancy."

"Of course." Nancy removed her oven glove and apron, placing them on a buffet table covered with a silver tea set.

"I was just telling AJ the good news," my father said.

"Richard, you know I wanted to tell her."

"Frances spilled the beans," I said. "With the baby block and all. She's excited."

Nancy shot Frances a reproachful look as she settled down into a dining chair. She cut into a slice of lamb. "Well, at least I can tell her about our vacation."

My heart sank. Vacation as a family meant only one thing for me. More babysitting. Although the alternative of being around specters and the strange feeling hovering over Addison High certainly made a family vacation sound much more appealing than in times past.

"Where are we going?"

My father and Nancy exchanged a quick glance.

"Oh, Richard." Nancy sighed. "AJ, we'd wait until you have a vacation from school, but I'll be showing in another month or two, and I won't be able to wear a bikini for a while. Your father and I will be taking Frances on a nice long trip to Bora Bora in two weeks. On a babymoon. This year is the most important year for your college applications, so you'll need to stay." She bit into another bite of lamb, staring down my father as she chewed. "The roast turned out perfect, didn't it?"

"It certainly did," my father said, nodding. Neither of them met my eyes. Frances climbed up into her booster seat.

I cut up a slice of lamb into tiny pieces, along with a julienned carrot. My mind raced with confusion as I pressed my lips together. I heaped a spoon full of mashed potatoes onto Frances's plate. Frances dipped her spoon into the potatoes, took two bites, and pushed her plate away.

"Yuck," she declared.

"Am I going to stay here alone?" I asked.

"Your father and I think you're old enough to handle it," Nancy said.

Fear welled up in my chest. They couldn't go. The thought of being alone in this house with whatever force had been following me around made me nauseous.

My father and Nancy stared at me from across the dining room table. They seemed to be a mile away. I felt like a set of strangers looked at me through some elongated lens. Even Frances stopped prattling about with her toys and stared.

"Caslin is sleeping over tomorrow," I said after a few moments of silence. "After her date with Johan. Whose twin sister is a total and complete b—"

"AJ!" Nancy's eyes widened. "Not in front of Frances. Or at all, for that matter. A real lady doesn't talk like that."

"Lady, talk!" Frances cried. She picked up the baby monitor and brought it over to Nancy. "See, lady talk."

Without a word, Nancy took the monitor from Frances and placed it on a side table.

"Lady talk every night," Frances sang.

"I'm glad you and Caslin are friends again," my father replied. Nancy helped herself to another slice of lamb and a teaspoon of mashed potatoes. Nancy and Dad spent the rest of the meal making funny faces and voices for Frances as she giggled. When she opened her mouth, Nancy shoved in a spoon full of food. Frances's pot belly peeked out from underneath her shirt.

****

Later that night, my father and I sat alone in his study. A soft light glowed from the totem pole lamp he had picked up during his residency in Juneau, where he once lived with my mother. The garish faces on the totem pole ranged from happy to sad to ghastly.

I stared at the wall, at a painting he picked up in Italy. *Il Prelivo.* The oil painting was black and slick, with the figure of a woman with her arms stretched out toward an open doorway, where presumably her mother crumpled on the floor forlornly reaching for her daughter, who was being spirited away by three shrouded figures.

"I've been seeing ghosts. But I'm not the only one seeing them. There is this guy at school named Ben Bach. He sees them, too. Frances sees them." I told him everything about the voices, the footsteps, The Magpie, and the lady in the baby monitor.

My dad placed his hands on my head as his fingers gently pressed into my scalp. Ever the doctor, his touch was comforting and healing.

He sat in his office chair across from me.

"Ghosts, while it is questionable that they are real, are really just pictures in the air, that's all. Just pictures."

"Just pictures. But the Magpie, she could put her hands on me."

"Did she put her hands on you?"

"She went to push me, but I moved out of the way. I guess none of them have actually hurt me. They're scary, though."

"You're no stranger to the darkness or being scared." His brow furrowed. "There is something I should share with you. About the day your mother died."

I leaned forward. "Tell me."

"You were barely four years old when your mother passed. You probably don't remember much of her. She was so beautiful. You have much of her looks."

I thought as hard as I could about my mother, about her comforting touch. "I remember… her hands."

"She seemed to have the power to heal in her hands. I was never so content or so calm as when she was alive and she would hold me." He placed his elbows on his knees and looked down as he spoke, blinking occasionally. Tears welled up as I watched him speak, his voice choked with emotion.

"I got the call at the hospital when we lived in Haines, Alaska. There was a landslide over our home, and you both were buried beneath. It was late in the morning on the seventh or eighth day of heavy rains. I had no idea such a thing could even happen, or I…" He paused to take a deep breath. "I rushed home, and the house was completely destroyed. Somehow, you were both unearthed. The people in town were standing around you, and you were standing in front of what was once our house, now a mound of sticks and debris, and your mother lay beside you. I have never asked you about any of this before, but I often wondered. Do you remember anything from that day?"

I struggled to remember. All I could see was the black dirt of the Takshanuk Mountains raining down upon us as my mother covered our heads with her arms. I remembered darkness.

I closed my eyes as I thought of Mother, my real mother, with golden skin and soft hands, her hair like a satin sheet covering me in the cool darkness as we lay covered by mud from the landslide. Her body formed a pocket of air over mine... I could breathe, but not much. The darkness enveloped me as the oxygen became scarce, and then a feeling of energy, as if I could burst. As if I could implode. A blue light grew within me, around me. I sensed Mother struggled to breathe, and perhaps I cried. Yes, I cried and sobbed, and then I felt the soft silk of her hair as I threw my head back and wailed.

Then, a blue light, gossamer wings beating as the blackness broke into pieces, and the sunlight met my eyes once again. Ultraviolet and blue orbs danced in the air. I could see sunlight again. The rays of the sky opened as if shining through a door...

I gasped.

"Something freed me from our burial place in the mountain. Something angelic."

My father smiled as if he were speaking to a four-year-old child. "This was so, for the villagers mentioned seeing such a thing as they struggled to make their way up the mountain to rescue you. But these are small-minded townspeople. They believe in ghosts and fairies and such things. Their memories could not be relied upon as factual and anyway, there was no proof of such a thing. You have always been a normal child, albeit special and wonderful to me.

"I arrived too late to save your mother. Her lungs had collapsed. As she lay there dying, you leaned toward her and gave her a kiss. She drew her last breath with her eyes upon you the entire time. She loved you so. She said your name, which I changed to the name you have now because when I found out the meaning of your Inuit name, I thought we should keep it a secret. I didn't want you to… be confused."

"What is my Inuit name?"

He hesitated, then sighed. "Maybe telling will make the ghosts let you be. Your name was Anirnaq Janguta."

"What does it mean?"

"It means 'Angel of Death' in your mother's language. AJ. Your mother insisted we name you that when you were born, as she told me you had special powers. Death is not regarded as such a bad thing in the Inuit culture. It is simply the passage of light from one state of being to the next. She told me I need not protect you from the darkness, for you were meant to bring the darkness to light, for you are the light. The newspapers, the townspeople… even I could not understand how you and your mom managed to dig yourselves out of the landslide. So many others died that day. I did not understand. We took it as a miracle that you lived, but it was not so much of a miracle because your mother died anyway."

"What does it all mean?"

He smiled gently.

"I think it means that you need to focus on the things that are real and disregard the things that are not. People deal with distractions every day. Yours are scary.

They are not like television or make-believe. But you can disregard them just as you do the images on television or anything else. Come to me, come to Nancy, if you are scared."

"Nancy hates talking about ghosts. She freaks out and starts drinking. She looks for any reason to drink."

"She has made great strides in her sobriety."

I shrugged. "I still can't understand why you married her."

"Because girls need a mom. And fathers need a wife. It's important for us to have a stable family life."

"Stable is not quite Nancy's forte."

"She's doing her best. I hate to leave you like this and go on vacation," Dad continued, "but I think you will be all right. You're strong. Most of all, you are young and you could learn from the responsibility of keeping to your own schedule and having the house to yourself. You're not fragile, like Nancy. She may not be the most... together person, but she's your stepmom. She has got her good points, too, right?"

Much as I hated to admit it, she did.

"She cooks good, she takes care of our home... lately, and she's given me The Talk and all that. The house is nice. Even my cherry sundae room is okay because she bothered to design it. I don't think it looks better, but it feels nice."

"That and a cat will ward off the ghosts. Babies, too. I think ghosts are afraid of babies."

"How would you know, Dad? You can't see them."

"I know they're there. I can feel them. Anyone who works in a hospital where people are dying all the time knows. They cannot hurt you. Remember that. If anything out of the ordinary happens, you pick up the phone, and we'll come right back. I swear. Do you think you can stay with a friend? The trip is ten days. That's all."

Memories of the epic fights I had heard at Caslin's house, with her mom shouting and her dad throwing beer cans against the windows and smashing appliances onto the kitchen floor, crossed my mind. They concluded with Caslin's dad snoring on his green La-Z-Boy armchair and Caslin weeping on the floor as we poured over college brochures. I didn't have the strength to go through that again. Not now.

"I'll be fine at home. I'm just a little scared." I clutched a throw pillow to my stomach to settle my nerves.

"Trip's off then. We won't go. I'll tell Nancy, and we'll take the trip after the baby's born."

"You don't have to do that. What does the Angel of Death have to be scared of, right?"

"We'll call the trip off."

"Nancy's going to flip."

"I'll take care of Nancy. Let me worry about her. You just keep on telling me when you... see things. We'll find a doctor for you if need be."

****

I watched the clock in my bedroom tick until two in the morning, then four, until my eyes finally closed. Thoughts of the ghost child with his big haunted eyes and black cap of silky hair plastered to his forehead walking down the halls of Addison High haunted me as I lay in bed. My mind played pictures of children running and laughing, and a woman with a long, embroidered dress festooned with full skirts came rushing to them, urging them to be quiet and hide.

Some of the children wailed in protest.

"They are coming!" the woman shouted. "Hide. You must hide!"

The older ones hushed the younger ones, but some of the younger children still cried. Voices echoed throughout the house as a pounding upon the door ensued. The woman brought a fist to her lips as a front door bolt came unhinged. She turned and ran through a door, slamming and locking it behind her. Footfalls pounded upon the steps as the woman and children ran into the basement. Gasoline was poured all over the baseboards and stairwell as men spoke in deep, ominous tones...

My alarm clock beeped over and over as my eyes flew open. The ceiling of my cherry sundae room was stark white in contrast to all the red picture frames, red roses on the wallpaper, and red cherry vine coverlet. I swallowed the bile bubbling up into my throat. Wrapping the sheets tighter to wave off the chill of the fog that constantly crept even through my closed window, I glanced at the clock. Nine in the morning. I heard the garage door open and knew that meant Frances was on her way to preschool, and I was late.

I jumped out of bed and threw on a sweatshirt and a pair of jeans. I ran a brush through my hair as I ran out the door. Turning back, I picked up the bag with my karate uniform and the dragon Katana inside and shut the door behind me. I would practice for at least two hours today so I could be ready for the talent show next week.

I dashed out onto the sidewalk in the direction of the bus stop. The sky was cloudy and dark, a typical early San Francisco morning. I thought about the child in the school hallway and wrapped my arms around my body, clutching myself tightly. Mrs. Faria watched from her window, and the flickering lights of her television illuminated the inside of her home. I reached a hand up and waved, and she lifted her hand to wave back. She shot me a questioning look and stuck her thumb up in the air, nodding as if to ask *Are you all right?* I nodded back and tried to smile as I quickened my steps.

I slowed my pace down to a walk, figuring classes had already started, and I would be late anyway, and then I found myself staring at the sagging brown boot house. I walked past, keeping a close eye on the windows and expecting a flicker of light or some sign of life from a house that seemed so ominous. The cold morning air chilled me to the bone, and I wished I had put on my gray thermal shirt and pants underneath my clothes before I left the house. A magpie flapped its wings far above my head in the dark gray sky. *Caw.*

My black Converse shoe came untied, and I removed the backpack containing my *gi* from my shoulders and placed it beside me on the ground. As I stood once I took care of my shoe, the hairs on my neck stood on end.

I turned slowly and saw her standing half a block away. The Magpie.

The black figure with her bunchy sweater and her wild hair. She clutched her sweater tightly around her, and I turned back toward Addison High. The school seemed stark and empty, but the sight of the stairs was welcoming. I took a few steps toward the school when I heard her call my name. The name my father had given me.

I whirled around.

"Who are you? What do you want?" I winced and scrunched my eyes together, trying to appear tough. "I know karate. If you come near me, I'll hurt you."

I sneered at her and she stopped in her tracks, just standing there, watching. I held her gaze. "I mean it. I'll really hurt you. I'm not afraid." My voice shook when I spoke the last word, so it came out sounding more like "afreed."

Idiot, I chastised myself. *I'm like some stupid kid in a horror movie who knows she's going to get hacked in little pieces but waits for her killer like a lost lamb.*

I turned away and faced the school. In a second, she stood directly behind me.

"You're going to die in there," she whispered in my ear.

"Please go away."

I prayed as something pecked on my shoulder. I closed my eyes. "Just go away!" I spun on my heel to face her, ready to use martial arts if I had to defend myself. I found her still yards away and reached a hand up to my shoulder, feeling my sweater for a button or tag, anything to understand how her finger had tapped me if she wasn't even near. She said my full name again.

"What?" I shouted so she could hear me.

Her left eyebrow moved up an inch or so with the rest of her face remaining devoid of expression. She lifted her arm slowly and pointed at the school.

You are going to die in there, she said without her lips moving.

She turned and shuffled away down the street before descending the steps into the sunken brown boot house where the front door was located below sidewalk level. The door slammed behind her, the sound sending magpies flying in the air into screeching *caws*. The mist blew in tendrils, almost like fingers clasping the air and warding all warmth away.

My teeth chattered from the cold air or from my encounter with the odd woman. I did not know. I turned back toward Addison High. The Magpie suddenly appeared in front of me.

She smiled, her teeth black and gray and green, smiled with a sick smell of rotten exuding from her gums like copper in sour milk. She transformed into a flock of clawing magpies, all fury and feathers, as they sank their talons into my hair and scalp, screeching. The pain from their bites seared my skin.

Their beaks tugged at the roots of my hair and the skin on my face, pulling chunks out. I screamed as I tried to pull one off, only to find another in its place, pecking bloody marks into my fingers until I sank to the ground, all the while screaming until all was blacked out by feathers and I could no longer breathe. A probing beak wriggled its way through my hands and pecked at my eyes as I screamed at the feeling of intense pain and warm blood coursing over my head.

My alarm clock beeped over and over again as my eyes flew open wide. I stared at the time. Nine in the morning. The alarm had been ringing for two hours. I threw off the covers and dressed for school, my hands shaking as I buttoned my jeans.

Chapter Nine
Hyannis Creeps

In Mr. Spinky's class, I felt a slight peck on my shoulder. *Stupid birds!*

I ignored it.

Mr. Spinky droned on about the anatomy of a cell, its birth and death, scraping the chalkboard with a stubby yellow bit as he lectured in front of a diagram. He faced the other half of the class and asked a question. Logan Worley raised his hand up, stumbling over the answer as he struggled to sound like a genius by adding in words such as "regeneration" and "exclusivity."

Logan and I had taken a few classes together at the karate studio before he stagnated as a green belt. He was red haired, portly, with a spatter of freckles over his cheeks and warty fingers and the ability to sneeze with snot flying in a six-inch trajectory from his nose. The girl sitting in front of him had gorgeous, wavy, auburn hair. I could have wept for her.

AJ, someone whispered. I looked over my shoulder, the smile that crept over my lips at the thoughts of Logan's snot torpedoes fading. Really, the closest thought to bright I'd had all day. Of course, nothing behind me but Gideon, who shot me a questioning look, his chin resting on his outstretched arm, his eyes bright blue. I shrugged and turned away.

The ghost is back. Just ignore it.

Logan Worley sneezed a robust, wet, and wheezy expulsion. I couldn't even look. His outburst seemed to have scared away any specter hanging over me, for throughout the rest of the school day, I heard the voice no more.

After school, Caslin came over to my house to study for the PSATs. Nancy and Frances had left for a gym toddlers class before I came home, so the house was quiet. Caslin and I marched up the stairs, intent on hitting the books I had borrowed from the library. Our conversation turned to Ben as soon as I closed my bedroom door. I unleashed the flood of thoughts I had been having about him. "Finally, we can talk alone. I am in agony over Ben. Why won't he talk to me? At least acknowledge me? I've done nothing to him. All I wanted was to know about his life. That's all."

"Ooh, Ben Bach and AJ Covington. Your nickname will be Baejay. Ba-jay-jay," Caslin said as she jumped up and down on my bed.

"You stink! Are you on your period?" I wrinkled my nose from my place as I lay on the floor. The Preliminary Stanford Achievement Test Study Guide lay open in front of me.

"Just crazy in love." Caslin climbed off the bed and plopped down next to me. "Like a skunk, an animal, horribly in love with Johan. Johan!" She threw her head back, screaming in a throe of passion so real, the sound made me want to cringe.

"You're sick." I laughed.

"I know. It's bad." Caslin rolled on her stomach as the metal barrettes that the sides of her hair in place bounced around. "I'm in love. It's ridiculous. Embarrassing. But so are you." She patted the tip of my nose gently.

"Yeah, the difference is you're dating. I think my love for Ben is more like an unhealthy obsession. He hasn't really given me the time of day since we had lunch on the first day of school. How was your date? You forgot to come over afterward. I thought you were sleeping over."

"I'm sorry. It grew late. Our date was amazing." Caslin turned onto her back and placed her wrist upon her forehead. "We drove out to Treasure Island after dinner and kissed so much I thought I'd faint. I went home and took a cold shower, and prayed for strength. Do people breathe when they kiss?"

"They're supposed to. Otherwise, they'd pass out."

"How would you know?"

"I've seen my dad and Nancy kiss. Last Christmas. I was helping them put gifts under the tree for Frances after she fell asleep, and I forgot one. I came downstairs, and they were kissing up a storm, with tongues in each other's mouths and panting and hugging. It was gross."

"Ugh! How could you look at them the same?"

"I've seen Nancy barfing in the toilet and then lying on the bathroom floor with her skirt around her waist. Being French-kissed by my father made her seem respectable."

Caslin laughed her trademark *hee-haw* chuckle that always brought a smile to everyone's face. She pinched my sleeve and grinned. "When are you going to plant one on Ben Bach? My guess is that if you kiss him, all will be better."

"I could stalk him in the halls. Or eat a gyro with extra onions and tell him, 'This is what you get for ignoring me,' before I shove my tongue in his mouth."

"Since he loves Mediterranean so much, he'll like it."

I smiled wistfully, then shook my head. "He doesn't like anything from me right now. All right, back to the books. Here we go. Oh, this answer is kind of funny. Name a major disease associated with cigarettes."

"A. Premature death."

"Did you study this already?"

"Yesterday. With Hyannis. I'm hungry. Do you have anything to eat?"

"Leftovers. Nancy food. Wheat germ muffins. Quinoa. Brown rice and steamed fish. Knock yourself out."

"Let's order a pizza. Oh, wait… actually, forget pizza. Chinese?"

"Too fattening. There's a little deli at the corner by the wine market. We could get a sandwich. Or we could make one here."

"Here's good."

Caslin hopped down the stairs, her feet practically levitating above each step with love bliss. She checked her text messages and giggled. "Johan." She smiled. She leaned against the wall and texted him back with a huge smile. I felt a pang of jealousy. *Requited love must be nice.* I wondered silently if I would ever experience such.

We opened the refrigerator. *Ahhh, deliciousness.* Nancy must have shopped that morning, for the fridge was stuffed with a pallet of fresh strawberries, packages of deli ham and turkey, an assortment of cheeses, and all sorts of fresh food. Caslin filled her arms with containers of sandwich meat, cheese, pepperoncini, mayonnaise, and pickles. She set the bounty down on the counter and began to work. I pulled a fresh loaf out of the bread box and laid the slices on a wooden cutting board.

Upon the counter sat the receiver for the baby monitor. I switched it on. A picture of Frances's empty crib appeared on the screen, along with a loud scream of static. The static subsided, and the screen glowed its customary greenish glow.

"I saw a face on the screen the other day. Someone in Frances's room. I ran up to check and there was no one there."

Caslin shot me a look of horror. "Get out. That is so scary."

"I did. An old woman saying hello and asking for help. I didn't recognize her face."

Caslin stood by my side and looked into the monitor. The crib looked still and serene, with little butterflies all over the sheets, the picture a blue-tinged black and white. "Did you say anything back?"

"I was scared to death! What was I supposed to say? 'It's a great time to be silver?'"

Caslin reached for the baby monitor and spoke into the little perforations. "I think you've been watching too much TV, AJ. Hellooo? Anyone home?"

"It's Hyannis McWolfe," I said in the deep, gruff voice of a wolf as I batted my eyelashes. "You have to be my best friend if you're dating my brother. It's a requirement. You can't date my brother unless you're my best friend because I'm a control freak, and I have to control everybody. Knock knock."

Caslin grimaced and giggled at the same time. "Who's there?"

"Control Freak Hyannis."

"Control freak wh—"

"Now you say Control Freak Hyannis."

Caslin switched off the monitor and resumed making sandwiches. "I know this won't be the last time I ever bring this up, but I swear you would like Hyannis if you just gave her a chance."

"No, thank you. She makes my skin crawl. Whenever she comes around, my insides just tighten up. I'm sorry. I just can't hang out with her."

"What about all the parties, AJ? She plans practically everything. She's on the dance squad, and she knows everyone. Can't you at least be nice so you can get invited?"

"And sell myself out by pretending she doesn't give me the creepy crawlies every time she comes near? By the way, you really should take it slow with Johan because he and Gigi the Barbie girl just might break your heart."

"I know that. Believe me, that's the only thing holding me back from saddling him up. I know how this game works. I'll have him eating out of my hand by the time the year ends, and then he won't be getting anything but kissing until spring semester, at least. I know how to satisfy myself in the meantime."

"You are really graphic lately."

"Yep." Caslin rolled up a slice of ham and bit into it. "But still a virgin," she said while chewing. "What are you going to do about the ghosts?"

"Ignore them, like I always did."

"You should see that psychic lady. Ruz or something? Remember, we walked by her storefront a couple of times. She sits in the window in that giant bird swing and talks on the phone all the time when she's not peeking into her crystal ball." Caslin shoved a slice of ham in her mouth, swallowing the meat in three bites. "You should talk to her. Don't even tell her anything when she goes. She's supposed to tell you everything the minute you hand her a twenty. She's the one with the shop near Pier 39." Caslin placed a sandwich on a plate, flattened it down, and handed it to me. "*Bon appétit.*"

I picked up the sandwich and took a bite. "It's good. Thanks."

"Ham and cheese for me, too. I love Gouda. So, will you see the gypsy Ruz?"

"Will you come with me?"

"No way. I don't mess with that stuff. I told Hyannis how you see ghosts, and she said there's no such thing, but I know better. Remember that time my cat died and the next day, the glass door upstairs by her kitty condo was broken. Shards of glass all over the floor, and a ball hadn't been thrown in. Nothing broke the glass. It was her spirit coming home." Caslin leaned up on her elbows as she ate. "I totally believe that."

"You told Hyannis I could see ghosts?"

"Uh-huh." Caslin ceased chewing.

"Great. Yet another reason for her to make fun of me."

"I think it makes her scared of you. Maybe she thinks you're a witch and can put a spell on her."

"Maybe she's going to torment me just to see if I am. Did you ever think of that?"

"She won't. Look, I'm sorry. It was late at night and we were chatting on and on, talking about scary stuff when we were kids, and then it just came up. She hasn't even mentioned it since. She probably already forgot. You never said not to tell anyone."

"Because I figured that kind of thing would be kept in confidence. It's like me saying, 'Hey everybody, did you know Caslin's dad is a deadbeat alcoholic who can't get a job because he has a felony on his record for rushing at a cop with a knife after he threw full beer cans at his daughter when she was eleven?' These are just not things you tell people."

Caslin's eyes filled with tears. I shook my head and sighed, staring down at the ground, my cheeks burning with shame. I blinked several times, trying to keep my own tears from falling.

"I wish I hadn't said that."

"Yeah, I know. Me too." Her voice sounded hollow. Caslin put her sandwich down and placed her plate in the sink. "I'm going to go." She walked to the door and I followed as she heaved her backpack over her shoulder. She opened the front door. "If it makes a difference at all," she said over her shoulder, "he's sober now. He hasn't had to go to the emergency room for six months." Her wistful smile broke my heart.

"I... I'm sorry—" I reached out to her, but she stepped away and shut the door.

I groaned and fell to my knees in a heap on the floor, hating myself for saying what I said to my best friend, hating Hyannis, hating the world. The world was mean, the afterworld was scary, and the air in this house was thoroughly ugly because I said horrible things to the friend I loved the most.

My soul seemed filled with blackness. As if I were indeed truly evil.

****

"Time's up. Pencils down. Congratulations, junior class of Addison High. You have completed your PSATs."

The school administrators shuffled about the multi-purpose room, collecting the test sheets.

"Stanford, here I come!" Hyannis exclaimed as she high-fived the lovely Gigi at her table. I bristled at the sound of her overconfidence. Chairs squeaked as they were pushed back, and students rose, collecting their backpacks. Caslin rose from her desk with Johan by her side. She glanced my way and nodded. I knew she had done well. I nodded back, for I was confident I had given the correct answers.

The clock hit the hour of noon, and the bell rang to signal an early dismissal. My stomach rumbled with hunger.

"Caslin," I called.

Caslin looked over her shoulder, her eyes forgiving. She grinned at Johan. "Be there in a minute." Johan acknowledged me with a chin up and hurried to catch up to Hyannis and their group. "How did you do?"

"I think I did pretty well. I crammed until late last night. I swear those were the exact same questions."

"I thought that, too. Next up the real SATs, then Stanford, here we come!" Caslin squealed. "You better be my roommate when we rush."

"Rush?"

"For a sorority. Hyannis has a friend in Theta Gamma. Best sorority at Stanford. Their members have been nominated as homecoming princesses every year since 1977."

"With Hyannis?" My voice was pained. "Really?"

"It'll be fun. I promise."

"Yeah, until you're passed out on a bed of newspaper in a frat house that smells like pee. Nancy was in a sorority. She said that the older girls stole their bras and panties and froze them, and crunched Cheerios and Froot Loops into her clothes. And she still wanted to be a part of their crowd. I'm not sure that's for me."

"Don't be so sensitive, AJ. Nancy is an alcoholic and a drama queen. That's just what happens to girls like her. It's textbook."

"Once she was in, she had to do stuff in her free time like string up toilet paper from the rafters for the dance and ride a teeter totter all night."

"That was probably a fundraiser. It's a group thing, AJ. There's safety in numbers. Either that or hiding out in the library all year."

"I like to read."

"You better start writing your own books because we've burned through all of the classics. Unless you want to regress and pick up Fatboy and Chum or Captain Underpants. I hear they're really good books."

Hyannis broke into a popular dance in the midst of her friends, her arms pumping up and down as if she rode a horse. Johan and Gigi exchanged glances. Johan murmured in a low voice to his twin sister, who stopped dancing and stood still, a self-conscious look crossing her face.

Funny. In that moment of silliness, to me, Hyannis seemed like a real person. Judging from popular opinion, that didn't mean much to anyone else. I sighed.

"Let me think about that one. What are you up to for lunch?"

"Not much, really. Are you going home?"

"I guess. I'll see you later."

I peered over at Ben as he said goodbye to Gideon and his friends. He stalked toward the exit. Apparently, I was still invisible, along with my ghostly friends. "I heard it too," he had said when we had first met in the theater. Oh, if only he would speak to me, and I could find out exactly what he heard. Why he heard it. And if he had been hearing and feeling the same things I had during classes.

"Okay, great. Well, I'd better go. Can't keep Johan waiting. For lunch, anyway." Caslin winked. She pivoted on her heel and walked away.

I gathered my bag and walked out of the room and down the steps of the school with a drove of other emos, rockers, goths, and young scholars known by Hyannis and her conceited crew as unapologetic dorks. Even they traveled in groups of at least two, but my father told me once that humans have a need to classify, so I suppose that didn't make me any better. They were what they were, just as I was what I was. Apparently, by all definitions, today, I was a complete loner.

I took a deep breath of the foggy air. A pang of hunger rumbled through my stomach at the thought of a steaming hot bowl of ramen noodle soup. I cut a left at the corner of the street The Magpie haunted and decided to catch a bus to my favorite hole-in-the-wall ramen house instead. I should have invited Caslin, but she was so wrapped up in Johan lately.

A few students with tight pants and dark bangs so slick they appeared to be coated with egg whites straggled onto the bus with me. The doors closed with a loud creak, and the bus shot out exhaust as it rumbled away from the sidewalk. The other high school kids had somehow found seats. I was stuck under the armpit of an enormous man who had an onion scent about him that was both fragrant and putrid at the same time. Bodies rocked against each other with the movement of the vehicle. At the next stop, an emo kid stood, loudly protesting at the string of pink chewing gum stuck to the bottom of his jeans. The fragrant man chuckled, the bushy bird's nest by my face shuddering and turning up his smell volume about ten decibels. I still couldn't decide whether he smelled bearably gross or outright sickening.

I stared out the window, sniffling. Never had I felt so alone, so invisible. I thought about Caslin and how I had hurt her with my commentary about her father's drinking. My insides churned with guilt and regret. She was so gentle about it, so forgiving, even though I knew she hid her disappointment about her dad's alcoholism behind her smile every day she came into school. Some warped idea of the movie *The Parent Trap* sneaked into my thoughts, where a sober Nancy ran off with Caslin's dad, and they lived the rest of their lives going to all-inclusive resorts during Spring Break and snickering at hopeless drunks while sipping Virgin Pina Coladas. Then Caslin's mom would be free to fix up the house instead of holding him over the toilet while he threw up the contents of his stomach, which consisted of whatever whiskey was on sale by the gallon at the local drugstore.

I had witnessed this at my one and only sleepover

at Caslin's house. When I told my father, he simply said, "Not again." Caslin slept only at my house from then on.

After Nancy shared the news of their vacation with Frances, he seemed fine with me going to Caslin's. I suppose he thought it was safer. Or he really wanted to go on his babymoon to Bora Bora with Nancy. I should just muscle up and let him go. *What's the worst that could happen? The ghosts can't hurt me. They are only pictures that can't hurt.*

The thought of the pecking magpies from my nightmare sent a shudder through my body. *Why did the pinch of their beaks hurt so much if the ghosts couldn't really hurt me?*

"It's all in your imagination, Andromeda Jayne," a man whispered.

I turned to catch the source of the whisper and found my nose almost buried in the bushy stranger's armpit. *Ugh.*

"The things you imagine actually can hurt you," the deep voice said.

Whatever spoke at that moment, I took for common sense, which had sprouted roots in my psyche sometime after the summer when I lost my best friend to Hyannis McWolfe. I shrugged as I gazed around at the other bus riders, their faces dour and bored, resigned to the fact that I would be spending this school year not only searching for valuable insight alone and having visual and auditory hallucinations. Perhaps I would not leave high school without going absolutely cuckoo, but as a junior with only one friend, there was not much to lose.

The blank eyes of my fellow passengers peered around me, their minds lost in thought. Outside the window, the fog stretched under the Golden Gate Bridge, miles away where the bay met the Pacific Ocean, with hills of gray rolling pavement in between houses so close they appeared glued together. I felt a tickle in my solar plexus as the bus began a steep descent. Going up and down the hills in these rickety vehicles reminded me of roller coaster rides.

The City Center, a strip mall that housed The Spot Pizza Joint and my favorite ramen house, loomed ahead on the right. I pulled the metal wire. A quick beep sounded as the bus driver looked up at me and nodded, veering the bus to the curb. I thanked him and jumped out, my rumbling stomach intent on savoring a bowl of soup to ward off the perpetual chill in my bones. A gust of wind blew my hair up. I shuddered and pulled my black puffer jacket tighter. The darkened clouds grew thicker in the sky. The air whistled by with the warning of impending rain.

A black motorcycle with shiny chrome parts pulled up behind the bus as it pulled away from the curb. The motorcycle engine chortled as the rider killed the motor. The rider removed his helmet and ran his fingers through a shock of brunette hair. I was face to face with my dark prince. *Ben Bach.*

I turned away and flung the nearest door open. *He ignored me at school and pretended like I wasn't even there? Well, two could play at that game.*

I balked at my surroundings, for instead of seeing leafy palm trees, ceramic cats, and oriental art on the walls, I was staring at Johan, Hyannis, Caslin, and an entourage of my peers at a long table filled with well-heeled, popular kids in the middle of a pizza place.

And they were staring right at me.

Caslin smiled, and she waved. She looked at Hyannis, who raised an eyebrow. Caslin waited as if she needed permission for something. Hyannis shrugged, and Caslin beckoned me over. I had no choice but to walk over to their table with their eyes upon me, scanning my face, my hair, my clothes, anything they could make fun of as soon as I turned away.

"I am so sorry," Caslin began. "I was going to invite you, but..." Her eyes darted to meet Hyannis's. Hyannis's lips curled up into a petulant smile. "I thought you had plans."

"I do." My false confidence succeeded in shining through my voice.

"What are you up to for lunch, AJ?" Hyannis said over her shoulder. "Table for one?"

I tucked a hand into the pocket of my jacket, my other hand wandering up to the side of my head to scratch as I prayed for the thought of something witty to reply. Hyannis balked as if I were infested with fleas. I stuffed both hands into my pocket as Caslin grew even brighter red with embarrassment. The whole table stared, with Gigi on the other side of Johan, tittering. For a fleeting moment, I thought Caslin would invite me to sit, an invitation I would have hastily accepted to duck out of the view of prying eyes. Caslin remained silent, her eyes fleeting from Hyannis's back to Johan's and back to the group's.

I was unwelcome.

"Just about to grab some soup next door," I blurted.

"Soup?" Hyannis giggled as if I said I was going digging for earthworms to make spaghetti. "Mmm," she drawled mockingly. "AJ's going to have some soup."

"I love soup on a cold day," Johan sang.

Gigi burst into laughter. I glared, and she stopped her guffawing. My face burned with anger and embarrassment.

I wished the den of Hades would open up and swallow Hyannis and Johan. If there were any justice at all in the netherworld, the devil himself would clamber out upon hooves and blow a long breath of steaming fire into Hyannis's hair, turning her into ash. No doubt she'd cackle the entire time. She'd probably marry him afterward, and I'd be sent to hell for all eternity for wishing such a thing, where she would scribble the word LAME all over me with a Sharpie pen, using my naked, tormented body as an eternal flyer advertising the Thursday Night Talent Show along with an ad for noodle soup.

A giggle slipped from my lips at the thought.

Gigi raised an eyebrow as if to confirm to everyone that she knew I was crazy. My reaction took Hyannis by surprise. She bristled with irritation. Waiters approached the table, carrying large pizzas with cheese, sausage, pepperoni, and assorted toppings.

"Can I get anything for you, miss?" a server asked. He pulled a pen out of his white apron and waited for my answer.

"She was just leaving," Hyannis said as she helped herself to a slice while pointing to a far corner of the restaurant. "Or maybe she'd like to sit at that table over there—"

"With me." Ben's hand touched my forearm. Hyannis's mouth fell open, as did the mouth of every girl sitting at the table. From afar, Ben was foreboding in his black leather and motorcycle gear. But up close, with his deep-set eyes and chiseled features, even the way his body was outlined perfectly by his black t-shirt and jeans, he was beautiful. Man beautiful and breathtaking. No one could deny it, even Johan, who stared at him with jealousy and perhaps a bit of interest before Caslin turned his way. Johan cleared his throat and helped himself to a slice of pizza.

"AJ saw you in here and wanted to say hi. We're going to leave now. You ready?"

His eyes were deep pools of safety, reassurance, a respite from the turmoil that racked my body only moments before.

I nodded.

"See you around," Ben said to the group, forever calm with a slight raise of his brows.

My heart flip-flopped at the feel of Ben's touch upon my skin.

"Come on, AJ," Ben said, his eyes earnest. He gently led me to the door. We burst out into the fog of a San Francisco day. I inhaled the moist air greedily, for the entire time I stood in front of Hyannis and her group, I had hardly taken a breath.

"The Ramen House, just as the lady said, right?" He winked.

Ben and I walked over to the next storefront and he opened the glass door. The bells on the door jingled and the waitress called out a warm greeting of *Irasshaimase!* We slid into a booth of burgundy seats with tiny white cracks in the leather. The waitress placed two menus before us and smiled through red lips and lipstick-stained teeth before she bustled away.

"When exactly do I disappear again?" I said as I examined the menu. "Since at school, I'm essentially dead to you." I glanced up at him. He was engrossed in the menu. "You see me. You look right through me. All for asking a question. One question. That's not very fair, is it?"

"I just answered one hundred and fifty questions on the PSAT, and you want me to answer another one. Is having this conversation right now that important to you?"

"Yes, it is that important." The waitress placed ice water with a slice of lemon and a hot washcloth rolled into a tube and on a square plate in front of each of us and bowed. I took a sip of the water, then unfolded the washcloth and wiped my hands. The warm water felt soothing. "Unless you want to care to tell me exactly what you heard in the theater on the first day of school. Because I'd really like to know why I'm the only person thus far at Addison High who knows for sure that the place is haunted. Why I'm hearing voices pretty much everywhere I go, including on a bus ride filled with people. And these voices know things, Ben. They know." I ran my hands over my head. "I sound crazy, don't I?"

There, I said it. I waited for him to put down his menu, fold his arms, and shoot me a look that said *Sure, Crazy.*

"No." He shook his head. "The drama between you and Hyannis. When did that start?" He folded his menu, placed it on the table, and wiped his hands with the hot washcloth. "She has it out for you."

I shrugged. "We've never been friends. Last year, I took to hiding out in the library with Caslin. Hyannis and Caslin became friends over the summer, and I became the odd girl out."

"Ah. The rivalry's the big secret, as girls always do."

"I'm not the only one with secrets."

"Here we go." Keeping his hands folded, he spread out his thumbs in a gesture that said exactly that.

Two different scenarios played through my head. The first was that I would press him for an answer as to what he did to make Hyannis label him as persona non grata at Addison High and everywhere else. After which he would get up and leave, possibly without even answering the question. The second was that I would casually bypass the issue of the ghosts of Addison High and whatever he had done in the past and continue to spend time in his company, to smell the clean scent of his masculine skin and the soft black leather of his jacket, to perhaps become closer.

Closer how? I wasn't quite sure. I could not let Ben leave now that I had him here in front of me. Beautiful, dangerous, glorious, Ben. The cool persona I portrayed on the outside contrasted with my screaming inner voice that refused to let him rise and walk out of that door.

I had to use what Nancy called feminine wiles when she clumsily gave me the sex talk the day I turned fifteen. "A lady doesn't always say what she is thinking," Nancy said, "because that information may be better saved to achieve her objective of something more than physicality. Physicality, for a *lay-dee*, must never be the objective, or you know what *they'll* say."

A picture of Hyannis had popped up in my head. Yes, I knew exactly who *they* were. The objective, I wasn't quite sure of, but I did know if he got up and walked away, my heart would sink somewhere below the pit of my stomach and die there for the rest of my life, or so it seemed. My lips parted as I ogled his profile. He glanced up sharply and met my eyes. I felt my eyes soften, knowing I looked desperate but too weary and hurt by my latest interactions with Caslin to care. My heart jumped, and even though I knew I gazed at him with desire, I was too overwhelmed to be ashamed.

"Why the puppy eyes?" he asked with a teasing smile. He pulled the collar of his leather jacket in mock discomfort.

My mouth fell open in dismay. "You wish! I'm just hungry."

"I can tell." He laughed.

I grabbed my backpack and slid over to the outer side of the bench, intending to leave.

"Wait. I'm joking. I really am. Please sit back

down." He rose to place himself in the path of the door so I would be stuck in my seat.

"I think you are so insulting to ignore me for weeks and then suddenly sit here and laugh at me! If I wanted to be ridiculed, I'd go sit by Hyannis and her horrible friends, including my former best friend Caslin Perez." Tears sprang to my eyes. The waitress quickly sashayed to our table, her pen poised in hand, placing her body in a way that helped block my exit.

"I'm sorry," he said, all serious now. "I really am. Can we just order, please, and have lunch together? Please."

The waitress nodded. "Yes. You eat." She gestured to the cushioned bench, the white tears waiting like a set of teeth ready to nibble my pant leg.

My choice was to either shove Ben aside and battle axe the skinny woman out of my way in order to get to the door or sit. I sighed, placing my backpack on the bench as I sat back down. "I'll have the *tonkotsu* ramen with chicken and vegetables." My anger dissipated like a receding cloud does in the bright sun as I sensed Ben was pleased. He ordered the same and slid our menus to the waitress, who sashayed away to the kitchen. I pursed my lips together.

"How do you think you did on the test?"

"Fine. How about you?"

"Fine as well."

"Really? You don't seem like the studious type."

"You'd be surprised what we motorcycle riders can do. It takes focus to operate a bike. The many facets of operating a bike is like answering a question. There is only one function that fits the request. It's kind of like a symposium of movement between rider and machine before the rider can finally take control. Symposium. Heh. Probably sounds funny coming from someone with the last name of a famous composer."

"Not funny."

"I didn't think so," he replied, suddenly fascinated by a pair of chopsticks. "It took me about three months to become good enough at riding where I could just breathe, and the machine felt like an extension of myself. Then I could just ride and feel the wind, smell all of the smells of the city. The eucalyptus trees when I ride by Golden Gate Park, the smell of fried food and garlic in North Beach, and the herbs and exotic smells in Chinatown. I swear, when I ride through the Financial District, I can even smell the scent of money. I used to, anyhow, in better times."

"You sound like a future politician. But you don't quite fit the mold."

"No. My dad does, though."

"Your dad is in politics?"

"He's a senator. He left us and moved to DC after he was elected. He said it was a career move."

"How long?"

"Seven years ago."

"Do you ever go out there to see him?"

"I have seen him once since he moved."

"Why?"

"He said it is for the best that we wait to have a relationship until he is out of office."

The waitress placed steaming bowls of soup before us. Ben reached for the Sriracha sauce and drizzled spicy red all over the top of the noodles. I wiggled my finger at him, and he passed the sauce over. "He never comes back to see us, either. Just busy, I guess." Ben shrugged. "My...uh, past being what it is... we talked before he left the last time, and he said it was for the best until his political career was over."

I blinked in shock. Ben stared at his bowl of

noodles, stirring them. I pressed my lips together and unwrapped my chopsticks, clicking them twice before pinching a sliver of chicken. We finished our meal in silence. When the check came, Ben snatched it away. "The fee for your soundboard services," he said as he placed two twenties down on the little black plastic tray and rose, wrapping his jacket around his shoulders.

I dug out my wallet from my backpack and held out a twenty-dollar bill. He backed away with his hands up and shook his head.

"You don't need to pay me to listen," I said. "I'd listen to you all day for free."

He chuckled and opened the door for me as the waitress called out a farewell and "*Domo Arigato*!" We stepped out onto the sidewalk. The sky, buildings, and concrete were awash in moist gray and the reflection of dark clouds. A tow truck driver was lifting Ben's motorcycle onto the truck bed, as it was still parked at the bus stop.

"Your bike's being towed."

"Yeah, I know. I called the towing company. The right handbrake busted. I had to let it roll to slow it down, and there you were. It's a quick fix. They'll tow it out to the shop, and it will be done by the end of the day." We stopped in front of the bus stop. People from all walks of life, bundled up and dressed in dark colors, waited on the bench and on the sidewalk. "The bus is going to be pretty crowded. Feel like walking? It's a good, healthy ten-block stroll to your house. Looks like rain, too. And if you're hearing strange voices on the bus, you should probably walk with me so you know exactly who is talking to you."

I smiled as I met his eyes. "It's mostly downhill. Why not?" We glanced over our shoulder at the pizza place, and Hyannis and her friends emerged from inside with Caslin in tow. "Let's give them something to talk about."

"What did you have in mind?" His eyes danced like twinkling lights.

I grabbed his arm and wrapped it over my shoulder. Ah, paradise, to be held close to the body of Ben Bach. We walked down the hill, and a delicious chill ran up my body as I felt eyes upon my back, but most importantly, his head close to mine. Our bodies fit together perfectly, for he was just tall enough for my head to nestle upon the soft spot of his shoulder.

"I saw your name in the headlines for the talent show," he said. His voice shook a bit. Perhaps our closeness made him not his usual calm and collected self. He kept his arm draped over my shoulder even though we knew Hyannis and her group were far behind us, perhaps already zipping around in Hyannis and Johan's convertible.

"Thanks to my stepmother, Nancy. I'm pretty excited about the routine. It's called Wu Shu. Do you know what that is?"

"The Chinese art of sword fighting."

"I have this plan of bringing in a steel Katana, not just a fake one. I want to do a routine and then take off a scarf around my waist, toss it up into the air, and let it fall onto the blade. The blade will be so sharp, it will slice the scarf right in half."

"Sounds dangerous, AJ. And illegal. I'm pretty sure you can't bring weapons to school." Ben nodded as we turned a corner near an apartment building and a restaurant that had gone out of business. The side of the building had been graffitied with unintelligible writing. The foul smell of urine rose from the corner where the wall met the curb. I blew sharply through my nostrils in an attempt to clear out the scent.

I began to talk after a few steps when it was safe to breathe again. San Francisco streets contained numerous pockets of smelly odors due to the vagrants who lived on the streets. I gingerly stepped over a used heroin syringe nestled in a crack in the sidewalk. "Motorcycle riding is pretty dangerous, too, you know. My dad is a doctor, and he said when he worked in residency, he treated all kinds of patients who hurt themselves in riding accidents. You're a good enough rider where you won't get into an accident, right?"

"Right."

"Well, I'm good enough at Wu Shu. I practice almost every day. I've been working with an instructor since I was eight. I have a black belt. I can nail this routine."

"There are no weapons allowed at school. You'd be breaking the rules. You could even get expelled. At best. Worst, you could slice one of your arteries and bleed out on the stage. All for three minutes of showing off. It's not worth it."

A magpie flew over my head, its black outline against the gray sky sending a chill through my body. "It's worth it to me. To show I can do something they can't do."

Ben slid his arm off my shoulder and turned to face me. We stood at the edge of Golden Gate Park. The eucalyptus trees lifted up and waved with a slight breeze, giving the park an ominous and eerie feel, as if the plants and foliage hung onto our every word. "Why take the chance of hurting yourself just because you want to prove something to Hyannis and her parasites? They're a bunch of mindless sharks swimming in the ocean, trying to bite someone, and you want to show them you can surf. What good would it do when you're setting yourself up to crash against the rocks?"

"That's a really beautiful analogy. You should take up creative writing. Try being excluded by your own best friend in favor of someone who said you look like a freak and your eyes are weird. Sure, she shuts up for a day or so, and then when I'm least expecting it, she drops a rude comment. Caslin said she doesn't mean to hurt my feelings—she's just blunt. The truth of the matter is that she is a mean, rotten person." I glared at Ben. "What do you want me to do? Say you're right like in some bad sitcom and run off to be Hyannis's best friend? Because that's what it sounds like."

His eyes were soft and caring, and I could do nothing but soften my own gaze. He placed his hands upon my upper arms, aware he was getting through to me.

"Where would that leave us?" I went on. "Hyannis hates you too, you know."

"Take up friendship with her or leave it. Doesn't matter to me. Just don't put yourself in danger to prove your worth to a stick bug dressed in expensive clothes. Promise me you won't do the performance with the Katana," he said, nodding as if to hypnotize me into doing so. "Promise me you'll use the fake sword." I shook my head. "Wrong answer." He grabbed me softly by the upper arm. "That's it. You're staying with me today. All day. Until you promise."

I had to force my lips not to smile. "I have... some reading to do."

"It's Friday."

"Caslin's spending the night tonight, too. I think. After her date."

"I didn't say I was spending the night." He smiled wryly.

"For your information, we're closer to evening." I blushed.

"She doesn't like me much, does she? Caslin."

"It's not you. It's the bike. It's a symbol of everything that's gone wrong in her life."

"That's what it's like when you own a motorcycle. Even when it's not your fault, especially when it comes to an accident, it's still your fault. Think people are just scared of things they don't understand. Little human history one-oh-one. You were at Oceanside, right? I went to Chula Vista."

"Those budget cuts stink, don't they?"

"Sure do. Half the school was redistricted to Franklin, the other half to Addison. Only five or so of my buddies came with me. What do you think of the people at Addison so far?"

Thoughts of Hyannis and her friends popped to mind, along with their snickering laughter and evil trust fund baby patois that excluded all but their immediate circle unless they had use for someone.

"They're people." I sighed as I wrung my hands. "In all shades of gray, good and bad all at the same time."

"My father would say that's a very diplomatic answer."

"And generous."

Great, I just ousted myself as a nerd. Ben was so handsome and easygoing that he fit right in with the rockers and the jocks and the pretty rich boys. If this date was a bomb, like our last lunch date, he would be gone for good and perhaps make a couple of jokes about how he saved me from an awkward situation. He would retreat into the blissful oblivion of the included while I spent my lunches hiding out in the library. *Nice going, AJ.*

"I need to tell my parents when I'm going to be home."

"Call."

"Where are we going?"

"Lake Stinson for a walk. Then dinner. No more questions."

I hastily called home, then mumbled the vague plans into the answering machine.

Nancy picked up and sounded aggravated. "I was in the shower—wait. Yes, Frances, I'll be right there. AJ, I was counting on you to babysit. Your father and I are going out for dinner."

"Say no," Ben said over my shoulder. I scowled at him, although a smile crept over my face.

"I'm sorry, Nancy. I'll be home—"

"Late," Ben said. "Around eleven."

"At eleven." I moved away, embarrassed by Nancy's tone of voice, which sounded like a hen cackling over a paltry serving of corn. "Yes, he'll come in to meet you and Dad. All right. Thanks." I waved the phone in front of me, trying to figure out a way to hang up. Ben grabbed the phone and pressed his finger lightly to the touch screen. He handed the phone back to me, and I stuffed it into my backpack.

The wind blew in with a mighty force. Ben and I decided to change course and take public transportation instead of walking to Lake Stinson. Tiny droplets of rain fell from the sky as we waited for bus number 34B.

I shivered from the cold. Ben placed his arm on my shoulder and drew me closer to him. I was enveloped in a heaven of the scent of leather and whatever spicy cologne he chose to use. Perhaps that was simply his scent, that fresh, clean scent that brought my senses to the surface of my skin, longing to touch. I blushed, for I knew this was the feeling Nancy had warned against, and even so, I knew I could privately revel in it.

The bus pulled to a halt before us, and the doors yawned open with a creak. A few people stepped off, their chins huddled deep into the upturned collars of their coats or squinting from the falling mist. We squeezed past the people exiting and climbed onto the bus. I hooked my hand into a plastic bus handle and kept the other entwined with Ben's. The bus rumbled as it pulled away from the curb.

The lights above the passengers illuminated as sleepy-eyed people rocked back and forth, their expressions somber.

"When I get my bike back, I could give you a ride home every day," Ben murmured.

"Never," I replied with a whisper. "I'll never get on a motorcycle. You couldn't pay me. Especially in this weather. We'll slip all over the road."

"Motorcycle wheels have great traction. Actually, you probably shouldn't. Not until we find out about this thing with Addison."

"What does riding have to do with Addison?"

"Some of the old ghost stories say that when the spirits stir somewhere, it means someone is about to die. When they make themselves vocal and begin to talk."

"How do you know?"

"Let's just say I've done some field work in the vicinity of the dead."

"That's morbid. Where?"

"I will tell you later. When I get to know you better. When we can fully trust each other."

The rain poured down in a thick sheet now. "Next stop, Palisades Drive," the driver called out. He shifted the bus into gear.

Ben's forehead crinkled in a brooding expression as he watched the rain patter against the windows. His bearing reminded me a lot of an actor playing the part of the rebel. Also, the fact that his mere presence inspired a torrent of raging hormones made him seem very charismatic upon sight. I wondered if he knew what kind of effect he must have on so many girls.

He raised an eyebrow as he met my eyes.

"What's wrong?" I said.

"Not the best riding weather. But it's getting late, and I need to pick up my bike before the shop closes."

"Can you pick your bike up tomorrow?"

"They'll charge me for storage. Then I'll have to work an extra ten hours to pay for it. Would you mind if we picked up my mom's car? Could you follow me after I grab my motorcycle? Then I'll drop it off at home, and we can get going from there."

"Sure." I softly punched his upper arm. "I didn't know you had a job. What do you do?"

"I work in the call center at a social network. Butterfly dot com. It's a lot like Facebook but not as successful. Yet. The cool part about it is that you can join all of these groups you have an interest in being in, so you can set up a profile and find out what runners, cyclists, bookworms, whatever are doing in your area. Then their outings show up in your news feed, so it's more than just pointless dribble every day."

I bit my lower lip, thinking underneath Ben's gaze. "Why don't we start a group called The Red Room of Addison High? See who joins."

Ben cocked his head thoughtfully. "That's not such a bad idea, AJ. The problem is, the group needs a moderator. I'd have to put myself up as one of the ghosts."

"Make up a profile. Can't be all that hard, can it?"

Ben's lips pulled back as he bared his teeth in apprehension. "I'd rather not mess around with that stuff. Declaring myself a member of the undead might stir up trouble later on, don't you think?"

"They can't hurt you, Ben. They are just visions that can't hurt."

Caw. The Magpie dream and her pecking birds, who left bloody holes in my skin, came to mind. I opened my mouth to discourage the idea.

"All right, let's do it," Ben said before a word escaped my lips. "We'll head over to my house and log in."

"Oh, actually, forget it. Maybe tomorrow."

"I think it's a good idea," Ben said. "If ghosts could communicate, the easy way would be through cyberspace. They'd just need to pick up a frequency and speak."

My level of curiosity surpassed my level of fear, even though my whole body shivered, from my shoulders to my ankles. "God, that is creepy. Although I think you're right. I kind of hope no one signs up."

"There will be quack or two who will. Hey, it might be fun."

He disembarked when the black screen above the driver flashed "Palisades" in lighted red letters. "I'll see you at your house in about a half an hour."

"Actually, meet me at Mrs. Faria's. I need to pick up her mail and sweep the porch. She lives across the street in the Victorian. Number 1250."

"Sure." He ran his hand along my arm. I acted on my first instinct and held his hand there for a moment. He smiled, then turned away and jumped onto the sidewalk. The bus doors closed.

LIZ NEWMAN

Chapter Ten
Mermaid Waters

Mrs. Faria's son Devon opened the swinging door that led to her kitchen with the side of her foot. He balanced a tea set in his hands, the cups and china clacking as her arms shook. Mrs. Faria sat in the living room in a pink flowered nightdress, staring off into space. The room smelled of a strange odor. Perhaps some would say the room smelled of the dying.

"Let me help you, Devon."

I wrapped my fingers around the tray, placing it on the table between us. Mrs. Faria's hair stood out at crazy angles that reminded me of the large, colorful springs in Frances's toddler toys. Her cotton sheath made a crinkling sound as she sat.

"There's not much the doctors can do about Mom," he said as I poured her a cup of tea. "No matter. She lived a good life, child. All I hope to do is that she leaves this world with the least amount of pain possible."

I teared up as I brought the cup to my lips.

I heard Mrs. Faria's voice clear as day. Her lips never moved, but she spoke.

Oh, don't you cry for me, darling. Why, if you knew the things I did as a young woman, you'd say her time should've been up about forty years ago. AJ, I'm eighty-seven years old, and I've got a lot of miles on this old clunker. It's about time for me to go.

I startled a bit and turned to Devon as he scrolled through his phone. "Did you hear that?"

"What?" he asked.

I shook my head. "I think I'm hearing things. Nancy's parents and my father's died before I was born," I murmured. "I never even met them. I didn't know what was a lie or what was the truth when it came to the people who raised me. Mrs. Faria is the only grandmother I have ever known."

His gaze was filled with sympathy as well as a sense of resignation. I gave him a tight-lipped smile to show him I could be strong, and I nodded in Mrs. Faria's direction.

The doorbell chimed a melodic symphony chorus. Mrs. Faria's voice sounded in the air again. *Well, there's your boy. Go now and enjoy life. The world belongs to young lovers.* In her eye, I thought I saw a twinkle, even as the rest of her body remained motionless as she stared into space.

"I'll ask him in."

Sweetie, I'd rather not see anyone right now. I hope you understand. Do you understand?

"Of course."

Devon glanced up from his phone again. "Did you say something?"

"Sorry," I said. "Just thinking aloud."

I held Mrs. Faria's frail body in my arms for just a second, afraid to press too hard lest I hurt her.

Turning away, I walked to the foyer and opened Mrs. Faria's front door. Ben waited there with a bouquet of orange lilies held in one hand.

"I know this is cornier than Nebraska, but these flowers remind me of you." His face flushed.

I took the bouquet into my hands. "That's sweet," I murmured, digging my head into the blossoms.

"I had to get them for you. Then I realized we'd be going right back to my house and they don't have a vase. How's that for thinking ahead?"

"I'm sure Mrs. Faria will love them. She's too tired to receive visitors."

"AJ," Devon said. "She's not tired. She's

catatonic."

"Yes," I said. "I understand. Ben, could you wait here?"

Ben nodded. I quietly closed the front door.

Mrs. Faria's head tilted to the side as she slept with her head resting in her hands on the dining table. I cut the stems of the flowers and placed them on a side table in an empty glass vase. Gently, I helped her to her feet and laid her out on the couch, nestling a pillow under her head. She murmured her thanks. Her head fell to the side, and she began to snore softly.

Crumpling up the cellophane, I tossed it in the trash. A half dozen or so bottles of prescription pills sat on the counter. The bottles were filled with pills. Pain relievers, from names like oxycodone and acetaminophen. Poor Mrs. Faria. She must be very sick. I heaved a sigh as I joined Ben at the front door. He opened the door of the passenger side and gestured for me to climb into his mother's red Lexus.

We drove a mere four blocks before he pulled into a long driveway lined with shrubs. He led me to the front step of a Cape Cod-style home with white trim. He dug through his pocket, coming up with a key, which he inserted into the lock and turned.

"Welcome," he said as we stepped in. "Mom?" Silence. "She must be out with her friends. They do some kind of ladies' dinner night on the first Friday of every month."

The home was impeccably decorated, with softly lit lamps and depictions of Parisian life. The fattest cat I'd ever seen curled around my ankles, purring. She was shaped like a football on furry legs.

"That's Phoebe," Ben said. "Phoebe's the dog cat."

"Why do you call her the dog cat?" I asked as

Phoebe sniffed my hand and licked my fingers. "Oh, I see why."

Phoebe jumped into my arms. I held her close to my cheek and sighed. Ben's eyes became soft as I met his gaze. My heart began to pound wildly. I cleared my throat and turned away as I walked with Phoebe in my hands, cradling her like a baby. Ben placed a hand on my shoulder, not saying a word, and I put the cat down as I followed him.

After logging on to his computer, Ben pushed back in his desk chair.

"You absolutely sure you want to do this?"

I took a deep breath, exhaling slowly. "Yes."

"All right."

Ben clicked Start A New Group and named the group The Red Room of Addison High. He pulled the image location of a picture of the front of Addison High School off the internet. The American Flag in front of the school's front steps seemed to wave in the still photo. He created a public group, skipping the request to add friends. "Bait's thrown. Let's see what bites." He clicked a button, and the page went live.

Ben rose as if he could no longer stand to look at the screen, clicking the monitor off as he turned away. I followed Ben to the garage.

He opened my door, gesturing toward the passenger seat. "Thank you," I murmured as I sat.

The tunes of a new pop song filled my ears as Ben switched the gear into drive. The car crept out of the garage and turned onto the street. Light sprinkles settled upon the windshield. A few miles later, Ben turned the car into the driveway of an auto shop decorated with old tires and a sculpture of spray-painted bent parts like some kind of mechanical art show exhibit. I scooted over to the driver's seat and waited. After a brief conversation with the mechanic, Ben took the key from a mechanic and then stuffed his hands in his pockets as he walked over to me. The rain had thinned to light sprinkles that glowed in the city lights. I rolled down the window.

"Meet you back at my house for dinner," he said as he slipped on his riding gloves.

Ben revved his motorcycle and pointed toward the street, signaling me to follow.

The stoplight flashed red. The car idled behind Ben, who looked over his shoulder. He nodded at me through his helmet and raised two fingers in a wave. I smiled and raised my eyebrows at him. I was sure he did the same.

The tune of Hello-oh-oh sounded inside the tan interior of the car. I picked up Ben's cell phone and read the name Kelly Rose on the display.

Who was Kelly Rose?

The phone's ring taunted me as I was tempted to answer. I sighed, resigning myself to respecting his privacy, even though I wondered who Kelly was. She could be a friend, an aunt, a sister, or a cousin, I reasoned with myself. If I asked him about the caller, I would sound nosy, not to mention like a jealous soon-to-be psycho stalker. Considering Ben's past apprehension, I should probably save those questions for later. When we were officially boyfriend and girlfriend, if that day should come. *Oh please, please!*

But who was Kelly Rose? And why was she calling on a Friday night? I should just come out and ask him, but first thing was first before he clammed up again. I needed to know who he tried to kill. Why he would try to kill someone.

Every man had a temper. Every woman, too. I'd seen a drunken Nancy throw a hot iron at the wall once when she yelled at my father about the long business trips he had to take. The iron bounced off the wall and left a V-shaped chip and a burn mark until a couple of days later when a handyman showed up to spackle and paint over the mark. God only knows how many times I had wished Hyannis would be covered from head to toe in permanent, itchy burning pox that caused all her hair to fall out or worse. Or that she would die in some painless accident. That was the best daydream of all. Although picturing how much Caslin would cry about losing Hyannis brought tears to my eyes.

Johan would be distraught at the death of his beloved sister and find solace in Gigi, the walking, talking Barbie doll who wouldn't play games. When time healed the wounds of a lost friendship, Caslin and I would walk home from school as Caslin's former chatter would return, and I would nod sympathetically, punctuating our conversations with witty remarks she wouldn't need permission to laugh at. We would go on to college together as planned, become roommates, and have coffee with an artsy, eclectic crowd that never uttered the words "lame" and "dum-dum." The world would go on all around us, but we would attend school bright-eyed and content without the abuse and hangovers that came from hazing, gossip, and false friends. The future could all be so easy, so uncomplicated. I thought of my vision with the words Hyannis liked to say.

It would be *just perfect*.

"How very perfect," I crooned and batted my eyes in the dark interior of the car. "*Just perfect.*" I silently wished Caslin was with me to share in the joke.

Everything with Ben and I was going *just perfect*, save for Kelly Rose, whoever she was. The mere nearness of him made my heart soar and my body shiver, and he must have felt the same for me, or he would have better things to do than come to my rescue as where I was the loner being eyed by the popular kids at The Spot. The idea of Kelly Rose loomed over my mind. I would find out who she was soon enough. I needed to know if I should be afraid of Ben Bach first, for if Kelly Rose was not, then what would I have to fear?

Thick clouds of fog floated past the front of the car like ghosts as I waited for the light to turn green. A goose walked over my grave, as Mrs. Faria would say when I shivered even though the interior of the car was toasty. Goose bumps prickled my neck and arms as my stomach sank. I switched on the headlights as tiny sprinkles dotted the windshield, just enough to press the wiper button every ten seconds or so to swab them off.

A minivan passed me on the right as I trailed closely behind Ben on Market Street. The frustrated minivan driver peered up at the signs with his left turn signal on. Turning left on Market Street was impossible until a driver reached traffic-congested Van Ness Avenue. The wheels of his car grazed the line dividing our lane.

The driver cut in front of me, moving close enough to Ben to sideswipe him right off his motorcycle.

My heart jumped into my throat. I shrieked as I laid on the horn.

Ben swerved his motorcycle to the right. The minivan driver glanced in his blind spot, and the driver swerved in the opposite direction just in time, veering back into his lane. I pulled up next to him and shot him a scathing look, which he didn't notice, for his neck craned forward into the windshield as if leaning in for a kiss. His eyes were big and heavy with puffiness, and his mouth was overly full like a bass fish. The errant driver seemed oblivious to everything outside his fishbowl.

Ben stopped at a red light. He looked over his shoulder and waved, his face covered by a slim helmet with a dark shade that made him look all the more libidinous. Elation and pride welled up in my chest. I had saved his life just now, perhaps in a small way since he was a skilled motorcyclist and would have probably gotten out of the way anyway, but for that moment, I felt a great sense of satisfaction in playing a part.

I followed Ben back to his home to drop the bike off and car off and then we were off on a walk to Lake Stinson. The walk was mostly downhill, and the weather was balmy now that the rain had cleared, very much like that moist yet warm East Coast summer air Hyannis had told Caslin and me about, experienced from her family's new five-million-dollar apartment on Fifth Avenue in New York City. The weather was warm enough that Ben and I could walk comfortably without windbreakers or heavy jackets. September and October were always the most temperate months in San Francisco. The sprinkling rain had transformed into moist air and an occasional dancing drizzle.

After paying for a boat rental, Ben handed me a brown paper bag filled with kernels to feed the ducks. I tossed the kernels out onto the grass as the ducks honked and pecked, their beaks a smile. I turned the bag over and let some kernels spill into my hand. Leaning forward, a little mallard duck, which I determined my favorite, pecked at the kernels. I looked up at Ben, who watched me with a pensive expression. I raised my eyebrows.

"AJ," he said simply, more as a statement of fact rather than a question.

I searched his eyes, waiting for him to go on. After a moment, he held his hand out, palm up. I placed my hand in his as the ducks squawked around our legs.

"Any more duck food?" he asked as he pulled me closer.

"Oh. Of course." I withdrew my hand from him,

but he held on gently. He held out his other hand, and I poured out a handful of kernels. We stood side by side, holding hands, until I overturned the bag as more ducks and geese pecked and pecked around us.

"Let's go," I said as I nodded toward the line of boats for rent that were tethered together by a rope.

I lay back upon the narrow wooden mast as Ben pushed the boat away and hopped in from the dock. Larks and a family of brown mallard ducks bobbed in the dark waters, honking and quacking at the rowboat veering into their path. I held my hands wide to show them I had no more food. They paddled on, some following us with hope. The air smelled of moss and brine from the ocean's shores nearby. Stately estate homes loomed over the water's shore like fine ladies watching the courting of two young lovers, and my insides tickled to imagine that one of the young lovers was indeed yours truly. And Ben.

Ben stopped rowing and leaned forward, placing his elbows on his knees. His black jeans were rolled up to mid-calf length, and his legs were tan and muscular yet lean, just as I had imagined. I squinted and looked away, afraid he would comment on my gawking yet again.

"You never want to be one of those fast girls," Nancy had lectured with her lips pursed and her eyes averted as if she were remembering a time when she knew one of those fast girls personally.

"Penny for your thoughts." He smiled. "Forget that. We live in California. I'll give you a tenner."

What do you think of fast girls? I suppressed my errant thoughts with a smile.

"I never took you for a boater."

"I'm a guy of many talents."

I inwardly chastised myself for being such a lovelorn fool and longing to succumb to the thoughts that sent chills up my back. Nancy had said love should be dance, and a *lay-dee* would only need to know how to back away, back away, back away, before advancing the moment a man thought to give up and leave.

Ben grabbed the oars resting inside the boat and rowed. A peacock from the nearby zoo cawed a melodic cry. I pulled my knees together tightly and leaned my head back, staring up at the sky. The sun burned behind the gray, faint clouds but almost broke through. The sun would lose the peek-a-boo game played with the clouds as it was growing closer to the west, where the shore of the sea and the setting sun lay less than a quarter mile away.

Ben rowed to the middle of the lake and we bobbed there for a few minutes in silence. I leaned my head onto my hands and watched the surface of the water as a bug skidded across the top. Ben hummed a tune as I closed my eyes, breathing deeply and giving myself fully to the moment.

My eyelids grew heavy, and my last thought was of a jewelry box I owned, with a pink ballerina that twirled around and around on her long, perfect legs. She danced and danced, all the while turning, never laughing or smiling. Turning and turning like a windup doll who couldn't stop until she broke. Her face morphed into Hyannis's face.

Why do I have to keep dancing? Oh, I know why. So everything will stay just perfect.

Her ghostly voice whispered as she turned and turned, faster and faster, the music becoming jangled and warbled, her expression changing from blank to frightened to angry. *Just perfect.*

I fell into a dark chasm of slumber. Images flashed behind my eyes. My home, my room, Nancy, the lake…

I dreamed I stared down at the slightly rippling

black water in the dead of night, watching my reflection. I looked pretty in the water. I liked that, for despite my cherry ice-cream sundae room filled with musical boxes of dancing ballerinas and flying fairies, I never quite measured up. I never really felt pretty, not like I knew Nancy felt when she was all dolled up with freshly highlighted platinum blonde hair, red nails, and red lips. When she knew she looked beautiful, she had the look of a woman who could devour a man with the flash of a smile. *Makeup makes all the difference. I should wear it more often.*

My skin was a golden beige, unlike my parents, who looked like the descendants of Nordic Vikings. Reflected in the water, my skin glittered with a golden sheen. I pointed toward my own image, and moonlight danced around my eyes. My hair sparkled with light.

Instead of trees, green foliage, and the grand dame houses of Lake Stinson, a stark white two-story building with a rounded cupola loomed in the background. Addison High.

My reflection and its pink lipstick smile thinned a bit. I reached a finger down and tapped my image ever so lightly, watching my face ripple.

A young girl's face emerged.

She looked a bit like me, with dark hair and full features, save for the dip under her belly button where her torso was wrapped in plants. Her neck and shoulders rose from the water, her face wet, and her hair slicked back. She beckoned me with the curve of her lips.

"Come closer." Her voice was thin and reedy.

I leaned my ear down to her.

"Don't you know we are already dead, and all this is just a dream?" she whispered.

I pulled back sharply as she laughed. Her skeletal hands shot out and grasped me by the sides of my head.

"One ending," she murmured, her breath odiferous with the brine of the ocean and moss and rot, "for all of us, it's the same. What we really are. All we are… is death. Can you see me?"

"Yes," I said. My cheeks became wet with tears. "I see you."

I pulled back sharply, and her face was a skull, her hair a tangled mass of seaweed and kelp, and her upper body simply bones jutting out from the water. A fish flopped within the cage of her ribs, struggling to find an exit.

I placed my hands on her shoulders and pushed her down into the water. Her face rose to meet mine again, and I pushed her again, but she kept popping up.

She pressed her toothy, skeletal mouth against mine as I breathed in sharply. Slimy, wet bone touched my lips.

I tried to wrestle her body away. Her bony face withdrew from mine as I finished inhaling a breath right before I was about to scream. Her bony fingers grazed my cheek. Her eyes receded back into her head and disappeared, leaving nothing but empty sockets. The bones sank back onto the water and floated for a bit, then slowly sank. As her head disappeared under the surface, her bones fleshed out. I beheld a familiar face receding, her hand tilting upward as if to say goodbye. I could not remember who she was or where I had seen her before, but I knew she looked familiar.

My throat caught. Something blocked my windpipe and melded with my own soul. My heart beat with such force I thought it would pop out. The reflection of Addison High School appeared upon the waters as if the building were watching me through its glass windows.

The soul I had swallowed emerged from my

insides. A flash of light sparked the sky. The clouds above parted.

The orb ascended to the sky, becoming part of the sun that peeked through the gray. The clouds closed again as I lay in the boat, weakened.

Wake up, I willed myself. *Wake up wake up wake up.*

My back buckled. I searched for Ben. I was alone on the lake with nothing but gray clouds overhead, convulsing with spasms so strong my back would have broken if I were not dreaming. *This is only a dream. Nothing more.*

I awoke with a start. My eyes flew open and beheld the puffy gray sky once more. The larks flapped their wings and lifted up from the water, calling out to each other to signal the retreating light of day.

"Can I take you, take you higher…" Ben sang softly with his eyes closed, his body reclined and completely relaxed. He opened one eye lazily. "You're awake. Sorry. I hope I wasn't singing too loud."

I sat up, disoriented. "I had a horrible dream." I peered over the water, half expecting to see that skeletal mermaid face in the depths. I beheld only a hint of the shadowy reflection of the outline of my head.

Ben's expression did not change. His eyes grew somber as he waited for me to go on.

"A woman in the water." My hand flew to my throat. I swallowed hard. The pain was so intense my eyes watered. "She was…"

He gazed up to the sky thoughtfully, then spoke. "Back in the late nineteen nineties, there was a murder out here. I won't go into specifics. It's not exactly date conversation." He spoke as if a bony woman in water was a normal occurrence.

"The Alisha Neil murder?"

"That's the one." Ben remained lying on his back with his eyes closed. "Anyhow, they say her body may have been wrapped in cement and weighted down. They never found her."

"Dark hair, kind of looked like me, like the girl in the dream."

"What dream?"

"She came to me in my dream just now."

"Her body was never found. They say her body was pulled out to sea if she was really killed here."

"She's here. Here under the water."

Ben drummed the oar with his fingers. If he thought I was crazy at this point, I was pretty sure he would have jumped into the lake and swam for shore. He didn't. He leaned his elbows upon his hands and waited for me to go on.

"I've been thinking a lot about Addison," I said as I pressed my hand against the lower part of my ribs. There was an emptiness there that sickened me. "There's something wrong with Addison High."

He shrugged as if the topic made him uncomfortable. "It's getting close to six. Should we grab something for dinner?" He gripped both of the oars and began to row. His knuckles slowly turned white as he scowled and shook his head.

"It upsets you. To talk about Addison. To talk about the ghosts. Why?"

"First of all, Addison is a place, not a person. Second of all, it's as creepy as King Tut's tomb and just as cursed, but all it is…" He sighed and stopped rowing, letting the boat drift and then idle for a few minutes as he stared at the houses, blinking as he tried to compose his thoughts. A team of rowers sped by, perhaps practicing for a college tournament. They called out a greeting to Ben and me, but Ben could only squint in acknowledgment. My heart pounded with fear, for I knew before he said it aloud. "The school is haunted."

"Obviously. But by what?"

"By shadows. Those who call out. I've heard them since…" he stopped suddenly, realizing he had not spoken about his fear out loud.

"At Addison, there were children. A fire. Children. They all screamed. A woman's voice loudest of all. Not so much in pain but anger. What is it? What do you think happened there?"

"We could try and find out. Don't tell anyone, though. I was on the other side once, for a minute or two, years ago when… but how can you see? Are your parents psychic? Anyone in your family. Or have you flatlined?"

"Flatlined?"

"A medical term for being pronounced dead."

I placed my hand on Ben's knee. "Ben, I've never told anyone this before." Ben's eyes hypnotized me. I couldn't stop speaking. "My father completed his residency in Juneau, which is where he met my mother. They married and had me, and she was convinced I had some kind of magical powers. There was a landslide in the town of Haines, where we lived while my father was at work. We were buried in the landslide. I remember the darkness. I remember her body cradling my own and how I could not breathe. I remember…screaming. Then, suddenly, we were on the top of the soil. Not buried anymore. But I don't recall how we managed to come out."

Ben observed me quietly. I turned away and sighed. "Okay, that was probably weird to hear on a first date."

"You can trust me, AJ. I'm not going to make fun of you. I'm not going to hurt you. I'll never hurt you. Trust me. I've had some hard knocks in life, and I've been around some bad people, but I'm a good guy."

"I know you are." I bowed my head, adjusting my hair to fall over one shoulder. The planks of the boat creaked over the water. Perhaps the skeletal mermaid waited under, listening. Perhaps her jaw was slack as she laughed silently in the depths. No, she was nothing but bones now. Her soul had been released. Because of me.

"I guess that's too much information for one day."

"Maybe just a California Moment."

"A what?"

"My dad calls that a California Moment. He said things are so nice out here we never diddle around about the weather and just go right into some deeply personal stuff that people in other states keep to themselves."

"With weather this good, who needs privacy? So, you don't think differently about me?"

"Truth be told, I like you even better."

"You're not going to pretend like you don't know me at school, are you?"

"Of course not. I'm sorry about that. They're just ghosts, and it's nice to know someone else can see them, too. These are things we can find out about in a history book. And somehow, they're at Addison High. They follow me, so I try my best not to be alone there."

"They're following me, too. They followed me home. Footsteps."

"So, we're both privy to specters. I knew we had something in common."

"Besides our dark, brooding personalities?" I smiled. "We should try and find out what's there. What went on in the building or on the land. Just so we know what we're seeing. If we both can see it, we can talk to it. We can tell it to go away." The waters of the lake were now deserted. The rowers had docked their boats and disappeared. Tendrils of fog crept in from the ocean like the fingers of a white witch enveloping the water. "Ghosts are cowards. They can't touch us. They can't hurt us."

"Some things are best left alone. I don't want to know. I'd rather pretend not to see."

"It's not just us, though. Mr. Spinky started out the biology lesson with the study of death. Why would he do that unless he could see them, too? The hallways are emptier since the beginning of the year. Some kids have transferred to other schools. Something is worming its way into us, and it could cause us trouble later. That's all I'm saying."

"AJ, some people feel and see nothing that isn't cold, hard reality. Most people do." Ben glanced around. "I don't know about you, but right now, eating for distraction sounds like a wonderful way to pass the time."

"I could go for a change of scenery."

"That settles it." Ben wrapped his hands around the oar handles and rowed toward the dock. "There's a diner up the hill. Great omelets and pancakes and stuff. Breakfast all day. Across from the zoo."

"I don't feel like breakfast. What else is there?"

"I could cook for you."

"I would love that."

With a heave from his strong arms and the oars, he ran the boat upon the grassy shore.

Ben held out his hand and helped me off as I teetered from side to side. He caught me around my waist to steady me. I hopped out and landed beside him on the grass. Reflexively, I grasped onto him to steady myself, and we faced each other, the closest we had ever been.

"Sorry. You're probably thinking, 'Get your hands off me.'"

I shook my head, unable to speak. My face flushed with heat. I tucked a lock of hair behind my ear and breathed a very tiny laugh. *Fast,* Nancy's disapproving face loomed in my imagination.

"You're all right."

Ben turned his back to me and reached into the boat for his leather jacket. He made a stunning sight, pulling the garment on over his striated muscles, the water and fog in the background. My dark prince.

He turned abruptly. "What?" He smiled.

"I was just thinking you'd make a great picture."

"I was thinking the same." He motioned for me to stand where he was standing.

"Really? Right now?"

"Yes, right now." He removed a slim phone from his jeans pocket and held it up. I silently prayed the picture would turn out good, even in the dim fluorescent light that the backdrop of fog provided, as the phone clicked and flashed. "Beautiful." He tucked the phone back into his pocket. "Hope it's not too presumptuous if I tell you I'd like to have dinner with my girl."

"Okay. Just call me when you get back home." He stood there, stumped as I laughed. "I'd be happy to."

My girl. The sweetness of the phrase made me want to throw my arms around his neck. For the first time, I worried about how our closeness might hurt him. For if I could send lost souls to the far beyond, what would happen if I kissed him?

Chapter Eleven
Shadow of A Man

"Building Site for Addison High." I typed the words into a search engine on a laptop as Ben pressed the edges of little pillows of pasta dough together. Phoebe, his football-shaped cat, lay on the countertop dozing, her tail twitching every minute or so. "It's canned pumpkin," he said, "but mixed with some basil and other herbs from the garden, it tastes as good as fresh."

"What's in the sauce?" I murmured as the computer searched.

"Cream, butter, parmesan cheese, nutmeg. Everything good and fatty."

"Mmm." A list of websites popped up. "Lee Sarong Associates, demolition of existing building to turn into 15,000 acres of school property. Delfini Partners, demolition site to become Addison High.And so on."

"Try 'existing building on Addison High site.'"

"Okay." The search engine churned as the smell of pumpkin ravioli filled the air. Ben measured out two tablespoons of vinaigrette dressing and stirred a salad with toasted baby pumpkin seeds, topping it off with a healthy sprinkling of parmesan cheese. "Feeling autumn festive, huh?"

"Don't you dare tell anyone I can cook."

"Lest it ruin your bad boy reputation?"

"Oh, you know what's going to happen now?" He placed the salad utensils on the counter and stalked toward me as I giggled.

"Do your worst."

"And more." He lunged, his hands holding my sides and tickling me until I screamed and begged him to stop. "Say it. Ben can't cook. You never saw me."

I squealed with laughter as his fingers danced around my shoulders, running up the back of my neck. "At least let me try the food first." The pressure from the twelve-ounce can of Diet Coke I had just consumed was overwhelming

"What? Again?"

"Stop!" He let his fingers loose with another torrent of merciless tickling as I shrieked.

A laundry detergent commercial on television ended. The news came back on. "We have some breaking news here tonight. The remains of a high school-age girl missing since 1997 were found floating near Lake Stinson this evening. Two joggers discovered the skeletal remains as they made their second lap around the lake."

One of the joggers came on the screen, his face pinched. "We saw something white in the water… long, white things which we recognized as bones."

"Our sources say the bones were easily identified with dental records. The body was identified as the missing remains of Alisha Neil, the victim of a kidnapping in the Potrero Hills District in August of 1999. Her mother issued a statement saying that while the family is in a state of grief, they are relieved that the search for their missing daughter has finally come to an end."

Ben looked up, his gaze fixed upon me as if he had never seen me before. I turned back to the computer.

The computer screen listed several websites. I scrolled down the headings.

"The Carrington House once stood at the corner of Washington and Fillmore. The historic mansion was once the home of Ibrahim Osman and Lady Auden Carrington, daughter of Dr. William Carrington and heir to the family fortune. The couple had no surviving children. The historic building was destroyed in a fire in the 1900s, restored, and held in trust. The Carrington House was once a refuge for immigrants from the hell for those born into poverty. Lady Auden Carrington was known to house children who were sold into slavery and prostitution within the slums of downtown and had escaped. The foundation of the mansion was leveled today to make way for the Our Lady Mary Church.' That was in 1958."

"That would be where the theater at Addison stands today. Try Our Lady Mary Church."

I typed the name into the site engine. A list of four websites came up. I clicked on the first heading. "Our Lady Mary Church opens its doors to worshipers in 1961."

Whoa. Do you really want to go there? A site advisor warning popped up.

I clicked BLOCK WARNING.

Whoa. Do you really want to go there?

I backed out of the site and clicked on the heading below it. "Our Lady Mary Catholic Church and Father Joe Simpkins."

Whoa. Do you really want to go there? Same site warning. I groaned.

Ben kissed the top of my head. "Maybe we shouldn't go there. Dinner's ready." He slid a plate heaped with steaming pasta and a salad with pomegranate seeds in my direction and sat on a bar stool with a plate of his own.

"They hold funerals at churches," I said as I sliced a ravioli pillow in two. I popped the half into my mouth. The taste was creamy and smooth, and oh so wonderfully pumpkin.

"What do you think of the ravioli? Beats that pumpkin latte, right?"

"Stalker. How did you know I love pumpkin?"

"Remember when I saw you at the coffee shop on Columbus Avenue with your karate teacher? The barista called out pumpkin latte. No big detective work there."

"Luis is my teacher. You eavesdropped about my coffee while ignoring me."

"Pretty much." Ben crunched on a bite of salad and shot me a tight-lipped smile. "Unless the church buried bodies somewhere in its walls, I'd be willing to bet that's not the reason Addison is haunted. It could be something else that happened while the place was being built."

"Or maybe something at the Carrington House."

"Maybe." We ate the rest of our meal in silence. Ben picked up the dishes and brought them to the sink. "Look, maybe we should just leave well enough alone. Maybe we should just ignore the spirits we're seeing. If we ignore them, they will go away. They have before for you and for me."

I shook my head. "I want to know who's following me. I want to call it out by name. I want to tell it to leave me alone or ask it what it wants and tell it I can help."

"You can't help the dead any more than they can help the living." Ben stood by the sink, frozen in thought.

"What are you thinking about?"

"Someone who told me that exact same thing before. Come on, I'll walk you home."

"What are you doing tomorrow?" I picked up my dish and our empty glasses and brought them to the counter. I nudged Ben so he would step away.

"No plans. I'll take care of the dishes."

"I'll help. So, tomorrow?"

"What do you have in mind?"

"The library."

Switching on the faucet, I rinsed the dishes. He held out a hand covered with a dishtowel. Without a word, I handed him the plates, and he placed them in the dishwasher.

When the dishes were done, I drifted back to the computer and logged into our social page, The Red Room of Addison High.

"Look. We have a new friend."

Her profile picture was the piercing stare on the face of a magpie. Her name was Avia. Ben switched the computer off. A shudder ran through his body. "I should delete that page. That's enough creepiness for one day."

"Let's check out her profile."

"Nope, deleted. Let's get you home."

****

Ben and I lay on my bed in the cherry sundae room. The house was silent and deserted, with my father and Nancy out on the town still and Frances probably at Nancy's cousin's house in the suburbs. Ben's hands were tucked behind his head as we stared up at the ceiling, and that delicious black leather and spice smell exuded from his body. I was pretty sure I smelled like briny lake water and pumpkin, which kept me at as much of a distance as I could muster on a queen-sized bed.

"Your stepmother made it all pony farts and fruit snacks in here." He laughed.

I lightly punched him in the shoulder. "Would you rather I painted the walls black?"

He turned over onto his side. "You and your room are perfect as is. Despite the fact that you don't ride motorcycles." He ran a finger down my upper arm, sending a delicious shiver throughout my body. Covering his mouth, he yawned. "I'm going to get you on that bike someday."

"Never. Never ever."

"Never say never."

"Did someone used to say that to you, too?" I curled my body into his slightly, just enough to be close. I rested my head upon the shoulder of his jacket, breathing in that beautiful leather smell. "Who?"

"My dad. Before he stopped coming back." Ben closed his eyes.

I glanced at the purple fairy clock on the wall. "Eleven thirty. Guess Caslin made other plans. Tomorrow, let's look up the archives on the Carrington House at the library."

"Let's forget about ghosts and go to the Palace of Fine Arts tomorrow. Some things are left better off alone."

"There's so much I don't know," I murmured as I closed my eyes. "So much more I would like to know about myself. Who I am. Why I see them."

Ben's breathing became rhythmic. "The past is all a ghost anyhow. Just a ghost in our mind until we breathe life into it."

"Or someone else does for us. Like Hyannis and her gossip."

Ben chuckled. He sighed with weariness. "There's that thing, I just don't like talking about my past. Goes along with the other thing. The thing about Addison High."

"Tell me," I whispered.

His voice lowered. His eyes remained closed as he seemed to be talking in his sleep. "There was an older kid, much bigger than I was, who was knocking me around my freshman year at Chula Vista High. I stood up to him as much as I could, then got sick of it and told a teacher. The teacher brought him into the principal's office and made him promise he wouldn't pick on me at school. He promised, all the while giving me this smirk that said he was going to get me.

"'Boys will be boys,' the principal said. He didn't tell our parents.

"There was a vacant lot down by Thurston Avenue, where the old blacksmith forge used to be. The historical place. Anyhow, I was walking home from school by myself. The kid pulled me into the lot that was all gated and there was this giant square in the ground. Nothing but cement covering the bottom. I guess it was the building's foundation. I yelled but it was pouring down rain. I grabbed him by the jacket. He gritted his teeth and showed me the knife he had in his pocket. I could swear he was going to kill me, so I wrestled the knife from him, but right before he sliced through me really bad. My arm started bleeding, blood just soaking through my jacket and puddling in the mud with the rain. I didn't even notice the pain. All I could think of was getting out alive. Something inside me just snapped. I rammed my body into his chest, slamming him into the gate one, two, three times. He bounced off the gate. It was one of those chain link fences that are portable and lunged at me the third time. I moved out of the way and he fell into the building's foundation, about twelve feet down. He landed on the cement on his back. I saw him hit his head pretty hard.

"I picked the knife off the ground, and that's when a man out walking ducked inside the fence and stopped short. He backed away when he saw the knife.

"'What did you do?'" he said as he peered over the edge and saw this kid lying unconscious on the pavement below.

"I was so scared." Ben's voice sank into a dreamy cadence. "I couldn't breathe. I couldn't think. I dropped the knife and ran down the hills toward the ocean. I didn't stop until I came to the wharf, and I slept there for a night before I went back home to face what I had done. I thought my house would be crawling with cops, news vans, whatever. But everything was quiet. I walked in and found my mom and dad sitting at the table with a couple of attorneys, and my mom had this lost, sad look. My father took me into my room and said the kid was rushed into surgery. The guy's parents said he had some kind of violent mental disorder. He thought I was threatening him with looks, even though I was sure he was always staring at me. He thought I was going to kill *him*. His parents had taken him out of an institution and placed him in school to give him a 'normal life.' They were afraid to tell the school that he had this disorder because they didn't want him to be treated like a psycho. They thought if he had problems with the other kids, someone would tell a teacher, and the school would tell them. I was raised to deal with my problems. I guess I just did. Crazy that out of all the kids in school, he picked me. Every time I would tell the story, people would look at me funny. I could read their eyes. They would always be wondering what I did to him and if I was just making up that he was mental. They would look at me like I was crazy, volatile, just some angry kid making up stories after he got off of trying to murder someone."

"I'm sorry."

His eyes opened sleepily. Then he yawned and buried his face back into the pillow. "Just the luck of the draw, I guess. My parents told me to visit the kid in the hospital and tell him I was sorry. He seemed okay. He was in a wheelchair and scheduled to have surgery to see if the doctors could make him walk again someday.

"My parents fought all night. I heard my dad say his career was ruined, that what I did would cause a scandal, and blaming her for the way she raised me because he was gone all the time working…" His voice broke. I placed a hand on his shoulder as he shook his head and composed himself.

"I walked out to Ocean Beach the next day when the riptides were so dangerous there wasn't even a surfer around. I walked in and started swimming, kept going out farther, as far as I could."

Tears welled up and began to fall as he went on, as if he no longer knew I was there.

"I kept swimming until the current pulled me under. The water was cold, biting cold, and I went numb as I told myself I'd just touch the bottom, just keep sinking until I touched the bottom, and then a Coast Guard person pulled me out, I guess. There's more that happened before I did that but forget it. It was just a dream. I found out the surgery wasn't successful. The kid was crippled and even worse off than when they took him in.

"After the emergency room released me, my mom called Hyannis's mom in a panic since she couldn't get a hold of anyone else and asked her to keep an eye on Phoebe while she drove me up to St. Helena and stayed with me during some teen wellness program. She didn't go into specifics. Hyannis drew her own conclusions. Ever since then, I've had a shadow that speaks. I can see the ghosts. I've heard them. They come like the sound of the ocean came from underneath, filling in presence yet hollow in speech, the tide like darkness washing over, and yet... that which lies in between life and death, once recognized, can't ever be ignored or put away. It's always there. Always. The voice is attached to a demon. Or an angel. Something in between. I had dreams about him, and I have never spoken his name before. Even in group therapy. I remember only the dream before I died in the water... just a dream. Then I came back."

"A dream of what?"

"A voice stronger than the rest. Calling me, telling me he could solve my problem if I just made him a trade. A ghost, maybe. Or a person. Not sure."

"Who was he?"

"Another lost person." Ben mumbled something unintelligible as he heaved a long sigh.

"What did you say?"

"Auroch."

"What?"

"His name is Auroch."

"Auroch?"

Ben's eyes flew open. He propped himself up on his elbow. I caught a look of panic in his eyes before a look of calm took its place, closing his expression as smoothly as a shutter. "I shouldn't have said that."

"What?

"His name."

"Why not?"

"It doesn't matter. Just forget you ever heard it." He ran his hand smoothly over my upper arm. Placing his fingers on my forehead, he touched the area between my brows gently. "Forget. Please."

"Why can't you say his name?"

Something slapped against my window with a loud *crash,* then knocked once, twice, three times.

Ben and I both started. A branch being blew about upon a gust of wind. Stupid oak tree. I wished Nancy would have the overgrowth trimmed already, especially before the storms came in December.

Ben's eyes cleared from his reverie, and he blinked several times. "Just a tree branch," I said. "That's all. Forget the name. Please. Never repeat his name to anyone. Do you understand?"

My head shook back and forth as I opened my mouth to speak. No words emerged. Auroch, the voice in my head whispered. *Auroch. Auroch. Auroch*. Ben's eyes darkened as if he could read my mind.

"He's no one. Nothing. That's not even his name. I'm going to wait here until you fall asleep and your parents get home. Then I'll sneak out so they won't see me. I'll be back tomorrow in the morning, okay? Stay here until I get back."

I swallowed hard, wide awake now. Outside the window, something felt awry. As if what had once been only a peaceful night had turned into something foreboding and sinister. The darkness loomed up against the window, the big oak tree outside a menacing specter. The whole world had changed with just one mention of a name. *Auroch*. I turned away from Ben, trying to make sense of the eerie feeling.

He stared at me for a minute as I inwardly longed for a kiss. "Go to sleep, AJ. I'll be here. You don't have to be afraid of anything."

My heart thumped wildly as I let out a long exhale. The sheets rustled as we settled into a comfortable position. He tucked his body behind mine. He was warm and comforting, and as excited as I was, the safety of his arms made me succumb to the opportunity to leave the day behind.

In my mind's eye, as I let myself relax into slumber, a black hole opened. I tipped into a chasm that swirled like a tornado of black ash. Tiny cinders flew as I fell farther down, my insides tickling. Despite the force of the fall, I descended calmly, simply watching as my hand flew up in front of my face to reach out toward the light at the top of the hole from where I came.

A flash of lightning blinded my vision. I stood before Ben. His eyes blazed with white-hot anger. His hand reached out and grabbed me by the neck as his other hand curled into a ball and pulled back behind his shoulder. I tried to say his name, but my throat closed before I could choke out the words. His expression flickered with uncertainty. I closed my eyes. Something struck me on the back of the head instead of my forehead, where his fist was aimed.

A warm substance trickled down the back of my neck. I was lying on the ground. In my mouth, I tasted the coppery taste of blood. My eyes flew open, and I stared up at the waving branches of a tree in the light of day, directly at a spot where the sun peeked through the clouds. Its rays moved back and forth, back and forth, with the wave of the branches.

"AJ," Ben said. My head lolled over in the direction of his voice. We lay in the middle of a residential street. My street? His motorcycle lay overturned in the middle of the road on its side. Birds in the trees sang the same plaintive song they always sang before the sun set into the evening, and in the sky, the light moved in flashes, filters of light shining through the branches of the trees. Ben lay on the ground. A red puddle bloomed on the pavement, the substance seeping everywhere. My hair was soaked with blood. The puddle was made of blood.

"AJ," he said again. He sighed. I reached my hand out to touch him. "I'm sorry. I'm really sorry."

"Why?" My fingertips touched the cool skin on his forehead. "You didn't do anything wrong."

A warm trickle seeped out of my eye. I pulled my hand back and wiped the corner of my eyelid. My finger came away covered in blood. Ben stared back at me, his gaze motionless, his body lifeless.

I awoke with a start. Ben kept his arms around me tightly as I bit my tongue to keep from screaming. "Just a dream, AJ," Ben said. "Nothing but a dream. Go to sleep now. I'm here."

THE ANGEL OF SHADOWMIST

"Ben, I dreamed you were—"
"I'm not. Go back to sleep

Chapter Twelve
Burn Them

I awoke from a dreamless sleep to the sound of my phone ringing. I picked the cherry red receiver off the cradle.

"Burn them," I croaked as I sat straight up.

"What?" Caslin said. "That's so weird to say right now."

"Sorry," I mumbled through my morning mouth. "What did I say?"

"'Burn them?' I'm sure you were referring to Hyannis and her crew, right?"

I groaned and threw my body back down on the bed. The stretched phone cord caught on my alarm clock and sent the cradle and clock tumbling to the ground. I swore as I picked up the mess and dropped it into a heap on my nightstand.

"Caslin?"

"Still here. Are you all right? Did the house fall in?"

My hand lingered on the side of my bed where Ben had lain. "I'm here. What happened to you last night? I thought you were coming over."

"Oh, let's just say Johan and I spent the entire night getting to know each other."

"You floozy," I joked. "Really?"

"We talked, AJ. We walked all around Fisherman's Wharf until around midnight. We had breakfast at The Three Pines, and then he snuck me into his house. The McWolfe manor, which has an elevator that stops on four floors and gold-plated rails everywhere."

"Ooh la la. Go on."

"We fell asleep in his bed with our clothes on. Hyannis walked in on us at five AM. She was not pleased. She said he forgot to give her back her iPad. He did, but she wouldn't leave. Kept insisting their parents were going to find out, and I had to go even though they were fast asleep, and Johan said they slept in on Saturdays. Then he drove me home. Do you think that she has something more than sisterly love for her brother? Something quite Greek?"

"Possibly." I twirled the phone cord around my finger. "She's a control freak. She probably was upset because she didn't know you'd be there."

"I can't believe she came in so early. Who gets up at five on a Saturday morning?"

"Possessed people, I think. They're up all day and night."

Caslin paused for a few seconds before she spoke again. "Hey, so about the pizza place thing... I am so sorry about that. I was going to invite you, but I know you and Hyannis don't get along, and I had no idea you would show up. I felt so bad."

"Actually, it turned out well. Ben and I are hanging out now."

"He's not exactly the most popular person at school, you know."

"I do know. And I know rumors are filled with lies and exaggerations."

"Did he tell you?"

"About what?" The name *Auroch* unwillingly popped into my head. I shook my head vigorously from side to side as if I could shake the name from my memory.

"About the guy he almost killed."

"Long story from his side. I'll tell you all about it if he says it's okay with him. Just understand that he's not the evil person the rumors paint him out to be."

"Wait. Hold on. Johan is calling on the other line."

A beep sounded. "Hiya," she said, her voice filled with enthusiasm.

"Sorry. Still just me." I couldn't believe Caslin just lied about Johan being on the phone!

"Oh, hang on. The line didn't switch over." She correctly switched calls. I waited for about ten minutes. Just as my finger hovered over the "hang up" button, Caslin came back on the line.

"So, tell me."

"I need to make sure it's okay with him. But just know that what happened wasn't his fault."

"And? Come on, I have to go soon."

I sighed.

"Seriously?" Caslin said. "You're not going to tell me everything. I'm your best friend."

"I know, so hopefully, you'll understand that you have a loyal, trustworthy friend who would not divulge *your* secrets."

Caslin made a disgusted noise. "Fine. What are you doing today?"

"Ben and I are going to the Palace of Fine Arts."

"I've heard enough. I'll see you on Monday. Ready for the talent show?"

"Not really."

"Little over a month left to practice."

"I need to."

"Good. Hyannis is dancing as the queen of fairies from *A Midsummer Night's Dream*. Gigi printed up the programs. You're on right after Hyannis."

"I'll bet she did that on purpose."

"You're going to be great, AJ. Your performance will appeal to both guys and girls and if anything, you'll have the popular vote based simply upon that. Hyannis cannot win her own prize, so you're going to get first prize, and then we'll all hang out at Hyannis's house in Maui and become good friends. She would never miss out on Hawaii. Control freak and all."

"I just want to be great on stage. At first, I didn't want to be on stage at all, but now I think I'm ready."

"That you will be, young grasshopper. That you will be."

We said our goodbyes and hung up. I stared at the heap of books and tchotchkes on my desk. My fingers found the alarm clock and set it upright on the nightstand. Nine thirty in the morning.

I switched my wall calendar to the month of October. Tempted to draw a red heart on each day Ben and I had hung out, I opted for a simple red dot. That would be my private little way of keeping track of the days he and I spent together.

The urge to glance through the curtains and out of the window was overwhelming. *What do you think, AJ? Could he be standing on the sidewalk clutching a bouquet of flowers? One can only hope. Actually, that's too corny. I hope he's not.*

Rising from my bed, I ambled into my bathroom. Turning the hot and cold taps on halfway, I cupped a handful of water and splashed my face. As I patted my face with a towel, the doorbell rang. I walked out of the bathroom and into my bedroom, then peered out the window. Ben stood on the front steps outside the open door, with four lidded paper cups of coffee on a tray in his hands and a brown bag presumably filled with pastries from the neighborhood coffee shop hanging from his arm.

"I'll get it!" I yelled at no one in particular as I grabbed a brush off my dresser and ran it through my tousled hair. Frances giggled from somewhere downstairs as my footsteps made hollow noises on the wooden stairs. I opened the door. Ben smiled that same smile that sent my heart reeling.

"Hi," he said. "I brought you breakfast."

I wanted to laugh, I was so happy, even though I knew I looked like a mess in my rumpled pajamas and robe. He was immaculately groomed as usual and sparkling clean, clad in a navy blue t-shirt that hugged his fit body, jeans, and that beautifully cared-for black leather jacket. I wished I could throw my arms around him and inhale his scent.

"AJ," Nancy said as she walked in from the kitchen. She stopped short at the sight of Ben.

"Hi." For a moment, I could even see a glimpse of the vivacious, perhaps even fast, girl she had once been. She extended out a long, slim hand and grasped Ben's. "I'm AJ's stepmother."

"Hello, Mrs. Covington." Ben was the picture of politeness as he shook Nancy's hand gently, letting her withdraw first and holding her gaze just long enough to be polite but not so long as to seem challenging. "Hope I'm not disturbing you."

"Not at all. AJ, are you going to invite your friend in?"

"Come in," I chirped as I stepped aside. Nancy's gaze drifted from Ben's black leather jacket down to his black boots with white stitching detail and back up again. She peered outside of the door. "Do you ride a motorcycle?"

"Yes, ma'am, I do. I believe in safety first, though. Always."

He ran his hand through his hair nervously, and his roving boot knocked over the umbrella stand by the door. The stand tumbled onto its side, and umbrellas rolled out.

"Sh-" he began, then met my eyes with a look of false panic. He bent down to pull the stand upright and tucked the rolling umbrellas back in their holder.

"That's all right," Nancy said. "It's a little unsteady. Come inside and have breakfast with us."

We followed Nancy into the kitchen. Ben set the coffee cups on the counter.

"I wasn't sure what you'd like, Mrs. Covington, so I picked us all up pumpkin lattes since they're AJ's favorite. Some muffins and pastries as well."

Nancy peered into the bag and shot Ben an impressed look. "Very nice. Thank you, Ben. Please, call me Nancy."

"Frances," I called. "This is Ben Bach."

Frances had a little circus party taking place on her play mat in the adjoining family room, as she spoke in a soft, high-pitched voice to her stuffed clowns and lions to stay quiet.

"Babach." Frances giggled. "Hi, Babach. Baba boo bach."

Ben's boots made a pleasant clomping noise on the hardwood floor as he walked toward Frances.

"What's going on over here?" Ben said.

"Clown party. You sit there."

She quickly pointed to a tiny pink chair. Her hand curled back into a fist under her chin.

"Sure." Ben set his paper coffee cup down on the floor away from Frances and picked up a clown doll. "What's his name?"

"Babach," Frances said as she placed plastic cupcakes on each plate. "Babach going to do jumps now. Aye Jay, Vay Jay, you want to play Jay?

Ben remained straight-faced, although he might as well have had a thought bubble pop out over his head that read *I'm going to tease you about that later.*

I hurriedly placed the pastries on plates and called Frances and Ben to breakfast.

"Piggyback," Frances cried as Ben rose. He lifted her on his back, and she giggled. Ben looked perfectly natural carrying Frances to the table and setting her down delicately in her booster seat.

Footsteps sounded on the stairs as my dad came down to breakfast, dressed in a robe and plaid pajama pants. He stopped short with surprise at the sight of Ben. He extended his hand as Ben introduced himself.

"Hello, young man. Pleased to meet you," Dad droned.

He picked up an apple muffin and the newspaper. He flipped open the newspaper and slipped on his glasses. Suddenly, being in the house seemed very awkward.

"Want to go for a walk?" I asked Ben.

"Sure," Ben said. He took a sip of his latte.

"Excuse me a moment."

I rushed upstairs to change and finish brushing my hair. I decided to pin the front part back in the middle of my head and let the length hang long over my shoulders. Hurriedly, I applied a coat of mascara and a coat of tinted moisturizer and gloss, willing my hands to stop shaking. My ears burned as I heard my dad's deep voice asking Ben a question. I only hoped he kept the conversation light. I brushed my teeth in a frenzy, then applied a dab of lip gloss. I pulled a long sleeve raspberry colored t-shirt on over my head. The neck hole seemed far too small, the arms far too long. With much tugging, I managed to pull the garment on. I threw open a drawer and yanked out a pair of jeans. I shoved my feet into them.

"Ben rides a motorcycle," I heard Nancy say to my father.

My legs tangled in my jeans. I fell over and crashed into the open drawer of my dresser. The voices downstairs quieted. The dresser teetered precariously. My arm shot out to steady the piece, even though I knew it had been bolted to the wall a long time ago in case of an earthquake.

"I'm all right!" I yelled before anyone could ask. My elbow had an angry red scrape mark.

"Great," I muttered.

I bit the edge of a Band-Aid wrapper and tore it apart. I ripped out a bandage and covered the scrape, then ran downstairs as quickly as I could.

"Ready?" I asked Ben. Ben was calm and cool, completely unfazed by my parents. He sipped his latte and nodded. "Okay, let's go."

"Would you like to borrow the car, AJ?" my dad asked. His bespectacled eyes glanced up from the paper.

My eyes met Ben's. He shrugged. "No, thank you. I think we'll walk."

"Ben, see that you do," my dad replied. "Beautiful day for a walk. Ben, I'd like to admire your motorcycle later on, if that's fine with you. Harley, right?"

"Street cruiser." Ben removed the keys from his jacket pocket and placed them on the kitchen table in front of my father.

"Feel free to take it for a spin. The helmet is in the compartment under the seat."

My father smiled. "I did ride a bit in my younger days. From time to time. My wild days are over."

"Well, start it up if you'd like. Feel it purr. It's an experience."

"Maybe I will. Nice to meet you, Ben. Thanks for letting me hang on to the keys."

Ben shook my father's hand and Nancy's. He waved goodbye to Frances, who responded with a cheery,

"Bye, Babach."

I closed the front door behind us and fell into stride beside Ben.

"Some weird exchange took place in there. Some male bonding kind of guy code thing."

Ben tucked his hands in his pockets. "I gave him my keys to show him he could trust me, and I trusted him. I am taking out his daughter, and I can tell he wants her to be safe. He wants his daughter not to be at risk. Not that you're his property or anything. It's just a sign of respect."

"Boys and their toys. So, where do you learn the guy code? I'm just asking so I can find out where to pick up the girl code. I'm having a bit of trouble figuring it out. I don't like Hyannis, but I'm supposed to be nice to her even though she is not nice to me. I'm trying to learn from Nancy, but it seems like there's only one thing Nancy wants to talk about, and that's—" I stopped short as Ben smiled at me knowingly. "Awkward."

"I want you to feel off guard with me. I like it. I hope you know you can tell me anything."

"I just can't ask you things about yourself, right?"

"Right."

I guffawed and slapped him lightly on the arm. "What I meant was, not if I expect an answer every single time. Just don't take away your company. That isn't fair."

"I had a hard time pretending I didn't see you at school."

"Didn't look that hard to me. Why?"

Ben shrugged. "Because I like looking at you. Because you're sweet. Because you're pretty. Because I knew you were looking at me, too."

I leaned in and teased him with a smile. "How could you know when you weren't?"

"I could feel you. Call it a sixth sense, a hunch,

whatever. I can see and hear ghosts, too. Of course, I could feel you looking at me."

"Maybe I wasn't. Maybe you were wrong."

"Then why are we here? Now. Together."

I secretly wished I was cleverer. That I could return comments with great wit and flirtatiousness. Honesty was the most I could channel. "Well, Caslin did ask me if I wanted to go to a party tonight and said she's spending her day getting ready. Much as I love doing my nails and hair—not—the jolt of caffeine I received from that tasty pumpkin-spiced latte you brought over put me in a chatty mood, so here we are, walking side by side, on a beautiful day."

"Yes, Miss Edith Wharton."

"I'm ready to talk about a demon. You won't find that in *The Age of Innocence*."

"Time for a subject change. Unless you want us to take a walk back."

I dropped my arms to my side and sighed in frustration. The sun shone brightly in a perfectly blue sky. A biker on a ten-speed rolled past us, dressed in a tight spandex shirt and shorts. He held up two fingers in greeting as he rolled past us. We strode past Ra's house, past Mrs. Faria's. The curtains of her red brickstone home were drawn shut.

"Where are we going?"

"I thought we could take a walk around Golden Gate Park. Maybe catch a movie later. There's a film that won Best Picture at Cannes. It takes place in the era of Britain's rule in India, and it was filmed entirely in black and white. A couple of great actors in it, too."

I shook my head with disappointment.

In my neighborhood, the homes stood side by side with small patches of lawn and greenery in front of each one. As we strode down the street and closer into the city, the remodeled Victorian homes gave way to homes with front walkways of solid concrete and stairs, so close together they seemed stacked upon each other, with shops and laundromats squeezed in between them and nary a glimpse of landscaping to be found.

The hill we walked upon began to incline sharply downward. In the distance, I could see the rising red towers of the Golden Gate Bridge jutting up from the bay and the Pacific Ocean with smooth rolling rocks rising up from the sea. We slowed our pace, digging our heels into the ground to take the hill more carefully. Ben placed a hand on my elbow to steady me. "Earth to AJ. Worried you might take a plunge?"

"A little bit. I thought we could go to the library and do some research." The breeze blew in strongly from the ocean. I squinted to keep the wind out.

"We should leave whatever is there well enough alone."

"What if someone gets hurt?"

"At Addison? Why do you think someone would get hurt?"

"Because misery loves company. So do ghosts." Our feet landed at the bottom of the hill where the sidewalk leveled. We passed a hot dog vendor.

"Hot pretzel?" I asked as we neared a cart.

"Sure," Ben said. I reached into my pocket as the vendor handed me the salted, steaming bread. Ben waved my hand away and had already withdrawn his wallet. "I've got it."

"No, please. Let me."

"We're on a date, remember? I've got it."

My cheeks flushed with heat. The vendor dropped the change into his hand.

"Thank you," I said to Ben.

"My pleasure."

We walked on the sidewalk along Golden Gate Park. Joggers, bikers, and couples with baby strollers past us, some smiling wistfully as if they were remembering better times.

I dipped a piece of pretzel in mustard and took a bite. The pretzel tasted yeasty and salty.

"Yum. Want some?"

"Sure."

I ripped a piece off and popped it into Ben's mouth, feeling strangely exhilarated watching him eat from my hand. "So, the library. There's one right around the corner."

"You sure you want to do this?"

"What harm would a little research do?"

Ben motioned to a vacant wooden bench facing the water. We settled ourselves in silence as we gazed out at the tall green grasses before us, waving in the breeze. He folded my hand into his.

"AJ, when you open your mind to something, you let things in. Your imagination is stronger than anything. Your mind can lie to you, trick you, manipulate you, all the while letting you believe you're in control. The things you and I see are more than our imagination, but what would happen if our imagination came into play? What would happen if what we believe we are seeing is more than what we are actually seeing?"

"I don't understand. We see, and then we know. We've seen ghosts. We know the ghosts exist."

"Yes, but do they care that we see them? If they do, if they really do care, what do they want from us? What are we willing to give them? Or are we seeing something with far more influence? Something that worms its way into our lives and causes such havoc we will never be the same again. It would be easier just to turn our backs on them than to acknowledge them. The more we know about the ghosts, the more they need us to bring them to life, and the more we need them to find a purpose. A solution. Something to look for when there is nothing to see. But there may not be a solution for the dead. They may simply be dead, and there may be nothing we can do to put them to rest. Nothing. We are wasting our time. Becoming obsessed even, with the idea that we can help them. That they can hear us, and we can hear them. What if it's all a trick from our own minds, or our interaction with them doesn't matter anyway."

I crumpled up the thin white paper my pretzel was served upon in my fist. Ben held out his hand. I dropped the ball and he tossed it toward a trash can, the wind arching the paper ball just right so it landed right in the center. The wind blew his dark hair up at a crazy angle. His full lips thinned a bit. "Please, Ben. I began seeing the spirits when…" There were words on the tip of my tongue that I knew would sound accusatory.

"When what?"

When I first met you. I feared I would lose him again if I spoke what was on my mind.

A look flashed in Ben's eyes. *Fear of guilt.* That's the look I saw.

"Nothing. Care to walk?"

"Sure."

We ambled along the path by the ocean. Ben stuffed his hands in his pockets as we chatted. "I'd like to know more about you. Not just the thing that Hyannis mentioned. We don't have to talk about that. Just about you."

"Ask away."

I asked him about his estranged relationship with his father. "You know, people out here try to make him out to seem like a bad guy. I know he sounds awful for what he did, abandoning me like that after the fight, but he did what he had to do so we could survive and live well. He had to keep the incident out of the newspapers. Let's hang a left here."

Ben pressed a button at the crosswalk, and we waited until the walk sign flashed. We walked across the street to the Palace of Fine Arts. The famous engraved rotunda of gold crowned the area behind a lake where a small fountain spurted in jubilation. I looked up at the underneath of the dark chamber roof as we neared the interior of the structure. A flock of pigeons nestled inside. The rotunda was cold and dank from the recent rain. The name of the demon Ben had mentioned the other day crossed my mind. *Auroch*.

"Auroch," a man's deep voice said from behind us. Ben and I whirled around.

Chapter Thirteen
History Repeats Itself

There was no one behind us. The air had gone still. Even the birds remained frozen in their perches, their heads cocked downward. All of them. Looking at us. The fountain near us continued gushing into the air, but the noise of the water splashing onto the lake was eclipsed by a hollow buzzing growing in volume, which surrounded us beneath the dome of the rotunda.

I swallowed hard and reached for Ben's hand. My throat was parched, and my voice hollow.

He gripped my hand tightly.

"Do you hear something?" I said.

"Let's keep walking."

"No. Let's stay here." I led him another ten steps to the center of the rotunda. Ben's hand tightened around mine as the birds above our head stirred. With a rush, they flew across the dome, cackling and cawing, one eerie tornado of birds above our heads, and all the while, that loud buzz eclipsed all other sounds.

Ben and I broke into a run and sprinted out of the shade and into the sun. Passersby turned with curiosity as we rushed over the paving and onto the grass. Abruptly, we slowed our pace as we neared the street and both laughed nervously at the same time.

"How long are we going to pretend?" I said. "Soon enough, I expect you'll tell me I'm not seeing the things I'm seeing nor hearing what I am hearing."

"I would never do that. That's why I like riding. I just concentrate on the bike underneath me, flipping gears, the sights, the sound of the motor. I don't hear anything I don't want to see or hear anything I don't want to hear. Except a siren once in a while. But even then, I feel like it's all under my control."

"The more we know about Addison High, about… Auroch, the more we will understand what we are dealing with."

"What do you suggest we do, AJ Covington?" Ben shook his head and stuffed his hands into the pockets of his jeans.

"Go to the library."

"I knew you were going to say that." He trudged beside me like a prisoner of war as we made our way further down Lyon and turned left on Palace Drive. A crowd of people crossed the street, weaving their way around us as they moved to the other side.

A wrinkled old woman with tufts of gray and black hair sticking out from her bald scalp and mottled skin with brown spots eyed us as she pushed a handcart filled with pink plastic bags in front of her. Ben spoke a greeting. She stood in the middle of the street and turned to look at us as we passed.

"Weird," Ben said as we watched her eyes narrow. She turned away. We reached the other side of the street and stepped onto the sidewalk.

A horn blared at the woman, and she jumped. A silver Mercedes convertible stopped just short of the woman with the sound of screeching brakes. The "walk" sign had changed, leaving an orange hand in its place. The elderly woman sneered at the car, baring yellow teeth with an enormous overbite. She grumbled and pushed her cart to the sidewalk slowly. I recognized the couple in the car. Johan and Gigi the Barbie Girl. Johan glanced at me, and a look of panic rose in his gaze. He gunned the Mercedes and sped down the street. Ben looked at me and raised his eyebrows.

"Should I tell Cas or not?"

"I would. Could just be an innocent car ride." We resumed our walk to the Marina District Library.

"He looked guilty, though."

"Or just bugged out. Johan acts really weird around me."

I pursed my lips mockingly. "Because you're a big bad motorcycle rider. With a history of violence. He's probably afraid of you."

"I think it's something else."

"Ah, are there more secrets you haven't told?"

"Nah. It's just another guy thing, I think."

"Well, are you going to let me in on it?"

"Maybe someday. If you choose to hang out with me long enough."

My heart fluttered as our eyes met, and he smiled that adorable smile again. I wished we were six months into our relationship, and he would bend forward and kiss me after every one of those smiles. I wished we could hold hands or touch somehow without feeling so awkward around other people. If it were just he and I alone, I would hold his hand, I would place his arm upon my shoulder, and I would curl my body into his every single time. But our relationship was merely blossoming, the stem uncertain and weak as it grew up from rocky ground, the petals fragile and timid of rain as they curled open to find the sun.

The rain was Hyannis, Caslin, and whatever elusive mysteries walked the halls of Addison High. Hyannis and Caslin, I could weather, for they were merely people whose flaws could easily be disregarded. Addison was something I wanted to fight head-on. I wouldn't let the school take over my thoughts. Thoughts I'd rather devote to Ben. If he was unaware of the ghosts, I could easily dismiss them as hallucinations until they would hopefully disappear altogether, but he saw them, too. He knew they were there. And the ghosts were keeping us together in all sorts of indirect ways.

"Penny for your thoughts," Ben said. We passed by a laundry where machines whirred and dryers beeped, as people milled about the counters and chatted while they folded, or some sat upon benches, watching the dryers as if the secret to life lay in the midst of their whirling clothing.

"Wait," I joked. "We live in California. I want a tenner." I held out my hand. Ben playfully brought his down on mine in a *pay-it-up* gesture.

"I was just thinking," Ben said, "that when we find out what's wrong with Addison, when we tell whatever it is to go away, we can get on to other things."

"Like what?"

"Like each other. Getting to know each other more."

Kiss me kiss me kiss me echoed through my head. Then, *Auroch*. The unwelcome name popped up, and I blew a breath out quickly.

"Should I tell Caslin about Johan and Gigi, you think?"

"They could be out on a date, but he could also be just helping her out with something. Just bring it up casually to see if she might have been sensing that something was going on between them. Let her know it could be totally innocent, and you didn't think much of it. She'll draw her own conclusion from there."

"They are friends. Johan and Gigi. Maybe he's just giving her a ride somewhere. I'll sound like I'm trying to stir the drama pot if I tell Caslin now."

"Just bring it up casually."

We came to a towering rose-colored building with glass doors.

"Here we are. A pretzel and the library. I gotta say

you've been one cheap date."

"Thanks, Casanova. You really know how to get the girls aflutter."

We climbed up the steps, and Ben rushed forward to open the door for me. He bowed, then stepped closer as he walked into the foyer and stood close behind me.

"I've only just begun," he whispered. There went my heart again. Flipping and turning as if I were having a coronary. He walked ahead to a table lined with computers, the soles of his boots resounding upon the marble floor. A homely librarian with purple-framed glasses looked up from her desk, her mouth set in a disapproving line. She started at the handsome picture Ben made as he leaned upon the table with his hands and tapped on the keyboard. She slowly buried her face back into the romance novel she was reading, with a paperback book cover of adults wrapped in loin cloths clutching each other.

Ben glanced up from the computer, the monitor's glow casting a pleasant light over his face.

"I'm not having much luck in the book section, although I found some archives on microfiche. Let's ask the librarian."

"You ask. I've gotta see this."

I ducked behind a shelf of books and peeked over.

"Sure," Ben said casually.

He ambled over to the poxy librarian, who looked up from her book with her mouth open like a dying fish. My head shot back into the space behind the shelf so she wouldn't see me.

"Excuse me, could you tell me where the microfiche room is?"

She swallowed hard, all the while staring into Ben's eyes.

"It's closed. The microfiche is so delicate. You

would have to make an appointment to see it if you want to see it. I'd be happy to show you the microfiche."

"Delicate. That's a nice, descriptive word. I like it." Ben smiled. The skinny librarian beamed. "I'd like to see it today. If you'd be kind enough to show me."

"Oh, I can't do that. Someone has to watch the front of the library, and I'm the only person on this morning. Our manager called in sick."

"Did she? That's too bad. I have a report due on Monday." He made a clicking noise with his tongue and leaned forward, placing his hands on the librarian's desk. "I'd really appreciate it if you could show me inside of the room. I could take it from there."

"I really shouldn't," the librarian said.

"I know," Ben said, fixing her with that piercing gaze that would make the world give him anything he asked for. "I won't tell anyone. It's a secret between you and I. By the way, what's that book you're reading?"

"*Never Love A Lumberjack*," she whisper-squeaked.

"Great read. What do you think of it?"

"It's... wonderful."

"I couldn't put it down. Especially that part when... well... about the microfiche. Can you at least show me the room?" The librarian placed a sign that read "Back In Five Minutes" on her desk. She extracted a key from a drawer and motioned for Ben to follow her. I placed the book I had thumbed through back on the shelf and walked behind them. She opened the door to the microfiche room. I retreated just a little farther into the aisle to hide myself completely from her line of sight and peered through a row of books. She looked around and closed the door behind them.

Minutes passed as I waited by titles in the Gardening section, such as *That's Not Fertilizer!* and

Turning Your Black Thumb Green. I tapped the plastic book covers with my finger, removed a book with pictures of flowers, and buried my nose in it as I waited for Ben to give me a signal.

"Oh, come on Ben," I muttered.

I shoved the book back in between the others on the shelf and was just about to give up my hiding place and knock on the door of the microfiche room when the librarian emerged. I pretended to be immersed in a copy of *Boot Planters for Kicks.* She hummed as she walked back to her desk.

I softly tapped the *shave and a haircut two bits* knock on the door to the microfiche room as she busied herself at her computer, her eyes averted. The door opened and Ben's hand emerged and pulled me in.

"Sit down," he said as he motioned toward a chair in the dark room illuminated only by the light from the monitor.

"You never read *Never Love A Lumberjack.*"

"I think my mom did. This is interesting."

"What?" The chair creaked under me as I sat.

He read aloud from a newspaper article.

"In the early nineteen hundreds, Lady Auden J. Carrington owned a mansion on where she hid several immigrant children who were born into a life of hard labor and exploitation. The lady of the manor, once along with her husband, Ibrahim A. Osman, cared for several immigrant children, teaching them how to read and live in the United States. There was an underground tunnel below the mansion, allowing the immigrant children to come and go as they pleased. She provided a safe house for the children and a place for them to rest and recover from the demands of city life. The Carrington mansion was burned to the ground in a suspected arson attack on November seventeenth. Lady Carrington and dozens of the children perished within. The crime was never solved."

"There it is," he said as he tapped the screen. "That's what's wrong with Addison High. The spirits are not at rest, and so they are haunting the school. And I will bet you a million dollars the epicenter of it all… is in the new theater." He turned a dial and flipped to the next article. "'The Carrington mansion was restored but subsequently deserted after changing owners several times until 1961 when the home was demolished after sitting empty for fifteen years. A Catholic Church was erected upon the site. This commenced a series of hauntings. Priests and nuns witnessed ghosts wandering the chapel and reported sounds of screams coming from the basement. They saw…'"

"They saw what?" I asked.

Ben swallowed. "This is crazy. Let's get out here."

"No." I placed my hand on the monitor. The light cast an eerie glow upon my skin. "They saw what?"

Ben gently removed my hand from the screen.

"'They saw the ghost of a woman floating down the center aisle of the church and crying out for help to save the children. The same woman would appear in the confessional booth during vespers. Often, she would peek out of the booth window at the nuns and priests and speak to them before disappearing. Her face could be seen in the stained glass at times, and at other times not. A nun named Anisette March Whittle… hung herself after she had reported several sightings of the woman's ghost to the Mother Superior. She was found in the basement near the door to the passageway. She tied a note around her neck, which she had slashed deeply after tightening the noose. She scrawled letters upon the wall in her own blood. Her note read 'Blood price.'"

"The blood price…" he murmured. He flipped to the next page of the article. "'Shortly after the body of Anisette March Whittle was discovered, in the year 1967, the church caught fire and burned to the ground. Again, on November seventeenth. The cause of the fire was unknown. The lot was used for debris storage until the county granted the school district the right to build a local school.' Sister March Whittle paid the blood price, so did the children…"

"What is the blood price?"

Ben parted his lips to answer, then seemed to think better of it. "The church burned down. The home before it. Now we know what happened there. Are you satisfied? That's how she put the spirits to rest. By giving her own life."

"How do we put them to rest?"

"By leaving them alone."

"Or paying the blood price. November seventeenth." I bit my lip. Something about that date seemed significant. The day before Thanksgiving break, but there was something else.

Little prickles ran up and down my spine. My mind sank down, down, down into a bottomless black pit where a blood-red heart existed, devoid of reason. I spoke without thinking, only feeling. There was darkness all around, surrounding me, suffocating me as I slipped into a peace separate from all that defined who I was outside of myself.

"The release of a soul is their reminder. It's the only thing that connects them to our world. The smell of it, perhaps it is all they can smell. The release makes them feel alive so they can forget that they are dead. They will do anything to draw it. That's why they speak to me. They know I can."

Ben turned the microfiche light up so the bulb

glared brightly through the darkness. He rose from his chair. "AJ." He snapped. I came rushing back to the surface. I stared at him.

"I'm sorry." I dug my toe into the carpet, moving my ankle around in a circle.

"There you go apologizing again."

I hugged my arms to my chest to quell the sudden shivers racking through my body. "Maybe you are right. We shouldn't mess with this kind of thing." I peered over his shoulder at the picture from the microfiche. The newspaper caption read *The San Francisco Daily*. On the screen was a picture of the charred house. A burnt frame that was once a peaked roof jutted only a few feet above the ground, with the rest of the home nothing but a pile of ash and cinder.

Something in the picture moved. First a hand, then a mouth, then a limb. The picture came to life as cinders lifted and danced above the ground in the picture. Ghostly children appeared as the white light from the monitor flickered. The children sang a song as they joined hands and danced in a circle.

The children circled around and around in the midst of smoke and ash, reminiscent of a program I once watched with my father on public television about the volcano eruption in Pompeii, where town folk were showered in ash as they ran away in vain, only to become skeletons with a look of horror frozen on their faces, found curled up in shallow graves.

A woman in a long, white flowing dress with an enormous flounce at the bottom of her skirt emerged from the gray background. In her arms, she clutched a child whose face glowed in a ghostly white. She rocked the child in her arms while standing in the circle of children. Then she walked forward as if headed through the monitor. As her face came closer, her lower body disappeared. Her head loomed larger. She gazed right at me. Then, the neckline of her dress caught flame as she dropped the ashen child and screamed.

I clapped my hands over my ears as Ben's eyes widened. He turned away, looking over his shoulder at the screen.

The screen cracked in half, the cracks spider-webbed across the black glass. I gasped, then turned and ran. My breath came hard and fast. My heart pounded with terror. Ben flipped the power switch. The monitor went dark.

"AJ!" Ben shouted as he called after me. I ran out of the door of the microfiche room and through the brightly lit library. The fluorescent lights stung my eyes. My footfalls echoed on the carpet, far too loud, but my mind was bent on escape as I passed rows of books, trying to gauge the direction to the exit.

"AJ!" Ben continued to call. I slowed down as people glanced up from their tables.

"Wait," Ben said. He leaned down to the homely librarian who sat at her desk. "The screen broke. I'm sorry, I'll pay for it." He pulled cash from his wallet and dropped it onto her desk, then trotted after me.

I paced away from him, hell-bent on getting out of the building as fast as possible. I turned a corner at a row of shelves and nearly bumped into a small child. The boy looked to be about seven years old, with shorn dark hair. He smiled. I maneuvered to move past him, but he moved to block my path. He was the child from the hallway at school. The ghost child.

"Can you see me?" he asked. He reached out and pulled on my upper arm. His grip dug into my skin. I winced with pain as I took hold of his small hand and wrenched it away.

He grasped for my hand yet again. I tore my arm

away from his fingers that dug into my skin. His nails left marks on my arm. Ben turned the corner at the shelves, where I rushed away from the boy. The boy's hand clamped tightly around my elbow. I whirled on him, ready to tear his arm away again as he softened his hold.

"Can you see me?"

"Yes," I whispered.

His dark eyes met mine, and my heart sank as I felt great sorrow for this little ghost child. My knees softened as I lowered myself so that we were facing each other.

His eyes narrowed as his fingers dug into my wrist. The boy burst into flames. The scorching fire enveloped my hand and wrist, making its way up my arms and my entire body as a searing pain caused agony beyond belief. I screamed as I tried to tear my arm away, fearing that my skin would simply fall apart into ash as I felt the flames alight my hair, and my scalp exploded with pain.

"Get off! Get off!" I yelled at the top of my lungs. I brushed my skin in an attempt to quell the flames, but the fire only coursed its way down my body and enveloped my legs, charring my skin to black as it engulfed the carpet and the bookshelves as the inferno devoured everything in the library. I howled at the top of my lungs.

"AJ!" Ben shouted my name, and the fire disappeared as if it was never there.

My whole body shook uncontrollably. I turned to where the boy had once stood, the space now inhabited by empty air.

"A child," I said softly.

"Let's get out of here." A crowd had formed at the end of the aisle. The library patrons stared, some reaching out as if to offer help.

"She's fine. She just isn't feeling well." Ben walked me to the end of the area between the shelves and out into the library's large hall. I caught a glimpse of the homely librarian. Her gaze was fixed upon me. Her face elongated into that of a slack-jawed, human-sized bunny rabbit. She smiled, her rabbit teeth pointy and red inside a mouth filled with blood. My eyes widened. I blinked, and there she was, just a librarian. Her gaze changed into that of a normal person disgusted by a crazy one.

Outside of the library, Ben flagged a cab down.

"A little boy," I whispered.

My hands quivered. Ben asked the driver for a tissue. The driver passed a smashed roll of toilet paper back to us. Ben raised an eyebrow and I gave a half a sob, half a laugh. He tossed the toilet paper onto the seat and offered the hem of his shirt instead.

"I can't go back to the house like this."

"You need to go back. But don't sleep. Have some coffee and stay awake. You need to forget all about this. About Addison."

"And Auroch."

"That's not even his name."

"Liar. Yes, it is."

"He's the least of your worries anyhow. Now that you know… now that we know what we are seeing at Addison, the ghosts will continue to reach out. They know we can see them."

"Should we call a priest?"

Ben made a clicking noise with his tongue. "Hard to tell. Some religious people are completely possessed by demons, strangely enough. Pretty sure a priest won't understand this situation."

The taxi cab pulled up to my family's Victorian home.

"I can't go in. I can't handle Nancy right now.

Can you take me to Mrs. Faria's?"

Ben commanded the driver to turn and pull into the driveway of Mrs. Faria's brownstone.

"I'll be by soon. Do not sleep. Do you promise?"

"Yes." My eyes felt heavy and tired.

I knocked on the door of Mrs. Faria's house. No answer. I twisted the handle and walked in. The cab backed out of the driveway with Ben's face peering out the window. I waved as if to signal that everything was all right.

"Mrs. Faria," I called. The house was silent save for the ticking of a clock.

Mrs. Faria lay snoring in the living room. One of her eyes popped open. Her hair crowned the pillow she lay her head upon in a wild coiffure. Her face and body looked so gaunt.

I winced.

"Hi," she murmured as she struggled to open her eyes. She ran a wrinkled hand over her frizzy hair, which stood on end. "I'm sure I look a fright. Make yourself at home."

"I'll make you something for dinner."

"No, no." Her head lolled to the side as she fell back to sleep.

I heated up some chicken soup and placed a bowl on a tray with a cup of Jell-O.

"Mrs. Faria." I brought the tray into the living room. "You should eat something."

She remained asleep, her eyes shut tight. I sat and spooned up a bit of the broth. My stomach rumbled. I devoured the meal quickly. I rinsed the dishes out in the sink and placed them in the dishwasher.

Padding on the soft carpet to the front door, I said goodbye to Mrs. Faria and closed the door softly. The night seemed to be waiting, expectant. A slight breeze blew as I strode past a neighbor's home. He sat at an easy chair in front of a wide living room window, smoking a thickly rolled cigarette. His head turned as he peered out at me and waved. I could tell by the blank look in his eye that he could not remember my name. I shook my head and smiled wryly as I waved back.

I was three houses away from my home when the footsteps began. *Clomp, clomp, clomp*, like a tall man wearing heavy-soled black shoes. When I reached my front door, I barreled into the home and slammed it behind me. Peering out the window, I saw nothing but the old craggy oak on our lawn waving and shedding its leaves with every gust of wind onto a deserted gray sidewalk.

****

Later that night, the phone rang. I sat up in bed with a third cup of coffee growing cold on my nightstand.

"Hello," I breathed. "Ben?" I whispered. "Last night, I dreamed you were dead."

"I'll be at your house first thing in the morning tomorrow," Ben said. "We need to be really careful now, AJ. He's coming after us. I can feel it."

"We have special powers, Ben. We'll know when he's coming. Or do you mean Au—"

"Don't say his name. AJ. Please. I'll explain everything tomorrow. You need to know how dangerous he is. AJ, are you there? AJ?"

LIZ NEWMAN

Chapter Fourteen
The Dragon Katana

Ben and I passed the weekend hours hanging out at Fisherman's Wharf. Droves of tourists ambled by with their backpacks and baby strollers, lost in their own worlds as they dipped spoons into clam chowders in bread bowls or licked the ice cream off chocolate-dipped waffle cones. Seagulls cried out in the distance. The smell of brine and fried food lingered in the air, blown about by the wind and occasionally interrupted by the smell of garbage or vomit. A pelican floated up and down over the surface of the water, its head craning for the light of the sun to peek through the clouds and highlight the day's kill.

Ben's eyes were rimmed with red from a lack of sleep, as were mine. He draped his arm around my shoulders as we stared out at the sea. He kissed my forehead. I intertwined the fingers of my hand with his.

Ben leaned forward and placed his elbow upon his knee.

"I caused this. I should have never told you his name. Saying his name opened the door. Now they can hurt us."

"They couldn't before?"

"They were just images." He lifted my arm and examined the scratch marks from the ghost child's nails. "Now they can hurt you. Me. And now he wants a trade."

"He wanted a trade from me before we talked about him, and he could hurt me before. Something hurt me in the library. I could feel the burning of my skin." I caressed my wrist, recalling the touch of the little boy's hand.

"It's because..." He leaned back and pulled a

tendril of my hair back. "Aur... the demon... he plays people against each other. To find out their weaknesses. I still think it's my fault all of this happened. Everything. I should have just stayed away when I met you in the theater when I knew you could hear them. But I want to be with you, AJ. I can't let you go."

"This is all so crazy. It's like we have something hanging over us, some unwelcome third party all the time. If it's not Hyannis or ghosts, it's some demon who's out to get us. Ghosts out to find us. I wish we could just disappear. Find somewhere else, start some new life. I want to be with you, too. How could any of this be just your fault? It's not your fault I can see ghosts. The woman in the monitor—"

"Did you recognize her?"

"No. She could be anyone. Any old woman who has passed away, perhaps the woman who drowned in Stinson Lake or..."

Ben shifted as if there were words on the tip of his tongue. "What is it?"

"Nothing. Just thought she might have been someone familiar."

"Mrs. Faria?"

"Perhaps when she is in the in-between, somewhere in her dementia state or another place."

"Did you tell Mrs. Faria?"

"She sleeps all the time. Has some health issues. I can't burden her with talk of demons and ghosts." I snickered. "Hey, excuse me, I know you're terminally ill, but I just want to let you know there is a purgatory, and there are some monsters in it that are horribly scary, and you might be going there in your sleep at night. 'Kay. Sweet dreams." I smiled weakly.

Ben's leather jacket rustled as he turned toward me. "Probably best to keep that to yourself." He exhaled loudly as if the thought burdened him. I shivered as the sunlight disappeared again behind a cloud in the sky as the San Francisco weather fought its never-ending battle of good weather versus bad weather.

After removing his leather jacket and revealing a black cashmere sweater that hugged his body beautifully, Ben wrapped the jacket around my shoulders. I brought it closer to me, reveling in the delicious smell of his cologne.

He looked off into the distance and scowled.

"What is it?"

"Nothing."

"Please tell me." I placed a hand on his arm. "Please. I'd really like to know what you're thinking."

A man dressed in jogging clothes stopped in front of the bench. "Excuse me. Mind if I sit down?"

"Sorry," Ben replied. "You can't."

"Looks like there's plenty of room." The man gestured to the seat, his eyes crinkling in the light of the sun.

"Sorry."

The man cussed under his breath and walked over to the next bench a few feet away. He sat and glared at us over his shoulder.

"Don't know why he couldn't sit there in the first place." Ben shrugged and placed his hand on my shoulder. "Just don't sleep, AJ." His voice took on an advising tone. "Stay awake as much as you can until we get this all sorted out. Try not to put yourself in danger. And forget about using the Dragon Katana for the competition instead of a foam sword. Now is not the time to be a badass at the talent show. This is serious. You could kill yourself, and Aur... *he*... would like that. Just trust me on this one."

"But think about Hyannis and her little ballet

routine." I paused to stifle a yawn. "To come on stage right after and perform with the Dragon Katana. I was going to wear a scarf, toss it up in the air as I posed with the sword over my head in one hand and the hilt held to the side, and let it gently come down after the performance. The Katana would slice the scarf in two."

"I know the plan. The crowd would erupt in thunderous applause, and Hyannis would be shown up completely. You and the Katana would be all anyone would talk about for months. At worst, you could accidentally slice your own artery. At best, you'd be suspended for bringing a weapon to school. Come on, AJ."

"There's a side of me no one knows, Ben. A side of me that is skilled. People see the quiet me, a good student, awkward at times, not very confident. Just another girl loner." I rose from the bench and strode toward the end of the dock, where the wind lifted my hair. I thought of the insult from Hyannis on the first day of school when Ben said my eyes were pretty. *The girl with the weird eyes.*

I propped my elbows on the bar and stared out to the sea. The gloaming sea, with the fog dancing over the surface in wisps as the water rose up to lap at it. Only a sand bar railing separated me from where the bay met the churning waves of the Pacific Ocean. I wondered if Ben would save me if the railing gave way, and I tumbled in and fell. There were sharks in the water, no doubt, as the yelping sea lions nearby would attest.

Ben walked over and stood by my side. He placed one hand on the railing, his body turned in my direction. He placed his other hand upon mine, his palm soft and smooth save for the spots under his fingers, where his fingers were a bit calloused from gripping the motorcycle handlebars. "I know exactly who you are. You're everything important in the world, the girl with eyes that sparkle like jewels."

I wrapped my fingers around his. We watched the waters in silence as cargo ships and sailboats floated by.

The sun broke through the clouds and illuminated the skin on our hands with a golden sheen. Our eyes met as we gazed at each other. Oh, the light in Ben's look and its warm softness, a blanket of warmth I could curl up and hibernate in. I smiled at the thought and he took me into a gentle hug as I tucked my head into the space between his neck and shoulder and closed my eyes.

We stayed there for a moment or perhaps an eternity, embracing as our hair blew all around us underneath the warmth of the sun, as waves lapped at the barrier to the sea below our feet. As we drew our faces away, we smiled the silly, stupid expressions of a happy couple. My heart soared with his closeness. I never wanted to let go.

That night, I struggled to keep my eyes open and drifted into fitful naps. I fell into a world of nightmares, where magpies cawed and crawled over walls thick with black feathers, three birds deep with scrabbling claws like insects. A phone rang and rang somewhere in the blackness of my mind. I answered. Then a child's voice whispered, "There is a dark home, red as the fire grows, and into the black she goes, she goes. Into the black she goes." Over and over and over again.

****

The karate bag over my shoulder tapped against my hip as it held the Dragon Katana, sheathed to the hilt. I walked briskly up the steps into Addison High School early on Monday morning. I covered my mouth with my hand as I yawned. Tendrils of fog drifted in front of the glass front doors of the school. The air made a moaning sound as I opened a door. I stared back over my shoulder as the *gloam* reached over the lawn of the school and drifted underneath the flag on its way to the ocean. A fog that seemed to encase drifting bodies and grimaced faces within its midst. I shuddered as I walked into the hall.

"Caw," said a woman's voice behind me. My mouth curled into a grimace. I dared not look back before I opened the glass door to the school and stepped into the hall.

The wide sign that took up almost the entire wall between two classrooms read "Talent Show!" in enormous blue and red letters. The mocking little epitaphs graffitied on the sign had been whited out with that sharp-smelling stuff the trailer park kids used to get high. The sharp scent made me wrinkle my nose.

I spent a few minutes locked in a bathroom stall, trying to breathe away my nervousness about breaking the rules and bringing a weapon to school. The bell signaling the start of first period rang.

I pulled open the door to Mr. Spinky's class and took a seat at my desk. Mr. Spinky peered my way, his eyebrows raised at my tardiness, but continued lecturing. I turned to Gideon. Gideon's desk was empty. The door opened behind me. Gideon shot Mr. Spinky a guilty look as he slunk through the aisles and into his chair. His chin rested upon his outstretched upper arm in his customary manner of sitting like a subject for a portrait of a school slacker. His other hand danced over a sheet of paper, where he began to draw a figure.

"Mr. Glazier," Mr. Spinky intoned in a British accent. "Gideon Glazier. Now that you have decided to grace the class with your presence, could you kindly give me the honor of your undivided attention? Where was I?" He placed his index finger on his chin, tapping lightly. "Oh yes, the British do not permit exoneration of the buried unless there is a solid need for DNA evidence that such exoneration is necessary."

I opened up my notebook and jotted down every word Mr. Spinky said.

The memory of last night's magpie dream caused my mind to drift back to a place where the sky was nothing but pecking beaks and the searing pain of claws. Something out of thin air pecked at the back of my head. I stifled a shriek as I reached up to my scalp. When I brought my finger back down to my desk, the tip was tinged with blood. The blood on my finger was warm and wet, with a bit of a scab sticking. The hairy unibrow boy was here, and the pretty girl wearing a letter jacket who glanced up at Mr. Spinky with full attention and focus and at Gideon, who doodled away on his notepad as he hummed a song under his breath. The class continued on, unawares.

I remained alone in a state of terror with a blood dot on my hand.

****

The dragon Katana lay in my half-open karate bag, its gleaming blade catching the spotlights hung over the top of the stage in the blood-red theater at Addison High. The end of school bell had rung an hour ago. The theater and halls stood empty of students, save for Ben and me. I stretched my hands over my head and twisted my body from side to side.

"AJ," Ben said as he pulled the sword out of the bag. "This isn't a good idea."

"It *is* a good idea." I hopped off the stage and gently pulled the dragon Katana out of his hands. "This sword is like my own right hand."

Ben shook his head and took a seat, stretching his booted legs out in front of him.

I unsheathed the dragon Katana. The light caught on to the silver and reflected off the walls. The thump of my footsteps reverberated as I walked up on the stage. Thrusting the sword out and leaning my weight onto my back leg, I sliced the sword through the air, enjoying the noise of the sound of the blade cutting through thin air. I flipped over and over, spinning around in the air as I held the sword close to my body. When my two-minute routine ended, I shouted a mighty "Ay-yah!"

Unsheathing a chiffon scarf from my *gi* pocket, I tossed the scarf in the air and posed with my sword.

The scarf floated down and, with a whisper, was sliced in half as it lit upon the blade on its way to the floor in two.

I bowed, then I lifted my head with pride and waited for Ben to speak.

Ben clapped slowly in a cadence that bordered on mocking. He breathed a loud sigh of relief.

"You can't tell me that was anything short of phenomenal."

"I thought you were going cut your arm off."

"Luis taught me that focus would make anything possible. I *am* performing this at the talent show."

Ben rose and strode in my direction as he brought me the sheath and motioned for me to hand him the sword. I complied. He slipped the sword into its smooth casing. "Let's return the sword to the dojo now and go have a coffee. Pumpkin spiced lattes. My treat."

"You go ahead. I'm going to stay and practice with the foam sword. You can leave the Katana there."

"You're lying. You're not going to practice with the foam sword."

"That sword is part of my arm now. Please don't be upset with me."

"You'll have to get a notice from the school principal saying that it is all right. Although that's pretty much impossible, isn't it? Weapons at school, AJ.

They're not allowed."

"Are you going to tell on me?" I bleated, a sound I knew was unattractive, but so long as Ben's ears were the only pair privy to the noise.

"It's getting late. Let's go grab a coffee."

"Nothing in here is going to hurt me. The Dragon Katana is not just a sword. It is the guardian of souls, the bringer of fire to those who are dead inside and have lost hope. This sword is perfect for me, Ben. Perfect for what I can do."

"AJ, power comes at a cost. Trust me, I know."

"How? Did he tell you? Aur—"

"Stop! I'm not leaving you in here alone." Ben picked up the sword and trotted down the stage steps, then sat in the front row with his arms crossed over his shoulders and the sword propped upon his knees.

"You know, Ben, just because we had a run-in with ghosts doesn't mean I need you for a babysitter."

"A babysitter? Come on, AJ."

"Leave the sword. I'll show these ghosts who has the real power. Since you're afraid to."

"This sword should go back to the dojo."

"I'll take it back." I jumped off the stage and reached for the sword. Ben did not budge. He stood and took a step back from me as I reached for the sheath. "You're like your mom telling you that you shouldn't ride your motorcycle anymore. How would you like it if your mom just took your bike away? Or your dad? I'll bet you wish he would so you knew he actually cared."

I regretted the words as soon as they left my lips. Ben's eyes narrowed at the mention of his father. "Maybe we both just need to be alone for a little bit," he said as he placed the sword on the seat next to him. "I'm tired. My fuse is short. Yours is, too. I'm out."

"Ben—"

"No." He held up his hands. "I'm going to take a walk. Some faculty members are hanging around after the teacher's meeting, so you'll be fine here. Practice with the foam sword so you don't get in trouble, but you obviously don't care what I think."

"Sure." My body bristled with annoyance and a sudden feeling of tiredness.

I had stuck my foot in my mouth. *Why, oh why did I manage to say things that hurt the people I loved the most.* "I'm sorry. I made a comment about Caslin's dad the other day, and look now."

Ben's eyes met mine. His gaze smoldered. I could see the temper that lurked underneath. "I'm not Caslin. I didn't betray your friendship or trust. Ever. What I told you about my family, I told you in confidence. I didn't think you would use it against me. You should come with me. We should leave this theater. Together."

"Don't stand there and act like I need saving. Leave the sword. You couldn't even save yourself in a fight." My irritation was roiled. "Get out!" My voice bounced off the walls of the theater. *Get out, get out, get out*! I startled, remembering the first ghostly words I'd heard in here when Caslin and I sat for orientation so many weeks ago. *Get out, get out!* Like an echo of my own voice.

Ben sighed with resignation as he lay the sword case upon the stage. He gave a double peace sign with two fingers up in the air as he stormed up the aisle without looking back. The doors closed behind him.

I crumbled to the floor and sat there as I closed my eyes and willed concentration to take hold. Breathing deeply in and out, I imagined myself practicing Wu Shu as my arms, legs, and the sword sliced skillfully through the air around me. After many breaths, I was calm. I felt complete. Even though I knew when Ben had left, a piece of my heart had gone with him.

Unsheathing the sword, I spread my arms out wide and quickened my pace as I flew through the air with the sword raised as a dragon taking wing. The danger of the motion, to have the blade mere millimeters at times away from my body, made my heart flutter as I spun through the air, crouching and lunging at an imaginary enemy. The enemy's face was Hyannis, at times Nancy, at times the darkness that threatened to envelop my soul. Then, my own face appeared before me, and I lowered the sword and stopped to catch my breath. Of course, there was no one there before me except the dimly lit theater.

The lights in the theater clicked off.

I stood in total darkness.

"Excuse me?" I called as my voice shook. "I'm in here! Could you turn the lights back on, please?"

Silence. Blackness. I imagined red eyes and pointed, gnashing teeth headed toward me, the evil fairy's teeth from the picture in my bedroom. My eyes shut tightly as I tried to block the imagery. "Ben?"

No answer. Not a shuffle or a whisper. My breath came rapidly as I reached my hands out. My surroundings were so pitch black I couldn't even make out an outline of my fingers.

"Turn the lights back on!" I held the sword out before me as I groped through the darkness, trying to walk toward the backstage area and find a light switch. My steps echoed in the theater, each thump causing my heart to beat more rapidly. Something soft and velvet brushed against my cheek. A curtain? I reached out with my sword in hand and heard the fabric tear. "Please." My voice sounded croaky and high-pitched.

"Can you see me?" a child's voice whispered.

"I can't see anything! Please turn the lights back

on!" I reached my hand forward, groping. "Please."

"You can see us, you can see, can you see." A chorus of children's voices echoed in the darkness. "Can you see me? Can you see me?" Invisible hands pressed into my stomach, my legs, my chest. "See me, see me, see me!"

"Stop it!" I screamed. "Leave me alone! Stop it! Stop!"

"Come with us, come with us, come with us..." Several children spoke now, their voices beating the air like flames about to unleash into an uncontrollable wildfire.

"Stop!"

The trapdoor opened beneath my feet. I clutched the empty air as I fell into the darkness, holding the sword above my falling body. The floor beneath me crunched and moved as if it crawled with thousands of beetles. I smashed my hands down upon their bodies. I consoled myself by the fact that none of the beetles crawled up my arms and legs. But beneath me, the smarmy darkness shifted and oozed.

A man's voice called out from the gloomy darkness, deep, melodic, and sensual. Thick as honey. "Be calm." The crawling floor transformed into cement. The cool, still layer underneath felt like redemption.

"Who is that?" I tightened my grip around the Katana.

"Someone who shares the eternal battle of light and darkness with you. Someone who speaks to you from within." His baritone voice was soothing. "Do you know my name?"

Auroch. I scanned the darkness, hoping to find a glimpse or a shadow, any hint that could tell me whether this man was indeed a man, or a beast, or a demon. "I don't want to say your name."

"Reach into the darkness and take my hand." I imagined a dark, hairy hand with thick fingers and black claws inching closer, ready to grasp my wrist. I wanted to sob. Instead, I sliced the sword back and forth in the empty air.

The voice laughed heartily. "Perhaps the children will show you the way out then." The voice laughed again before the sound faded. A great whooshing burst forth as the blackness swirled and receded. My hair was lifted up by a wind and brushed about my eyes. The space before me was inky.

"There is a dark home, red as the fire grows," a child whispered. "The red a mess, crawls up her dress, and into black she goes she goes. Into black she goes." The child's voice grew louder as if someone spoke into my ear, and then other children's voices joined as they repeated the poem again. Tiny hands pressed against my ears, my face, and my neck as I slashed the Katana in mid-air as the children giggled. "This way." They laughed as they pulled me up and pushed on my hair and my gi, then pulled me in several directions at once. "This way. This way."

I yanked at smooth hands and limbs, slightly filmy with the moist skin of children and their luminous bodies. A blessed ray of light filtered through from somewhere, perhaps from the children themselves now that I could see them up close.

I gasped.

These were not children. They were burnt corpses. Blackened skeletons grinned as bony fingers scraped at the skin on my arms and legs. Glimpses of their faces hovered below me, grinning charred black smiles. I screamed.

"This way. This way," one uttered with the metallic voice of an insect as the bony, grimy hands grasped at me. "You can come too. You can come and live with us here."

"Aurroooocch!" I screamed out his name as a drowning person would cry out for help before succumbing to the water. The voices of the children immediately ceased. "Auroch!"

The hands disappeared, as well as the ghastly faces. I was cast into silence with nothing but the sound of my own breathing to fill my ears.

"This way," the man said. His voice faded to a mutter of numerous dark, deep voices.

I sheathed the Katana, backing away from the voices and the darkness until I bumped into a wall. My hands scrabbled along the surface of the wall. "You don't scare me at all!" I shouted. This is some kind of joke. That's all it is."

"You will leave this place and go home if only you would reach out and take my hand." I whirled in the direction of the voice in the darkness. "Take my hand," he insisted. His voice became a low guttural growl of a beast. "Take my hand."

I lowered my sword, reaching forth blindly. A thick, hairy hand grasped my lower arm and pulled.

The lights flashed once, like lightning. I glimpsed the red eyes and grinning face of a giant red wolf with gigantic curved horns. The lights flashed again as I turned and ran. I leaped into the darkness, falling flat on my face as I tripped. I reached my hands up and felt the opening on the trapdoor. I climbed through it and lay on the floor to catch my breath before I looked over my shoulder and saw the monster underneath clambering after me like a giant spider as I slammed the trapdoor shut and locked it.

The emergency lights switched on. I sheathed the sword and gathered up my things. Blood dripped from three slashes on my wrist. I must have slipped with the sword, or perhaps the claws of the beast had cut me.

I ran out into the eerily lit hallway, past the mopping janitor, who seemed half comatose as he mouthed two indiscernible words. I thought about the way his mouth moved and tried to read his lips in my mind. *I remember. I remember?* He stared in dismay at the blood dripping from my arm as his thirsty mop lapped up every trace.

My legs and arms pumped as I fled through Addison High School's glass double doors and out onto the stairs. A lace of my black Converse had come undone. The errant lace tripped me, and I fell forward. I held out my hands to brace my fall, bashing my knee into the cement. I rose back to my feet and dashed up the street, past the sagging brown boot house. The Magpie lurked somewhere near. I didn't doubt that at all. I kept running all fifteen blocks until I burst into my home, a mess of sweat, welts, and bruises.

LIZ NEWMAN

Chapter Fifteen
Death Wish

Panting, I slammed the front door of my home behind me. I backed against the wall, trying to summon up the courage to look out of the window next to the front door. That monster face. The red eyes. Perhaps he... *it* ...whatever it was staring into the window right now. I clutched the hilt of the dragon Katana. Whatever the creature was, could I kill it with this weapon? I wondered. Or would it take me, baby Frances, and my entire family down to whatever hell it had crawled out of?

I shivered with fear.

Frances's voice rang down from upstairs. "Jay Jay," she murmured. Nancy said something softly back. I unsheathed the Katana and threw open the door. Our brightly lit walkway was empty and still, save for a crumpled autumn leaf blowing by in the wind. No ghost, no specter, no horrifying creature.

"AJ," I whispered to myself. "You have one hell of a runaway imagination. Or you should hope."

"AJ?" Nancy said from the top of the stairs. I whirled toward her with the sword in my hand. "What is that?" She recoiled with disbelief.

"A prop." I pulled strands of hair dripping with sweat back from my face. "For the talent show. I was practicing."

"Looks heavy. Are you sure that's just a prop?"

"Yes," I said as I sheathed the sword. "They make them look really real nowadays."

"You look filthy. Rough day at practice?"

"You could say that."

Nancy's eyes widened at the blood dripping from

my arm onto the travertine floor of the foyer.

"AJ!" Nancy shrieked. "You're bleeding!"

I shook my head, unable to speak.

Nancy stepped down to the landing, her fixated stare upon me the entire time. "Come on to the kitchen. Let's get you bandaged up."

A short while later, I sat on a barstool, pressing gauze pads and ice to my wounds. Nancy bandaged my arm. Her breath smelled like asparagus.

"AJ, despite what you would like to believe, you are a lot like me."

"How?"

"I was a cutter, too."

"A what?"

"A cutter. I would slash my arms in high school and make them bleed. Just little slashes. To remind me that I was real."

"Nancy, I'm not a cutter. This was truly an accident."

"Sure, sure. That's what we like to say now, isn't it? You may as well pick yourself up a shopping cart at Riley's on the corner and make your way over to the Tenderloin because that's how little girls with big bad demons who they never face live out their lives. Right now, you're so mired in your own denial you can't even admit that you need help. Once upon a time in my life, the only place I felt safe was at home, drinking, numbing everything. Your dad was my anchor, and now I'm well. I'll be here for you, your dad will be here for you, but *you've* got to be there for you, and you won't be there unless you start realizing the truth."

"What truth do I need to realize?"

"The truth about your status in this family."

Just when I thought Nancy and I were having a heart-to-heart talk like a real mother and daughter, there she'd go again.

Everything's going to be okay, AJ. Ben's image quickly popped into my mind. Ben's slow, half smile. The smell of Ben's leather jacket, the scent of his hair. The nearness of him and how good it felt. I needed to text him and tell him what happened.

"Thanks, Nancy." I rose to go up to my room.

"By status, I mean by becoming a part. Being involved as a daughter, as an older sister. An older sister who would care for the home while your dad and I are on vacation," Nancy called after me. "I miss you calling me 'mom'!" She sighed as she leaned back and examined her fingernails.

"You aren't my real mother."

"I'm the only mother you ever had."

"I'm not a cutter, and we are nothing alike. I'm not popular, sorority girl, Miss Country Club, future PTA queen. If it makes you feel any better, I still love you now as much now as I loved you before." A lump welled up in my throat. I knew I sounded hurtful. The distant, unfeeling look in Nancy's eyes told me she wasn't as hurt as I felt. And that had always been the worst part of our relationship. Real mothers hurt for their daughters. Real mothers, whether by birth or circumstance, reflected the pain their daughters felt and did their best to remedy.

"I'll keep going to meetings and accept that I might always be this way. But I need your help to not drink, AJ. I need you to stay healthy and strong, and sane."

"That's not my responsibility!" I shook my head. Nancy sounded so creepy.

"Fine," muttered Nancy. Her hand remained on her pregnant belly as her gaze drifted. "Let's not speak of this again, then." Nancy rose and sauntered toward the kitchen without giving another look, then stopped short.

She turned and rushed up the stairs to her bedroom, sobbing.

****

Ben and I had spent every lunch at school together the entire week, sitting or walking together and talking. I told him about the ghosts, the pictures. Ben listened sympathetically, always nodding, always responding with just the right amount of understanding. We knew we were both not perfect. That gave us the freedom to share everything. The weekend loomed ahead, and on Friday, we sat in silence together in the common as people around us chatted. Ben placed his chin upon his hand and sighed as if he had something weighing heavily on his mind. I knew exactly what it was.

"I'm going to perform with the real Katana. And that's final."

Ben leaned back and tilted his head back to the sky. "You ever worry you might chop your own arm off? Because I do."

"Ben, I could start in about the motorcycle, but I won't. I have total control over the situation. You're just going to have to trust me."

Ben touched the area on my arm just below the bandages.

"That was not… from that."

"Then what? Tell me. How did these cuts happen?"

I wrinkled my nose as I met his eyes for a second, then looked away. *If he knew about… the monster, he would blame himself. He would blame Auroch. And I just can't hear that name right now.*

"This is unbelievable." Ben rose from the steps and paced in front of me. "To ride a motorcycle, you have to take lessons, get a certification and a license. To perform with a sword, a lethal object, you can't just pick one up and start swinging it around in a public place."

"To perform Wu Shu, you need a black belt and years of training. Same thing if not more intensive."

"Could you just not perform with the Katana for me? Could you just promise to perform with a plastic sword just to make me feel better?" He sat beside me and held my hand. "What kind of boyfriend would I be if I let you do this?"

"The kind every girl wants." My eyes pleaded with his. I needed to perform with the dragon Katana, needed to show everyone in the audience the stunt I had planned by tossing up a scarf tied around the sword's hilt and letting it fall. Letting the sword slice the scarf in two. "This isn't about popularity or showing off. This is about me being able to do something no one else out there can do. That's what a talent show is about, isn't it? It's not just about swordsmanship. It's about showing the world what I'm capable of. I want... I want them to know I have talent. Forget about them, even. I want to prove to myself I have the guts and the concentration to carry something like this off."

"What about the ghosts?"

"Funny you should mention that because I kind of wanted to show them too."

"Look, just promise me that if you feel like something in the theater is going to mess with your focus or trip you up somehow, you'll stop performing. Just cut it short. Or toss the sword and do some flips or something. Promise me you won't get hurt. Just promise."

"I promise."

"AJ Covington, when are you going to tell me your full name?"

"Soon enough."

"Like when?" He wrapped his hands around my

waist, drawing me close to him so he could gaze into my eyes.

"Like when I know you love me." The words fled my lips so quickly that I blushed the moment I spoke them aloud. Over the course of the past few weeks, I had wondered whether the sidelong looks I caught him giving me, whether the electrical charge that shuddered through my body when his hand touched mine, and I hoped was shared, whether the tenderness that guided his every move near me translated into such. Love. I had hoped, wished, and dreamed of the moment he would say he loved me. Now, I'd practically forced it out of him. In the cell phone area. At school. I groaned and pulled away. "Oh, forget it." I buried my head in my hands. "If you're going to say it, please don't say it here."

"Do you have plans this weekend? Because if you do, I'd like you to break them."

"Why?"

"Let's take a walk. Someplace special. Unless you want to take a ride on the motorcycle?" He smiled that sideways, mischievous smile that sent my heart tumbling.

"No, Ben."

"If you'd tried, I think you would love it. The wind whips through your hair, you can see the tall buildings and all the sights of the city as we ride without anything in your way. You would love it. I just know it."

I sighed. Yards away, Johan sprinted down the basketball court. He held his hand up at a fellow player as he caught the ball, then slammed dunked it through the net. Hyannis, Caslin, Gigi, and several other girls chatted in a circle at the picnic benches, oblivious to everyone except themselves. All around me life went on, with people who chatted about school reports, homework, and weekend plans, while I sat here far and away from it all, exhausted and afraid of ghosts. I needed to take chances.

I needed to start living.

"Okay," I said, nodding. "You do have an extra helmet, right?"

"I have everything. A leather jacket, a do-rag, girls' gloves. Everything you need. I'll bring them over."

"Why do you own a pair of girls' gloves?"

The bell rang before he could answer, signaling the end of lunchtime.

Ben's phone jingle sounded. He pulled the phone from his pocket and checked the screen. "I need to head out. I've got some things to do after school, too. Pick you up at ten in the morning."

Ben's phone rang again. He shifted his weight from one foot to the other.

"I have to take this call." He turned away quickly.

"Hi, Kelly," I heard him say into the phone under his breath. *Kelly Rose.*

I waited there, tapping my foot. He sneaked away, walking and talking. I think he felt my gaze upon his back, for he turned around while he was still on the phone. He muttered something in closing and stuffed the phone in his pocket. He walked back toward me with his hands spread wide.

"What's up?"

"Who is Kelly Rose?"

Stuffing his hands in his pockets, he shifted his weight from one foot to another. Anger swelled up inside me. If I wasn't getting shirked and shortchanged by my former best friend Caslin, it seemed I would be shirked and shortchanged by my own... boyfriend. Who very clearly might have another girlfriend. The digital screen of my phone popped into my imagination with a WTH! which I almost uttered in the longhand, profane version but thought better of it.

He ran a hand over the top of his head in

frustration. This gesture succeeded in only making him look even more handsome by spiking his hair up.

"Kelly is…" He waved his hand as if conducting the first few bars of a pre-recorded symphony. *Ha, of course. Ben Bach, giving me the old song and dance.* Seemed like an excuse was coming. "Can I just explain that to you better another time? It would be better if I showed you in person."

"Wait, you would like me to meet another girl you have been talking to *in person*?" Ben laid a hand on his head. "Have a headache? Oh, I'm sorry," I said in a sarcastic tone to mask the hurt. "The mysterious Kelly Rose, whose calls take you far away and make you rush off somewhere so you can talk in secret. Who is she?"

Ben closed his eyes and sighed.

"I wish I could be somewhere else, too." I spun on my heel and stormed toward the entry to the school. The sound of Ben's phone ringing tormented me, as well as the sound of his hushed greeting as I entered the school.

"I'll see you tomorrow, AJ," Ben called. He resumed talking on his phone.

Chapter Sixteen
Accidents Happen

My eyes popped wide open the next morning. Saturday.

Carlos the cat stretched out one black furry leg with a white paw as if he dreamed of flight among the clouds. I wiped the sleep from my eyes with the back of my hand. Last night, I dreamed of darkness and hands over my eyes, touching my face and cheeks, more hands. I shivered.

The house was quiet.

I opened the door of my bedroom and peered out into the hall. Silence. As I brushed my teeth in the bathroom, I called out. "Dad? Frances? Nancy?" No answer. Perhaps they had gone out to breakfast. Nice of them to invite me.

I pulled on a pair of jeans and a black tank top. My heart did flip flops in my chest as I knew Ben would be picking me up for another date today, perhaps with a helmet tucked under his arm. I sighed with relief, knowing that if my parents weren't home, I could just jump on the motorcycle without hearing them try to talk me out of riding. Maybe Ben wouldn't even show. Maybe his conversation with Kelly was so captivating he would decide to make *her* his girlfriend.

His *girlfriend*. My heart tinged with pain. I picked up my cell phone.

Wait and see, I told myself. *He called you his girlfriend, which means you are his one and only.*

That's what it should mean, an impish voice inside my head piped up, *but you didn't ask him to clarify, did you?*

The fog was thick today, so thick I couldn't see Mrs. Faria's house across the street from my bedroom window. I hopped down the steps to the kitchen to pour myself a glass of orange juice. I knew if Ben actually showed up for our date, he would want to go to the cafe on the corner, or he would bring lattes, so I decided to skip breakfast even though my stomach rumbled at the site of yogurt and granola parfait in the refrigerator and the oat nut muffins on the counter. I sat in the living room in front of the picture window and waited for my phone to ring with a call from Ben to tell me he was on his way.

Chainsaws roared to life across the street as a tree service company chopped down an old oak that must have been diseased. The workers fed the chopped branches into a chipping machine. *Clack clack clack clack. Chirrrrr.* The sound could be heard even through our double-pained windows. A dull headache wrestled its way into my forehead.

My cell phone rang its familiar jingle to notify me that I just received a text. I smiled, expecting a message from Ben.

From Hyannis McWolfe, my cell phone read.

A picture of Hyannis, Johan, Gigi, Caslin, and their crowd popped up, all at a breakfast diner, making funny faces at the camera. Underneath the picture was the caption, "So happy you're NOT here, AJ!"

Swearing under my breath, I tossed the cell phone onto the couch. Enough already.

I looked outside of the window to see Hyannis in her designer skinny jeans walking next to Caslin, whose lips moved on and on in oblivion. Hyannis pocketed her cell phone with a smug smile as she glanced at my home and shimmied her shoulders with delight. I picked up my cell phone and tucked it into my back pocket. I would show Caslin what a bully Hyannis really was. If Caslin chose to ignore this slight, I could no longer consider her my friend.

I threw open my front door and stalked down the steps, calling Caslin's name over the sound of the wood chipper. She continued on with Hyannis. Both girls were about to turn the corner.

"Caslin!" I yelled when the wood chipper machine lulled.

Caslin heard me call her name and turned around to face me. The chainsaws roared to life as Hyannis opened her mouth in laughter.

I stormed toward them, my arms and legs tearing into the space over the street as I held my cell phone in hand.

"AJ!" Caslin stood in the thick fog, waving her hands back and forth.

I jumped reflexively over the serrated yellow line in the middle of the road, scowling down at the yellow stripes. I had to keep my cool throughout this confrontation. I couldn't let Hyannis see me crumble. I couldn't let her see me cry. The inclination to weep was overwhelming. I squelched my feelings down and widened my eyes, pacing forward in their direction.

Caslin said something at the top of her lungs, and I raised my head. Her arms swung about wildly as she pointed to my right just before the machine lulled again. A high-pitched screeching sound cut through the noise of an oncoming bus as my head whirled around in its direction.

The bus careened toward me, an enormous lethal force of steel. The bus was so close I could see the driver's eyes widen, his teeth bared as he pulled back on the steering wheel as if that would make the brakes work better and keep the vehicle from plowing me down into the blacktop. The bus swerved to the left. I folded my arms over my head and closed my eyes, praying my death would be quick and painless.

Then came the sound of a motorcycle revving along with the acrid smell of burning rubber. I whirled around in time to see a motorcycle fly through the air toward the bus. The motorcycle swerved in front of me, blocking the way between my body and the oncoming bus.

Ben slid the motorcycle on its side as he slammed on the brakes and skidded on his back tire with the intention to wedge it under the bus's tires. The sound of the bus brakes screeching made a sickening, high-pitched wail. Smoke emanated from the heel of Ben's boots as he dug them into the ground to bring his bike between me and the bus. The side of the bus flew in my direction, an angry honking beast of metal and tire and steel as I realized at that moment just how dead I would both soon be.

Pop! The bus bumping the motorcycle made an explosive sound like a volleyball being spiked by an iron fist. I flew back with my hands in the air, a millisecond too late, for the motorcycle handlebar punched my chest. The force of momentum threw me into the ground as the back of my head crashed against the pavement. Ben's head smacked against the ground loudly as the material of his helmet cracked open. He lay beside me in a heap of torn leather, motionless.

The smell of a burnt rubber tire assaulted my nostrils as I lay on the ground, my legs splayed off to the side with my hand at the sides of my face. A pool of warmth spread under my head, wetting my hair.

"Ben," I moaned. "Oh, God, I'm sorry. I'm so sorry."

Hyannis spoke rapidly into her phone as Caslin rushed out into the street and crouched by my side. She picked up my cell phone. I watched as the illuminated screen of my cell phone, with the picture Hyannis had sent, faded to black.

"AJ!" Caslin screamed. "Someone is coming to help you. Hold on, okay? Please hold on!" Tears coursed down her cheeks as she grabbed my hand.

"Ben," I moaned. "Oh, Ben." I could taste blood in my mouth.

Caslin rocked from side to side as she knelt before me. Her eyes ran with tears. "She's bleeding. Can someone please call an ambulance? Somebody call an ambulance!"

The driver of the bus emerged and knelt by Ben's side. Ben lay on his back. I couldn't see his eyes. I didn't know whether he was alive or dead. I tried to lift my head up, but my hair was stuck to the ground. The intense pain slowly faded into a dull throb, then faded again into numbness, which overcame me as I lay there. Caslin and the bus driver's voices faded as my mind closed down.

"Ben," I whispered. "I'm sorry."

Hyannis casually strode over to my side. She appraised me coldly with disgust as her gaze traveled up to the top of my head.

"What was she thinking running out into the street like that?" She turned her head to the side and surveyed Ben with that same grimace. "This is so poetically tragic." She reached out a foot and tapped Ben's helmet with the pointy toe of her boot. "He's definitely dead."

"Don't do that," Caslin protested. "You never touch someone who's injured. You could hurt them even worse." Hyannis's eyes widened at Caslin's chastising. Caslin shot Hyannis a dirty look for the first time, *hallelujah*. Caslin's turned back to me. "You're going to be fine, AJ. Just hang on."

A siren wailed in the distance, growing louder as

it drew closer. I stared up at the sky. There were white puffy clouds floating in a backdrop of cerulean blue. The vision was one of the most beautiful San Francisco skies I had ever seen. No fog. No gloom.

Hyannis moved into my line of sight. My gaze that had held the blue skies dulled over with an intense hatred. If the emotion could have manifested itself in my surroundings, lightning would have flashed in thick, dark clouds. Rain and hail would have poured from the skies and pelted Hyannis into a pulp. I focused every ounce of hatred in my being on her face. For a moment, just a moment, her eyes widened with fright. The cords in her throat protruded. She looked as if I held my hands around her neck and was strangling the life out of her.

Two ambulances screeched to stop on the street, and her eyes became blank and unfeeling again. Caslin moaned my name over and over. Two paramedics, one with her dark hair pulled back into a ponytail, and a handsome, muscular man with long flowing hair hovered over me. The man placed a box of medical supplies on the ground. I tried to speak.

"This is your fault," the paramedic said to Hyannis. I could hear him speaking without his lips moving. "Everything is your fault. *Kill yourself.*" I looked up at Hyannis, who had locked eyes with the paramedic. The paramedic looked down at me and smiled.

"How are you doing, AJ?" he said. His voice was deep, fatherly, and troublingly familiar. A demon's voice.

"I'm all right," I said. My mouth tasted like copper.

"*Do it, Hyannis,*" the paramedic's deep voice said as he looked up Hyannis. "*Kill yourself.*"

But his lips did not move. "Who are you?" I said.

"Who are youuuu?" the paramedic giggled softly.

"Shhh. You're going to be okay. Hang on."

No, that was not the paramedic's voice speaking to Hyannis. But then, who was it?

Kill yourself, Hyannis. Kill yourself.

I could hear the words spoken clearly, and by Hyannis's ashen facade and widened eyes, she could as well. She turned and walked away quickly, like a hit-and-run driver leaving the scene of the crime.

My mouth forgot how to move. I lay there like a fish gulping air. Something pushed down on my chest, hard, then harder. I searched for the paramedic with the deep, familiar voice, but he was nowhere to be found. There were others now, firemen and policemen and more paramedics with bandages and tourniquets and a stretcher. Another set of paramedics lifted Ben up onto a stretcher, helmet and all. A man in a blue uniform fastened an oxygen mask over my face, even as I continued to watch the ambulance with Ben inside driving away.

I sank into a world of darkness.

LIZ NEWMAN

Chapter Seventeen
Demon World

I ran a hand over my lower lip, removing the white stuff that no doubt stuck the corners together. All was quiet. Perhaps death is as peaceful as they say.

"Somebody help me," I whispered. "Somebody. I can't see."

Besides the pain of my throbbing hip, I felt numb. Even terror ceased to strike me as I realized I was blind.

Andromeda Jayne, called the voice. *Come with me.*

The voice from the theater. The voice of the paramedic. The deep male voice, soothing yet terrifying like the feel a drowning person must have as they take their last gulps of water before drifting into eternal peace.

Why should I follow you anywhere? I could hear my voice in my mind but not with my ears, much like the drowning person I had imagined.

Either me or the darkness. Take your pick. Come with me. I will answer all of your questions.

My eyes stuck together as I pried them open with my fingers. The dirt on my fingers stung the insides of my lids. I was lying down on a wooden floor, my legs sticking out at all angles like a broken doll. Above me was an alfresco of angels soaring in picturesque blue skies. The dome-shaped ceiling reminded me of the Palace of Fine Arts, yet the structure was walled off instead of open on the sides. On the outer edges of the dome, angels frozen in expressions of terror and woe instead of peace and tranquility looked over their shoulders at dark clouds coming in.

Pushing down on the palms of my hands, I rose to a sitting position and surveyed my surroundings.

Tapestries hung from the walls, and a lattice cut detailing in iron covered the windows. I stood and brushed my hands on my dress. Ugh, taffeta. I despised the seafoam color and the glittery detail of the frock I wore. I walked to a window and stared out. I was at least two floors above ground, perhaps three. The sun shone in from a grassy knoll, reminding me of a picturesque valley on a box of breakfast cereal come to life. The grass was so shiny it almost appeared to be made of plastic, the sun so bright and the sky so blue and clear it shone like a five-dimensional hologram painting. This world seemed to be made of Technicolor candy. Even the air was clear and without a breeze, unlike the usual misty fog hanging over San Francisco. I ran my hand over a bleached wood chair, antique in design, yet I could not pinpoint the era in which the chair had been fashioned. The room was furnished in opulent style, with the smell of lush flowers and freshly oiled cherry wood in the air.

A roaring fire burned in the hearth, although the weather outside appeared not to warrant such warmth. A muscular man with a thick dark braid down his back stood in the dark shadows in front of latticed windows, his hands upon his hips. I approached, expecting him to turn and acknowledge me, afraid that if I called out, he would turn and reveal the face of the grinning red-eyed monster in the theater. His hair appeared thick and luminous in the shadows of the firelight. I expected his hands to be black and hairy with claws. He clasped them behind his back. His golden-tanned hands were smooth and perfect, with shiny, smooth nails and thick masculine fingers.

Birds chirped from somewhere inside the room. I gazed upward, seeing a collection of doves, sparrows, and even an owl watching me from the rafters. A magpie hugged its wings to its body, and a bird dropping fell from its bottom, disappearing into thin air before it hit the ground.

I suppose I'd be a bird person, too, if they didn't make such a mess in real life, I thought.

"Perhaps we all would," the man said. He chuckled, then turned and faced me. He was extraordinarily handsome, perhaps about ten years older than I, with chiseled features and piercing hazel green eyes.

He was a man at the peak of his life, muscular yet lithe. He exuded sensuality. I gasped as I gazed, for he intrigued and scared me all at the same time. He was the type of handsome a man should be, without overly perfect features but all arranged in proportion and accord. *Man Beautiful* is what Nancy would call him.

"We all would what?" I stopped next to a carved wooden table and ran my hands nervously along the smooth polished oak and the dragons, cheetahs, birds, and feathers carved upon the surface.

"Be bird people. They are fascinating creatures. Someone once told me birds are inhabited by the spirits of the dead. What do you think of that?"

"It is possible. Truly possible as this world is possible."

"Exactly what I thought you would say. So here we are, Andromeda Jayne. Here we are."

"Auroch?"

"I am." He bowed in a grandiose gesture.

I curtsied half-heartedly in response, just because it felt like the right thing to do. A mocking smile crept over his lips. My face flushed red with embarrassment. "I thought you would be…"

"Ugly? Hideous, with an awful face? Why no, dear Andromeda Jayne. No, no, no. The world in which you live is ugly. People can be so ugly. We in the otherworld are actually quite charming."

"I hate this dress."

"Perhaps because you have not seen how beautiful you are in it. Pleasure to be in your presence. Enchanted, really. I am delighted that you reached out to me. I have been waiting for you for quite some time. You will find that, indeed, if you ever need me, you simply need call, and I shall be there. By your side." He poured a glass of wine from a decanter into a goblet and held it out to me. "For you, to take the edge off our first meeting."

I peevishly wondered if anyone had ever said that to Nancy during her Alcoholics Anonymous meetings and chuckled. "No, thank you." I had never drunk alcohol before and wasn't about to start now. I narrowed my eyes and raised my chin. My dress rustled and I looked down to truly examine my clothing for lack of anything better to do other than stare at Auroch. I discovered I was now clad in an elaborate blue crystal-encrusted gown rich in layers and tulle that would make Cinderella weep with jealousy. My shoes were extraordinary as well, glass, yet within them, my feet floated on air, or so it seemed.

"Perhaps this color is more to your liking," Auroch said.

"Seafoam green has never been a favorite of mine."

"Better now?"

"I really don't like dressing up." I gazed down at my hands, now with delicately painted nails, not the bare surface I usually maintained. My hands reached up to my neck and hair, feeling my strands had been tamed into silk locks, and my neck was covered with a light coating of powder. I pressed my lips together. The sticky stuff I had wiped from my lips earlier turned out to be gloss, not blood. "I know you're not a true mind reader, or you would know I hate dress clothes."

Auroch wore black leather boots that hit just below the knee and clomped pleasantly as he walked toward me and reached for my hand, resplendent in an embroidered tunic and impeccably tailored pants. "It is of no matter at all." He led me to a balcony that was larger and longer than my entire home. "Welcome to the land of Shadowmist."

The view was something out of a princess movie. Even Hyannis would gasp if she saw this.

I was inspired but not thrilled by the view. The presence of Auroch, standing beside me and observing my gaze with his own, brought a sensation of heat to my cheeks. I wished he would stand farther away. I wished I could go back in time, hit delete on the picture Hyannis had sent with her nasty text message, and simply wait for Ben to arrive at my home. I wished Ben and I were riding his motorcycle on the Embarcadero, with joggers, bikers, and couples pushing baby strollers in the background. This world was too pristine, too beautiful. This world was somehow a trick.

I shrank away from Auroch and his prying eyes as he scanned my expression. "Do you wish me to stand farther away from you?"

"Yes." I looked down at my hands. "I mean, no. Actually, yes. Look, I don't mean to be rude. I just—" I sighed as I gazed out at my surroundings. The hills were studded with cherry blossom trees, and between them bubbled a sparkling river. The world of Shadowmist danced in bright hues, with grasses rolling perfectly with the breeze and the sunshine radiating out in cadenced rays. Auroch reached for my hand and grasped it, holding it up high as the sun illuminated his face, bringing out flecks of light brown in his dark hair and endowing him with the shining aura of a god. "I don't understand what this is or who you are. And I hate this dress, too."

I glanced down at my body and discovered I was naked. I shrieked in dismay as I covered my private parts with my hands and backed away while Auroch looked off to the side and gave a merry laugh. My fingers touched the reams of silk and lace that encompassed my previous dress as my mind raced to find the most biting, stinging words I could use to cuss him out.

"Where we begin, we are sure to end. Remember that, Andromeda Jayne, before you reject any more of your dresses. I have existed here for decades, and I come to assist when I am called upon. I wait here for people such as yourself to find me so I can teach you."

"What could you possibly have to teach me?"

"About life. How to fix the links in the broken chain, keeping one so delicate in mind as yourself from breaking beyond repair. To teach about that which is unseen and unheard, yet so essential to your being you cannot exist without. For when the flowers close their buds and rest at night, they recognize not that the night keeps them from burning, wilting, and dying from the perpetual heat of the sun. In their blindness, they worship the sun and forget about the darkness which sustains them. It is the night which shields them, saves them, allows them to survive."

"I'd learn better if I could wear my regular clothes."

"The dress suits you. You'll learn to love the clothes you wear here after a while. I guarantee it. We have quite some time to get to know each other, you and I. I like you, Andromeda Jayne." He placed his hand just below his ribcage and bowed. "I am the master of this land. All you see before you and all that stretches beyond is the land of Shadowmist. My domain."

"This is some kind of hallucination from morphine or something. Let me guess. The hospital found me half dead and wailing about burnt children in my hospital bed. Now I'm drugged up and shuttered in a looney bin. I just had my eighth dose of lithium."

Auroch shrugged. "Perhaps." A smile danced around his beautiful, full lips. He stood, appraising me, sizing me up. My cheeks burned hot. The corner of his mouth lifted in a smile. He knew I thought him beautiful. That I wondered what he thought about me.

"I'm going back inside." I walked quickly and purposefully into the lattice windowed room. Auroch must have stayed behind, for I did not hear his footsteps glide after mine. I whirled to see what he was doing on the balcony.

"Ah!" I exclaimed. He stood right in front of me.

"Go ahead. Explore your new home."

I swallowed hard and reached out to touch anything I could place my hands upon. I picked up a silken cloth from the table with a design that looked like a map sewn upon it. The needle pricked my finger. A bead of blood bubbled up from the wound. I dropped the cloth to the ground and reflexively sucked on the tip.

"Apologies, my lady."

"So, who does needlepoint around here? I wouldn't have thought you were the type."

"You thought correctly. I am not." He clasped his hands behind his back once again and looked up at the birds. The Magpie flew from one rafter to the other, flapping its wings. "Yet as time goes by, I find myself in need of new hobbies."

"Strange," I said as I eyed the offerings on the table.

"What is so strange, Andromeda Jayne?"

"They won't fly down and eat the bread. The birds."

"They are very well cared for. Very well fed. But

they are unimportant. We must only dwell upon the important things, Andromeda Jayne."

"Stop saying my name." My voice sounded paper-thin and wispy. Weak. I cringed at the sound. "I can't stand hearing my real name spoken aloud. I go by AJ."

"Ghosts call out what you hide. You know that. They want you to know that they know. They know everything. What you do when you're alone, all of your secrets. The ghosts know. I know. AJ is such a nothing name. Neither masculine nor feminine nor beautiful or even intriguing. A nothing name. It disturbs me. Andromeda Jayne is fascinating, interesting, hints of the mythical and exotic. You were named for the stars."

"If you expect me to listen, then call me AJ."

"I shall not address you that way. I shall call you my lady, then."

"I am not your lady."

"You mean you are not *a* lady. Yet. And you *will* listen for what else will you do besides stick your fingers in your ears and sing la la la for hours. We have an eternity here, in this dream. You and I. You will go when I say you go. Or you shall stay for an eternity. Therefore, I shall refer to you as *she*."

I stuck my fingers in my ear and did just that. I sang and hummed and chattered to myself. *We'll see who wins this battle of wills.*

Auroch sat and covered his ears with his hands, miming the placing of a set of headphones, before resting his hands on his knees. Quietly, he sat there for minutes upon minutes as I continued my chatter. I continued on and on, watching the light outside the window turn into a dark night with stars, then back into dawn, then onto day, then twilight, over and over, days passed as I sang and sang, and the days passed by quicker. I sang Top 40 songs, pop songs, old rock songs, and some of the jazz songs I could remember from my father's CDs, and when I could not remember any more songs, I sang them all again. I thought for moments, or was it days or hours, that if I kept on singing, I would go crazy, that if one more day passed, I would break, but the days seemed to pass by in a matter of minutes.

The birds on the rafters hooted and chatted with me, singing and singing along. "Wake up, AJ," I said to myself over and over. "Wake up, wake up, WAKE UP!" Soon, the birds picked up the phrase, clamoring and hooting and chattering.

The Magpie flapped its wings and flew from the rafters in a circle, screeching something that sounded like, "Wake up! Wake up!" She flew down and pecked my hand.

"Ouch!" I shouted. Blood trickled down my palm onto the floor.

Auroch rose to his feet and cleared the room in a few long strides. He deftly reached for my throat. My heart pounded. This was the moment he would grip me by the neck. Then, I would snap out of this dream.

The handsome man simply waved his other hand over mine. The blood disappeared.

"It could have been worse. Now, are you ready to listen? For a change, as dear stepmother Nancy would put it?" He held up a finger as I began to retort. "Names by any other name are still simply names. The important thing is that you, she, is here and I am here, and we have much to discuss as to why, for I am sure you are curious. Would you care to dine?"

"After getting bloodied by a bird? You must be joking."

"No matter. I will wait until she is hungry."

"Who?"

He glanced at me dismissively as if I were the

dumbest person in the world.

"Perfect." I examined the smooth, high walls of the palace, searching for a way to escape, even as my stomach growled and gnawed upon itself. I was starving. I was so hungry I could have reached up and eaten one of those birds, for all I could think of looking at them was roast chicken. The room was wide, the size of Addison High's gymnasium, and laden with furniture and expensive knick-knacks. I ran my hands along the buttery silk tapestries, peeking behind them. Auroch chuckled. He sat in a high-backed chair facing the window and turned away from me. Probably some comedy show playing in those invisible headphones, I thought. *Why not? Next thing I know, he'll be telling me he's Lewis Carrol back from the dead, and we're stuck here for an Eterni-Tea. Ha ha.*

Behind an opening between high, lush velvet curtains, I found the escape I was looking for.

Three wooden doors with gold knobs lined the wall. I wrapped my finger around one of the knobs. The heat seared my skin. "Ouch!" I shouted in surprise. Pulling my hand back, I scowled at the solid wood panel that refused to budge. I had expected to throw the door open and run.

"Not a wise choice to touch those quite yet. In any event, you never exit through those doors unless you are given permission."

"Who gives me permission?"

Auroch peeked over the back of his chair. "Your host. We can tarry here for hours, or you can choose to sit with me. If not, perhaps the Other shall take you if you stand too close."

"Who is the Other?"

The man sat back in his chair. His voice carried over the seat back loud and clear. "At times a beast as one you have never seen, at times an angel. At times, a monster. One can never tell, but when the Other takes someone, they never come back. Have you ever seen the work of art titled *Il Prelievo*?"

The work he spoke to sprung to mind. *Il Prelievo*. The Taking. The Baroque-style painting in my father's study at home, in which a young woman clothed in a few skillfully draped cloths with ivory beige skin and chocolate brown hair had been lifted up by a crowd of darkly shrouded beings. The beings lumbered away with her as another woman, presumably her mother, kneeling on the ground. A man in an executioner's garb stood behind the weeping mother. The woman's hand reached back in a perpetual gesture for help, her face turned toward the hooded figure in distress, but none would be given.

"Those are the Others," Auroch intoned. "Trust me, you do not want to see what is under those shrouds." He rose, standing to his full height of six and a half feet. Perhaps more. "Sit with me, and I shall provide explanation."

He gestured to the table, laden with platters of meat, bread, cheese, and fruit. The grapes looked so swollen, purple, and juicy that my mouth watered at the sight of them despite my torrent of emotions.

"I'd really just rather go back home if you don't mind."

"There is no home to go home to. Not quite yet. We shall dine together. For what else do you have to do besides wait? You will learn what I mean very, very soon." He pulled a chair out for me on his right, then took his place at the head of the table. I sat obediently, all fight subdued by my curiosity.

Auroch snapped once. The doors flew open, and into the dimly lit room strode servants in white wigs dressed in layers of taffeta, with puffy sleeves and hats that looked a bit like turbans but were not wrapped about their heads. Straight out of a children's book, they seemed to appear, almost comical in short pants, but their faces were so serious and intent on serving. Held high in their hands were platters of seafood, roast beef, and a whole suckling pig with an apple in its mouth. The suckling pig was placed before Auroch.

A servant snapped the neatly folded napkin on the table open and placed it across my lap. A tureen was placed before me, and a servant lifted the lid to reveal a heap of steaming mashed potatoes. I resisted the urge to shoo the servant away. He bowed, then took a step back in retreat.

I looked up at his face. He had the face of a tusked boar. I gasped and dropped the fork. The servant snorted, his split hoof reaching out and placing a gleaming new piece of silverware by my side.

"No need to be rude," Auroch said, hiding his smile behind a large bejeweled emerald ring.

Another servant whipped open a napkin. He lay the cloth over Auroch's lap. The servant looked up and met my eyes. His face was that of an enormous monkey, his mouth stretched into a grimace. He whooped as his eyes crinkled, and he hopped backward a step or two. I was grateful for the dark shadows in the room, grateful that I did not have to see the monstrous faces of the other servants who were farther away from me.

Auroch raised two fingers and gestured at the servants to leave. They disappeared from beyond the curtains from which they came.

Auroch ripped a piece of skin off the top of… *surprise*… an entree of suckling pig and crunched on it, the greasy fat coating his lips with a gloss that strangely made him all the more handsome. He chewed. I remained still, watching him, trying desperately to understand what sort of dream this was and why it felt so real. Why the smell of roasted pig and pungent cheese filled the air. Why the scent of wine rose from the glasses before us when this was all a dream.

"Where are my manners, dear child?" Auroch said. "Please, eat." He paused, waiting. I picked up a fork.

Auroch grabbed a ladle, ready to heap food onto my plate. He gestured for me to hand my plate to him. I declined. Auroch sat back and surveyed me with one finger resting upon his chin. "She does not eat," he stated. "Perhaps that is why she is far too thin."

"I am not—"

"Silence." Auroch raised a finger. "I am a host who is insulted quite easily." A smile played about his lips. "A warning. She does not want to make me angry."

"What happens?"

"She does not want to see."

I folded up my napkin and placed it back on the table. "I would really like to know why she's here."

"First, she eats. Then I will explain. Is the meal not to your liking?" I shook my head. "Then we shall fix it." He gestured to my place at the table. I looked down, and before me was a steaming hot pepperoni and olive pizza with a ramekin of ranch dressing on the side.

"Now, eat." I tried to resist, but my stomach rumbled with hunger.

The appearance of the dish induced a feeling of calmness, as now I knew this was a dream. This had to be a dream, some hospital painkiller-induced dream that had me craving pizza. *Pizza for dum-dums*. The food brought Hyannis's smug smile to mind. I placed the slice back on the plate and pushed the meal away.

I glanced up at Auroch. His playful expression

made me feel as if we shared a private joke, although what that joke was, I had no idea. I looked down and could swear I felt him sitting still and watching me. I looked up again. He delicately lifted a fork with a sliver of pork fat to his lips. When I looked back down, a slice of chocolate cake had replaced the pizza on my platter, dripping with hot fudge and served with a fresh scoop of vanilla ice cream.

"It was you. You spoke to me in the theater at Addison High?"

"Yes."

"You looked like a monster."

"I tend to be theatrical. We were in a theater, after all."

I took a bite of the moist chocolate cake, oozing with fudge filling. The delicacy was so rich and decadent that I could almost feel a pimple about to sprout from my chin. I placed my napkin on the table.

"Maybe I do, too."

"And who are you?" His grin spread wide, the grin of a shark about to devour its kill. The butterflies in my stomach and the sick feeling in my throat made me the complete opposite of the ever-calm, hookah-smoking caterpillar in Alice In Wonderland who asked the same question. *Whoooo are youuuu?* For try as I could, I could not shake the feeling that Auroch was someone very familiar.

"You tell me first."

"Whoooo are youuuu?" he said, just like the caterpillar intoned in Alice In Wonderland.

I startled. Could the demon read my thoughts?

"Mr. Auroch, I—"

"Just Auroch. You have to mind your comfort level. I know I will."

Handsome or not, he talked like a creepy old man.

"I think I hit my head in an accident."

His eyes flickered as if to say go on.

"Is this… the afterlife? Am I dead?"

Auroch's canine teeth were pointy, a striking contrast to his handsome face. His eyes narrowed on his plate, and he devoured every bite of the meal. He ate so much that there was no more meat left on the bones of the suckling pig and only tiny bits of cheese and crumbs of bread on the serving platters. He filled himself so vulgarly that I wondered to myself how he could not weigh four hundred pounds if he ate every meal in such a manner. The nagging feeling that things were very out of sorts made my stomach nauseous, which disturbed me yet again with the certainty that this dinner was more than a dream.

"Come with me." Auroch threw his napkin down, rose, and ambled to my side of the table. "Take my hand." His deep hazel eyes hypnotized me. I had no choice but to place my hand in his. His large hand made my body feel delicate as he wrapped his palm around the side of my waist to lead me to the edge of the balcony. I gazed over the precipice, hundreds of feet over the rolling hills below, with only an occasional rock rising from the landscape to break my fall.

"Why am I here?"

"Because where we begin, we are sure to end."

"Help me begin."

I was sure at this moment he would push me off, and I would go tumbling down. But he only positioned his body in front of mine, looming over me. Why was his nearness so enticing rather than disturbing? My cheeks grew hot with the nearness of his flesh.

"You are one of the lucky ones, a dreamer. So many languish in darkness in life, in that in-between place somewhere in the middle of life and death. Some go straight to where they are destined to go. Only a chosen few are drawn to me, and I to them. We are both keepers of the light and movement in the shadows." He sighed and shuddered. I found his show of emotion moving as his lack of command over his body in that instant made him seem tender, more human.

"Who are you?"

"One who understands. For I lingered in dreams once, too. And now I am the master here." He placed his hands on my shoulders. "Someday, you too shall be the master of your own realm. And I shall see to it that you have your heart of heart's desire."

"I already have everything I want or need." I pulled away from him and placed my elbows on the ornate rail of the balcony, hearing the train of my dress shuffle as I leaned forward and contemplated this picturesque world. "Why am I wearing this again?"

"Be truthful."

"I hate this dress."

"No," he said as he stepped toward me. "Be truthful. Do you have your heart's desire?"

"Yes." My voice wavered with uncertainty.

"She is lavished with attention from her parents. One can see she is the favored child. Especially after the little Frances arrived. When she is lonely, which is quite often, she stares out of her window at the street, where fine cars with happy families inside drive up and down the block. Not one person sees the lost girl watching them from upstairs. There is a shadow of her in the window even after she is gone, and this is how I found her. Sad people have shadows that linger."

"So what?"

"Even her own father feels a twinge of guilt every night he arrives home for not loving more what will never truly be his wife's own. He wanted his new wife to love her, the relic of a relationship lost. Cruel nature, which rips a mother from her daughter far before her time."

"What is your point?"

"Care, care, young lady. The world is filled with poetry and likenesses. Those who are able to envision the likenesses have the makings of genius. The dusk crowns the end of a day, the dawn heralds it, the young lady rages silently. One thing is so very much like another, you see. So alike and yet so different, all of us. But god, monster, or mortal, we all desire the same thing."

"What?"

"Death to those who betray us."

"I'm sorry, but I don't know what you're talking about." I pinched the sleeve of my dress, pushing the fabric in so I could feel my skin. Pain resounded throughout my arm as I gripped a tiny bit of skin as hard as I could. "I wish I could just wake up."

"I can help you obtain what you want most in the world. The thing you most desire. You only need ask."

I hoped that was true, for Auroch was far too charming, as if he knew exactly what I needed, even when I did not know. Far too handsome and cajoling. He radiated an aura that could bring a saint to its knees, and here he was, standing in front of me persuasively. *What I wanted most...* I tried my best to squelch the thoughts, yet so many popped into my mind. The faces of those I harbored strong feelings for swam about my mind. Ben, Caslin, and... Hyannis.

Auroch smiled. A plush chair was situated on the balcony. He walked over to it, sat, and crossed a black boot over so that his ankle rested upon his knee. A platter of cheese and fruit lay on a plate on the side table next to the chair, along with a cutting knife and a goblet of wine. Tipping his head back, he tilted his face into the warmth of the sun.

"Nothing will ever be as it was. You will never wake up unless I permit you. I am disinclined to do so as things stand now. You have a problem with giving, Andromeda Jayne. I need you to *give*." His entire body relaxed as if he were about to take a nap.

"Give what?"

His eyes remained closed even as his lips parted with a sigh. "You missed your chance, Andromeda Jayne. You missed your chance to become a real person, but you never had one. Because you are a dead woman's child. You never had a chance at all. Call it fate, call it unfair, call it the plain and simple fact that whatever fate created us doles out gifts unequally, but you never had a chance. Even though you try to be perfect. *Just perfect.*"

I lunged toward him, picking up the knife on the table beside him and holding it to his throat. "If this is just a dream, I could stab you, and your blood will spill all over this pretty balcony of yours, and then I'll wake up, won't I? Then maybe I'll never see you again."

His eyes opened, and his mouth curled into a lazy smile. I froze, suddenly conscious of how close my face was to his. He wrapped a hand around my waist and pulled me even closer while he gripped my wrist firmly.

He pressed his lips against my ear softly, perhaps a hair's breadth away from touching my skin. He breathed an enticing scent. I could almost feel the softness of his lips upon my face. Even worse, I wanted so desperately to feel them for just a moment. I both desired and despised him at that moment.

"I will take all of your pain and sadness if you will just call upon me in the world of the living. Give me your anger, your heartache, your sadness, your deepest, darkest desire. Make a bargain. Make a trade. You will know when the time comes."

I sliced the blade across his face, then gasped. The

beautiful skin upon his cheek opened, but nary a drop of blood spilled. The seam closed just as quickly.

"I knew you had a death instinct within you."

His hand shot out as he clamped his fingers over my other wrist, hard, his fingertips pressing into my skin. There was no pain, only the pleasure of being held tightly within his grasp. My hand lost its strength. My will became his. The knife clattered to the marble floor.

I sighed with resignation and crumbled as much as his grip would allow me to. His barrage had beaten me down into sheer exhaustion. I wished I were in Mr. Spinky's class, listening to him drone about immortal jellyfish. I wished I were in the school library, nose-deep in a ratted paperback copy of *Long Story Lost*. I wished I were lying down in my room on the cherry sundae bed, listening to Nancy bang around a hundred pots and pans as she made a cup of tea in the kitchen. I hoped this nightmare would end soon. Perhaps if I flattered him, he would let me wake.

I sank down to the floor, a heap of dejected taffeta. "Fine. You're stronger than me, smarter than me, living better than me in this grand palace of yours. What else does it say in your crystal ball?"

"Your heart is betrothed to the one who brought you to me. The mysterious Ben Bach."

"He didn't bring me to you."

"All he had to do was say my name. Once my name is spoken, then I am no longer there. What a wonderful time for a riddle. Once the name is spoken, I am no longer known. Who am I?" He waited as I glared at him. "The answer is Silence. Silence becomes you."

"You're some figment of my imagination in a dream that doesn't make sense."

"This will all soon make a great deal of sense."

"Then why not just clear up who you are now so

we can move on."

Auroch crouched down beside me and offered a hand to lift me up. "Tell me your desire. The thing you want the most."

He brought me closer to him so that my back pressed against his front. The thought of resisting paralyzed me. I couldn't resist. He was a spider, and I was trapped in his web. My head lolled to the side, exposing my neck. Exhaustion overcame my body as I closed my eyes. He could have sunk his teeth into my neck, ripped me apart with his bare hands, or stabbed a knife through my back.

"Consider that I have the power to grant you what you desire the most," he murmured softly in my ear.

He sighed in a way that I knew I had touched a nerve inside him. Surrounding my waist with his hands, he used this as an opportunity to hold my body close to his. "I am pressed for time. Another soul makes passage to this place. I must make room quickly, and you must leave. Simply grant me a small request."

"What?"

"Allow me the courtesy of visiting you, of watching over you in your dreams. I shall serve as your guardian. Say yes."

This is only a dream, I told myself. *Only a dream.* Still, he had no business in my dreams or my life. "Yes, but—"

"Yes?"

"Yes, but I have a few more questions—"

"You said the word. They heard you." He gestured to the birds sitting upon the rafters. They cocked their heads, gazing quizzically with round eyes. One stretched its wings out and flapped them. The Magpie cooed a long, sad sound.

"Off you go." Auroch gestured to the far end of

the room where the wall curved as if we were truly under an enclosed version of the dome at the Palace of Fine Arts. "Go to the stars. For you were named for the stars. "

I shuddered. His haunting words seemed a premonition.

Three doors were widely spaced apart upon the curved wall. "The next time you visit, which shall be soon, you will be allowed to make a choice. You will be given the chance to obtain your heart's desire. Through one of these doors, you shall find what you want most in the world. Through another, you may find the apparition of all human fears. The Other. The Taker, who will certainly spirit you away to a horrifying place. Within the third, you will find a reward. A reward which will reveal the cost that shall set the spirits at Addison High free. And deliver your enemies to your hands.

"The next time we see each other, you will choose one of these doors to leave. My regards to your adored Ben. Today is, at best, is a beautiful memory. At worst, forgotten with the passage of time. But you shall not forget me."

"What do you mean my enemies' lives?"

"Our time is finished. Avia will show you the way out," Auroch dismissed with a wave, striding toward the window and staring out at the valley. "It will please me to see you again soon."

The black magpie descended from its perch on a beam, flying down and flapping to signal me to follow.

Behind the curtains from whence the servants had emerged, a set of double doors with an *A* crest emblazoned upon crystallized glass opened and closed on their own for our passage. The hallway stretched out long and dark. The shock of cold hit as we walked further away from Auroch's domain. The magpie's wings flapped in front toward a dim light at the end of the hall.

My mouth tasted coppery, perhaps from the air in the dank hall. More likely from whatever medication the hospital had doped me with.

Steps before the end of the tunnel, The Magpie turned and landed. She lit upon the ground and pulled her wings over her head. As her wings pulled back, a young woman stood. Her hair shone in dark rivulets, and her lips were rosy and pink.

" I will help you to understand," she said in a hushed tone.

"Why?"

"I know what he wants from you. You are his now, but maybe we can help each other find a way out. For both of us. He'll hold us until…" She glanced over my shoulder. A look of terror crossed her face. "He's coming." She transformed back into a magpie, flying fast away from me through a tiny opening in the hall ceiling and high into what looked like a candlelit sky.

The sound of sandpapery feet scraping upon concrete resounded within the narrow cylinder. I whirled around. An enormous spider scurried down the hallway in my direction, its massive, hairy body taking up so much room it had to crawl up the walls to make its way, going around in circles as it neared. My mouth opened to scream, but no sound escaped. Red eyes. Fangs opened wide and closed, the points coming back together.

I bolted toward the opening, feeling one spider limb scratch my ankle as I reached the exit. I jumped, then fell quickly, all the while falling, falling. Auroch's palace was made up of one high floor that floated above the candy land terrain, with nothing above or below, just illusions. Just one circular floor suspended in midair above all.

I hit the ground hard. My body bounced on the grass as if I had landed on an inflatable jumpy tent cushion. The force pushed me back up high into the air with arms and legs swinging to grasp something, anything.

The spider loomed over the exit, all beady eyes and fangs and wiry hair. The thing surveyed me with a cold glare as its fangs opened wide. With horror, I watched the enormous arachnid drawback and leap high into the air over me, floating and falling over me in the feathery way that only spiders can. In a second, we would collide. In seconds, the creature would clutch my body in its spindly legs, trap me down on the grass, sink in its fangs, weave a web immediately over my body, and hold me entrapped as its next meal.

I screamed.

Chapter Eighteen
Awakening

The hospital machines beeped in rapid succession as I screamed and bolted upright. I pulled the intravenous tube from my arm. The puncture in my wrist spurted out blood and a clear fluid for a second or two before the gush stopped. The gash it left looked like a spider bite. I leaped out of the bed and backed up against the wall. I turned and screamed at the feel of something brushing against my shoulder, coming face to face with a sheet of paper reading "Your Flu Shots, Facts to Know." Air from a vent lifted the corner of the paper, causing it to reach out at me like a spidery leg. As the edge of the paper brushed my upper arm, I screamed again.

A searing pain shot up from my arm as my legs crumpled beneath me. I fell into a heap on the floor with a loud clunk and another shock of pain. The burst of adrenaline shielded me from the pain of my injuries. Now, the agony radiated full force. I moaned. My hands found their way to my head. I sighed with relief at the feel of my hair. Perhaps they had only shaved a few of my locks off to stitch the head wound.

A gray-haired nurse and dark blemishes rushed in and pressed a button on the machine. The machine stopped beeping. "Your vein might have collapsed." She made a *tsk!* sound with her tongue. "Back to bed now."

I obeyed. "My wrist hurts. And my legs."

"You were in an accident. Nothing that requires bandages or stitches, but you will feel pain for a little while. Just a little sprain in the wrist is all."

I reached to feel the back of my head. There were no wounds or lumps. "I bled all over the pavement."

"Blood? No. You merely hit your head very hard,

that's all." She stuck the needle back into my arm. Tears burned in my eyes as I felt the sting, not so much from the pain but from the thought that the giant spider had somehow shrunk and was lurking in the sheets, perhaps manifesting its presence through the itching I felt.

"Was all of the blood from Ben?" I shuddered.

"Perhaps. It's okay if you want to sleep," the nurse cooed as she reinserted the IV tube. "They'll be releasing you soon to go home."

I stayed awake, forcing my eyes to remain open until a doctor in a white coat strode in. He reminded me of an actor Nancy was fond of in the old daytime shows she used to watch in a drunken haze. Some guy with a hairdo straight out of the 1980s that looked like an angel's wings curling over his forehead and scalp.

"I've given you the okay to leave," the doctor declared. "The nurse will give you a release packet. Your family has gone on vacation, but they gave me instructions to release you to your neighbor, a Mrs. Eleanor Faria."

"Mrs. Faria? But what about my parents?"

The doctor cleared his throat. "That's all I am authorized to tell you. Mrs. Faria is right outside the door. Elise," he said to the nurse, "would you grab a wheelchair for Miss Covington, please?"

"Where is my father? Can he come to pick me up?"

"I'm sure Mrs. Faria will explain everything to you. I can help you with questions about your condition. As it is, you will be discharged, but you must stay home from school until further notice. You write with your right hand? Is that correct?"

"Yes."

"You have a mild sprain in your right wrist that will need time to heal. At least six weeks. Mrs. Faria used to be a teacher at the Community College of San Francisco before she retired. She's a very pleasant woman. I'm sure she'll be happy to keep you up to speed until it's time for you to go back." The doctor's eyebrows raised quizzically. "Are you not willing to go with her?"

"Willing? Willing!" My voice bordered on hysteria. The *wh wh wh* sound escaped from my mouth half a dozen times before I could form a sentence. "Where is my dad? Why can't he come for me?"

"This is outside of my jurisdiction, AJ. The papers on file say we are to release you to Mrs. Faria if your custodians are absent. Perhaps it would be best if you speak to her. I'll send her in."

Hospital visits always reminded me of bad high school plays, where one character came in and then another only to refute or reinforce what the other actor just said. Everyone who had a part seemed to be trying to make themselves as worthy as possible. I couldn't wait to leave. The nurse came in, as expected, and pulled my IV tube out gently.

"I hear you'll be going home now, darling. Be happy. Some stay here for a very long time." Her blue eyes shone thoughtfully, staring off into space. She chuckled. "The transition from here to home will be quick for you, I promise." She pressed a button and the bed hummed as the half underneath my back rose so that I was sitting upright. She squeezed my foot and smiled before she left the room.

Mrs. Faria breezed in through the door with a gentle expression, wearing a pastel pink suit that made her look as if she had just come from an English tea party.

"AJ, my dear. Oh, my darling dear." She perched on the edge of my bed. "Your mother and father left yesterday on their honeymoon. They called it a babymoon. I hear your stepmother is expecting. They had no idea you'd come out of the coma so quickly. I'll stay with you and house-sit while your parents and Frances are gone." Her mouth seemed set in that worried zigzag on pencil drawings. "They'll be home soon, and when they come home, I am sure they will explain everything."

"I was in a coma, and they left me?" The sentence contained not a note of bewilderment or any expression. It simply emerged flatly from my mouth as if I were saying *Carlos the cat went outside*. I liked the fact that outrage at their neglect simmered underneath Mrs. Faria's eyes.

"Come now. I'll take you home and make you a nice pot of chicken soup, and all will be better soon. You'll see."

****

Mrs. Faria wrapped her arms around me and led me through the open door of my home. She hung her Easter Egg hat up on the coat rack. I buried my face in my dad's brown wool overcoat and sniffed back a tear. Mrs. Faria removed her gloves and patted me gently on the back. "I made a room for you in the guest room," she said, "so you wouldn't have to trudge up and down the stairs. Would you like me to bring down your bedspread from home?"

The thought of the comforter with stems and cherry fruit all over it made me think of Nancy, and hurt coursed through my body. "No, thank you."

"All right." Mrs. Faria opened the door to the guest room, which looked warm and inviting, with a fire burning in the hearth and a bed with a simple blue coverlet and some practical pillows. I had never spent much time in this room, as no one had, really, since Nancy had terrible anxiety when guests were scheduled to come over. Over the past few years, we had stopped having company altogether. Nancy refused to keep in touch with her parents, and my father would fly out to his hometown and stay in a hotel to see his ailing mother until she finally passed away last year, as his father did before I was born.

"Lie down and rest. I'll be back with some supper and a sponge bath."

I stretched out on the bed and stared up at the ceiling, praying the feeling of emptiness would go away and I would understand why my father wasn't here to welcome me home. The more I thought about what I would say to him, the more the emptiness twisted and stabbed inside the pit of my stomach, and then the tears began. I cried, all the while listening to the sounds of pots clanging and Mrs. Faria humming in the kitchen.

Auroch's words crept into my head. *You missed your chance to become a real person, but you never had one. Because you are a dead woman's child. You never had a chance at all. Call it fate, call it unfair, call it the plain and simple fact that whatever fate created us doles out gifts unequally, but you never had a chance.*

Oh, to hell with you, Auroch, I vowed to say when I saw him next. To that, he would merely smile, that devilishly handsome yet terribly condescending smile. *But of course.* I struggled to stay awake even though I was tired. I didn't want to see Auroch ever again, or Avia. All I wanted to do was talk to Ben.

I picked up the handle of the decorative vintage phone on the nightstand and dialed his cell phone number. The line rang ten or twelve times before I slammed the phone back down on the receiver.

"Mrs. Faria," I called into the kitchen.

"Yes, hon?" She appeared in the doorframe with half of a mostly peeled butternut squash cradled in her hand.

"What happened to Ben?"

She looked puzzled. "Ben?"

"The boy who was with me during the accident. The boy on the motorcycle. He was injured, too. He was bleeding."

Mrs. Faria pressed her lips together in that worried zig-zag line again. "Oh. Yes. The boy." She sank down next to me on the bed. "Maybe we should talk about this another time. You've been through so much. The doctors watched over you for over a week. You were in a coma, then you woke up screaming. They said you looked coherent. I even went in when they said you were up and fine. Talking again. Then you began screaming. Sometimes, they would sedate you. Sometimes, you would pass out."

"Screaming about what?"

"None of that matters right now. What matters is that you woke up, and you're here now. I listened in on the conversations amongst the doctors, and they were unsure whether to keep you in the medical facility or to transfer you to a mental hospital. Perhaps you should take a nap."

"Please." I grasped her free hand in mine. "Tell me what happened to Ben."

Her expression was enough. Her eyes told me everything I needed to hear. "AJ, Ben is not in the same place as we are."

"Why? How? He had a helmet on!"

"Oh, sweetie. It wasn't enough. He didn't make it through." She stroked my hair with her hand. Her crepe paper skin smelled like baby powder. "You know, sweetheart, I've lived in the house next door all of my life, I have. It was my father's house and his father's house before him. The place was built in 1910 after the Great Quake and has always been ours. Dagan has a pretty house of his own in a sunny city south of here. He'll probably put the house up for sale when I'm gone. I wouldn't blame him. Why, the money he could make off that house would set his kids up for life. College tuition, a nest egg, some money to invest, everything. AJ, my dear, I'll stay with you here as long as you need me.

"I saw it all the whole accident through the window of my home. I've never seen an accident like that one in all my life. Never seen a boy who would want to protect a gal so much he'd try to stop a bus."

I shook my head once, twice, then again. Surely life couldn't change so quickly, from learning I was adopted to losing Ben and suffering injuries that would keep me home for... how long? The doctor said I'd regain the use of my hand in six weeks, but what about...?

"When can I go back to school?"

Mrs. Faria's lips pressed tightly together. "Not for a while, sweetheart. It's possible you may have to skip the rest of this year. Let's make this promise to each other. We'll do our best to keep up on your schoolwork together. I teach, you learn. Our goal will be to get you back to school after Winter Break. How does that sound?" I nodded, feeling like the real me was hovering somewhere around my body rather than inside it. "Good. Take a nap, and we'll have some dinner. Then we'll hit the books. Unless you feel like you should rest?"

"I just... I don't know. Maybe I should rest for a bit. Has Caslin called?"

"No, sweetie. I'll go to the cell phone store as soon as I can to pick you up a new one. Just give me a few weeks. I'm supposed to stay and observe you and call the doctor every day to let him know how you're doing."

Mrs. Faria and I dined on a meal of homemade

chicken soup and warmed sourdough bread with butter. I wandered back into my room, falling into a dark, dreamless sleep. When I awoke, I stared at the ceiling with the first light of morning seeping in through the window blinds. "Ben," I cried. "Oh, Ben." My head ached, my arms and back ached, my whole body reverberated with pain. The worst pain pierced my chest, where my body met my soul, perhaps. The loss of Ben was intolerable.

"Can you see me?" a voice said.

I startled. Was that really a voice or my imagination. I pressed down on my elbows and sat up. Swinging my legs over the side of the bed, I rushed to the blinds and yanked them open.

The scene where the accident had taken place looked calm and tranquil, just one wide tree-lined street in an affluent part of the city, with tourists ambling by and a city bus rumbling in the distance. I could almost see Ben there, parking his motorcycle and pulling off his helmet. I could see him. I could see ghosts. Both of us knew that.

"Ben," I whispered as I leaned my forehead on the cool glass. "I have to see you.

I glanced at the calendar on the side table. October 30. Tomorrow night was Halloween, where the veil between the living and the dead was at its thinnest. I would go to Ben's home when Mrs. Faria fell asleep and find his spirit there.

Chapter Nineteen
Halloween Night

So there I was, standing before the mirror in Ben's bedroom on Halloween night with his ghostly facade staring back at me. Oh, the agony of being worlds away from him was too much to bear.

You don't have to die to know a thing or two about death. You shouldn't have to. I could see them. The ghosts. Perhaps I always could. Sometimes, there's just one incident in life that turns our minds inside out in such a way that maybe thins the barrier between our souls and our physical bodies, and there they are. And when we can see them, we realize they were always there, dancing around like flames above our heads waiting for us to notice them. Wanting, wishing, waiting to ask, "Can you see me?" Because everyone wants to be seen.

Our fingers touched through the glass. Tentatively, I allowed his palm to meet mine as his face was slowly revealed in the mirror. He clasped his fingers around mine. Ben stepped through the mirror with a bewildered smile. My eyes filled with tears as I felt his fingertips upon mine, the feel of his skin so acute his fingertips could have very well printed themselves on my hand. But he didn't have fingerprints anymore. Because he was dead. Because he was a ghost.

"AJ." He sighed. He wrapped his arms around me. He may have even kissed me on the head, but I felt nothing. Of course, I felt nothing. He was a ghost. "AJ?"

I clutched him in my arms, nothing but empty air. I could see him. That was enough for now. "Ben. I'm sorry. I'm so very sorry."

"No apologies. You did nothing wrong."

"I did." I sank down upon the navy blue coverlet on his bed. "This is my fault. If I hadn't been so angry, I would have heard you coming. I would have seen the car. Hyannis sent me a photo of herself and Caslin and everyone in their crowd making fun of me, and I was blinded by anger. All I could think about was showing the picture to Caslin and exposing Hyannis for the horrible person she actually is. Then it all happened so fast. The accident."

"What happened wasn't your fault."

"It is Ben. You deserve life."

Ben placed his hand upon mine.

"Can you feel my skin?" I said. "I can't feel yours."

"I can feel yours. I can feel it the way it used to be, soft and sweet. Every time I touched you, I could feel my heart quicken inside of me, and I feel it now. I'm telling you this because I may never be able to tell you again. I'm telling you this because I don't know when I'll see you again, if we'll ever get to speak like this, if I'll stop being able to feel your touch after some time. From the moment I met you, I wanted nothing more than to be with you, always. For my entire life. You know that now, don't you? You know I would do anything to be with you."

I nodded. Tears fell as I gazed at his hand upon mine. I wanted to be able to feel him, to touch him, to bring him back to life. "My father told me the name I had been given in the village before I had been cast out was Anirnaq Anguta."

"I'm glad he changed it." Ben grinned.

I laughed, then clutched his hands and grew somber. "Listen. The name means Angel of Death. Remember the skeleton woman in Lake Stinson. She kissed me, and I released her soul."

"I remember. Don't kiss me. Otherwise, we might not be able to visit again."

"Please don't make jokes."

"I'm sorry. I was suicidal once. Remember? I'm all about humor now. You know what's funny?"

"What?"

"Jokes. Okay, I'll stop. I promise." His glowing eyes stared into mine.

He was silly as always. How could he be dead?

"It hurts me because of the way we are now. *You* should be alive, not me. You died saving me. Just put your arms around me and hold me tight. If you can feel me, that's good enough."

He embraced me and held my body close to his. I wished I could feel the warmth of his body or what I remembered his warmth to be. He was dead and cold, nothing but air. I cursed Hyannis and her horrid ways. Tightening my lids together, I cursed her with all my might. I cursed her with every ounce of hatred for as long as I could. Then I cried and cried. Hours passed as we lay intertwined.

"Kiss me. I won't breathe in."

"You know we can't take that chance, AJ."

"You're right. Probably not the best idea. So, when's the funeral?"

Ben shifted his body so he lay a few inches away and not right up next to me as he was before. His entire body glowed with an ethereal light. "It has not taken place yet, but when it does, I'm sure relatives I've never seen before will show up. People will cry. Idiot cousins will do some underage drinking while their parents are in the other room and throw up in the bathroom, and no one will notice. It will be a pretty basic funeral."

"Do you need some time alone?"

"No, stay right here. As long as you can, with me.

There are some things I need to explain to you. Better yet, I'll show them to you. Let's take a walk." I heard a car start in the garage on the first floor of Ben's home. The garage door closed. "Coast is clear," Ben said. "Not that she could see anyway." He rummaged through his drawers and pulled on a t-shirt and jeans. I marveled at his glorious body as he dressed.

All I wanted to do was lie down with him and place my head on his chest yet again. Perhaps the sensation was only a memory, but I could hear his heart beating in a rhythm so enchanting and beautiful, a song that made me want to weep. He stood and gazed at me for a long, long time.

"Come on," he said. We walked down the stairs.

I did as he said. We trudged out of the house and up to the sidewalk. His steps were heavy, naturally, with the walk of the dead. I linked my arm through his. He shot me a wistful smile. We headed toward a neighborhood on the border of Chinatown. A grocery store cart filled with vegetables and spiced exuded an exotic smell. The vendor acknowledged us without looking up as he removed stacks of celery from a cardboard box.

After rounding a corner, we came to a hospital. "St. Simon's Convalescent Home," the sign read. The glass double doors parted when we stepped on a wide front mat. Ben strode inside, past a desk where two elderly ladies in pink uniforms chatted. We walked down the hallway to an area where people shuffled behind plate glass. A husky guy, perhaps a little older than Ben, sat in a wheelchair before a game table.

"That's Kelly," Ben said. "Kelly Rose."

Kelly's head lolled about and faced our direction. He lifted up his hand in greeting. Ben and I waved back. "He sees them, too. The ghosts. He has met Auroch before. Now he lives here, crippled, brain damaged. We talked about the in-between world. I took him for a walk last week, and we saw The Magpie. I know who The Magpie is now."

"Who is she?"

"She was the daughter of the family that owned the sagging brown boot house we passed on our way to Penatisimo, the Mediterranean restaurant I took you to. She came back from her first year at St. Charles University. Something terrible happened to her there, something so terrible that for years, she wore the same clothes all the time and painted her face with the same makeup she wore the night of the incident. The house began to slide into a sinkhole. Her mother and father begged her to pack her things when they were going to move, but she was convinced that she was unsafe outside of the home. Convinced that if she left, whatever happened to her would happen again. Her mother packed her things for her. The night before the moving van arrived, she hung herself from the porch. She was sent back to the sagging brown boot house by Auroch to walk an eternity upon the earth in search of her lost soul."

"How do you know?"

"I thought she was going to act crazy, so I started to tell her off, but Kelly started talking to her in that friendly way he has, and she softened. She didn't feel threatened by him."

"Her name is Avia. I met her in Shadowmist. Part of her lives in Shadowmist with Auroch, and part of her must live here as a ghost. She hasn't realized she's dead, I don't think."

"Yes." Ben nodded. "We spoke. She thinks she is dreaming. She thinks she still has a home with a computer and that her parents like to keep her room dark because that's what she likes. She thinks she dreams of

Auroch every night because he once asked her if he could see her in her dreams while she was still alive."

I shuddered as I remembered the words Auroch had spoken to me. *Allow me the courtesy of visiting you, of watching over you in your dreams. Say yes.*

I had said yes.

"She looks so much older than nineteen."

"Of course. She rots here on earth. Her soul lives with Auroch. And she is a beautiful soul."

Ben's gaze fixed upon Kelly. The thick scruff under Kelly's chin made him look menacing, even in a wheelchair. He stared intently at a chess board as he played with a man with heavily hooded eyes he struggled to keep open. His head slowly turned again toward our direction.

"Hi, Kelly," Ben whispered. Kelly pointed, his voice a mere murmur behind the glass wall. In his excitement, he knocked the chessboard over and sent the pieces scrambling all over the floor.

"Kelly Rose is the boy you got into a fight with. The boy who fell from the wall."

"He's in that wheelchair for life. Still has mental issues, only they are much worse. He awoke from the surgery with serious brain damage. His mother had to quit her job to take care of him full-time, taking him back and forth to hospitals. His father left their family. Just as my father did. All that anger I had inside over what happened with my father brought Kelly to the same end. Anger revisited one hundred-fold upon someone else. During my first visit to the hospital, before they operated, Kelly was fine. I apologized, and we shook hands. I swam out into the sea, and… when I came to visit Kelly again, his mother told me how he fell asleep and didn't wake up the same. Said the docs told her he might, so every time Kelly went to sleep, she prayed he'd wake up better. But he never did. His mother wheeled him in and he grinned like I was an old friend. He doesn't remember any of the fight. He thinks I'm his friend and that we've always been friends. I owe him what little I can do to make up for what I stole from him.

"Because when Auroch offered me a choice in Shadowmist, I gave him Kelly. I traded Kelly for my own life. I was declared dead after I tried to drown myself in the sea. Auroch gave me the dark gift of life, and Kelly was my trade."

I placed a supportive hand on his shoulder. "No one will answer when Kelly calls your phone. Oh God, Ben, this is my fault yet again. Can you find a way to put Kelly and I in touch? I could help him any way I can, but at least be a friend to replace losing you."

"You can come visit him anytime. I know he will appreciate it." A nun shrouded in a white habit rolled a cart stacked with medication down the hall. She shot us a quizzical look. "Let's go." Ben placed a hand on my elbow. "There's one more thing I have to show you. Then you must make me a promise."

"Anything."

Ben waved goodbye to Kelly, who flailed his arm back and forth over his head, reminding me of the audience in the Brazil and USA soccer camp match that my dad watched on television back in the Nineties. *Ole oleeee... ole oleeee!* My hand flew up in a goodbye wave as well. Kelly shot me a wary stare and returned to his game of chess.

We walked out of the hospital. The thick, gray fog had rolled in over the streets. Ben kept his head down and his hands in his pockets. The pedestrian signal peeked through the mist. The flashing red hand on the pedestrian signal seemed to be the only thing that stood between us and becoming flattened out in the middle of the city street. Well, between myself and such a fate. The car would likely pass through the ghost of Ben.

I watched him from the corner of my eye. The ethereal, fluorescent light surrounded him again. "AJ," he said without looking in my direction.

"Yes?"

"Nothing. Just making sure you're still there. The fog is pretty thick."

"Where are we going?" I asked as we passed through North Beach and the giddy crowds of evening revelers dressed like superheroes and fairies and go-go dancers. The lights from the restaurants illuminated our path. We turned down another street that was dark, with only a few residential buildings looming over us. Church bells clanged the hour of nine o'clock at night.

"My mom gave me some tickets for a Halloween party cruise on the Hornblower," Ben said. "We could go for a boat ride if you'd like."

"Sure. If that's what you want to do. I'll feel a little awkward on a boat by myself."

Ben stared straight ahead as he walked on beside me. "The boat might be pretty empty. There haven't been many parties on it since that guy fell off and died last year. Mostly tourists. I don't think many will be going out on the bay on a weekday Halloween, especially on a chilly night like this."

As we approached Fisherman's Wharf, colorful lights twinkled from the shops hawking cheap glassware and shirts proclaiming "Alcatraz Escapee or Fresh Off the Rock." The smell of fried fish hung in the air. A seagull bounced upon the pavement, its beak tinged with blood. Auroch's lair in Shadowmist sprung to mind with his collection of rafter birds. I turned to Ben, wondering if he remembered Shadowmist. He stared straight ahead at the churning water over the pier, once again exuding an air of inner struggle as he resisted meeting my eyes.

We strode onto a ramp and boarded a ferry boat cruise. Our footfalls echoed on the stairs as we climbed to the third level of the boat. We stood at the edge and stared out at the water. The black sea foamed as the boat pulled away from the dock.

"What if someone checks?" I asked.

Ben withdrew two Hornblower cruise tickets from his pocket. He held them out so that they flapped in the wind for a few moments.

"Then we'll need only one." Our footsteps sounded in metallic echo as we walked up to the highest deck.

Ben shoved both tickets back into his pockets. A cheesy narrator's voice came over the loudspeaker, talking about Al Capone's time on The Rock. A lone couple in skeleton bodysuits carried plastic cups in their hands and squeezed by us. "AJ, I need you to promise something to me. Right now."

"Anything, Ben."

He grasped my hands in his. We settled down into a bench at the top. His voice sounded hoarse. "Promise me, no matter what happens while we are on this boat ride, you will not leave my side. You will stay with me. I'm going to show you something you aren't going to expect. The fog lifts the spirits, remember?"

The heady wind blowing in from the Pacific Ocean whipped my hair against my face. I pulled a few strands free from my lips. The boat horn honked loud and long, a melancholy protest of a journey into the rough tide.

"Whatever you're going to show me, I've already seen!" I shouted. "Shadowmist. Auroch and his bird pets! The three doors!"

Ben leaned his head back and shot a look up at the

sky before fixing his gaze upon me again. "The three doors! Tell me you didn't open one!"

"I didn't!"

"The three doors represent three wishes, but you only get one! Through one of the doors, you will find the thing your heart wishes for the most!"

"Then I will find you! I can bring you back to life again!"

"You might or you might not. It's a trick, you see. Auroch is a trickster, a demon, a monster. He is all of these things. He will tell you what you want to hear. He is all of these things because *you* want him to be all of these things."

"What do you mean? Did you see him before you died? Did you pass through Shadowmist?"

"We all pass through Shadowmist. All of us who hover in between life and death. Every single one. Through the next door is where the Others lie."

The Italian painting of *Il Prelievo,* The Taking, flashed through my mind. "The Others are the takers."

"They take whoever opens the door to hell. I've seen it happen. It's horrible. When they reach for someone, these hands pop out of their robes. Scaly hands like rat feet, but huge." The boat turned at the Bay Bridge which was strung with more twinkling clear lights. San Francisco's ferry building came into view with its huge clock tower shining like the full moon. I shot a glance up at the clouds. The real moon was eclipsed by the thick, black clouds in the sky.

The Blue Fleet passed under the supports of the Golden Gate Bridge. Their majestic pillars looked desolate and gray, the famous towers braced with dark wire veins suspended from blackened blocks. The ship rocked with the force of the open ocean's waters.

"Behind one door is your eternal reward. Or so he

says. Do not walk through the doors if they are empty! Do not open any of the doors! When it's your time, I will help you. But you have to find me, AJ! You have to promise me you will not make the choice without me!

"When it was my turn, I made the choice alone. Afterwards, I thought, 'When my time comes, I only hope to be judged fairly, when there are only two doors remaining when I pass from this life to the next. That my heart will choose its eternal reward rather than the Other to take me to some deep pit of hell.'"

Ben's eyes met mine. The revolving light on the boat illuminated him from behind, this boy I loved, appearing in flesh and blood as real as the torment in his eyes.

"I chose to give Kelly to Auroch so that I could live. Half of his soul is in his body. Half of his soul belongs to Auroch." His hand clenched into a fist, which he rested on the metal bar as he gazed at the black sea.

"Promise me something," he said. Make it the most important promise you will ever make."

"Anything."

"That we will find a way to connect like this, that we can find each other and speak just enough so we won't begin believing we're crazy. Promise me! Just trust me when I say that you must stay with me. Don't go. No matter what you see right now. Don't get scared. Don't go. You need to know the truth about what I am now. About what you are. I'm going to try my best to be with you forever."

A blast of white sea spray shot up into the air as the boat turned around at the Golden Gate Bridge. The water churned and slapped on the posts with a pleasant slopping sound.

"Ben!" I raised my voice so he could hear me over the wind, then shook my head with chagrin. "Hear me!" Of course, he could hear me. He was dead. There was no need to raise my voice. Somehow, I knew he could sense me, hear my every word even though the boat engine huffed and churned and jazz music lilted from the galley below. "I would do anything to stay with you, to see you as I'm seeing you now! What if holding you to the earth is the wrong thing to do?" My eyes filled with tears. The wind blew them onto my cheeks before I could blink them away. I swiped them with the back of my hand. "If I make a promise like that, you might have to walk the earth for an eternity as a spirit! How can I live with that?"

A man dressed in a black-and-white suit and bowler hat cleared his throat. A freshly lit cigarette hung from his black lower lip. His face was a ghastly gray. "Excuse me," he said to Ben. He tossed the cigarette into the water, then spun on his heel and trotted down the steps to the galley below.

"Another ghost seer," I stated the obvious. Ben's form was backlit by an ethereal moon. The wheels of his mind turned behind his eyes. He had a decision to make.

I placed my hands upon his. They were warm. Perhaps too warm. "I think you're alive, and this is all a bad dream. Isn't it? You're warm. I can feel you. Pinch me awake."

He tucked a bit of skin on my forearm between his thumb and index finger, squeezing gently. "I can't feel a thing," I said.

He chuckled. Rising to his feet, he strode to the edge of the boat. I followed him and stood by his side. He placed a hand on the rail.

"Will you stay with me?" He grasped my hand in his. I could feel his fingers wrapped around mine.

"Yes," I whispered. He smiled that wry, crooked smile that made my heart tumble, touched my hand, then withdrew and jumped over the side of the boat and into the dark waters.

LIZ NEWMAN

Chapter Twenty
Ghost Voices

"Ben!" I screamed as his body splashed into the churning onyx surf below. He disappeared beneath the surface.

I climbed up the railing. My heart pounded in fear of jumping, fear of these shark-infested waters, fear of drowning. I turned and sped down the metal stairs, searching for the captain's galley. I ran around the sides of the ship, peeking in windows and maneuvering around benches. No one but a few tourists who stared morosely at the waters, as if they, too, were already done for and unaware that a fellow passenger had left the ship.

I took the landing down to the bottom deck and discovered the captain's galley. A lone, beefy man with a white captain's hat steered the ship. A pair of earbuds hung from his ears.

"Sir!" I screamed. "Man overboard!"

His hands moved back and forth slightly at the wheel as his back remained turned.

"Ben is in the water! Help, please!"

He nodded. I sighed, relieved until I realized he nodded to the sound of his own music. I groaned in exasperation.

"Sir!" I walked up behind him. I tapped him. Slowly, he peeked over his shoulder. Surely, he saw me standing behind him. He shrugged. He turned and looked out at the shimmering black ocean.

I strode toward a red button on the side of the boat and slammed it down to the console with all my might.

Red lights came on everywhere as an alarm sounded. The captain switched the engines to idle, then turned to face me. He donned a life vest and grabbed a flashlight. He strode in my direction, his mouth pressed together tightly in a line.

"Sir! Ben fell into the water! Over the left—"

The captain ignored me as he spoke into his radio, ordering a deckhand to the wheelhouse. He walked toward me, his eyes blue and cold.

"I'm sorry, sir," I said. "My boyfriend fell…"

The captain walked right through me. As if I were made of thin air. As if I were a ghost.

I whirled around after the captain, confused at his retreating back. Ben was the ghost, I reminded myself. Not I. But where would the waters take him? Why did he jump in? Did he want me to follow him and die there?

I felt my body. My angles were still there, the fabric of my jeans, my shirt. I was human. I was solid. How…?

Before I could think or even take a breath, I ran to the left side of the boat and jumped in after Ben, flying through the air, through the mist, toward the water. His head broke the surface. He stared as I hovered.

"Follow me, AJ. Follow the course of *the gloam*. It will take you back to the school, back to Auroch, back to where you can choose a door. I'm going to drown. I'll be there with you when you make your choice."

The mist held me in the air a few feet above him.

"You're not going to drown!" I shouted. "Someone is coming to save you!"

"No, AJ! Let me come with you. There is a chance for you… to live. I need to be there to help you!" A wave overtook him as he coughed and sputtered, continuing to struggle against the heavy tide. His head dipped below the surface.

"Ben!"

The alarm continued to blare as a spotlight switched on from the boat. Ben surfaced, coughing and spitting up water. His lips were blue.

"There!" the captain to the steward said as he jumped into a raft. The steward dived in and grasped Ben around the chest. Ben tried to swim away, but he was weakened. I floated above Ben as the captain hopped from the boat into an inflatable raft and tossed the ring to the steward as he pulled on Ben's upper body.

Ben flailed, half drowned, coughing and sputtering. The steward wrapped an arm around his body and swam with him to the raft.

"You're gonna be all right, kid. Killing yourself is not the way. You're gonna be fine."

Ben shook his head as if he were shaking water out of his ears.

Reality crashed in as the whitecaps slammed upon the raft. The captain could see Ben. The captain walked right through me in the galley. That meant I was... *I* was...

A ghost.

"Listen to me, AJ," Ben said as he climbed into the raft.

"My name is Mike," the captain said. "What the hell are you thinking jumping into the water like that?"

I reached for Mike's hand, confused as to why I floated in the air. Mike jumped as if he felt my touch. "What th..." he trailed off and ordered the steward to row for the ship.

"You're trapped by the mist, AJ," Ben said, ignoring him. "The gloam. The gloam will move, and you should move with it. It will take you back to land. You can travel in it. Wait for me because you will find—"

The foghorn of the ship blared, drowning out Ben's words. A heavy wind blew in from the Pacific. I grasped for purchase upon something, but Ben's hand reached for mine far below me now.

"AJ!" Ben shouted. Farther away now, the captain named Mike asked Ben if he was crazy. The fog spirited me back to the shores of San Francisco near the Embarcadero. The mist broke up between the buildings and floated away, high into the lights of the skyscrapers where I couldn't see it anymore. If I had feet, they would have set upon the sidewalk. But I didn't have feet. I didn't have legs. I had nothing. I knew that now.

I was a ghost.

I gritted my teeth. Teeth I didn't have. Teeth I only imagined feeling. A couple rolling a baby stroller with a sleeping child inside stopped suddenly in front of me. They maneuvered the stroller around and walked the other way, pulling their jackets tighter around their bodies. They knew I was there. They sensed a bodiless soul. My coldness, my transparency. Maybe they even heard my voice saying *help me help me help me.*

With the lack of a physical body came a quickness of movement I had never before experienced. I took giant step after giant step, every step perhaps ten yards long. I strode through the city streets, through the Financial District, through the seedy Tenderloin, where some drug-addled transients gazed at me as if I were nothing they hadn't seen before.

A homeless woman nibbling on something wrapped in foil met my eyes. "Finally, you're here," she murmured. She dropped the foil packet and lurched toward me with grimy fingers outstretched. "Take me. I want to die now!"

As her hands reached for me, I flew as far and fast as I could up the city streets. I was scared, frightened out of my mind. Lost in a world of the living dead. Cold, restless, and robbed.

I wanted my body back. I wanted to lay next to Carlos the cat and feel his warm body curled up near my hip. I wanted to bury my face into Frances's hair and smell her plumeria-scented shampoo. I wanted to sit next to my father as he read the Wall Street Journal at the breakfast table and bit into a croissant.

"Give me back my life!" I screamed into the gloam as I climbed hill after hill, heading toward my Pacific Heights neighborhood.

I pictured Auroch in Shadowmist, sitting in that high-backed chair with one finger smugly resting upon his chin as he waited for me to return. I flew by the sagging brown boot house, where Avia the Magpie swung on a porch swing. The brown boot house was no longer sagging. Now, it was a charming two-story brickstone with lighted windows. Avia's hair was combed in a stylish but dated hairdo. Her skin shone with an ethereal glow. She smiled and waved. She was one of me and I was one of them now. She no longer feared me.

Addison High School loomed before me, the American flag waving in the breeze. Black clouds eclipsed a moon that had turned blood orange behind the clouds. The dark building of Addison High towered like a golem ready to strike. Hesitating, I closed my eyes.

"Wake up." I slapped myself. "Wake up! Wake up! This is all a bad dream, and Frances is going to jump on your bed any minute now and cuddle close to you with her face in your ear and say, 'Jay Jay.' Ben will be waiting downstairs with a cardboard container of pumpkin lattes while Nancy eyes his motorcycle jacket and my father has his nose buried in the newspaper. Wake up, AJ! Wake up! *Please wake up!*"

Stillness. I opened one eye because I still believed I had an eye, for just a little peek. Addison High in the darkness. High glass windows with the small ashen faces of children inside, some burnt beyond recognition, watching me. This was no dream. *This was real.*

I glanced back over my shoulder at Avia's home. The brown boot house had turned back into the sagging, decrepit mess with a new ornamentation. Avia was only a skeleton hanging from a porch rafter, her hand raised in an eternal wave in the direction where we had first glimpsed each other half a block away. Her neck creaked as she turned toward me. Her mouth was a black beak that fell open in a greeting. "Caw."

Something black and shiny rose scrabbled upon her chin bone. A magpie poked its beak out from between her grinning skull. The bird's beady eyes flashed red in the darkness. A flock of magpies burst forth, splitting her bony beak jaw in two.

Her skeleton shattered in pieces as emerging magpies blew open her breast cage. The magpies flew in my direction, their eyes bright red as they caw, caw, cawed. I rushed into the school. The breath of the flock's wings beat down upon me as they flew closer, their beaks nipping at my hair and shoulders. For one fleeting moment, I thought the doors of the school would be locked, and I would pound desperately on the glass as the birds tore me apart.

"I am a ghost!" I shrieked at the birds as I reached for the doors. I covered my head with my hands. "You can't hurt me!"

So are we, a blip in my subconscious answered back. Or maybe it was the damn birds talking. Some kind of twisted telepathy from specter to specter. *We can hurt you! And we will. We will! WE WILL!*

There was no time to open the doors. The birds dove upon me. I flew into the glass, half expecting to smash my face there and slide off with my lips stuck to the smooth surface like a dumb cartoon. I passed right through the glass. The flock of birds followed me through.

I ran down the halls of Addison High as they chased me, their wings flapping furiously. Their cawing now sounded like cries of "See me! Can you see me! See me! See me!"

Bolting for the theater, I threw open a door and threw my body inside. I slammed the door shut. Peeking out through a circular window, I saw them flying around and around in the school hallway, their black wings flapping like delirious bats. "See me. See me. Caw caw caw!"

The theater was dark save for a few dimly lit recessed lights. Blood red velvet seeped over chairs, stairs, everywhere. Whoever designed this place must have had a hell of a fixation for the Phantom of the Opera.

The school janitor mopped the floor down in the little hovel that passed for an orchestra, where the school band played its warbling tunes. I crept... no actually flew, or perhaps even ghosted, because *tada!* I was a ghost now, down to where he pushed a mop back and forth, back and forth. Earbuds were stuffed in his ears. The tune of *Good Times* lilted in the air as his head wobbled in what looked like a neck movement-only version of the chicken dance.

For the life of me (*ha!*), I couldn't remember the janitor's name. I wanted to shout to grab his attention. I wanted to know if he saw me. Instead, I simply stood next to him and said, "You! Can you hear me? Can you see me?"

No response. The music from his earbuds sang through the darkness, a wiry voice warbling about good times. His eyes widened slightly.

"Hello," I said again. Seef. Siftly. Sievely! His name was Mr. Sievely!

"Mr. Sievely!" I shouted.

He plucked an earbud off his ear and threw the piece down on his shoulder. His eyes were wide with torment.

"Mr. Sievely, I need your help. What do I need to remember? You mouthed that to me, that I needed to remember something. What should I remember?"

He continued to push and pull, push and pull with the mop until the orchestra pit shone. "Remember? Remember November," he murmured. "When you will all die."

"What about November? What happens in November?"

He rested the mop handle upon his shoulder and tucked the bud back into his ear.

"Mr. Sievely—"

He pointed in the air. "You don't know what I will do if you don't stop talking. Stop talking!"

He picked up his bucket and mop and headed up the stairs.

"Mr. Sievely—"

Sievely drew up his mop and swung the end in my direction. I shrieked, dodging out of the way before I realized I had no flesh for the mop to bruise. Mr. Sievely's face was bright red even in the half darkness, and spittle emerged from his pursed lips as he snarled and swung.

He threw the mop to the ground, tossed the bucket aside, and pushed open the door to the orchestra pit. I half expected him to begin screaming as the magpies bit his skin and hair. Silence.

I folded my arms. The school janitor was the smartest person here, it seemed. Had I only not listened to the voices or to Auroch. Had I only not replied.

November seventeenth. The day of the talent show. The day Lady Carrington's house burned down.

The day the church that once stood here burned down in the 1940s after the body of Anisette March Whittle had been discovered after she hanged herself.

A premonition... no, a certainty now, came to mind so strongly I began to shiver. On November the seventeenth, Addison High would burn to the ground, killing everyone inside. The students, teachers, and faculty would all perish, their souls perhaps being called on by Auroch as they searched to find meaning to their deaths. No one would be set free, not Lady Carrington, or her children, or the hundreds who would die. For no one could free their souls but a trade.

Or perhaps me.

I hopped up on the stage and parted the curtains, making my way to the trapdoor. I would find him there. *Auroch.*

LIZ NEWMAN

Chapter Twenty-One
Angel of Death

I hovered over the trapdoor on the floor of the stage.

I groped for the handle. Darkness eclipsed my surroundings, yet I could see perfectly. Like a cat or vampire or any other creature of the night, I slinked within the darkness, perfectly comfortable in my element with no heed to thoughts of shame or pretense. For in death, all pretense is meaningless. Shame as well. The thought that the same knowledge applied to a life well lived crossed my mind.

"Now you tell me," I murmured to myself. "Or maybe now, I finally believe you."

I wondered if ghosts spoke aloud and if the attuned human ear could truly hear them every so often.

Mist escaped through little cracks in the opening. If I were alive, I would actually hope that geeky drama students crouched underneath with a fog machine, giggling. But I was dead. I was dead, and this was not a dream. I was a ghost in need of a path to the underworld where all would be explained by the master, the teacher, the demon Auroch.

Where we begin, we are sure to end.

And this... had all begun here.

I pulled open the trapdoor.

A burst of sooty smoke escaped, blowing my hair back. The heat bit my face sharply. Reflexively, I brought my hand to my face. *What face?* I giggled, feeling one frayed thread away from sanity. If a ghost went crazy, who would even care?

I wished I was Jacob Marley in Scrooge with a set of iron chains to rattle around. Wouldn't that be something at the talent show? I wondered if Hyannis would break character while on pointe. That wasn't the only thing I wished she would break. I hoped she would break her neck, for she was the cause of all this.

A deep, melodic male voice laughed with pleasure. I jumped. He was here somewhere. Auroch was here.

I dropped through the trapdoor. A bright orange light flickered just around the corner, perhaps a hint of a fire that blazed a few feet away. I drew back in fear.

My body yearned to jump out and run away. Where would I go? Would the Others find and take me? Auroch was my only source for answers. Even Ben would not know as much as he did.

My hands reached up to the top of the door to guide me into the belly of the stage. Embers of fire danced into the crawlspace. The embers singed my eyes and brows. I pressed forward as I coughed. Smoke burned my nostrils and lungs. What nostrils and lungs, I couldn't help but think. *Ha!*

Screams of agony pierced the smoky air.

I clapped my hands over my ears as the shouts and wails of children who cried for their mother, for anyone to take the pain of burning flesh away, resounded throughout the crawl space.

A woman's voice sobbed, "All will be well. Your father shall come and save us. Good men always come to save us. You will see. Shhh. Shhh…" The children's sobs turned into wails. "Everything will be all right."

Lady Carrington appeared, her gown and hair on fire as she clutched a child under her arm. I rushed to her and patted my hands upon her in a feeble attempt to suppress the flames. The flames were quelled, although my hands seared with the pain of burns.

Her eyes widened at the sight of me. "There

now," she said to the burning child she held. "See, someone has come."

The fire receded, and we stood face to face in the basement of a Victorian home, complete with a sewing dress form for both women's and children's clothes in the corner. The child under her arm slowly released his death clutch upon her. He stared at me with wide brown eyes.

She placed the child on the floor and reached out to touch me, her hand traversing the contours of my face that reminded me of the kinesthetic manner a blind person would have greeted new acquaintances with. Yet in her eyes shone clarity. She could see me.

My breath sighed in a cool vapor. As the air from my lungs touched her dress, I watched the fabric dissolve over her heart. Her body became so transparent I could see her heart, encased in small flames.

"The blood price. The blood price was paid for you, but you stay. Why?"

"We live, and we burn," Lady Carrington said. "Live and burn. We never know when the fire will come, but eventually, the heat does. And with the heat, the pain." Tears coursed down her chin as she looked at the children. "We did nothing to deserve this. And I am worried, so worried, about the children's father. Where is he?"

"Please, Lady Carrington, don't be afraid. I'm going to try something." I leaned down toward the boy, taking his chin in my hands. "What is your name? I want to release you from this misery." I looked up at Lady Carrington for approval. She nodded, a serene gaze on her face.

"My name is Jin." The boy's eyes shone wide and soft. I caressed his face with my hand.

"When I breathe out, you breathe in. Okay?"

He backed away.

"Do not fear, Jin," Lady Carrington said. She gently pressed a hand upon his back. "Go."

Gingerly, he stepped toward me with a look of apprehension. I exhaled before he could turn away. He drew in the vapor from my breath. His skin turned an ethereal pale before his body dissolved into air. The macabre sadness that was his soul transformed into a purity I could sense. The semblance of him diffused until his presence disappeared. I breathed in, feeling our souls connected, even as the boy's had gone.

Lady Carrington blinked. "Who are you?"

My voice was gritty with ash and smoke. Yet, for once in my life, I knew exactly what to say. I didn't know where the words came from. I simply knew they were on the tip of my tongue, and if there was a time to give them voice, that time was now.

"I am Anirnaq Anguta, the daughter of a mortal man and a mystical being. I guess my purpose now is to release the souls restrained to the earthly plane."

"I am sorry. Who?"

"Just call me Andromeda Jayne. It's easier."

She let out a long, low exhale. "We have burned for so long," she said. "So long. These poor, sweet little children." She caressed a little girl's pale face as she gripped her charred skirts.

"Lady Carrington, pleased to meet you." I half curtsied in an attempt to mimic the custom of the time.

Her hands shook. "My manners fail me. My apologies." The crazy thought that she spoke much like Auroch crossed my mind. "We have been burning for so long. Why has God let this happen?"

"I'm not sure if this is something God has done." My senses pricked up as I tried to remember all I had learned in Sunday school and whether or not I spoke with words that would help my soul reach paradise or be damned for all eternity. "I'm terrible at theological conversations. I think I can help you as well. I think I can send you somewhere better."

Lady Carrington caressed another child's cheek, then sunk into a sewing chair and stared off into space. "I must wait for my husband to return."

The smell of smoke wafted from behind the walls. Dark smoke seeped in through a tiny vent at the edge of the floor.

Her head turned toward the entry. She jumped up and placed her hand on the chair. "No. Not again."

A hand grasped mine tightly.

"Ah!" A little girl with lush brown hair and lashes looked up at me.

I stepped closer to Lady Carrington and clutched her hand. "I will help you save them. Stay with me."

Dark smoke billowed up through the vent now. Slowly, the screams returned, mere whispers at first, then increasing in volume. The little girl clutched Lady Carrington's hand. "No more," she pleaded. "No more fire."

Lady Carrington wrested her face away from my grasp. "Save the children. Please. As many as you can. I must find the others. If you are as you truly say you are, do what you can for the child, but I will not leave until every one of these children leaves by my side."

"Lady Carrington," I shouted as she ducked into the black clouds of fire. "Please don't go back into the fire! Come to me!"

Lady Carrington turned as a flame licked the bottom of her skirt. The lace detail at the hem began to char and turn black. The fire crawled up her dress, igniting. Her face began to char, yet she remained calm. Grotesquely beautiful even. "These children are like my own. I will not leave them!" She gripped the top of her skirt and pivoted on her unburned heel in a rush to the children who screamed for her.

The remaining children followed their lady mother into the fire. I could do nothing but watch the fire catch their clothes as I gritted my teeth in desperation.

The blaze roared about, advancing. Soon, the flames would consume me. The smoke filled my lungs as I coughed into my hand and collapsed to the floor. Rolling onto my stomach, I saw dark red trickles of blood and phlegm in my palm.

I coughed. The smoke became thick, black, punishing. My eyes stung as I blinked several times, seeing nothing but gray. And then the heat. Heat so powerful and searing my skin screamed with pain.

Call my name. Just call my name. I will take the pain away. All of your pain and sadness, if you will just speak my name. Give me your anger, your heartache, your sadness, your deepest, darkest desires. Call upon me. Call my name.

With my last breath, I shouted his name as loud as I could. "Auroch!"

Chapter Twenty-Two
Difficult Choices

When I opened my eyes, I found myself face down on white bedcovers. My eyelashes were stuck together. This had to be the sheets underneath my cherry sundae bedcover.

"It was all a dream," I consoled myself as I flipped over and stared at the white ceiling. "I am alive, and it was all a dream."

"Not quite," said a melodic male voice.

Auroch sat in a chair by the fireplace in a lavishly decorated bedroom. My hands pressed into the mattress as I lifted myself to sit up on the bed. I wore a high-necked Victorian gown made of heavy cotton and lace.

"Haven't I told you I hate wearing this stuff!" I tugged and tore the neck of the gown, unbuttoning the top two.

"A bit rash, would you say?" Auroch said.

"I have eczema!" I threw the covers off the bed and swung my feet around, pushing myself off onto the wooden floor with a loud *thunk!*

Auroch laughed as if I'd just told the funniest joke he'd ever heard.

"Did I save the child? Jin?"

"You have no power to save children, for you are merely an apparition. Save for maybe the power to be seen like some do, the power to make mildly consequential movements the same as the breeze, but nothing more. You thought you were saving their souls. You really just invited him inside yours." He laughed and laughed until his face turned red, ugly laughter which should have made him hideous but instead even more handsome.

A feeling of heaviness settled in my chest. Fullness. Jin's soul was inside of me. "But I thought…I thought—"

"That you are dead? That you have magical powers? The funny aspect I find about people your age is that they always think they know. They always think they have the scenario figured out. Surprised, oh so very surprised to find that what they believed to be true was not all along. Andromeda Jayne. May I call you Andromeda Jayne now?"

"Only if you can find me a black tank top, jeans, and Converse sneaks."

"Done." Auroch gestured toward a marble bathroom. "Dress, and I shall explain all. Now that you are willing to listen."

I slammed the door of the bathroom, then unbuttoned the rest of the nightgown and threw it onto the floor. A fresh new frock in teal green taffeta (ugh!) hung from a hanger on the back of the door next to a hanger decorated with a worn black tank and dark blue jeans, just as I demanded. Just for good measure, I tore the teal green taffeta thing off the rack and crushed the material in my hands, then threw it down to the floor. After I slipped on my shoes, I pulled at the fabric and stomped upon it. My fit helped dispel my intense anger. I dressed and stormed back out to the bedroom, which was no longer a bedroom but Auroch's great room, where he stood at the tall arabesque-style windows with his arms behind his back, staring out at Shadowmist. Exactly like the first time I had met him.

"My dear Andromeda Jayne, would you care to—"

"Get to the point, Auroch. What do I do now?"

"I love when you speak my name."

"No more games. This is my life we are talking about."

"Your life, Andromeda Jayne? I thought we were speaking of your death."

"I am alive. I never really woke up from the accident, did I?"

"Memories. So much time I have spent in here renders memories as mere torture."

"What memories could you have possibly had?" I grumbled.

"So many memories of a past life. I was once a prince, once a pauper, a husband, now a king in a world of the animals, and yet I feel like an insect. I ruled and I served, I loved, I groveled and I obeyed, I ordered beatings and took them. Try as I did, time and time again, I used each life to avenge the previous one until neither the dark lord nor the universal light would take me. I created Shadowmist to suffer my memories, to grasp onto each soul who passed through in hopes of meeting another one. Soon, your beautiful face shall be another such memory. Would you stay with me, Andromeda Jayne? Would you? You are fond of me, as I am of you. I see such in your eyes, you want to be with me here, down in the depths up above and somewhere in between or below. Why chance the saccharine sweetness of heaven or the bristling fires of hell when you could be here with me, and we could dance our eternal dance?"

His eyes were mesmerizing as he strode toward me, holding out his hand. Everything about him screamed unearthly perfection. His skin, his scent, the way that he moved. If I were any other girl, perhaps I would have fallen under his spell. But only one boy enticed me, and that was the one who was so perfectly imperfect, so tenderhearted, tough, and fragile all at the same time. Whether Auroch knew it or not, I knew in my own heart that the best of me wished for none other than Ben Bach.

"You called upon me to take you away from your fears. Now, you and I have made a pact. All you must do is abide with me on a few and fleeting occasions."

Auroch's hand circled my waist. He pulled me close. My lips hovered inches away from him, and still, all I could think of was Ben.

"My own memories are too strong to accept anything you have to offer, Auroch."

"Oh, you are pondering your lover boy." Auroch uttered a high-pitched giggle, which strangely sounded sophisticated coming from his closed lips. His lashes fluttered slightly as he stared down at the ground, releasing his tight hold on my waist. He sighed. "What is memory but biased perception? What is life but a shared hallucination? Words are a simple breeze. Some feed flames, but most dissolve into air. What are words but the wind, and yet words consume the time in which they are spoken. And time for the living, my dear friend, is priceless. Perhaps you have always been dead, and your life was only a dream."

"How do I make a trade?"

He turned to me and smiled, his mouth curling up at the corners. "How do you trade for what, my dear?"

"Trade with the blood price. To get my life back."

"Would you not rather stay here with me?"

My voice shook even as I spoke the word. "No."

"You know what will happen if you make the wrong choice? The Taking or something worse. Stay here with me, Andromeda Jayne. Leave behind the confusion. I promise when you look at me, you shall see nothing but beauty, the reflection of your better self, of the one you imagine yourself to be. Beautiful, powerful, important. Worthy. Keep your eyes on me, Andromeda Jayne, and forget a world which does not want you."

I thought of Ben, of my father, of Frances and Caslin, and even Nancy. Could they go on without me? Perhaps. Could I go on without them? No, I could not.

"Auroch, I insist. I must have a chance to have my life back. Let me open a door. I cannot live like this, here with you. Shadowmist is beautiful, but it's just an illusion. It's not real."

Auroch's eyes widened. For a split second, an emotion flashed behind them. Something that looked like…

Fear.

Closing the space between us, Auroch pressed his hand to my back and all but shoved me toward the hanging draperies that framed the wall of doors. "Pity. I shall miss you, Andromeda Jayne. Choose." He gestured to the wall.

Three doors were lined up. Three choices.

"Up above, beyond the basement of Addison High, you lie asleep. Ben Bach, your prince, has kissed you not once, twice, but three times as machines keep you breathing in a hospital. Each time, he weakens. With each breath you release, you bring his soul closer to you. Closer to death. Down to the depths. Down to Shadowmist. Only he doesn't know it. He only knows that he feels an urge to destroy himself. The urge grows stronger and stronger with each passing day. It began with a desire to speed up while riding upon his motorcycle on a foggy day, speed up closer to cars driving errantly. Another to drown himself in your presence, to draw your worlds together by crossing over into death. And now dear Ben's thoughts turn to an idea even more insidious."

"Such as?"

"Fire."

I shook my head.

"The truth is a bitter pill to swallow. But that is the world. Anger wells up from the soul. How to right that anger equates into savagery turned outward or upon oneself. That is where I come in. Your movies up above have it all wrong. With true love's kiss, the spell deepens. It does not break. The spell deepens and worms into the soul. Human nature has a humorous way of turning traitor and destroying those romantic notions. That is simply who you are. Now you have company in that body of yours. You have whisperers. Others."

"The children I tried to save. They are inside of me now?"

"They may make you strong enough to fight your way out of your useless body. They may make the fight harder. I have a way out for all of you. But I want something first. Well, two things, actually."

"What do you want?" The three doors seemed to stare at me like the mentally ill facade of Addison High. Nothing about the doors seemed pleasant.

"The first is that you will promise to come here to Shadowmist should I give you back your life. Your dreams shall belong to me. Souls enter, they choose a door, they leave. Some are taken. Some go willingly. All tell me their name, stare at me with bewilderment sometimes, perhaps even infatuation. As you do now."

"I don't," I murmured.

"Yes, you do."

He caressed my cheek, letting his hand linger a second too long. I ducked, then glared at him.

He shrugged. "Another time, then. No sense in argument. Souls leave through a door, or they are taken. Either way, they leave. They choose a door, and I am left to ponder this place alone. How I long to escape these walls, even for a moment, to see the outside world. To hear your music, wear your clothing, feel the passion that you feel when you look in the eyes of one who adores you, to move, to gather, to learn." His voice choked as he looked up and blinked back tears. "To hold my sweet wife again. So much pleasure have you at your fingertips. You cannot know how fortunate you are. Even your silly bare arms and your ugly shoes appeal to me in some way. I would like you to replace me as guardian of Shadowmist, if only for a short while. Promise before you choose a door." The soles of his boots echoed on the tile as he stopped in front of me.

"Andromeda Jayne, Angel of Death, mythic, guardian, goddess, human… do we have an agreement?"

I stared at the doors.

Behind one door lies the thing you desire the most in the world, behind another lies your eternal reward, behind perhaps hides the Other ready to spirit you away.

A vision of the painting in my father's study popped into my mind. *Il Prelievo*. The Taking. The woman holding her arms out to her mother as the shrouded ones hold her over their shoulders. Her mother down on her knees, weeping as the reaper stands over her. No one would weep for me.

"Yes," I whispered.

"Andromeda Jayne, which door do you choose?"

"What if I choose not to choose?"

"However long you spend here is no matter to me. I have come to enjoy your company. If I gathered the feeling was mutual I would sit down and order a meal for us even. Perhaps even take a nap. But you are restless. You long to leave me. That is fine. I take no insult. My only consolation is that a part of me shall go with you when you walk through a portal. When you open the door, should you find your heart's desire then you will simply walk through. And within the other door, death awaits. Like Avia, when you open that door, your earthly body will die, and maybe, if you're lucky, your ghost will allow you to remain in some familiar places. Your soul will stay here with me for all eternity. Lest you open the third door where the Other is waiting. Then they, him, she, *It*, whomever chooses to show their ugly face shall take you without question. I do hope that will not happen to you. I find The Taking a horrible sight."

His wide grin stated otherwise.

I took a long look at each door in turn. They were identical, plain wooden doors with brass doorknobs. Doorknobs that reminded me of Alice in Wonderland. Waiting in expectation like the Mad Hatter or the White Rabbit sitting at a table with hands clasped in anticipation. Waiting to reveal my *Eterni-Tea*. Oh, if only one could talk and tell me if there was doom lurking behind or the thing I wanted most. Life. Ben. Home. An awakening.

Ben would be behind one door. He will find a way to come for me. He is standing behind a door, and he will rescue me from this terrible place. He will take me back to life, and we will talk about how he found his way into the world of ghosts over coffee shop pastries and pumpkin lattes.

"Follow your heart to choose a door. Your heart will always guide you to the right one. To the one that houses your deepest desire. Your most fervent hope."

Follow my heart, follow my heart. Where my deepest, darkest secret exists. Beyond which lies what I desire most.

My hand reached out to the door in the middle. I touched the cool brassy knob. A flutter of panic released in my chest as I pulled my hand away. "No." My fingertips grazed the door on the left, then the door on the right, then the door on the left again. I rested my ear against the wood of the door on the left. Silence.

I glanced at Auroch. A small smile played about his lips. He knew.

Striding to the door on the right, I gripped the knob in my fist. I twisted my hand and pulled the door open.

LIZ NEWMAN

Chapter Twenty-Three
Back to Life

Hyannis McWolfe swung by her neck from a thick rope tied to the chandelier of the cathedral ceiling of the walk-in closet of her bedroom. Her face was black and blue, and her hair stood on end. Once a crown of onyx silk, her strands hung from her head in dried-out masses of sweaty tangles as if she may have clutched and pulled at her own hair in the throes of death. Her tongue lolled out of her mouth, black as a parrot's. Her ballet slipper feet swung from side to side as she swayed in one final dance. Her voice echoed in my mind. *Hey, Dum-dum. I hear this is your favorite.*

I slammed the door closed. A force behind the door pushed back, and the door flew back open. I cursed and kicked. The wood panel would not budge, and the door remained open. Hyannis's body rocked slightly from side to side.

"This is not my choice!" I shouted. "This is not what I wanted most in the world!"

Auroch remained still and emotionless. Neither pity nor glee nor sympathy shined in his eyes. His pupils remained as cold and dead as a snake's.

"You chose," he said. "Only you make the choice. The decision is made in the recesses of your heart, in the dark place where the fire grows. No one else chooses for you. I have no bearing as to what you will discover behind these doors. Make no mistake about it. You are murderous, AJ. You wanted her dead.

"Every one of you asks me the same thing. Every single one who passes through. Some before the Other takes them before they receive their eternal reward, that which they have earned for the acts they have committed in life, before they walk through the door which holds what they wanted most in glorious submission, acceptance, or are pulled in shrieking and fighting. All question. I can see why your higher power tires of you. For you question even upon the succession of your very own quest. Walk through and return to your world. Hyannis McWolfe is mine and will be judged accordingly. And remember, this is what you wanted."

"This is not my wish!" I said. "This is not my doing. I want my life back. I want Hyannis to have her life back. I want Ben. And he wants me." I wiped the tears streaming down my face. "I want it back!"

"Therein the great dilemma, Andromeda Jayne. The moment Hyannis infused you with murderous anger was the moment she gave up her own life. The moment she took glee in your accident was the moment her days were numbered. As you wished her death long before. One cannot inspire such ire in a Mystic, the Angel of Death, and expect to live. You took nothing from her. She gave you her life because she coveted yours. Your friend Hyannis… well, it was only a matter of time with her abhorrent attitude that she would give herself over to eternal damnation. We all know what a piece of work she was."

I shook my head, confused. "Hyannis was rich. Beautiful. Popular. I had nothing that she could want."

Auroch collapsed onto his high-backed chair and propped his feet up on a velvet ottoman. Seemed to be all in a day's work for the master of Shadowmist.

He sighed. "You had everything that she could want. You had great power and talent. The power of fury, the power of anger, the power to change the world with the energy of your emotions. Those without power or talent will always find something to covet. Like Hyannis.

"Go now, Andromeda Jayne, push aside her body

and leave her with me. Return to the life you want. Forget about Shadowmist. Return to a life without Hyannis McWolfe, and let her take your place in death. Live a life where you're free to live without sadness. Go, Andromeda Jayne. Walk through the door. We'll see each other in your dreams. This I promise you. Or reject me and go to the stars for which you are named."

Hyannis's eyes bulged out of her sockets as she rocked back and forth, back and forth. Those white marble eyes with the fuzzy brown pupils seemed to torment even in their stillness. Tags hung off a row of brand-new designer clothes still hanging inside her bedroom closet. "I suppose she will not be needing those," Auroch said. "The new clothes with tags bothered you so! What excess to make purchases and never use. Reminds me of a life of a lowly cog out west trying to make his name in the world and a nice home for his beloved wife." His laugh was so titillating in contrast to the grisly sight of Hyannis's dead body.

"What will happen to Hyannis?"

"What do you think will happen? She is not meant to serve as decor. When you trade your life for hers, she will abide with me. Perhaps she will be a pet. Perhaps she will choose a door. Perhaps the Others will take her."

I glanced up at the brown magpie Avia. Her head cocked as she cooed, forlorn and watching me. I wondered who traded her life for their own.

"Walk through and awaken back into your life. Go now. Or the door will close. The choice will no longer be."

My steps started into the door frame before I could think. Hyannis's body smelled sour and old, like the beginning of rot.

I closed my eyes. This was wrong.

"I will not." I turned away from Hyannis's body

and strode to a latticed window. Shadowmist gleamed with all of a fantasy land's sunny brightness.

After several minutes of silence, Auroch spoke.

"Hyannis will remain alive and well if you do not walk through that door. You will remain with me. At times, we must push aside one life to save our own. Do you believe hers to be more valuable than your own?"

"There must be another way."

"If you remain, we shall have plenty of time to talk about it. Your physical body will only last so long. In your hospital bed, you shall wane. Your muscles shall atrophy. Your mind shall deteriorate into soft matter. I suggest you return to your body immediately. Do not hesitate."

I sighed as I shook my head.

Auroch strode toward me and stood over me as his voice rose. "Take her life in place of your own! Do it! Return to your home, those you love, all you hold dear. Give her to me, Andromeda Jayne! You shall never have to see me again while you are awake, even at the end of your living days. I will operate in the shadows of your mind. I will live in the darkest chasms of your heart. But for your own life, there is a cost to be paid." He grinned, devilishly handsome with a wide smile, gleaming teeth, and sparkling eyes. "I would gladly trade your life for hers."

The doors lined up on the far side of the wall stared back, one open with Hyannis's body. My feet froze to the ground. I couldn't do it. As much as I despised her, I couldn't make the decision that would take her life away and doom her to an eternity with a demon. I reached deep, deep down inside myself to find mercy, for my first inclination was to save myself. Hyannis's life, or any life for that matter, was not mine to take.

The doors began to shimmer. Auroch sank into

his favorite high-backed armchair as he watched my stone-faced expression. The portal with Hyannis's body creaked shut slowly, her blackened tongue moving back and forth as if to taunt me.

I cried out and sank to the floor. The doors faded into the wall panel and disappeared.

Auroch's eyes dulled like dirty glass. He curled a fist under his chin and shook his head in disappointment.

LIZ NEWMAN

Chapter Twenty-Four
Resignation

"How sweet. Young love. And so tragic," one nurse murmured to another as they watched Ben stride through the hospital foyer. The nurse, clutching a diet soda in her hand, looked in my direction as I followed. Perhaps she could feel my presence. She blinked twice, then turned back to her computer.

I passed the doctor and nurse who had spoken to me on Halloween night when I thought I had awakened from the coma.

The nurse smiled softly as she moved with her wide hips, shifting from side to side. The doctor went about his business with his brow furrowed as he tucked a pen into his breast pocket. He might know he was dead, a mere ghost, or he could be oblivious. Either way, they both seemed content going about their day among the living, pretending that they were still interacting with patients when they were really interacting with the dead and dying.

I floated through the double doors as they opened for Ben. He seemed to know I was there beside him in the parking lot. Ben started up the bike's engine, same as he left the hospital for the fourth time in two days. As he rode out of the parking lot onto the street, I followed, only needing to glide upon the wind to keep up as he drove onto the city streets. I jumped upon his back, clutching the sides of his leather jacket with hands made of mist and shadow. One of his hands reached down as if to stroke mine.

I thought for sure I would wake up today. I thought Auroch would have given me the chance to come back to life and settle upon a choice, or at least to prepare for the night of November 17.

When my time comes, I only hope to be judged fairly when there are only two doors remaining when I pass from this life to the next. That my heart will choose its eternal reward rather than the Others to take me to some deep pit of hell. That is what Ben had said.

My mouth might be permanently turned down at this point. I could feel the curves of it pointing down to the shiny asphalt I glided over. I'd probably have a very scary ghost face, the face of a specter moaning in agony while caught in the unseen world.

The leaves on the trees had turned brown and yellow. Autumn was always slow to develop in California. A leaf fell off and flew up above my head, or where my head should be, twirling around up into the sky. My spirit, for an instant, became a part of everything I passed. When I passed a river, part of me was the rushing water, feeling putrid and grimy from pollution. When I passed a stone, part of me was encased inside, immovable and constricted. When I passed a tree, part of me was the wave of leaves and branches. I heard other ghosts in the sound of the wind. I wondered if Ben could truly imagine that I was sitting behind him on the motorcycle with my arms wrapped around his waist as I spoke softly into his ear.

"I'm here, Ben."

"God, I miss you, AJ. I wanted to drive into the hills, take my helmet off, and perform the ultimate motorcycle stunt, and ride into a forest of oak trees in an attempt to jump them all until my bike crashed. I had to steer myself onto Sixth Street toward the onramp and almost doubled over as I breathed the urge out of my body. All I am, and all I want is to join you wherever you are."

"Don't even think about suicide," I said. "The

minute you die, I would probably come back to life. That is the type of trick Auroch would play."

He rode his motorcycle into the school parking lot and slipped into a space. Placing his hand where my arm would have been, he turned slightly and spoke under his breath. "Come back to life now. Come back to me, AJ. Anything can happen if we wish hard enough."

We walked together through the parking lot and up the stone stairs to the front of the building, through the glass doors, and down the hallways until he arrived at his homeroom. He turned and gave me that sideways, tight-lipped, corner-of-the-mouth smile that made my heart tumble. Somberly, he threw open the door and walked in.

Life continued on at Addison High.

Caslin Perez didn't seem to be the backstabber I had her pegged for. She spent some of her time hiding in the library. She had branched out into different groups and made new friends. I saw her at lunch, often sitting alone, staring off into the distance as other kids passed by her and said a casual hello. She twisted the cap off a bottle of water as she stared at the bench I used to sit at the few times we lunched across from each other. Then sadness and hatred would flash behind her eyes as she glanced up at Ben.

I knew that look. My eyes had been filled with so much sadness they hurt. Caslin always gave me a break by looking away before Ben could really feel the intensity of her hatred. Misdirected, yes, but neither of them would come out and say it. They both didn't really know for sure why they despised each other.

I think Caslin realized Hyannis McWolfe somehow drove the events on the day the accident occurred. Hyannis dripped with the same aloof, utter *stuck-upness* that she was famous for. Yet the Monday after I realized I was now the undead, a specter walking the earth as a guest from the in-between world, I found Hyannis standing in front of the door to the theater at Addison High, staring into the circular window after she collected the attendance sheets from the classrooms. Her face was frozen with fear as she pressed it up to the glass.

She turned to me. Perhaps she could see me. Perhaps she could feel me. Perhaps she could feel how close she had come to her own death and how her life had somehow been in my hands. I saw a flicker of terror in her eyes before she fixed a look of annoyance to the sky as she rolled them. Maybe she could see the ghosts now, too. I looked forward to her performance at the talent show on the seventeenth. I'd like to see how graceful she would be dancing among the dead.

In my hospital room, my physical body lay, atrophying. The raw unfairness of Hyannis still being alive and me in a coma, hanging by a thread to life in a hospital room, twisted my heart. The muscles of my physical body were limp from lack of use in my bed, my hair dried and withered upon overly starched sheets. My soul seemed drained, replaced by blackness. Replaced by anger. Replaced by a call for revenge. This black heart would be what I would take to the afterlife unless I could find a way to come back.

I stood behind Hyannis, longing to reach out my arms and squeeze her slim neck until it snapped like a twig.

Can you see me? I whispered to Hyannis.

She heard nothing. I knew she felt something, for a frown darkened her face before she turned away. Her fingers intertwined around her charm necklace as she pulled hard, leaving a mark around the nape of her neck. I could not squelch the thought of yanking out her heart and throwing it down the trapdoor in the theater where the spirits lived so I could come back to this life. If only I had the hands to do so, I might have to give it a try.

There was never enough time to think or time to plan, even for the dead. For the dead, whether physically or spiritually dead, are manipulated by that feeling of perpetual out-of-body experience. The powers we possessed could not be activated without focus, and there was too much about life to miss to stay focused.

Auroch's words came to mind.

What is life but a shared hallucination? Words are a simple breeze. Some feed flames, but most dissolve into air. What are words but the wind, and yet words consume the time in which they are spoken. And time for the living, my dear friend, is priceless.

I followed Ben home as he rode his motorcycle with my ghostly arms wrapped around his body. At times, I floated up next to him as he rode, caressing his cheek with my hand like a touch of wind. He smiled and closed his eyes for just a second. When he breathed, he would breathe me in. The Angel of Death. I knew my presence might be depleting his soul, but just once, I wanted to let him take in my essence. Just once. But to do so would be quite dangerous.

LIZ NEWMAN

Chapter Twenty-Five
The Secrets of All Souls

"Say something, Hyannis. Anything."

I followed Hyannis up and down the halls of Addison High as she collected attendance sheets for the school office. She brushed her onyx hair back over her shoulder, her white gold and diamond bracelet jingling.

"I know you can hear me. Say something."

Hyannis pressed her lips together. She reached for the door to Mr. Spinky's biology class. Before she flounced inside, she turned and looked around. I glared at her with all my ghostly might, hoping she could feel my gaze.

She hissed at the empty hallway. Then, she walked inside the classroom.

I watched her through the window in the door. Mr. Spinky's lips widened into a smile at the sight of her. I forgot people could be so dazzled by Hyannis's beauty, for I knew her to be such a mean person her looks didn't match a person who could be considered lovely in my eyes. Even Gideon watched her with admiration. Perhaps I had commanded such a look on occasion but was too wrapped up in thoughts of how my physicality did not quite measure up to feeling perfect that I could never bask in it.

Just perfect.

My lips pressed together in a wry smile. If I inhabited a physical body, I would have sighed with melancholy. Hyannis walked to the farthest end of the classroom and exited through the door farthest from me. As she strolled out into the hall, her fiery eyes gazing in my direction. She turned away quickly. Her shoulders pulled upward, almost hugging her neck, as she ducked into an adjacent classroom.

I passed through the door, stealth in immateriality. Mr. Spinky paused in his lecture. He seemed to be able to see me, but no, he couldn't. Could he see me? Could he? I flew up quickly from the front of the classroom to the top windows, where the sunlight filtered through.

In the gleam, I could see outlines of my arms and hands the way one might see dust motes dancing in the sun, only they had taken on a shape. Tendrils of my hair floated around my face. I stayed up in the air, feeling an elated feeling at being so high above the students and desks.

Mr. Spinky glanced up as he talked. His gaze remained transfixed in my direction as he lectured. He cleared his throat. His gaze zeroed in on Gideon, who was scribbling furiously.

"Gideon," he called, "the lesson is taking place at the front of the room and not in your notebook." Mr. Spinky walked down the aisle to Gideon's side.

"Right, right," Gideon said. He clicked his ballpoint pen shut. I flew down to his row and peeked at the page. Mr. Spinky also did, a clicking noise escaping from parted lips. Gideon had drawn the basketball court outside the window with a view of the city skyline behind. Larger than all, in the background, Gideon had drawn me as a ghost, looming as tall as the sun, my hair blowing past my ears and down my back.

"A sad situation, indeed," Mr. Spinky murmured. "Do put that away and try to focus. Would you like to talk to one of the counselors?" Gideon shook his head.

The entire class seemed to shift, as everyone knew he was talking about me and the accident.

Mr. Spinky resumed his place at the front of the class as well as his lecture.

I leaned down.

"Gideon," I said into his ear.

No response. Not even a flicker of an eyelid. He propped his chin upon his hand, blinking sleepily at Mr. Spinky's droning lecture about the properties of a living organism's cellular function.

The bell rang, signaling the end of class. Students stuffed books and sweatshirts into their backpacks. "Chapter seven and eight tonight, class. Review questions at the end. Typed, please."

His words were lost on the students who somberly trailed away, some tittering in an attempt to lift the heaviness from the room. Death. Death was all around us, in the tension, in the gloom, in the fear that if it could almost happen to me and perhaps would inevitably happen to me as I lay comatose in a hospital bed, then it could happen to anyone.

Mr. Spinky shook his head.

He sat at his desk as the room cleared. Having nothing better to do and nowhere to be to do it, I settled down in a chair at the desk in front of his.

"Mr. Spinky," I said. "Can you see me?"

Mr. Spinky gave the space I inhabited a long look. He reached into his pocket slowly and removed his earphone case, popped the buds in his ears, and touched his phone screen. The soft sound of classic rock filled the classroom as he bent his head toward his computer and began grading papers.

"AJ," a boy's voice said.

I immediately knew who the voice belonged to. "Jin!"

"Yes."

"Where did your soul go?"

"What is a soul?"

"Nothing. Where are you?"

"Same where you are. Here. In the air."

"Do you think Mr. Spinky could hear us if we spoke together?"

"I know he does not hear us. But someone has to. We have to tell them that the school will burn down on November seventeenth. I heard you when you spoke to the papa man."

"Auroch?"

"I hid because he is scary. Do you think he is scary?"

"Not really. I feel sorry for him. He's stuck there, in the in-between world."

"At least he's somewhere," said Jin in a pouty voice. "Not like us. We are not here or there or anywhere."

Jin appeared beside me, sitting on top of another desk with his head bowed. His dark hair tilted forward like a fan of silk into his eye as he sat with his legs crossed on the linoleum floor with one hand propping up his chin. He looked lost, forlorn, perhaps weary from hundreds of years as a ghost.

Mr. Spinky paused his corrections. His head lifted slightly and cocked to the side. Jin and I ceased our speaking and waited. Mr. Spinky resumed his work, his pencil making scratchy noises as he wrote in comments for his students.

"He is what the mama, the lady who cares for us, who burns with us, calls husband," Jin continued. "He does nothing but talk. The men who came to destroy my home could do more. They were stronger."

"Auroch? He is the man the mama lady calls 'husband?'"

Jin nodded. "He cannot leave. He cannot do anything. He mad at us. Angry with us."

"How does Auroch even know you exist?"

"He is the papa man. He is supposed to be. But

the mama lady says he does not want us."

"If he knows about you, why doesn't he let you go from here?"

"The mama lady say he cannot because he is the bad papa man, not the man she married. The mama lady say that only an angel come for us."

"How?"

Jin shrugged. "Until then, we sleep, and we wake by day sometimes, by fire other times. The nightmare is not always there. We live like we always did, like animals in a hole, but we have food, and we read and we play, and we sing. No one hurts us anymore. It is only when you come that the nightmare begins again, and we burn. But I bet right now everyone else is singing, playing, or eating the dinner that the mama lady prepare."

"Why don't you leave?"

"We cannot. But the mama lady says an angel will come and save us."

A pang of jealousy fluttered within me. Perhaps Auroch had once murmured in his wife's ear, pressed her back close to his front, and gazed at her as if she encompassed everything beautiful in the world. Inwardly, I cursed myself for falling prey to his charms.

Lady Carrington was the sweet wife Auroch had spoken of!

"He has no power," Jin said. "The bad papa man. That's why he so angry. Because he still in love with the mama lady."

The realization that I was truly a young girl, naive to the ways of the demon Auroch, overwhelmed me. I had fallen into the trap of his offers, from which I assumed there was no alternative to refusal. I had been fooled into believing that we were consubstantial when, in reality, he was bound to the world of Shadowmist, and by his own words, he wanted everything I had. The power to travel the world, hear music, taste and sample earthly pleasures. Pleasures only feasible to the living.

Now I knew he was once human.

My reactive nature, my anger, my jealousy, all qualities which the demon Auroch had fed upon, had destroyed me.

"It's not true. He's more than just a man," I murmured, even as this dialogue of truth ran through my mind.

"You could leave, but you did not try."

"I tried!" I shook my head. "I tried to drown out his voice…"

"Leave. You did not just leave."

"There were no doors save for the ones he presented. The ones with the choices."

"He has no power," Jin said with exasperation as if I were the dumbest person alive.

I bristled, mildly insulted that a boy of ten would think so. "Tell me about Auroch. Tell me everything."

Chapter Twenty-Six
Tunnel Vision

Jin sat and leaned against the wall. I floated down and sat across from him, my back propped up against a desk. Our seating positions reminded me of a crackpot social studies instructor who once insisted that a desk only existed because our minds validated such, but if we were to deny the existence of the desk we sat upon, it would cease to exist. I finally understood the lesson.

In a lilting voice, Jin told me the story of Auroch. I could see the man he was clearly in human form in my mind's eye, disembarking from a passenger ship in San Francisco in 1892, a young man with a devilish twinkle in his eye and fifty dollars in his pocket and a bar of gold hidden away in his luggage. In my mind's eye, I could see it all.

****

The fine young gentleman was clearly a royal. He stepped down from the gangway in a resplendent suit, a gold-tipped walking cane in hand, as he tipped his top hat to a beautiful woman in velvet and fur whose sleek hat was adorned with feathers. The man gazed up at the city of San Francisco, seemingly a hill peppered with buildings here and there that rolled higher and higher as the elevation before him increased sharply. This was a city to be conquered, a city in which he would make his fortune.

"Take what is in your traveling chest and never return," his father had told him sternly, mere days before he made passage for America. They spoke their last words in his father's study as a fire roared in the hearth. His father stared out of the floor-to-ceiling arabesque

349

windows with his hands on his hips. Auroch pinched a throw blanket between his thumb and forefinger as he stood patiently listening to his father's tirade, his only show of emotion as his father disowned him for wanting to venture out on his own as a young man of twenty-two years. His father had placed one gold bar in the chest, a bar shown to him by his uncle years ago with tales of rivers that ran with gold in the New World. His uncle, now lying dead in their family mausoleum, which was perched in a cemetery on a hillside overlooking the Caspian Sea, gave Auroch's father the one-kilogram gold bar as someone with billions of dollars in their bank account would dole out a new car.

To his father, the bar was merely a party favor. To Auroch, it was a ticket to a new life. Even now, as his father berated him, he recognized the value of that gold bar, and he would not speak a word in rebuke to his father, knowing this gold bar was his ticket out of this prison of a palace and into the real world as a businessman. His worst nightmare was to live the life his father and his father before him had, the life of one who existed in a palace day by day, without industry or motivation, perusing the works of generals and philosophers while servants attended to his every need.

"Your place should be here, by my side, as my last only and living heir. Instead, you have rejected me and all that I have offered you and so you will learn to abide in the world you seek, a world of charlatans and thieves. You shall never meet my eyes again."

Auroch's eyes had moistened at his father's words, but he was resolved. He ordered the servants to pack his bags, and out west, he sailed. His accommodations were first class, for all one needed to do was mention his family name. Their lines of credit were vast and recognized worldwide for his family's contributions to industry and textiles. It would take months, perhaps years, for his father's men to catch up with him, for hoteliers and restaurateurs to recognize that he was now a disowned son and disavowed of the family name and all its privileges.

Standing on the edge of the dock in San Francisco, Auroch turned and took in the sight of the vast bay with boats and ships all along its waters. A nearby liner sounded its horn, loud and melancholy in the distance. Auroch bristled with annoyance at the intrusion into his soliloquy. In short order, he commissioned a man to assist him with his luggage, and soon, he was ensconced in a suite at the Palace Hotel on Montgomery Street. He set to work on making himself a fortune. After a good sleep, a long bath, and a shave, Auroch left his hotel room the next morning to meet with Patrick Leahy, the president of the Harbor Commission, and begin his appointment as a foreman for the city of San Francisco.

Against his father's wishes, Auroch had studied civil engineering at a prestigious university in his exotic homelands. His specialty was tunnels. The city of San Francisco, the city surrounded by the Pacific Ocean on one side and a vast bay on the other, was in need of infrastructure to support its growing population. Tunnels were the answer to everything this city needed.

"As we discussed in our correspondence," Patrick Leahy intoned, "I have a project for you. An underground tunnel system leading from a place called Chinatown and connecting to various other tunnel systems in the city. Complete this assignment to our satisfaction, and your place within the commission of the City and County of San Francisco in this great state is assured."

And satisfy he did, for the next three years was spent ordering a team of five hundred men to dig and blast, dig and blast, all the while keeping the surface ground intact. Auroch created a vast network of tunnels that stretched from Grant Avenue through California and Sansome Streets and into North Beach, even as far as the stately homes of Pacific Heights. Men died in the blasts, and accidents happened, but with steadiness and lack of feeling, Auroch completed the job and soon found himself on the board of commissioners. As a commissioner, he amassed a fortune in kickbacks and bribes from builders. All the while, the gold bar sat in a safe deposit box at the Palace Hotel. He had no need to barter it for cash, ever.

One Sunday afternoon, when there was no work to do and no unanswered letters on his desk, he ventured forth into the financial district for lunch. After a sumptuous meal of champagne, escargot, and beef wellington, he adjusted the waistband of his fine trousers and caught a glance in the mirror. At the age of twenty-eight, he filled out his suit finely. He noticed he was a good-looking man, finally noticed this after all these years of thinking only of building and industry.

He caught the eye of a young lady who dined with her family. She glanced at him, giving the type of smile one gives to someone who they only tarry with before they go on with their lives. However, she did notice him, and for that he recognized that perhaps he should find a wife. But where does one without an established family go to find such a woman in a city of men and dust and tar smoke?

He traversed the streets of San Francisco on this brisk October day until he turned a corner. A sleazy barker informed him he was now entering Maiden Lane, and he could choose from any bevy of beauties to chat with him. Scantily clad women called to him from behind wooden screens as they attempted to reach out to him. He dodged them, recognizing he was in the wrong place and near the wrong types of women.

A dame dressed in soiled white tatters shoved herself into his arms. He backed away as she began to shout, demanding a nickel for the touch. He shook his head as he turned to leave in haste and came face to face with the most beautiful woman he had ever seen.

"Do not bother to wager, for I am not one of them," she said briskly, although her eyes were gentle. She turned away, a basket filled with glass bottles balanced upon her hip.

He followed her. She was a magnet to him.

"I did not think so," he said in a nervous voice, which did not sound like him. He introduced himself and asked her if she could help him find his way back to the Palace Hotel.

She laughed, then turned and took another look at him. She surveyed him thoughtfully even as her body moved to turn away again. She smiled a wry and tired smile. "As I said before, I am not... as you know. But I would be happy to help you as soon as I dispense the rest of these medications."

He waited patiently as she completed her work. They walked in the direction of Montgomery Street as she shared with him that her father had recently passed away. He was a doctor, she said, and as part of his charity work, he would visit the undesirable areas of the city to assist those who were less fortunate in preventing disease. She explained to Auroch that she would be leaving the city soon, for when her father died, his debts were called in, and she had no way to pay them.

****

Days later, Auroch turned in circles as he surveyed the vast and empty mansion on the land that would someday be the site of Addison High School. The mysterious lady stood by his side, her hands grasped together in the front of her body as she told him the history of her family home.

"The fine furniture has been sold at auction, but it is a beautiful home nonetheless. I will miss this place greatly," she said. "I spent every year of my life here. After Maman and Papa died, I am now forced to sell the home back to the bank."

Auroch stared out of the high picture windows at the sloping magnificence of the city of San Francisco with its budding skyline, rolling hills, and clear and crisp view of the Pacific Ocean. "If I may suggest," he said in his most debonair voice, "another option."

In less than a month, they were married. He crossed the threshold as he carried her in his arms as she laughed gaily. They set about making the home into a fine residence that resembled the Palace Hotel. Years later, they welcomed a son, but he passed away at the age of two, much to Auroch's heartbreak. Another year after that, a stillbirth girl baby as beautiful as a cherub, even in death, to join her brother in the churchyard as his childless wife sobbed in his arms.

Shortly afterward, Jin and the lost children found their way to the home through the tunnels.

It started out as a mild nuisance at first. Auroch would return home and find his beautiful wife downstairs playing music on the Victrola record player as she danced around with three or four orphans. Plates with pie or some other dessert would be stacked on a side table as she laughed merrily. "They are such poor, sad little children. Coming here is their only joy in life." As time went on, she found out more about these children and the sweatshops they worked in or the brothels they were sold to. Soon, the basement of the home was filled with children. Children who did not want to go back to their parents. Hungry children, more mouths to feed, pint-size strangers with dirty hair calling him *Papa.*

One day, he'd had enough. He returned home and informed his wife that, in a fortnight, they were leaving for an affluent suburb called Hillsborough, where the rich now built their mansions. She refused to leave. "You will, or you may no longer regard me as your husband. Should you refuse, I shall never lay eyes upon you again. I will sell this home, and we shall part ways as quickly as we joined." His heart tugged as he said the words, recalling similar cruel words that were once spoken by his father, but he hardened his heart and turned away. Tenderly, she walked over to him and allowed him to take her in his arms.

"I shall go with you," she whispered in his ear. "I shall follow you to the ends of the earth and back, my beloved husband."

That evening, in a dark hovel in North Beach, he met with an associate of Patrick Leahy's, a man known around the city to *take care of problems.* "It is the idea that she may want to come back that vexes me," Auroch said, "that is why you must eliminate the home completely. Burn it to the ground. She will be with me at that time at our new home. In a month or so, she will have forgotten all about it. I have built her a palace in Hillsborough."

"All will be burnt to ash," Patrick Leahy's man promised. "It will be as if the home never existed."

November seventeenth was the moving day. The fine furniture, chandeliers, tapestries, and other household items were being placed in the expansive new estate in Hillsborough. Auroch received a telegram from his wife that evening as he waited for her to sit down to supper. *The children are here,* the telegram said. *I have thrown a goodbye party for them. Please do not be angry with me. I shall join you at our new home tomorrow in the morn. All of my love, forever and ever.*

Auroch rushed to the stables and ordered the coachmen to ready the horse and carriage. He grew impatient and jumped onto the carriage, beating the horses as they headed out for San Francisco. He whipped them until their backs were streaked with blood, the whip snapped, and still he could not reach the home fast enough. When he arrived, the home was already burnt to the ground. He turned around and round, his hat in his hand, doing some horrific dance of grief in the ruins. All had turned into cinders with only a pair of marble pillars standing. It was indeed a horrific site, with bones and the smell of burnt flesh with tatters of children's clothing buried in the ash. Auroch fell to his knees and pawed through the rubble in the darkness as he cried out in agony for his wife.

****

"It is there I died too." Jin finished his story with tears.

I sobbed as I wiped his tears away as well as my own. I cried and cried for Auroch, for Lady Carrington, for all the children that had died in the fire. So many innocent lives lost, so much sadness.

Outside the high classroom window, the fog eclipsed the sun, making the room as dismal as my aching heart.

Chapter Twenty-Seven
Ghost Games

I stared into space as I contemplated Auroch. He was a brilliant man, a lord, a businessman, and a tyrant. A man who set in motion a plan to burn children to death because he could not stand the thought of his wife's affections being divided. A man who fell to the ground and cried, raking his face with soot as he stared at the home where his beloved wife met her death inside. And he had given the order.

What kind of man was this?

"Why," I whispered. "Why would he do such a thing?"

Jin shrugged. "We tried to make him like us. We sang songs, we played games, we shined his shoes and helped to cook him dinner and still he never wanted us. 'Get out,' he screamed at us once when the mama lady went to buy treats, 'leave my wife alone, you monsters! You demons.' Leave my wife and I in peace.' But no one in the world was as sweet and kind to us as the mama lady. My own mama, she die in the streets trying to keep me warm and I cry and cry until these men came and say I am to work in a place where I would bring wine and smoking sticks, people would always be hitting me or locking me into something."

Jin sniffled and wiped his nose.

"We would sneak through the tunnels, laughing when we knew we were getting close to the mama lady, and she would greet us with hot chocolate and peppermints and take turns rocking us on her lap while the music boxes played. I remember. I remember her sweet scent, the most beautiful in the world. I remember I felt not just okay. I felt…"

"Love," I sobbed.

Jin thought for a moment. "Yes. I did not know this before. At least here, that is what we have."

I told him the story of my own mother, of the avalanche crashing down upon us and her body collapsing as she drew her last breath. I told him of the winged creature, beautiful in electric blue and violet rays, of the soil above me exploding into the atmosphere as I screamed in fear and anguish at the death of my mother, and found myself unearthed with hands clenched and head thrown back, howling at the stormy, unforgiving sky.

"Angel birds," Jin said. "The mama lady used to love her angel birds.

"What kind of birds are around here? Magpies?"

"Lots of them ugly. I don't want to talk to you anymore. You make me angry. You say you come to save us but you take me away from home to this shiny place and I do not want to be here. I want to be home with the mama lady and the brothers and the sisters. Can you take me back home?"

"I'll try, Jin. I'll try."

I leaned my head against the front of Mr. Spinky's desk. I heard a shuffling noise and the squeak of his chair. He peered over the desk, right to where I was sitting. His eyes seemed to look right through me. His head receded back as his chair protested again while his weight settled.

"Do you think he can see us?"

"No," I said. "Otherwise, he would have run out screaming."

"I think I can get his attention. I did this once in the church that used to be here. Look."

A rush sounded through the air as Jin's presence

flew up to the desk, dashing Mr. Spinky's papers onto the floor. The teacher's hand shot out as they fluttered to the ground. He mumbled something unintelligible as he reached down and crawled under the desk to pick them up. Suddenly, Mr. Spinky shrieked and drew back, bumping his head upon the bottom of the desk.

Jin's spirit flew back to my side. "I touched his hand." Jin chuckled. "He was not expecting it."

If I had a hand, that hand would have been stifling a giggle from my lips. It was my turn to peek. Mr. Spinky's fingers danced over his skin on the back of his hand. His lips pouted out in a look of puzzlement and fright.

"I can make him see me," Jin said.

"How?"

"I will show you." Jin began to run circles around the room, faster and faster, until his spirit became a blur. His soul became the wind.

The wind that was Jin picked up the blinds as they flapped wildly when he passed. Mr. Spinky's papers flew into the air in a tornado-like fashion as Jin flew about the room faster and faster. The teacher's hair flew up wildly around the pattern bald spot in the middle of his head.

Jin swooped down from the ceiling and opened and closed the desk drawers, slamming them as he giggled. The unlatched windows also flew open and closed, sounding as if a hundred feet were marching, marching, intent upon a death on the battlefield. The force that was Jin swarmed faster, knocking on walls and the doors.

Mr. Spinky's face grew alabaster white. His eyes were wide open pools of fear.

"Jin! Stop!" I commanded. "Stop! Enough is enough. He's scared."

The knocking noises ceased. The windows slammed shut and remained still. The air in the room seemed to wait with expectation.

Mr. Spinky panted. Beads of sweat dampened his brow.

I felt as if I could hear the blood pumping through his heart, thicker, rapidly… too much. Too quickly.

"Mr. Spinky," I whispered.

As if he moved through clay, Mr. Spinky's head turned to meet my eyes. I reached a hand out to him. He drew back in fright, looking at the space where my hand would be. My body was in the shadows. I could see the bones of my arm and hand almost touching Mr. Spinky's skin. He drew back as if he were looking at a dead person. And indeed, in many ways, he was.

Mr. Spinky fell to the ground, clutching the left side of his chest. His left arm bent into his body, overcome with some kind of paralysis. He leaned on his side, moaning.

Jin was gone. I could no longer feel his presence.

I flew through the doors in a panic. The halls were deserted. School was over for the day. The milky faced janitor propped the boy's restroom at the end of the hall open with his cart. A loud soul melody echoed from his headphones.

I spirited toward him. "Mr. Sievely, listen!" I said with as much power as I could muster. "There's a teacher dying in room eleven. Please!"

The janitor shook his head. "I'm not listening." He reached up to a knob on his headphones and turned up the volume to its loudest level.

I rushed away toward the school office. Before I reached the door, I came to an emergency switch. Forgetting I did not inhabit a physical body, I pulled the switch downward. The fire alarm blared. The school secretary emerged from the office, her mouth pursed in a disapproving tone, her hair wild and curly with funky purple streaks through dyed auburn. The color of her hair matched the floral pattern on her dress almost exactly.

Jin's spirit returned. I felt his wild presence in the air.

"Where have you been?"

"I'm sorry," he said.

He flew to the door of room eleven and threw it open. The door slammed against the wall with a great deal of force. The secretary started at the loud noise, then rushed to the doorway to investigate. She screamed as she found Mr. Spinky, motionless, on the floor.

LIZ NEWMAN

Chapter Twenty-Eight
The Weather Tax

"Jin?" No answer. "Not here," I said as I lay beside Ben upon his bed. Ben's mother murmured softly elsewhere in the home as she spoke to a client on the phone, her voice unintelligible through the solid wood doors of Ben's room.

Ben stared up at the ceiling. He lay as if he had a heavy weight pressing down on his chest. I ran my hand up his tanned arm. His bronze color slowly faded as warm October days in San Francisco had turned into blustery bouts in the atmosphere between blue skies and gray. The gray skies outside were winning outside, but inside Ben's mind, the battle was long over. His eyes were dull, the light behind his pupils swimming rather than illuminating as they once did.

"Ben?"

He turned to look at me. I could see love in his gaze, and intense sadness.

"Penny for your thoughts? Wait, we're in California. Make it ten dollars for weather tax."

The corner of Ben's mouth turned up in a wry smile.

"Can you speak to Auroch?" he asked. "When I sleep, do you sleep too? Do you dream?"

My insides tumbled with fear. For what would Ben do if he knew I remained in perpetual motion. Restless, unable to turn my soul off to the world. I could feel nothing. As the days went by, even the mere concept of touch became obsolete, for touch and hunger and cold and warm were all just memories. I was part of the air now, nothing but a breath in the wind. Try as I could to repeat the force I had summoned outside of Mr. Spinky's classroom, force enough to pull the fire alarm, to reach out and touch Ben and run my fingers down his sleeve, soft yet firm enough so that he would pull back in surprise, perhaps reach for where my hand would be, I could not. I could not summon the strength to do even so, and I knew this was largely emotion-based. Much as I loved him, much as I could feel my passion for him, my love could not manifest its energy as strongly as my hatred, jealousy, and fear.

"I walk. Or I ghost, I guess. That's all I can do."

"Are you tired?"

"I'm weary from nothing because everything is nothing. Except you."

Ben's eyes were glassy as he turned his head away. "I wonder what it would be like to join you. Three doors. One has my eternal reward. I want you as my eternal reward."

"Ben, don't say that. Don't even think it."

"I've been wondering how I can pay the blood price. Because if I did—"

"Stop! You can't even consider it."

"I can. To be with you, I can. And I am. Please, AJ, hear me out. If I paid the blood price, I would save the school. I would clear the demons."

"Sister Anisette March Whittle, the nun, hung herself, and the church still burned."

"Without anyone inside."

"Just understand me when I say this," he went on. "I talked to your doctor. You are probably going to have an embolism soon. You have so many internal injuries your veins are clotted, and one of those clots is on its way to your brain. They said no one can stop it. The clot is lodged at the stem of your brain and is traveling upwards."

I thought back to a scary Japanese anime film

about the ghost of a girl who was murdered upon a rock on a road between Kyoto and Tokyo. The murder was said to be so grisly that her spirit became trapped inside the rock. At night, the rock would weep.

"I wonder if I cry while I lie there."

"You do. The tears make your face dry and give you these deep lines on the sides of your eyes. I brought you some lotion. I put it on when I visit."

"Thank you."

"Of course." Ben placed his hands behind his head so his elbows fanned out in a v behind his head. "If you won't come back to me, I'll come to you. What am I hanging on here for?"

"Ben. Who is putting these ideas in your head? Are you dreaming of Auroch?"

"You and I. We belong together. We can see the ghosts. Whether we are in this world or the next, we'll be together."

"If you kill yourself, you may not be able to be with me."

"You're wrong. Anisette March Whittle killed herself. She's in Shadowmist, with Auroch. Although she has not spoken. She has not spoken."

Jin's words echoed. *He has no power.*

I placed a hand on Ben's chest. Ben looked down as if he could feel a slight flutter. "Auroch could not hold me in his lair. I chose to stay there. Auroch said I could only leave if I chose a door, but I did not try to leave. All I did was feel the walls, solid walls that were part of an illusion. This notion of being trapped is an illusion. The notion of finding a passage is an illusion. The notion of fear is yet another illusion. Ben, maybe the burning on November seventeenth will not happen. Maybe that is an illusion as well."

"I'd hate to just wait and see. AJ, I'm not afraid to

die. Things have been terrible without you. I miss you. I want to be with you. If I pay the blood price, I could save the school and we could be together."

Before I could pull away, he brought his lips close to mine. The warmth of his skin overwhelmed my better judgment. I pulled him close, placing my mouth upon his, inhaling deeply, feeling his soul fill me from the inside. My mouth parted as I opened to his touch, a touch borne perhaps solely of imagination, but a touch divine and ethereal, bringing me to a secret place of light shared by us alone. His breath filled me. I breathed in.

A shudder coursed through his body. My eyes flew open. Ben's pallor had become ashen and gray. He fell back onto the bed, clutching his body and gasping.

Angel of Death. I was truly the Angel of Death.

My hands had become cold tendrils of mist, swirling where my fingers should be. I reached out and caressed his mouth. The tendrils entered through his parted lips. He gasped and coughed even more, his body racked with convulsion.

"AJ," he whispered. "Don't go." He reached for me. I drew back and became part of the air in the room, lifting myself high to the ceiling. "Kiss me again," he said.

"Ben?" Ben's mother called out from the hallway. "Are you all right?"

Ben's body racked up and down. His hands clutched the top of the covers on his bed. Slowly, they released their tight grip. He flipped upon his back and blinked several times.

"Ben?" His mother opened the door.

I flew through the window and hovered outside.

"It's so cold in here." I heard her remark as she entered the room. I spirited above the city street. Ben was all right, but I could not take the chance of dragging him into my world. I needed answers, and quickly.

"Avia!" I called as I rushed down Thornberg Avenue, then through Pacific Street. I flew high up into the sky. The sunlight blinded me, brutal and searing to my coldness as it set. I felt myself dissipating into several parts, evaporating over the roofs of the tall houses that made up San Francisco.

I swooped down into the brown boot house and walked around under its decrepit roof. Jagged panels of light shone into the interior. The house groaned and creaked. Somewhere inside, there was a dripping noise. I floated through empty halls and rooms.

I sighed and sank to the ground, feeling the depravity of my situation. Caught between life and death, no good to anyone, and poison to my beloved Ben. I wished I could disappear, then laughed at the irony of the thought.

A scrabbling noise came from within the home. Then a sound as if someone were speaking in a normal voice. "Caw."

I jumped up, pressing my back against an exposed beam. A *drip drip drip* noise sounded. My gaze darted from left to right as I sunk into the darkness. What manner of creature had I become, slinking in the shadows, fearful of every noise and the elements of the earth.

A fat rat scurried out from under a dusty floorboard. The rodent lifted itself up upon hind legs, sniffing the air. It squeaked before ducking into a hole in the wall. That explained the scurrying. Now, to find the voice. I knew with an ominous feeling exactly who the voice belonged to.

The house creaked again. I felt a slight tipping as if I were suddenly off balance. I stared out onto the sidewalk, which was crooked.

Through the window, I saw Ben and I walking. I was wearing the outfit I wore on the first day of school. My hair was flat ironed, my eyes pretty with mascara and a touch of lip gloss. This was the day we had lunch at Penatisimo. I pressed my face close to the broken glass. The form that was me looked in my direction.

"What's up?" Ben said.

The form that was me mouthed the same words I spoke inside the sagging brown boot house. "I think somebody is watching me."

"You're right," choked a woman's voice in a whisper behind me.

I jumped back from the window and turned.

"Hello, Andromeda Jayne."

Avia stared at me with one eye slack from asphyxiation. Her face was bony with the skin stripped away completely over one side of her jaw and cheek, her flesh gray and streaked with dark blue eye shadow and bright pink lipstick. Her body was clothed all in black. The Magpie.

"Welcome to the party. Would you like a cup of tea? Eternity?" She giggled.

Eterni-tea. Welcome to your Eterni-tea. I squeezed my eyes shut to squelch the thought.

"I need to know how to stop the burning. I need to know how to save the school."

The Magpie surveyed me with black eyes that glittered. "Why should I help *you*?"

"I offer... I offer you a release from this place. I can do it. I know how. I will bring you up into the sky and breathe your soul into heaven."

"Hmm." Her bones creaked as she turned away, nothing but a tall, broomstick figure with a cricked neck from the hanging.

"You want to leave. That is why you approached

me."

The Magpie grinned, her teeth black and rotting. A scraping sound came from the wall.

A tiny claw poked and wiggled its way through a hole in rotted wood. The claw retracted and an eye peeked out, then a beak. A black bird squeezed its way through and emerged from the wall, followed by other birds that cawed sinisterly as they squeezed themselves into the room. Magpies began to fly in from the holes in walls and the windows. They pecked their way through the floorboards. The air stank of bird droppings and feathers. *Caw caw caw!* screamed the house as the birds flew toward me, black eyes intent on pecking out my own.

I swiped my arms and hands about shooing the birds away. They kept coming, attacking, forcing me down to the ground.

Rage rushed through my ethereal body. Suddenly, I unfolded into the air, into the room, and I was the room. I screamed with all my being. The birds were blown back in a sonic boom as their feathers scattered everywhere.

All was silent. Avia had disappeared. I was alone.

"I will not go until you tell me how to free the children!" I yelled.

"Piss off, Drammeeeda!" I heard The Magpie scream from outside. I ran to the window and saw my past self shoved down into the street as The Magpie outside broke into a run.

Ben reached down to help me up.

"Show me!"

A weary voice spoke from the shadows. "I just did."

I whirled around. "How?"

Avia's gaze back at me was forlorn. Her mouth was downturned as she watched the past Ben and me from the abandoned house, as she beheld her sad form in The Magpie, dirty and dressed in tattered clothing.

"I wish I could return to the past," the Magpie said as the bones of her chest seemed to sink in. "I wish I could undo my greatest mistake. I painted my face over and over again, I wore the same clothes, and I have waited. At times, I see the past as you do now, from a mirror or a window. The same story plays over and over. It never changes. If I could come back to life I would change the events, and so I wait here for my chance because someday it will happen. Someday, if I wait long enough, I will be able to correct the mistake."

"There's no going back, Avia. The only release is in acceptance. Take my hand and leave here with me, but just tell me first how to stop the burning."

"I am not ready to go. Leave me alone."

"Only if you tell me how to stop the burning."

The Magpie appeared to yawn as her jaw opened. Her mouth gaped even wider, past the point where her jaw would remain hinged. My heart pounded as I watched the scrabbling claws gripping the sides of her lipstick-stained mouth, pulling ever wider as feathers emerged. Dozens of birds burst forth. I shrieked as I turned and ran.

The birds flew all about me again, cawing and pecking and gripping at pieces of my hair. I was blinded by black beaks and drips of blood, all the while twisting and turning to rid myself of their grip. I shrunk down to the floor, convinced they would tear me to pieces.

I flew up into the air and rushed to the window. I would be out in a second, flying down the street and back to where? Where could I go? What could I do? Ben was far better off without me. The entire world was moving on without me. No, I had to stay and find a purpose. I had to stop the tragedy at Addison High.

Perhaps fear is an illusion.

I needed to know how to pay the blood price without anyone else dying. The Magpie might carry this wisdom, she might not, but if I left now, what if she was not here when I summoned the courage to return.

I whirled around and, again, gathered my energy into a ball that formed under my ribcage. I rose high up into the air near the ceiling, and then I let the force go with all my might. A blue light radiated out into a circle around my upper body, throwing the birds back. They dissipated as their originator sunk to the ground, her teeth gnashing like an animal.

I collapsed to the ground like a child learning how to walk and stumbling with overexertion. As I lay there, my eyes widened with the realization that I possessed a true power, one which I could see. One which could assist me in fighting Auroch and his evil influence.

I stood and lifted my head high with courage.

The Magpie hid in the shadows somewhere. I could feel her apprehension. I could feel her fear. I could feel her awe at my display of power. For she, like Auroch, knew her power to scare was nothing but an illusion.

"Avia! I know you are still here. I know that is you. In here exists your shadow side. In Auroch's layer in Shadowmist, you are a beautiful bird with a broken wing. But the break is a lie. You can fly away. The ceiling is an illusion. The walls are an illusion. The idea that only something in his lair can set you free is an illusion. You are free to go whenever you please."

Avia's head convulsed with a shudder. Her pink-stained lips parted.

"You lie!" she spat. "Auroch sent you to find me, didn't he? Don't you tell him I'm here. Don't you tell him where to find the rest of me. I'll wait here until I get

371

my life back."

My hand reached up to the hair on my scalp, as I pulled my hair gently with frustration. "Avia, you will never have your life back. You are dead. You hung yourself on the front porch because of something terrible that happened to you in college. You were sad and afraid and hurting. You felt guilty. You felt alone."

Avia reached out a bony hand and slapped me across the face. The blow stung like a brick. I cried out. Lifting my hand up to my cheek, I touched a spot of warmth. I drew my hand down. I expected to see blood, for I could feel it, but there was none there.

She shoved me by the shoulders down onto the ground. Her skeletal body straddled mine as she pushed me down to the concrete floor. I pulled on her arms as her hands enclosed around my neck, strong as a vice grip. Her weight pressed my back down into the floor, and I registered pain oddly enough since a ghost should not feel pain. Yet we were in a world that made little sense, where we were just as real to each other as the dust dancing in rays of sunlight that peeked through the slats. A dizzying feeling overtook me as her hands pressed tighter around my neck.

Gasps emitted from my throat.

Minutes passed as she crushed my throat with her grasp. The choking noises subsided as I forgot how I was supposed to feel and focused on what was really happening. And what was really happening was nothing at all. Despite what my imagination insisted I sensed, I realized I could not feel her death grip. My mind went inside my own body, or lack of.

Avia's grip tightened and tightened. My eyes filled with calm as I stared at her. The look of menace in her gaze faded into that of surprise.

Somehow, I knew at that point as I lay in the

hospital bed, the embolism started.

With my last breath, I choked. "You wanted to die." She squeezed harder. "Please. I know what that is like."

Avia's shoulders slumped. Her head lowered as she grunted softly.

Her grip relaxed on my neck. I rose slowly, my hand out to both appease her and defend myself if need be as I backed away. I stopped short of a comfortable distance with my hands wide apart in a gesture of surrender.

"Avia, you have been dead for almost seventeen years. You're nothing but a ghost. Just a shadow of your former self. Auroch convinced the better part of your soul that you are a magpie. He keeps you with him in Shadowmist. Your shadow side stays here to scare people who are capable of seeing you. Like you were scared when you parted this world. Auroch likes that. He is able to see them through your eyes. With your soul, you feel. With your shadow, you exist. When one part is tortured, the other is diminished. Tell me how to stop the burning, and I will set you free. For as Auroch sees through your eyes, so can you see through his."

"You already know what to do." She sank to the ground with one hand holding the hinge of her mouth wide. Her bony fingers drifted down to her lap. Her eyes closed. She appeared to be sleeping.

I settled upon the dusty concrete and waited. She stirred and reached out her hand to me. I took it and held it close to my chest.

"Only forgiveness shall stop the fire," she said. "Only love shall douse the flames."

"How?" But in another second, I understood exactly what I needed to do.

Avia's eyes met mine. She was no longer a ghost

or a skeletal figure or The Magpie. She was a girl close to my age with shining skin and eyes.

I squeezed her hand. "Thank you."

Tears began to flow down her face. "Am I really dead, AJ? Am I really?"

I sniffled as I caressed her shoulder. "Yes," I said as I swallowed back tears. "Yes, it is true."

"Oh no," she sobbed. "Nooo. What did I do?"

"Avia, you felt alone, that's all. Sometimes, a moment of loneliness is all it takes." I struggled to hold the tears back, but they fell down my cheeks anyway.

"I will come back to life someday. I will. Auroch said we must persist in what we want to achieve anything. I want to stay home."

"Take my hand, Avia."

We looked up at our reflection in the glass. In the shadows, my hand appeared to be shrouded in a black cloak. My fingers were skeletal. Avia's eyes widened in fear.

She disappeared. "Avia," I called. No answer. Resigned, I turned to leave.

"Let the devil come and take me," she whispered. She was nowhere to be seen.

As I walked on the path away from the front door, as I floated upon the misty fog, I noticed a sign tacked to the sagging brown boot house that I had never seen before.

"Condemned," the sign read. "Demolition scheduled for November 17th."

Auroch's words echoed in my mind.

We only see what we want to see.

A rumble sounded in the distance. I took one last look at the house in the light of late morning. The dusty windows, some collapsed, once again looked like the anguished eyes of a person caught in the throes of some severe mental illness. The rumbling noise grew ever closer as I fixated on the home, unable to move my gaze.

A great metal beast tore through me, but I was nothing but air. The demolition began as a bulldozer tore through the home, snapping wood and piling brick into piles, its operator unaware that he had torn through the last remnants of life that Avia had hung on to.

Today was November the seventeenth. Tonight was the talent show at Addison High.

LIZ NEWMAN

Chapter Twenty-Nine
The Angel of Death

I lifted myself high into the air and glided over the city streets. I needed to find Ben immediately. For if he was foolish enough to believe he could join me in this limbo, he would attempt to pay the blood price. The thought flashed through my mind that he might attempt to burn down the school. I knew he would not do something so savage as to intentionally kill people, but I knew he was capable of harming himself as he had in the past.

The school. I could find him at the school.

I swooped down Sutter-Hayes Street back past the bulldozers and wrecking ball mess that was once the brown boot house, Avia's house. Landing in the front lawn area in front of Addison High's glass doors, I watched the windows. Again, came the eerie feeling that the windows were watching *me*. I rushed past the doors, through the halls and heard the muffled voices of teachers as classes took place.

I pictured Ben in the theater where we first met, as life was cyclical, and where we began, we were sure to end. Into the darkness of the theater I crept, and with a surreal sense, I found that in the darkness, my hands and arms transcended into bone covered by black robes. I glided past a brass panel near the tiny orchestra section. My reflection was a skeleton, a reaper, the Angel of Death. I gasped in fright and watched my own skeletal hand reach up to cover my mouth.

A cry of terror rang out, subdued yet apparent.

The janitor stared at my horrible form reflected in the brass with wide eyes. He dipped a cloth into a bucket, wetting it, and then worked on my reflection.

"I don't believe in you," Mr. Sively muttered.

"I believe in you." I laughed.

"And I won't respond. Never, ever, ever."

I moved quickly toward the stage and down to the trapdoor. This is where I would find Ben.

Either dead or alive.

Minutes later, down I fell through the trapdoor of the stage. There was no dusty floor beneath, no hard area where my feet could steady myself upon the ground. The feeling of vertigo prompted me to close my eyes. I was sure I was falling to my real death. Perhaps the embolism had done its destruction, and my soul was separating from my body. Perhaps Nancy and Dad decided to pull the plug.

I fell faster, far past the point where the floor below the stage would be. I unfolded my fingers, now I could feel them, the stretch of my bones, the tips of my fingers upon the air. I was back in my body, or at least I thought I was.

I hit the floor with a thud and fell onto my side, the side of my ear banging and punishing me with a ringing noise. Slowly, I peeled my eyes open.

Auroch sat facing away from me upon his high-backed chair before a roaring fireplace, one finger dangling over the side conducting music only he could hear. The back of his chair had a diamond pattern, which brought back to mind the fancy living room setup of a restaurant as my family and I waited to be seated for Mother's Day brunch last year at a fancy hotel. I shook my head to ward off the thought.

"Andromeda Jayne," Auroch drawled. "To jest of you dropping in would be droll. So welcome. Welcome. I see you have found out exactly who you are. I hear you are spreading the good word, as the holy people might say." He remained seated with his back toward me, lifting a hand in a grand gesture upward and high in the air.

Avia the Magpie flew down from the rafter and alit upon his outstretched fingers. A tiny patch of breadcrumbs lay in the webbing of Auroch's hand between his thumb and forefinger. Avia's beak pecked at the crumbs. She looked up with big, black, beady eyes and blinked. A pleased trill emitted from her throat.

"Discuss. What made you think you could better me?" His voice was soft, deep, and melodic, a voice that still inspired a physical response. "What made you think you could stop playing the game?"

A breath of movement whispered, lightly lifting the hair on the back of my head. I whirled around quickly. The wall began to shimmer, and three doors appeared.

"Where is Ben?"

"I am not his keeper. I could be yours. Leave your soul here and I shall return your shadow to the world. It is there that you will put a stop to the burning of Addison High. Allow me your soul so that you may save many."

"I am never trading with you. Ever. Is Ben here? Is he behind a door?" I turned back in Auroch's direction to his tidy sitting room lavished with animal furs and all manner of comforts. He remained in his chair. I could see the top of his head, crowned with shiny hair,

"First, we have business to attend to. A solid deal to make between you and I. You promised you would allow me to visit you in your dreams. You became involved in a terrible accident. I gave you the grace of exchange, Hyannis McWolfe's life for yours, and you refused me. Who do you think you are?"

I pressed my lips together as I attempted to summon the courage to speak. "You are the shadow of a man who once existed. You are an illusion. You are nothing but a mask."

Auroch's thumb lifted to pinch Avia the magpie's

claw. Avia made a protesting noise. Her head ducked down and came up with another beak full of grain. Auroch remained silent.

"You were once a human, the Imperial Prince Ibrahim Auroch Osman," I continued. My voice wavered. "Husband of Lady Carrington. Father and savior to the children she saved from the horrors of the Barbary Coast. Or you should have been. You are a liar, a demon, a manipulator. You have no power."

The fire crackled, and I jumped. Avia flapped her wings. Auroch held her claws fast to his fingers, pressing so hard Avia cried out in pain. I remained rooted to the floor as Avia's cries grew loud and desperate.

"Stop!" I said. "Leave her alone."

Auroch relaxed his grip but would not release his hold upon Avia's front claws. Resigned, Avia rested there. Her eyes closed tightly. Behind her lids, her black bead eyes darted fitfully.

The voice uttered from Auroch's throat was that of a beaten old man who had experienced years of hardship. Gone was the smooth, cajoling cadence that wooed me from the moment I heard its baritone melody. Replaced by it was a guttural rasp.

"Andromeda Jayne, angel of death, angel of stars, angel of release from misery and this thing called life. You are a pretty child with exceptional powers. I ask myself why did you come to me? Why, out of all the demons you could have chosen, you chose me."

"I chose you?"

"You did."

"You can't get to me anymore. You won't take Ben. You will free Avia."

"You cannot steal from a demon." He laughed. "That is not how it works. The demon steals from you. Ask Avia. She told me what you are looking for. She told me that you tried to set her free as a bargain for information about me." Auroch remained forward, talking more to the fire than to me. His thumb came down on Avia's front claw, and again, she uttered a small cry. "The truth. Why do you want to know the truth about me? What business is it of yours?" he growled.

I advanced toward him. I intended to pry his finger off so that Avia could fly away.

I raised a finger up to my lips as Avia's black eyes blinked. *Shhhh…*

I strode toward Auroch seated in his high-backed chair, determined to dig my nails into his wrist and fight for Avia's release.

Avia cawed and cried out in warning as Auroch remained still. "Silence," he said in that beautiful, deep voice.

He released his hold on Avia as she flew above me, back to her perch on the rafter. I was so close to him I could see his shoulder but not his face.

"We hide behind masks of deception, humans and demons alike. Masks which protect others, for their own good and for our own interests. Perhaps it is time I take my mask off so you know how powerful and scary I can be. When you see, you will be begging for my grace. Would you like to see, Andromeda Jayne?"

My voice constricted. I could not move or speak. My hand reached out to grasp him, strike him. I lost all consciousness of why I was reaching out.

"You have no idea just how scary I can be," he murmured.

His hand glided up and pressed against the front of his face, which came off in his hand as easily as if he were removing a mask of plastic. The removal of his hair revealed perfectly smooth white clay. "So now, Andromeda Jayne," he snarled, *"can you see ME?"*

He turned his head and glared at me over his shoulder.

I screamed.

He gnashed at me with the face of a wolf, although his face was rather wide than pointed, and huge, his teeth bared with slobbery red gums, his eyes wide and glassy and terrifying. From the chair, he jumped to the ground on all fours, his body still that of a man but crouched over like a beast. I turned and ran as fast as I could toward the door, glancing over my shoulder to see him leaping onto all fours and pursuing me.

I reached for the first door, then the second. Ben would be behind one, but which one? Which one? I whirled around. The legs of the werewolf churned with a mighty force and stopped short, reeling back upon hind legs ready to pounce. In a crouched position, the demon rocked back and forth, teeth dripping with saliva. He would jump upon me at any moment and tear me to pieces.

I grabbed the knob of the door on the right, ready to twist. The Other waited behind one, Ben possibly behind another. Which to choose, which to choose. Or perhaps Hyannis, and if I ran through the door, I would condemn her to a fate of death.

With a mighty snarl, the werewolf leaped up and bared white teeth advanced with such force I could feel a breath of air move just in front of my nose.

I released the doorknob and jumped high into the air, hovering above the ceiling. The wolfman jumped as well, snapping and growling. I lifted myself higher and higher. Before I spirited through the roof, I looked back and saw Avia the Magpie flapping behind me in an attempt to escape.

The wolf's jaws closed upon her bent wing, and he pulled her back. The crushing of her bones resonated with a loud snap as he bit down.

LIZ NEWMAN

Chapter Thirty
Eternal Fire

"Avia!" I screamed as I awoke. My gaze darted about in terror. Four stark white walls surrounded me. The darkness of the room and the sky outside bathed everything in an eggshell blue light. The sheets under my hands were scratchy with too much starch. A blue machine with dozens of little green lights beeped next to my bed.

I jumped off the bed onto the floor. Turning around and around, I tried to get my bearings. For a moment, I felt dizzy and nearly stumbled, picturing my head crashing down onto the white metal brace that was part of the frame of the hospital band. I would be knocked out cold, heh! They'd probably put me right back into that bed and pull the plug.

Throwing open the set of tall wooden double doors on the closet, I found a black tank top, jeans, black and white Converse sneakers, and the dragon Katana propped up against the wall and sheathed. I tore off my hospital gown.

Ben pushed the door open with a Styrofoam cup in his hand. He gazed in disbelief as I stood before him in bikini underwear and struggling to pull on clothes. His mouth dropped open, his eyes widening in admiration and something that pleased me very much to see. Love. Pure, shining love.

"We have to hurry," I said as I pulled my bra on. The determination to stop the destruction of Addison High was too great to feel self-conscious now. He watched for a moment, then cleared his throat and turned away. I pulled my tank top over my head and stepped into my jeans.

"AJ." He strode forward, taking my face into his hands. "Are you really alive?"

"I am." I embraced him and kissed him back softly.

"You're not," he said. We turned to my hospital bed. Sure enough, my physical body still lay there connected to the machines. My heart rate monitor continued to beep.

"I guess I'm still a ghost then. I only have powers when I'm almost dead it seems. There is no time to lose. The school will burn down tonight, and everyone in it, if we don't stop it."

His arms wrapped around my waist as he gazed at my face, my hair, running his hands up and down my cheeks and shoulders. "I can feel you. How is this possible?"

"Oh, Ben, I have so much to tell you. But right now, we need to get to the school." I spotted the dragon Katana propped up in the closet where my personal belongings were stored. "Take the sword. We might need that."

The digital clock read six-fifteen. I racked my mind as I tried to remember the show's start time.

"Seven," Ben said. He read my mind.

"We need to go. Quickly."

Ben threw open the door, peeking out. He raised a hand up to his lips and waved me into the hall. I crept out, squinting from the bright light.

"Nancy and your dad are in the chapel. The priest is meeting with them before he was to come up and give you the last rites. You had an embolism, and your doctor said you are brain dead. Are you sure we should go to the school now?"

"We have to. There is no choice."

We slunk down the hallway, passing an elderly

person in a wheelchair whose body hung limp. His eyes were filled with resignation. "Angel," he rasped as I passed by. "Take me."

My hand caressed his head as he clutched his chest. His arm fell to his side, his body slack, yet he wore a small smile.

"He's at peace," I said to Ben. I could feel a smile creeping over my lips. "He's not in pain anymore."

"AJ, that's an amazing power."

"Thanks." The elevator doors opened. I leaned against the wall. "Just don't get too close."

"God, I want to kiss you."

"I wish you could, Ben."

My ears burned as we walked through the lobby. I was convinced one of the security guards would rise from the desk and drag me back to my room. The double doors to the entrance parted, and we burst out into the night.

"Are you sure we shouldn't catch a cab?" Ben asked with a wry smile as we hurried out into the parking lot.

"We ride."

Ben's eyes lit up with admiration as he straddled the bike and strapped the Katana sheath across his chest. I jumped on behind him.

"Let me breathe you in," he said. He took a deep breath, and he and I became one. I could see, touch, and smell everything he sensed.

The wind blew our hair as we sped over 19th Avenue and up the hills toward the Pacific Heights neighborhood. At times, I floated above him, enjoying the softly lit streetlights. Then I became a part of him again and listened to the sounds of cars humming with music, people talking on the sidewalk, and the smells of spices coming from Chinese and Italian restaurants. No wonder Auroch longed to be alive and walk among the living. If only the living knew how extraordinary their everyday existence was. I realized that they had forgotten because they had lost touch with their senses. True death is the cessation of all sense. Many people were already dead inside because of this very reason.

Ben maneuvered the motorcycle into the parking lot of Addison High. The fog began to gather in droplets. Inside, I could hear the lilting piano playing an introduction. Hyannis would be taking the stage at that very moment, gliding out upon her tippy toes as she held two hands folded under her chin.

Ben strode up the front steps. He did not slow his stride as he grabbed the handles of the double doors and threw them open. I gulped the misty air, for it felt so good to breathe again, if only through Ben. For so long, I had existed in a state of death. The area under my ribs, Ben's ribs, felt so alive, it hurt. Or perhaps the feeling was my heart, which pounded with fear at the terror we were about to face.

Silently, we crept into the darkened theater. Hyannis performed the last steps of the routine. She lifted her hands in a grand gesture as she bowed and smiled.

Ben and I slid along the red-paneled walls. We climbed a set of hidden stairs and ducked backstage as the curtain closed. The applause rang out as Hyannis slipped through the red velvet curtains, presenting herself for one more round of cheers. A strange chemical smell hung in the air and gathered strength as we neared the trapdoor. Ben slipped down under first, and I followed.

He lowered me down by the waist into a space eclipsed by complete darkness. The chemical smell was even stronger down here. A ray of artificial light shone around the corner. I waved Ben closer. He took me by the hand and insisted on going first as we turned the corner and into the long, wide room where I had first discovered

Lady Carrington and her children.

She sat in a rocking chair, her hands clapping as the children danced. A Victrola record player turned with the resounding notes of a happy song. The room was draped with long, beige curtains, with doilies and quaint figurines on all the oak tables. A side table was littered with the remnants of an afternoon tea. All around her, children were playing on the floor with tea sets and wooden trains, blocks and doll figurines. I looked up at Ben and smiled. Both of us did not want to intrude upon this peaceful scene.

Lady Carrington looked up out of the corner of her eye. She jumped up in surprise.

"You are here," she breathed. She turned to the children. "Quickly, go hide, and Mommy will come fine you. Go." The children scampered away up a staircase commenting with giggles on the clothes Ben and I wore and our hairstyles. Lady Carrington's eyes were large and round when she faced me again. "Please, let us not scare them. They forget, you know. They forget the burning. Are you here to take us away?"

"I will try."

"There is another here. Someone who the children fear greatly, but she is very sad. All she wants to do is stand in the shadows and watch us."

I already knew her name.

"Sister Anisette," Lady Carrington said, "come out and meet our Andromeda Jayne."

Looking tired and as if she were weighed down by heavy chains, the nun Sister Anisette rose from the shadows with a benevolent smile. "The best of me is still here," she said simply.

"We must hurry. Someone has come to pay the blood price. We must get you and the children out before—"

A large splashing noise sounded nearby. The chemical smell was overwhelming. My nostrils burned, and my eyes teared. Lady Carrington's head darted about in fear. "The children! They have never been alone during the burnings. I must go and find them. I must keep them safe."

"There's a sprinkler system on the panel on the right, just past that exit," Ben said to me. "We need a key for it."

Lady Carrington appeared at the foot of the staircase with her dozen children in tow. "We will come with you," she declared. "We cannot stay here. You will save us this time. I know it."

My mouth fell open in despair. If they followed us to the source of the fire, if I could not save them, if they were doomed to burn again, I would be devastated. What would happen to their souls? What would happen to Sister Anisette, who had stayed in limbo for so long and lived in a state of anguish and regret?

"Let them come," a voice inside whispered.

Jin? Is that you?

"Yes. Let them come. It is the only way to get them out.

How do I know this is you?

"AJ," Ben said. "I hear the voice, too."

"What if it's Auroch?"

The ghostly image of Jin wavered as he appeared. "He has no power," Jin said. "I already told you that. I went to the place you tried to send me, Andromeda Jayne. I know how to release the souls. Just take them with you. Take everyone with you."

"Jin, if I make the wrong decision, the mama lady and the other children…"

"There isn't much time. The man who cleans is going to make the fire worse."

"He's right," Ben said. "We can't waste any time. The smoke is thick. They might not smell it in the theater until it is too late."

Ben and I strode to the far entrance of the room. We stopped short and jumped. Mr. Sievely, the school janitor, blocked the doorway, his light brown hair plastered to his head, his sallow skin shining with moisture. He wore a fire suit doused with a foul-smelling liquid. The smell was gasoline. Gallons of gasoline.

His eyes were those of a dead fish.

"You're the ghost," he said with mild bewilderment. "The man said the voices I hear are inside, and the only way to get them out is to burn them. Burn them all. You. The kids. The whole school because this is an evil place that shouldn't exist." His slack, grayish pupils scanned the room. "Burn all of the ghosts and the students, too." Around his neck hung a silver key. I silently prayed he held the key to the sprinkler system. He grinned with yellow teeth. "All the doors are locked. We're all going to burn, burn, burn." His thick fingers dipped into his jeans pocket and emerged with a book of matches. "Move," he growled. His breath smelled of rot and tobacco.

"Please listen," I pleaded. "You don't have to do this. The man who speaks to you has no power at all. He told you to do this, but if you do, you will never leave. Did he offer you a choice of doors? It's a lie, you know. It's all a lie. Which door did you choose? Which door did the demon Aur— what door did he offer you?"

Sievely shivered in terror. "Don't say his name, or he will come! He told me to pick because something horrible was behind the other two. That's what he said. I asked him which one I should pick, and he kept saying the ghost children who try to make you hear them talk, you want to keep them quiet, don't you just want to get rid of them, make the ghosts go away. He said he couldn't tell me what to choose, but I told him he had to, he had to because I was really scared and he needed to choose for me because I was so scared. He gave me. He told me. He told me he would give my life back for theirs."

Ben pounced on Sievely and tackled him. He landed a punch on the man's face, then pulled his fist back, wincing in pain. The man's teeth had sliced through the top of Ben's knuckles. I knew the gasoline inside his wound had to have stung. Ben unsheathed the Katana and advanced toward Sievely.

Sievely jumped up, pulled a fire extinguisher from the wall, and flung it at Ben, knocking the sword from his hands. The Katana flew across the room and clattered on the floor out of reach. Sievely grinned, a waxy crescent moon from ear to ear, as he lunged and grabbed Ben by the throat and pinned him to the ground.

I ran up and delivered a swift kick to Sievely's side, but my ghostly foot found no purchase. Ben landed another punch just above the man's temple. He pushed up and regained his position, crushing the man under his body. The man's hands flailed around this way and that, a match in one and the book in the other, ready to be struck.

A magpie flew in from the trapdoor and hopped along on a broken wing. The Magpie turned into a beautiful young woman. *Avia.*

Avia picked up the key from the floor. She clutched it in her bony hand. "Avia, give me the key. I need to turn on the sprinklers."

She backed away, still clutching the one small piece that would save everyone in the school.

"Avia, please." Ben and Mr. Sievely struggled on the ground as Lady Carrington and the children watched in horror. "Give me the key."

"Please," Lady Carrington said. "Do not let these children burn yet again."

"Then you will go away," she said as her eyes moistened. "You will all go away, and I will be alone. The best part of me has died. My house is gone. I have nowhere to go."

"The best part of you, the only part of you, is right here. Everything about Auroch is an illusion. A dream. All you are and all that you will be is here. Set yourself free. Please, Avia, give me the key."

Sievely snarled as he threw Ben off him. Up came the match, and he struck. He lay on the floor as he shot me a look of triumph. His fingers opened, and the match fell upon his chest. His body erupted into flames, but he did not scream. He simply rose to his feet, a pillar of fire and intense heat.

He was going to break into a run to rush past me up the stairs and into the theater, where the students were locked in. I was the only barrier between him and the theater. And there, everyone would burn.

Lady Carrington and the children screamed. Ben backed away, looking in the direction of me and the children, trying to decide who to attempt to save.

I felt a movement in the air. Jin began to swirl, surrounding me with the cold. "Tell them," Jin said.

I didn't have to say a word, for Ben heard Jin's voice, too. "Surround AJ," Ben said. "Hurry!" He took Lady Carrington by the hand and led her to me with the children in tow.

Lady Carrington remained fixated on the burning man. Her voice was frantic. "He will kill us all again and again, please—"

"Lady Carrington," he said as he looked deep into her eyes. "Stop being afraid of what he will do. Do what you need to do. Follow Jin. Make the children follow you. Fly around AJ. Fly as hard and fast as you can. Now!"

Avia dissipated into the air and swirled around me as Jin did. The ghosts of Jin and Avia formed a thin shield of cool, a barrier from the flames.

Sievely advanced toward me. His fire suit was likely to be burning through to his skin by now. "You'll go to hell first."

He advanced upon me. Fear overwhelmed me even though part of me knew I would not feel the fire. In my mind, I was falling, falling, back into the chasm where I would finally perish. I stood, unsure if Sievely was more afraid of me or if I was more afraid of him.

Auroch's voice echoed in my mind. *Call upon me when you need me. Call upon me, and I shall save you in your times of deepest trouble, anger, fear.*

"Call him!" Jin yelled. "Don't be afraid. You are the angel, and he has no power!"

Sievely advanced closer, ready to run past me. I could feel the fire of the flames singeing the air I occupied.

"Auroch!" I cried out as Sievely broke to run through me. "Auroch, I call upon you!"

Thunderous footfalls resounded as Auroch charged into the room. He appeared in the towering beastly form that haunted the theater, the hideous minotaur with large gnashing teeth. Avia dropped the key to the sprinkler system as she turned into a flock of magpies and flew into the tunnel.

"She is mine!" Auroch growled as he slammed his beastly arm into Sievely's body, which flew against the wall. The wall burst into flames as the children screamed. Their exit was trapped by Sievely and the beast Auroch. The fire spread rapidly, licking the wall and shooting across the ceiling.

"Ibrahim," Lady Carrington said softly.

"What!" Auroch snarled as he pounded his hoof into the floor and turned to glare at her.

"Ibrahim, is this you?" Her eyes glistened with tears.

"It is," he breathed. His chest rose and caved with his breath.

"Ibrahim," she said as she reached toward him. She touched the shoulder of the beast. And still, the fire licked and burned and consumed the room around them. The children remained silent, their eyes large and round.

"It is me." He peered into her eyes.

"No, this is not you," she said.

His eyes moistened. He glanced at the children over her shoulder and threw his head back in a guttural howl as he ripped her hand from his shoulder as she backed away in fear.

"Yes, it is me! In all of our years together, you never knew me!" He stomped toward her, his mouth snapping open and shut with his shouts. "Away with these bastards! If you knew me, as my wife, you would have known how to make me happy, to give me a living child as you promised. Leave me be. Leave this place or die here again as you did before!"

Another rush of air enveloped me as the children took flight, fleeing round and round all across the room, their coldness tempering the fire. A light surrounded me, a light that traveled all around my body and through the air, shielding me. I strode toward Auroch, the horrible beast man, and clutched the sweaty, beastly face in my hand, and closed my eyes as I placed my lips upon his terrible teeth and breathed in.

The beast's talon fingers reached out to grasp me as his fingers closed upon my upper arms as if to crush me. Ben stepped forward. With the last burst I could summon, I withdrew all of the energy I could from his body as his fingers dug into my flesh.

I exploded into light, sending the cool shield of Avia, Jin, Lady Carrington, and her children into my surroundings. The energy illuminated the room brilliantly. As the underworld comes for blood, so does heaven come for light. The sky opened through the ceiling. Through the opening, a land that looked like Shadowmist waited beyond. A land of lush vineyards, flowers bursting from plants, and trees waving in the breeze. Avia, Jin, the children, and Lady Carrington gazed at the ethereal blue orbs that danced in the dazzling illumination of celestial rays.

I turned toward where the beast once was and there stood Auroch, the real Auroch, the Imperial Prince Ibrahim Auroch Osman resplendent in his top hat and suit ensemble.

"Ibrahim," Lady Carrington said. She ran to him and embraced him.

The sky in the room seemed to fade. He stood there, disarmed, silent for many moments, and only a man, the beautifully handsome man he once was. "Auden, will you forgive me? Could you find it in your heart to forgive the man you love? I am sorry. So sorry."

"Hush now, Ibrahim. We are together again. The pain is over."

The children surrounded him. With hesitation, Auroch placed his hand upon their heads, his other hand embracing his wife. "Let us go now. All of us."

Auroch reached for my hand, grasped it, and kissed it, then smiled at me with that devilishly handsome grin. He led his wife by the waist into the light as the children followed them. Lady Carrington turned toward me, gazing through the light with gratitude before the opening faded completely, and they faded.

Ben removed a fire extinguisher from the wall and sprayed Sievely, the janitor, as he rolled on the ground, his flames completely doused, with charred blackened skin on his neck. He shouted from the pain, crying and screaming.

There was a commotion as the trapdoor opened, and footfalls sounded. Students and faculty rushed into the room, with Hyannis leading them. She scowled at Ben.

"You ruined it!" she screamed. "Everyone ran out because you burnt this place up! I knew you'd find a way to ruin the whole show! Now I can't even *give* away the trip to Hawaii!"

My energy had been almost entirely depleted. I collapsed, just a sad and lonely ghost on the floor. Ben picked up the key to the sprinkler system.

"Benjamin Bach, do you have anything to say for yourself?" Hyannis demanded.

"Yes," he said as he placed the key in the sprinkler system in case anyone had any ideas about lighting another match. "It was *just perfect*."

He turned the key. A flood of rain poured down on Hyannis as she glared at him with her eyeliner running down her cheeks and her silk tutu sopping wet.

I lay there, completely spent, waiting to die. Waiting for the ceiling to open up again and come take me into the sky. Footfalls and commotion were all around me as I simply dissolved into nothingness. Teachers rushed down into the space as they attempted to treat Sievely, who flailed around, still shouting about the blood price.

"AJ?" Ben said.

"She's in the hospital in a coma, you idiot!" screamed Hyannis.

"AJ! I can't hear you. Talk to me, AJ. AJ!" Ben

rushed to the stairs, no doubt on his way to the hospital.

I could not float. I could not move. I could not speak or even attempt to connect with Ben. I had lost all strength. What will I had left to exist had fallen away.

"Andromeda Jayne." I heard a whisper. The ghost of Sister Anisette crouched over me, one soft hand on my shoulder and the other caressing a rosary. "It is not time for you to go. You will go to God closer to when *he* does. You are still needed here."

"Who…?" escaped my lips.

Her soft, white hands caressed my shoulder as she lifted me to my feet. "Fly, little bird," she soothed. The lights in the theater flipped on, and before me stood a nun with a purple face and bruised black eyes. Yet her smile was benevolent and beautiful, and her touch so kind and gentle.

"In a hospital, thy parents weep over you as a priest performs the last rites. Go back to your body, child. Go back before it is too late, or you are doomed to haunt these halls forever. Peace be with you, child."

"And with you," I said weakly as she faded away. And then I prayed for strength.

Sirens roared in the distance.

Chapter Thirty-One
Everlasting Peace

"Thy kingdom come, thy will be done on earth as it is in heaven. In heaven. In heaven," I prayed.

I crawled upon the floor as I dragged myself to the opening in the trapdoor. Paramedics were all around me, working on Sievely as he groaned on the floor. "She's still here! The ghost is still here!" he screamed over and over as they subdued him with medication. "The blood price must be paid. It must!" The IV dripped into his arm, and he finally quieted. The dragon Katana lay on the floor in the corner of the room, unnoticed.

Auroch's voice echoed in my mind. *Where we begin, we are sure to end.*

I had to get to the hospital. I had to return to my body and send some kind of sign to my parents and let them know that I was alive. *I am alive.*

To end, he said. *Sure to end.*

"Jin," I cried. "Jin, are you there?"

No answer. He had gone into the light I had opened up. And now I was left here all alone with no one to help me return to my body. I heard sobbing. "Avia?"

"They have all gone, and now I am alone," Avia said from the shadows.

"Avia, I need you to help me. Please."

"Why should I help you," she cried. "If you return to life, you will leave me, too."

"There isn't much time," I gasped. "I'm weak. Please go to the hospital. Go there and find my body in room 612. Come back and tell me what is happening. Just be my eyes and ears, and please don't let them kill me. Please."

"You'll leave me…"

"I won't leave you! I will find a way to help you, I promise. Please go now, or I will die!"

She whirled into the Magpie and flew up through the trapdoor. I could only hope she was on her way to the hospital to do as I asked. Like some kind of blob, I seeped up through the trapdoor and across the stage of the deserted theater. I heard Ben calling my name.

"Ben!" I cried.

He rushed up the stairs to the stage. "I started riding to the hospital when I realized you would still be here. Let's go, AJ. You can fly fast and far in the gloam. Let me breathe you in, and I will breathe you out into the fog."

"Wait, take the Katana!" I shouted. If I were going to die tonight, I wanted to at least have Ben return the dragon Katana to Luis. Ben lifted the Katana and draped the sword in its sheath. He slung the sword over his shoulder.

He leaned forward and breathed me in deeply, then rushed out to the hallway. He threw open the doors into the night and stopped short.

The night sky of San Francisco shone clear without a cloud or tendril of mist in sight.

"Oh no," I said. "I'm going to die, aren't I? We will never make it there in time."

"We will," Ben said. "We have to. Stay with me. Let me think."

The flag on the flagpole in front of the school waved in the slight breeze. It may have well been the old Jolly Roger. I was done for.

"We'll take the motorcycle," Ben said. "It's the best we can do."

He ran down the steps and jumped on his motorcycle, revving it up as the engine churned. We sped into the night. Just as we passed the demolition site of the brown boot house, Avia appeared as a bird.

The Magpie lit down upon us and whirled back into Avia.

"The last rites are being read, and they are about to cover AJ in a burial shroud," Avia shouted. "You'll be too late if you use the city streets!"

"Then how?" I said.

"Follow me," Avia said. "There's a tunnel entrance below my home. It's how Auroch found me. Don't ask me how. One goes directly to the hospital, but we have to move fast." Her eyes grew frightened. "But beware. There are monsters in there."

She flew to the gaping opening at the center of the wreckage, which was covered with "Caution!" tape. Ben turned off his motorcycle and maneuvered the bike down into the opening and soon we were in the middle of the tunnel with the starry night sky above us. The inside of the tunnel loomed as dark, dank, and mysterious. Ben switched his headlight on.

I gasped. All around us, the walls crawled with beetles, spiders, and other mysterious bugs. Webs festooned the walls. "I can't, Ben. There has to be some other way."

"This is the only way," Avia said. "The fastest way. Straight down and then you will come to the end and turn right. Go down that way about a mile, and on the piping on the ceiling, you will see numbers... 404... 505... 710. At 710, you will turn left and go around five hundred feet, but go no farther. The gutter above will be right below the emergency room steps. Don't be afraid. He knows what will scare you."

I thought of the monsters of Shadowmist, of insects and minotaurs and all sorts of scary creatures. "Ben..." I said, my voice shaking.

"You can do this, AJ. We'll do this together."

"Don't let me die, Ben."

"Never." He planted a kiss on my forehead. "Are you ready?"

I nodded.

"Follow me!" Avia turned into The Magpie and flew.

Ben revved the bike, and we sped into the tunnel. The tunnel wall loomed up in front of us. Ben swerved to the right. All around us were indiscernible drawings and foul writings scratched into the wall. A scribble of an awful creature with horns above an epitaph read, "The Devil was here and his Papa too."

I shuddered.

A smell hung in the air, a smell of rot and perhaps a campfire. Just ahead, a group of creatures huddled crouched around a pit of fire. They looked up as the motorcycle approached. "I'm not stopping," Ben commanded. "Move!"

Snorts and guttural noises emitted from them as they rose. Ben prepared to swing his motorcycle upward to travel the curvature of the sides of the tunnel to avoid them. Avia flew ahead and buzzed the group. They reached up and *clawed* at her. Their faces were the faces of rabid boars, monkeys, and rats, much like Auroch's servants.

Snarling teeth gnashed at us as we rode forward. Inside Ben's body, I reached for the dragon Katana and swung at them as Ben roared past. A rat face with a dwarf's body sprang onto the front of Ben's motorcycle and gripped the handlebars. Its head dipped as it bit down upon the arm of Ben's leather jacket. Ben swerved upward into the tunnel, traversing the circle. The rat monster lost its grip on the handlebars and fell to the ground.

A hairy claw lunged in the air and almost grabbed

Ben's wrist. I sliced downward with the dragon Katana and heard the sickening sound of the blade as it cut through flesh and bone. The claw was severed from a wrist, its hairy, bony hand landing on the concrete with a soft thud. The creatures hopped into a run as they set out in pursuit of us. The speeding motorcycle left them quickly behind as the darkness of the tunnel eclipsed them.

"710!" I called out as Ben turned the bike to the left. Only a few more feet until we were at the hospital. Ben slammed on the brakes, and before I could ask why, I knew.

There it was, the spider of all nightmares. The big and horrible black creature this size of a horse who had lit upon me in my dreams. "Turn back!" I screamed to Ben, but it was too late. A web, thick as a rope, flung out in our direction and slapped Ben off the bike. He slammed to the ground, and my soul left his body. The spider advanced toward us and released another web, which pinned Ben to the floor.

I jumped back into Ben's body and armed myself with the dragon Katana. The spider hesitated. Its fangs opened and closed as if it were thinking. I slashed the Katana forward, slicing off one of the spider's fangs as it screamed and lunged at me. I fell back into Ben as I screamed. The Katana fell out of my grip into the darkness. The spider descended upon me, all red eyes and teeth and menace.

A flurry of magpies swarmed the spider and attacked. I groped around the cement for the Katana as the magpies vexed the spider even as it attempted to ward them off with its legs and lone fang. My fingers closed around the Katana. I jumped up and sliced the rope webs from Ben's body. The warring spider and magpies stood between us and the exit to the hospital. From the direction we came, I heard the snorts and howls of the animals that were coming to slaughter us.

"We'll never get there," I said. "It's over."

The light from Ben's motorcycle illuminated the tunnel. "I'll never let you leave me. Do you understand that? Ever!" I waited for the creatures to light upon us, the Katana held in my other hand. Waited for the final death. I was too weak to do anything else.

The spider warded off most of the magpies, and the remaining birds were moving past the opening, deeper into the tunnel, as the spider stabbed them with his fang, annihilating them one by one. On hairy legs, the spider ran toward us. Ben stood his ground, our ground, as the spider jumped. Reeling back, he drew the Katana over his head and thrust the sword into the spider's belly. The spider recoiled and dropped to the ground, its insides oozing goo, which smoked as it seared through the cement.

The creatures turned the corner as Ben and I sprinted for the ladder. The magpies turned back into Avia, bloodied and bruised but ethereal and beautiful. She turned and ran deeper into the tunnel. "Go through the opening! Go!"

Avia drew the creatures deeper into the tunnel. "Go!" she said. "Live the life I can't." She sobbed and disappeared around the corner with the hideous shrouded monsters from the *Il Prelievo* painting in pursuit.

Ben slammed the gutter grate, and we were suddenly at the surface in front of the emergency room. With his last bit of strength, he lurched up at the steps and ran down the hall despite the protests from the hospital staff. He shot into a waiting elevator and pressed the number 6. We rode the elevator for what seemed to be an eternity.

Without waiting for the elevator doors to fully

open, he rushed out into the hallway and into room 612, where my father, Nancy, a priest, and the doctor watched my limp body. The machines had been unplugged and there was no activity on my heart monitor.

"Excuse me," Ben said as he shoved everyone aside and leaned toward my body.

"What are you doing?" the doctor said.

"Are you crazy?" Nancy said.

Ben kissed me, fully and deeply, and breathed my soul back into my body. I wailed and shot upward as I came back to life and sat up in my bed. Nancy fainted. The doctor slammed a button on the wall, and loud beeps sounded as nurses rushed in. The priest reached into his pocket for a cigarette case and shook out a rolled cigarette with his hands shaking. He lit it and took a long, deep inhale as he clutched his cross. He removed the rosary from his neck and passed the cigarette over to my father, who sat dumbfounded. Ben gave me a wry smile, then collapsed onto the floor.

LIZ NEWMAN

Chapter Thirty-Two
The Last Shadow Dance

"Strike it down, that other boughs may flourish. Where that perished sapling used to be. Thus, at least, its moldering corpse will nourish. That from which it sprung - Eternity."

An *Eterni-tea*.

"Emily Bronte," Ben declared as he closed his textbook for English class. "That's the reasoning behind the blood price." Weeks later, we sat on the banks of Lake Stinson as the misty air from the nearby sea floated past, hugging my legs to my chest. The late afternoon sun peeked through spots in the fog before becoming eclipsed again.

"The very mantra of the death instinct," Ben continued. "To clear the way so that others may live. The theory, at its core, is the reason all wars have been fought. All atrocities committed. You could say they are the work of demons like Auroch."

"People are driven by principles or demons," I mused. "The ones driven by the demons work the fastest to destroy. Have you seen the ghosts of Addison High lately?"

"Not after the talent show. If I don't hear them, I don't look for them. Have you?"

"They are quiet. All of them are quiet."

"Even Mrs. Faria?"

"Even Mrs. Faria. I brought flowers to her grave and sat there for a little while. Nothing."

"Are you happy?"

"I'm at peace. Calm. Avia was the true angel. She saved our lives."

"She did." Ben wrapped his arm around my

shoulder. I breathed in his clean smell of leather. Sinking into his chest, curled my arm around his waist. "What did your doctor say?"

"He thinks the clot may have traveled elsewhere in the body and that I may have problems in the future. I'm like a walking time bomb. Tick tock tick tock. Guess that makes me appreciate life all the more."

Ben's lips tightened. "That's not funny, Andromeda Jayne."

"He also said I'm young, and I'm otherwise healthy, and I shouldn't worry."

"That's more of what I like to hear. You won't leave me alone in this world, you know."

"I'll stay as long as I can. I think things will be fine."

"How do you know?"

"Just a feeling. Like the same one I get when I feel a ghost. A feeling that I'm absolutely sure this is real." I tilted my face up to his and gazed into his eyes. He leaned his head down and we kissed, long and soft and sweet.

"Caslin should be here any minute," I breathed as we drew apart.

"I'm glad you are friends again." He embraced me as he stared out onto the water.

"Me, too. You know, I never told her about the picture Hyannis sent me. The *We're so happy you're not here* message."

"Why?"

"I didn't have to. She figured out Hyannis soon enough. Sooner or later, everyone does. She might be pretty and popular, but anyone reasonable will finally understand that she's a bully. She needs me to talk bad about her so she can attack me. Isn't that crazy? So, I just won't." I shrugged.

"Good move, AJ." Ben kissed me on the top of the head. "You hungry?"

"I'll take a soft pretzel."

"Be right back." Ben rose from the blanket. I watched him stride to the snack shack, glorious in his jeans and a black t-shirt. I chuckled. The guy who worked in the snack shack was a junior at Addison High. He looked like a surfer, judging from his lazy bangs and his fingers, which were curled in a perpetual hang-loose position. Ben became engrossed in their conversation.

Ben and I didn't wear the exact same clothes every day, but there was a certain uniform we adhered to because our style was comfortable to us. That's how we liked it. I felt lucky to find someone who understood that, who didn't feel caught up in the rat race of needing to have different outfits and new clothes all the time. Somehow, we were just comfortable being who we were. In tune with spirits, in tune with each other, and above all the noise and tension that encompassed being a high school kid in the twenty-first century. We liked what we liked, we saw what we saw, we did as we knew we should. By seeing ghosts, by being afraid, we began to look within where we found Auroch hiding. And where we could finally defeat him. Fear had opened me up to his influence, the fear of not being good enough, rich enough, loved enough. Without fear, the negative forces could no longer touch me.

I lay back on a soft blanket and stared up at the gray sky. The song Ben sang to me on our first day here lilted through my head. *Can I take you, take you higher…* I sang the first line aloud before I realized that was goofy and looked around to see if anyone heard me. A family of three lounged on a blanket beneath the shade of a eucalyptus tree, far out of earshot.

I closed my eyes. Perhaps I sang the line one

more time as I heard my own voice in my head. *Can I take you, take you higher...*

****

As the darkness enveloped my mind, I found myself in the dark, round hall where the spider lurked. Auroch's voice lilted with an echo. "Can I take you, take you higher," he sang in his husky voice. There was a hollowness to his tone.

I whirled around in search of an exit. The cylinder was closed off with black cement. There was no bright light at the end of this tunnel, only another side where I knew Auroch waited as he gazed over the land of Shadowmist. My footsteps echoed as I walked toward the opening. I shrank back into the curved wall. Taking a deep breath, I forced myself to be brave. I lifted my head up high and walked into Auroch's palace.

Gone were the tapestries, the ornate rugs, the luxurious furniture, the heavy drapes. In their place was nothing but cement floors, chairs, and tables, all stark and bare. Auroch sat at his high-backed chair in front of a fireplace that was now a cold and empty cave, yawning with the misery of destitution.

"Come closer, Andromeda Jayne." I could see his once sleek hair that peeked over the back of the cement chair was mussed and dry.

My steps thudded on the concrete, all sound absorbed by the vortex this room now seemed. A feeling of pity for the demon overwhelmed me. As I approached his side, his brown eyes, now soulful and sad, gazed at me. Behind them, a small gleam of glee flickered before the hurt look eclipsed his gaze again.

Even in his pallor, as he sat clutching what looked like a scratchy wool blanket around his shoulders, he was beautiful. His lips were blue but full, his skin pale but luminous, his eyes forever feathered by lush, dark lashes.

I sat on the ottoman near his chair, as if a student to teacher, finally ready to listen to him speak.

"So," he drawled, "you delivered the wayward spirits to heaven and saved the school," he said with a wry smile. "All hail Andromeda Jayne. Angel of Death. Reaper of souls." He fixed a pointed stare upon me. "She who does not repay."

"Auroch, I owe you nothing."

"On the contrary, you owe me everything. For without me, you are a wanderer, a philanderer, a person who knew nothing of her powers nor cared to know. You are someone so much like your equals, finding diversions to pass the time and ignoring your real powers. Powers that make the world the place that it is. I found you, I spoke to you, I tried to give you everything in exchange for just a few souls, just a few souls, and you could not even give me an insignificant cleaning man or a spoiled, insolent ballerina girl. You are greedy, you are of poor character, and you are not as good as you believe you are. You are not as strong as you believe you are."

"Are you speaking of me, Auroch?" I gestured around the room at the once magnificent room. "Or are you speaking of yourself?"

He shivered. Even as he did so, the scratchy wool blanket turned to ash and disappeared.

"Ah," I said. "Now I know the source of your power. Me. And you are the source of mine. Because every time you take someone down to your depths, you bestow on them angel powers. Or so it seems."

"Stay with me, Andromeda Jayne," he begged. He began to fade, his once magnificent clothes tattered rags. "All I can give you, all we can accomplish together if you just stay with me. If you just believe. Angel of Death. Reaper of souls. We are one and the same. Stay with me."

"We are nothing alike." I watched him fade. "The

best of you has gone on to heaven. And all that remains is a monster who no one is afraid of anymore."

He could not fade fast enough. For my heart tugged at the pleading in his eyes. I reached out my hand to caress his cheek, knowing this was our final goodbye, and yet I could not help but feel sad to see him go. For I had been captivated by him, entranced by his resplendent wickedness, I had loved him the same as I would have loved a part of myself, which he once was. But he was a part of myself that was toxic. A part that had almost killed me.

"Stay," he said over and over again. "Please, stay. I would give you everything if you would just come and see me, allow me into your dreams from time to time."

He faded, then he was gone.

"AJ," Caslin said from somewhere beyond the dream. "AJ, wake up."

I took one last look at Auroch's concrete room. Beyond the window, I could see Shadowmist, the sunny land of emerald hills and misty skies where all was *just perfect*. I could have walked to the window to take one last look. I decided instead to close my eyes and bring myself back to the place where I would find Caslin and Ben.

****

"AJ," Caslin said as I opened my eyes. Ben stood behind her with a salted hot pretzel in one hand and his cell phone in another. A lark upon the lake flapped its wings and took off into the air, making a great splash that shoved me out of the world of Shadowmist and back to Lake Stinson, where I was surrounded by the two people I loved most.

"You're awake!" Caslin squealed. "Oh my god." She hugged me tightly. "Are you all right? I've been nervous ever since the accident. I'll be nervous about you for years." She brushed a lock of my hair out of my face and smiled.

"I'm good." I sat up all the way and reached for the pretzel.

"Thanks," I said to Ben. His eyes shone with concern. He knew where I had been. I winked to let him know everything was okay. Caslin lay down by my side. She twirled a daisy around in her hand, plucking out the petals and throwing them onto the grass.

"I finally just stopped talking to Johan. Finally. No communication. It was the only way to get rid of him. He was texting me and calling me after I broke up with him the first time, the second, the third. He kept telling me his sister was mad at me for leading him on, and I told him, 'You know, Hyannis is a manipulator, and so are you,' and then he hung up and kept calling and calling, and I kept telling him never to call again, but after that, we'd have a conversation. Johan McWolfe! More like Johan McDirty Dogface. I heard he's already seeing Gigi. They were all over each other last weekend." Caslin chatted on and on. Her voice was the melodic, friendly voice that sang to my soul.

"Do you want a diet soda? I'm going to go buy us sodas."

I nodded.

"Ben?" Caslin said. "Would you like anything?"

He reached into his pocket and pulled out a ten-dollar bill. Caslin waved his hand away as she patted her purse with another and turned and walked toward the snack bar on the other end of the lake.

Ben lowered himself down on the grass. He took my hand in his. His grip was firm but gentle. I leaned my head into the crook of his elbow.

The shore of the lake gleamed like emeralds in the daylight. The water shone like diamonds. Magpies frolicked in the eucalyptus trees, their flapping wings like a hundred beating hearts. A thick mist floated past, made translucent by the sun. In the mist, I could see ghosts dancing and twirling, content to be exactly where they were and in search of nothing but the time to perform their pleasure. For time for living and time for the dead, although experienced in different ways, was still quite precious.

Words are a simple breeze. Some feed flames, but most merely dissolve into air.

"I see them, too," Ben whispered. "I think it's time for me to tell you what my power is. I think you're ready to know."

I looked up and met his eyes.

"I regenerate. My body fixes itself, given a little bit of time. That's why I wasn't injured after the motorcycle accident."

"Then that means you can kiss me. Now that I'm truly alive."

"Yes." Ben's eyes stared into mine, beautiful blue-gray pools of longing and desire.

"What took you so long? Kiss me."

Our lips met, a most glorious meeting that was true, a meeting in which my mind shut closed, and all I knew was the softness of his lips and this feeling of closeness and goodness and *now*.

The effect Ben Bach had upon me, one soul to another and yet joined as the same, made my heart beat faster with the beats of love.

Auroch's voice echoed in my mind. *When the student is ready, the teacher appears.*

While the demon was a teacher who encouraged pettiness, I would be a teacher who encouraged greatness. While he was a teacher who encouraged bitterness, I would be a teacher of forgiveness. While he was a teacher who sought gratification, I would be a teacher of gratitude. Auroch's power had existed only in the power I gave him. I vowed to give myself and these souls who needed me so much more. I had not the time nor energy to waste upon the demon, for I was needed and knew my calling.

For where we begin, we are sure to end, but there are no endings for beings of light.

There are only beginnings.

The End

www.DrElizabethNewman.com

Evernight Teen ®

www.evernightteen.com